No Place Left

Sean Watkin was born and raised in Liverpool and studied a BA and MA in Creative Writing at Liverpool John Moores University. He has been shortlisted for Fresher Writing Award, Book a Break Prize, Bristol Short Story Prize and the McDermid Debut Award. His writing has been featured in *The Gay UK magazine*, and *The Content Wolf* e-zine, as well as other LGBT+ publications. Sean lives in Liverpool with his partner and two dogs.

Also by Sean Watkin

DCI de Silva Crime Thrillers

Black Water Rising
Better Off Dead
No Place Left

SEAN WATKIN

NO PLACE LEFT

canelo
CRIME

First published in the United Kingdom in 2026 by

Canelo Crime, an imprint of
Canelo Digital Publishing Limited,
20 Vauxhall Bridge Road,
London SW1V 2SA
United Kingdom

A Penguin Random House Company
The authorised representative in the EEA is Dorling Kindersley Verlag GmbH. Arnulfstr. 124, 80636 Munich, Germany

A CIP catalogue record for this book is available from the British Library.

ISBN 978 1 835981 344

Cover design by Andrew Smith

Cover images © Shutterstock.com

Printed and bound in Great Britain by Clays Ltd, Elcograf S.p.A.

Look for more great books at
www.canelo.co | www.dk.com

1

FSC
www.fsc.org
MIX
Paper
FSC™ C018179

To the other legs of the Tripod: Amanda and Jenny.

One

Southport

11 February

Snow came down in clumps, soft and silent as ash. The wooden boardwalk creaked like old bones as DCI Winifred de Silva dragged her thick, curled auburn hair back into a messy ponytail. She pulled the white protective crime suit over her legs, knowing it would offer no warmth against the biting February cold, and considered what was ahead of her.

At this hour the place was as quiet as the dead. No seagulls circled or swooped for scraps, there was no laughter from children excited to be at the beach or the fairground, and the orange glow of lamp posts were circled with halos the colour of winter citrus. The police cordon tape, blue and white, rippled like scraps of cut ribbon in a breeze de Silva was thankful felt like barely a child's breath.

It made her think of that song her dad would sing to her when she was little. The one where the girl prays for some ribbons and then later, the dad from the song, who de Silva always pictured as her own father, looked in on his daughter. There were scarlet ribbons there on her pillow. The girl's prayer had been answered.

If only all of our prayers were as simple as ribbons, she thought, *maybe God would answer them all.*

The call from Detective Superintendent Murphy came while de Silva was sitting up in the office she'd made of the box room at the back of her house. The one she locked after herself and never let her sister Laney or niece Bonnie go into when they were visiting. Behind that closed door were the abominable things that had circled her life these past few years. The things that had reached into her home, into the nearness of the people she held dear. The ones she trusted most.

De Silva had left the papers, the crime scene reports and the manuscript that had become a key piece of evidence in her ongoing case into the alleged offences at Rainford Lane School for Boys, and closed the door, turned the key and pocketed it. She found herself thinking about it all of the time, even right then as she was on the phone to her boss. The institutional abuse that had led to so much violence, and she'd witnessed it all right there on the page, in the words of one of the victims, the now deceased Jacob Meeks.

'I'm afraid it's a bad one,' Murphy had said, her voice cold and crisp as any northern February morning. 'There will be media interest. Outcries no doubt,' she said. 'Outrage.'

And she'd been right. Someone had tipped off the local press, though she hadn't yet noticed that little idiot Joel Matthews from the *Liverpool Journal* near the exterior cordon. Usually, he'd be the first one there, his toothy grin that made de Silva feel queasy, and the stink of that aftershave he seemed to bathe in.

De Silva had collected herself on the landing, could hear Murphy doing something down the line, moving about, getting ready to leave her house maybe. 'Will you be there when I arrive?' de Silva asked, padding through to her en suite and grabbing her toothbrush.

'No,' Murphy had said. 'I have a meeting with the assistant chief constable. I'll await your update in my office later this morning.' Murphy hadn't told her what to expect, just that she should head to Southport pier immediately. Then the line had gone dead. Murphy never said goodbye and de Silva couldn't figure out why. An inefficient use of time? Wasted words? Something else? *Maybe it's a southern thing*, she thought.

The roads from Prescot to Southport had been icy; even the M57 had shone in her headlights like the glitter de Silva was still finding around her living room even all these weeks after Christmas.

De Silva used to think of times like Christmas and New Year as pre-Ritchie's death and post-Ritchie's death. The first Christmas since he'd died. The second birthday. The upcoming third Valentine's Day. With him gone and her mother in a care home forgetting herself, forgetting her life, these festivities and celebrations had seemed trivial. Unimportant.

But after spending this last Christmas with Laney and Bonnie, de Silva was glad they'd put their differences aside. Whatever the reason was for their falling-out, it all seemed to be over now. Since last year when Laney came to stay with de Silva for a while, after splitting from her violent, abusive cock of a husband. De Silva got to see how lovely having family at Christmas could feel. How magical it was for Bonnie.

She felt thankful for that. Warmed by it.

She'd made it down the Formby Bypass in one piece, but the snow had started to fall again as she turned left onto the coastal road. The sand dunes started to look like they were ice caps and de Silva wondered whether the snow would last. The weatherman on the news yesterday had seemed to think so.

As she drove, she thought of the victim left on the pier. In de Silva's mind, the victim was just a grey shape in the form of a human being right then. She didn't know any particulars like gender, age, race. But when she did, that grey blob would take on something more solid. More real. She wondered whether they'd celebrated Christmas in a warm home surrounded by a family who had loved them, before they were left for dead on a pier high above the Irish Sea.

She shuddered and turned on the radio.

'—disgraced retired MP Jeremiah Sure has died. In an official statement released by his family, Sure died in the early hours of yesterday morning when a fire broke out in his home. In an interview with the BBC, his daughter Meredith said: "I blame the police for this. Merseyside Police told lies about him, about his affiliations with that school. All of it unfounded. There was no evidence. My dad was beside himself. He'd become careless. Forgetful. They hounded him and now look."

'Sure, whose legacy includes fighting for free school meals for children from deprived areas of Merseyside, and the introduction of a sleep-away summer camp in Devon, was assisting Merseyside Police with their inquiries following a leaked list of apparent sexual predators who are accused of abusing children from the now-closed Rainford Lane School for Boys in the 1980s and 1990s. The fire department are still investigating—'

De Silva turned off the radio. She'd heard enough. How a fire breaking out was the fault of Merseyside Police was beyond her understanding. But this case was everywhere. It had been her entire life for the past few years. Bringing to light the truth of historical systemic institutional abuse of minors was no easy task, and on more than one occasion, de Silva questioned whether she was up to it. Just last year, she had uncovered the truth that her own husband had attended that school.

Regardless, Sure's death was a blow for the investigation, given that most people from the list leaked to her by a do-good internet sleuth hacker, were already dead. De Silva didn't even know the hacker's name, though they'd called themselves 'Breaker', which had made de Silva roll her eyes. She'd not been in touch since, and they'd never been able to track her down.

De Silva slipped on the blue shoe coverings and stepped out from the under the pop-up tent. From here, she could see the glare of lights below her, the flashes of cameras. Her every move was being watched.

She glanced down to the left of her, where some white chipboard had been torn off a make-shift frame. A laminated notice had been stapled to it: *Pier off limits. Closed for maintenance.* There was a clear, filthy mark on it, probably from an average-sized trainer.

She was sure she'd read somewhere that the pier had been closed for years, and she wondered what the hold-up was. Underfunding or an indecisive local council? Maybe both.

The frame was splintered and nails stuck out of it, threatening to claw at anyone who passed it. Clearly, whoever had wanted to get onto the pier wasn't going to let a piece of chipboard stop them. She could tell that it had been dusted for prints; black streaks of dust had begun to clump together in the snow and cold.

'Morning.' A voice ahead of her, so low it was almost a whisper. De Silva almost slipped on the ice. Area Forensics Manager Adam Brennan pulled down the hood that covered his head and removed the protective goggles. 'Careful there, Win,' he said. His hair was thinning at the temples, and he had that type of complexion that made him look like he'd just stepped off the plane from Corfu, no matter the time of year.

'You scared the life out of me there, Brennan.' De Silva shook her head. She'd worked with him on so many cases, and she admired him. He cared about the victim and that was important to her. He also had a reputation for sneaking about like a bloody cat.

'Sorry,' he said with a smile that told her he wasn't sorry at all. 'Look, it's not pretty down there.' His face changed, becoming solid and grey as stone. 'It's not going to be easy.' He stared at her with dark eyes in the gloom of the early morning and shook his head.

'You tell me a time they ever are, and I'll buy you a pint.'

'You're right,' he said. 'Bloody smart arse. I still want that pint though.'

'So, that door back there…'

'We already dusted it,' he said. 'Found some prints, so we'll run them when we're back at the lab. We got photographs of the shoe print on there, too.'

Good. 'Barclay here?'

'Boy Wonder? He's down there already.' Brennan gestured with a thumb over his shoulder. 'You know what he's like. First on the scene and—'

'—and last to leave,' de Silva said with a smile.

'Do me a favour,' he said. 'Stay to the right railing going down. There are footprints down the middle. Some blood too. A fair amount, actually. Trying to get an impression on the footprints, but you know... snow...'

Foot, de Silva thought, *not shoe.* 'The victim was barefoot?'

'No,' Brennan said. 'Well yes, the vic is, but we're not sure who those prints belong to. That's your job.' That childlike, wicked smile that cut halfway up his cheeks. 'Some blood on the railing, too. A full palm print. We've got a sample, but don't touch it until the team's all done, will you?'

'Yes, sir,' she mocked. De Silva ducked under another section of cordon and walked down toward the crime scene rigging at the end of the pier, held on to the chipped white metal railing and passed two Scientific Support officers covering a footprint with a plastic casing.

They're tiny feet, de Silva noted. Much smaller than her own. If she were to guess, she'd say four or four-and-a-half. If they weren't the victim's own, then who did they belong to? She shivered when she realised there was only one set of prints. In, not out. Maybe Brennan was wrong; perhaps those prints did belong to the victim.

Then there was the blood. Brennan hadn't been kidding about that. The deepest red de Silva thought she'd ever seen. Set against the quiet white of the snow, it looked like violent blots from some grim Rorschach test. Not in drips or drops, but jagged lines and smudges, as though the snow had open wounds of its own.

The lights ahead were brilliant white, the harsh kind that pricked at de Silva's eyes. As she looked ahead to them and felt them calling to her like some terrible lighthouse on a faraway shore, she almost slipped on some ice. She gripped the railing and, even through the blue nitrile gloves, the shock of the cold metal stabbed through the middle finger of her right hand. It had started to ache in the cold since autumn, especially around the scar, and if the weatherman was to be believed, this Arctic blast could last weeks. Snow the heaviest the north-west had seen in thirty years. The pain in her finger now rang through her entire hand, and she hissed at it.

The surgeon had told her to expect that, just one of the lovely new experiences she had to endure as a result of reattaching her finger. 'You could leave it,' the surgeon had said, 'get a prosthetic.'

'Why don't I take yours and see how you get on without it?' she'd bitten back, without intending to. It wasn't supposed to be missing. It was supposed to be part of her. If there was a chance, a remote possibility that a reattachment surgery would succeed, then she was taking it.

'You okay there?' The gruff timbre of Barclay's voice brought her back to herself. Even if he hadn't spoken, she'd know it was him from the hulk of his shoulders. DS Ben Barclay was a tall man, with the frame and build of a rugby player. Despite that, he jogged toward her, moving across the ice like a gazelle in grassland.

De Silva steadied herself just as he arrived. 'I'm at that age where falling is scary, Barclay. I've said it before, and I'll say it again. I'm a week away from sensible footwear, I know it. I'll keep Clarks in business.'

'Well, as long as you don't start wearing *Hush Puppies*. Besides, you've got the reflexes of a cat; look at that. You held on for dear life.' His eyes smiled under the hood of his white suit.

'At what age do you stop having fallen and started having had a fall, do you think?'

'Oh, I think you're a good five or six years off.'

'That's a relief.' They walked down toward the crime scene, where Barclay took her elbow and she batted him off. 'Get away, you soft sod.'

'I used to have to do this with my nan when I took her the bingo.'

'Are you looking for a demotion, Barclay, because I can make it happen.'

'Well just be careful.'

'I was being careful! Anyway, were you just heading off? I don't blame you. You'll want to get in the warm before you freeze your knackers off.'

'No, I was coming to get you.'

'So, what're we looking at? Murphy told me nothing.'

The smile and shine in Barclay's eyes went out, like a shadow passed over them and put out the light that was there. His shoulders rose and tensed, his back straightened. A physical change in him that de Silva had seen so many times. His professional switch, preparing himself to report on the findings. The facts. The matter at hand.

'There's no obvious cause of death.' His voice was clipped and muffled under his mask. 'By that, I mean there are no apparent injuries. Brennan thinks exposure.' He looked around at the fallen snow and hardening ice. 'I'd have to say I agree.'

De Silva kept her eyes on the ground, one foot in front of the other, and listened. 'Exposure? So, we're talking minimal clothing then?'

'The victim's naked,' Barclay said. 'Exposure and...'

'And what?'

'Well, she's young.' Barclay looked out over the railings at the coastal road. 'Very young.'

They walked on to the end of the pier which jutted out over the beach, where the sea had left the sand dark and wet when it receded. They passed the pavilion, boarded up now, but de Silva remembered arcades and laughter and hot drinks in polystyrene cups. Warm chips and runaway scarfs on bitter Irish Sea winds. Ahead of them, the bright white lights of the crime scene.

To de Silva, the light rigging felt like a gateway, like something she had to pass through – physically and emotionally –

to get to the other side. To the awful, dreadful nightmare that would always, inevitably, lie beyond. She steeled herself for the transition from nighttime into the clinical light of the crime itself.

A tent had been pitched against the railings, and it trembled in the breeze. De Silva stepped into the white light and there she stopped, took a few deep breaths to settle herself before she stepped into the tent.

Barclay pulled back the flap and de Silva felt something crawl up her spine. A cold, harsh chill, and then she knew why the crime scene tent had shivered. Her breath caught in her chest, and she could hear the desperate thrum of her heartbeat in her ears as she peered down at the young victim.

The umbilical cord was attached.

She took deep breaths to steady herself, and took all of it in. The cord wasn't cut with pristine precision. The end was rough, frayed almost, like an old rope.

Like it was bitten through, she thought. Next to it, a mass of red, and for a minute de Silva wondered whether it was a twin. She took a step closer, felt bile rise and burn in her chest, but couldn't look away.

The placenta, de Silva thought. *God, she must have been just hours old. If that.*

De Silva knelt down next to the baby, her skin turned blue in the cold air. She looked back down the length of the pier in the direction she and Barclay had just come from. One set of footprints in. Nothing heading back out. She glanced over at the railings, searched them until she found the red patch of a palm print which Brennan had told her about.

She closed her eyes and let the scene around her form in the blank canvas space of her mind. She quickly reconstructed an approximation of the pier, of the boardwalk, of the beach below where the tide was so far out, she couldn't see it. Snow drifted down onto the pier and then there were the feet. Those small size fours, naked, cut, filthy and cold. Then came the blood.

It dripped down from between her legs, slid down them like rivers toward the sea. The woman with the small feet shivered in the cold.

The baby would be in her arms, either cold as stone or screaming, wailing. The mother would be in pain. Agonising, excruciating, and de Silva wondered if this was where the baby had died, or where she'd been born. In her mind, the mother put the baby down, kicking and in need of comfort, and she'd laid down next to her daughter as her body pushed out the placenta.

'Are you all right?' Barclay's voice caused de Silva's eyes to snap open, bringing her back to the present for the second time that day.

'I think she jumped, Barclay,' de Silva said. 'Whatever happened here, I think she jumped over the railings.'

'It's not that big a drop,' he said, moving to the railings and peering down. 'Broken bones at most, do you think?'

De Silva joined him at the railing then looked out to the open plane of the beach and said, 'Not if the tide was in.'

She thought again of the footprints walking in, the blood. 'Maybe her baby died, and she couldn't live with it.'

'Or maybe she left her here to die, and she couldn't live with *that*?'

'We need a search team,' de Silva said. 'Now.'

Two

Barclay had come to question his beliefs. The things he'd always clung to, the way he was raised as a kid. The truths he knew as absolutes. That God protected the good and the righteous. That evil is an entity, a thing that slithers from street to home, from bed to corporate boardroom. How could he not believe, given the things he saw daily? His work – the terrible, awful, heartbreaking things he witnessed – the constant churn of the things that people do to each other.

As he was standing there over the tiny baby girl, he knew the truth he'd tried so hard to rally against stared him in the face: everyone has the capacity to do evil.

Beyond his beliefs was his detective brain, his training, his reasoning beyond a Catholic upbringing. There was a kind of comfort in the binary of good and evil, the black and white of it, that the detective in him couldn't reason with. In reality, Barclay had come to know that things were more nuanced.

Barclay thought of his own daughter, eight years old now, and going on eighty. She'd be fast asleep in her comfortable bed in the home Barclay once shared with his husband. *Then there's all of that*, he thought. He knew that their marriage was over, that they'd been unhappy for some time, and that unhappiness had led them both to sleep with other men. But he'd never really understood the reasons why they were unhappy. He didn't know what had changed. There was that nuance again.

His marriage. The awful things from his past that he could never give a name to. Everything he'd seen in his career so far was exemplified and amplified in that little baby girl, dead, naked, and alone on a boardwalk above the wild Irish Sea. It would haunt him in his dreams, along with everything else.

Sure, he'd tried all kinds of therapy from talking to eye movement desensitisation and reprogramming techniques, and nothing had really worked for him. Instead, Barclay had found his own way of coping. Medication. Sometimes even that had drawbacks. It was more obvious in situations where he knew he should be feeling something strongly.

Like right then, staring at that baby, he should feel angry. He should feel hurt. He should feel… something. Instead, he had just a sense of those emotions, but they weren't solid. It was as though they were smoke. Like they were far away, and he could see the light of them through cotton wool.

'We're ready to go.' Brennan's voice came from nowhere. Barclay hadn't even heard him approaching. 'Have you got everything you need?'

'We're done, I think,' de Silva said.

Barclay wanted to say something, anything, but his brain couldn't quite catch up. He nodded instead.

'Did you manage to get an impression of that footprint?' de Silva asked.

'We did,' Brennan said. 'And the photography team have been all over the scene, so we're ready to, er…' His eyes locked on the baby on the floor, and for a moment the only sound was the flapping of the crime scene tent.

'Should I?' de Silva asked.

'I've got her.' Barclay swooped her up into his arms and wished he could make her warm again, turn her skin back to a healthy pink and breathe life into those tiny lungs.

As they headed back down the boardwalk into the dark, Barclay felt de Silva's hand on his back. He didn't want to think of what would happen to the baby next, but he knew that everyone who had to work with her, on her, would treat her with the respect she deserved. With care. With feeling.

Something she didn't have in her short little life, Barclay thought.

When Brennan held out his hands to take her the rest of the way, Barclay didn't want to let her go. Didn't want to give her up. 'Take care of her,' he whispered.

Brennan nodded and took the girl into his own arms and held her close. Maybe he felt the same. Maybe he wanted to warm her, too. In that moment, there was a flash of a camera from somewhere below. The thought of cameramen and journalists relishing this moment flustered Barclay but surely they couldn't see anything from down there. Not at that angle.

When they were alone, they removed their crime scene kits. 'Who found her?' de Silva asked, reaching for her black padded coat and pulling it on quickly. 'Did anyone take a statement?'

'It was a drone,' Barclay said.

'I'm sorry?' De Silva took out her phone and tried to dial out. 'For God's sake. No service, and I left my radio in the car.'

'Yeah, me too,' Barclay said, taking off his protective shoe coverings. 'Come on, I'll tell you all about it somewhere warm and we'll call in. I could do with a brew.'

-

He pulled at the car handle with his little finger and spilled some of his black coffee onto the ice. Not his first choice, but he doubted McDonald's did an oat milk latte, and he didn't want to embarrass himself by asking.

De Silva was sitting in the passenger seat, one hand over the heating vent, her radio in the other. 'Thank you,' she said. 'Over.' She put the radio away on her holster, the one she hardly ever took off, and grabbed one of the coffees from Barclay. 'They're putting a team together, but with this weather, it's going to take a little longer than normal. Meanwhile, that mother could be on that beach.'

Barclay climbed into the car and closed the door against the cold. The engine hummed lightly, and the headlights illuminated snow banked against the kerbs of the carpark.

'I know what you're thinking, de Silva, and the answer is no.'

'I don't remember asking you a question, Barclay, and I don't remember you being promoted to a position where I need to ask your permission.' De Silva took a sip of her coffee and winced, placed it down in a cup holder near the handbrake.

'Well, it's still a no,' he said. 'You're not going off trundling down Southport beach in the dark looking for a missing woman on your own. You know I'm right.'

'I know the right thing to do is to be out there searching for her.'

'And we will. When the team arrive.' Barclay took a swig of his coffee, and it tasted burned. He swallowed it and put the cup in the holder next to de Silva's. Still, at least the car was warm.

'So, this drone then?'

'Yeah,' he said, picking the coffee back up just so he could feel its warmth. 'There was a fella out here flying his drone. Mitchel Whitley.'

'In the middle of the night?'

'Well, technically it's early hours in the morning, but yeah I do see your point,' he said. 'Uniform took a statement. He said he was trying to capture some footage of the beach and the pier with the snow coming in for his social media channel. He's well known for sharing drone footage, "showing the people a look at Merseyside as they've never seen it before". He's done flyovers of the Bramley Dock construction, abandoned buildings. All that. He's very popular.'

'Lord have mercy. Please!' de Silva said. 'You know, I always wonder what these influencers would have done in the nineties when the lecky went and their mum didn't have enough in the emergency.'

Barclay laughed. 'Imagine livestreaming on dial-up.'

'Kids these days don't know what dial-up even is.'

'I can confirm that's correct, and let's not even touch on floppy disks.'

'You can keep your floppy disks to yourself, Barclay.'

'Besides, Mitchel Whitley isn't a kid,' Barclay said and took another sip of coffee despite himself. 'He's in his thirties. "It's Whitley, Mitch." That's the name of his social media channel.'

'No, you're taking the piss.'

'I'm not. I think it's a take on Britney—'

'Yes, I get it. That name though… seems familiar.'

'I'm getting there.'

De Silva glanced at the clock on the dashboard and said, 'So, he was flying his drone around hoping to catch some snow rolling in. Are they even waterproof those things? I mean, I'd assume so.'

Barclay shrugged. 'Wouldn't know. I'm sure they're hardy. Anyway, he was flying over the pier and spotted something lying there.'

De Silva cleared her throat.

'He thought she was a doll at first,' Barclay went on. 'You know, a toy? Something someone had left there.'

'Someone did leave her there.'

'Yeah.' Barclay looked out of the window and wished he'd chosen a better turn of phrase. He reasoned with himself quickly that there was no time to sit and overthink every word that came out of his mouth. 'He flew the drone down, took a closer look, called the police right away. Thank God he had the presence of mind not to go up there himself.'

De Silva stared out of the windscreen and Barclay followed her eyeline to where the snow had turned shrubs and bushes white as clouds. Barclay knew that her mind would already be in motion, already looking for holes in Whitley's story.

'I know what you're thinking,' he said.

'Again? You're getting good at this.'

'You're thinking, "How would he have the presence of mind not to go and help if he thought a baby had been abandoned in the snow."' He grinned. 'Am I right?'

'You give me the creeps sometimes, do you know that? You've started to think like me and it's worrying. It's like you're learning who I am so you can become me. Are you some Musk-created AI robot that's infiltrated Merseyside Police?'

'No, I'm just getting good at reading you,' he said. 'Anyway, I've got an answer for you if you want to hear it.'

'Yes, Detective Sergeant GPT, I want to hear it.'

'Mr Whitley could tell, or had good reason to believe, that the baby had… well… that she had already passed,' Barclay said, stumbling over his own words. 'In that case, he knew not to go up there himself because he used to be one of us.'

'A bobby?' Her was voice high and incredulous.

Barclay nodded. 'That must be how you recognise the name. A bobby turned social media professional a few years back.'

'Well, who did he work for?'

'I'm not sure,' he said. 'But he was uniform when he left.'

'That's quite a change, isn't it? Uniformed officer to social media personality? Still, I wouldn't mind speaking to him myself.'

Barclay looked down at his lap. He had answers, but not all of them.

'Let's call him,' she said. 'See if we can get him out to the OCC for questioning. I don't mind coming to him if I have to, but I'd rather be on our turf.'

De Silva's radio fizzed and buzzed from her klick-fast, and she drew it out. A scratchy, fuzzy message that the Coastguard had put together a team and that she and Barclay were to meet them. 'Roger,' she said. 'We'll head over now. Over.' She reattached the radio to her holster. 'Come on,' she said, already climbing out of the car. 'Let's get this woman found.'

Barclay wanted to remind her that there were no guarantees. They might never find the baby's mother. *That, after all, was the point of her jumping, wasn't it?*

Three

'Do you know anything about tides?' de Silva asked Barclay as they crossed Marine Drive toward the path that ran parallel with the beach. It had stopped snowing again now, but the sky was dark with the threat of more.

'Oh yes,' Barclay said. 'I'm a regular sailor.'

De Silva laughed, one loud 'hah' which echoed down the street. 'I'm not even touching that one, Barclay. But you want to thank your lucky stars McLachlan's still off, and O'Connor or Braxton aren't here. You'd never live that one down.'

He took out his phone and tutted. 'You know what I meant.'

'Oh, yes, I know what you meant.'

'Any news about McLachlan coming back?'

'Not yet,' de Silva said. 'He's been in and out of hospital with that Covid pneumonia.'

'Poor fella,' Barclay said. He groaned. 'Bloody signal's awful. Never mind dial-up, Wi-Fi in 2025 is just as shocking. High tide was 11:51 p.m. last night. It says high tides happen around twelve and a half hours apart. Takes about… six hours for the water at the shoreline to go from high to low, and vice versa.'

'What time was the drone footage from?'

'About 1:30 a.m. So, we're talking high-ish tide. Say this woman can't swim, or she's hit her head,' Barclay said, putting his phone away. 'She could have been swept out to sea.'

I think that was her intention, de Silva thought. *But why?* 'Maybe she didn't want the baby. Maybe she was stillborn. Maybe she panicked, left the baby and tried to take her own life? Anyway, let's not get ahead of ourselves. Anything could have happened.'

They headed toward a small roundabout at the bottom of Marine Drive, where de Silva could make out some headlights through snow-capped shrubs. De Silva sighed. 'I've been dreaming of some beach time, but this isn't what I had in mind.'

'You and me both.'

De Silva had considered calling in the helicopter, but reason had kicked in. They'd never lift off with the threat of snow still in the air, even for a missing person. Still, even if they would, the cost of the thing would tear right into her budget. And that, she decided, was the awful, messy, political state of things: finding the truth, protecting the vulnerable, solving the worst crimes imaginable, all came at a cost.

Every penny would be scrutinised by accountants, raked over by the finance team in HQ who'd never investigated a crime in their lives, and all of it had to make sense when de Silva filed the final report on the case. Spending public money was a serious business.

As they turned right on the roundabout, the Coastguard unit was sitting there waiting, a white Mitsubishi, decked out in reflective markings and with lights on the roof. A man leaned against the hood, bundled up in a thick coat, and on his head was a green beanie, the colour of forests in summer.

He stood up straight when he saw them, flicked a cigarette on the floor and stumped it out with the toe of his heavy boot. He eyed de Silva with a frown then looked at Barclay and said, 'You the DCI I'm here to meet?' his voice made hoarse by what de Silva guessed was years of smoking. 'De Silva?'

'I'm DCI de Silva,' she said. 'I know it's early, so thanks for making it.'

The man shrugged. 'We were on call. Just sorry we couldn't mobilise quicker. This weather, you know.'

De Silva looked into the car then, where a woman was sitting in the passenger seat, her dark hair tied back into the ponytail inevitably adopted by long-haired women in emergency response. She waved, her smile Cheshire cat-like.

'Anyway, I'm Ste,' the man said, shaking their hands. 'That's Sheryl. You ready to go?'

De Silva and Barclay climbed into the back seat of the car. She made herself comfortable while Barclay fastened his seatbelt. The diesel engine whirred, groaned, and chugged as they moved off the roadside and onto the sand.

The beach spread out in front of them and in the dark, de Silva could barely make out the open expanse of wet sand until Sheryl pushed a button on the dashboard console and the beach was illuminated in cold, white light. Patches of fallen snow scarred the landscape in ripples, like it had healed wounds left by the ebbing tide.

The sea was so far away she couldn't make it out, and though she could hear nothing over the engine, de Silva could imagine that it was deathly quiet out there when no one was around. De Silva knew the sea was out there somewhere, rolling over itself and crashing onto the shore. It was there. Like *she* was. The baby's poor mother. Probably pulled out by gravity and tidal motion and maybe dropped somewhere at the bottom of the Irish Sea, her flesh and bones peeling away layer by layer.

Snow began to fall again, and de Silva knew their time with the Coastguard would be cut short. Flecks moved past so quickly it reminded de Silva of that scene in *Star Wars* when the *Millennium Falcon* goes into hyperdrive. The flakes were stars rushing past them as they moved forward.

Barclay leaned across the back passenger bench to de Silva and said loudly over the engine, 'There's a lot of ground to cover here.'

'I'm hoping the weather clears soon,' she said. 'Get that helicopter out. But the more time that goes by...'

She didn't need to finish the sentence, assumed Barclay knew the implication of it. The more time that went by, the more likely the mother was dead. Two lives gone in a matter of just hours and for what?

De Silva turned back toward the window, was convinced the seat under her was wet and had begun to seep through her coat and jeans. The last thing she needed was a chapped arse on top of everything else. They passed under the pier, its ancient structure shining black under the light from the Coastguard vehicle, and thick with barnacles. Then, something caught her eye.

'There!' she called out. The car stopped.

'It's a snow drift,' Ste said over his shoulder. 'Your eyes play tricks on you out there in the dark. There're torches under the seat,' he added. 'You know, I knew a man who was convinced he'd seen a penguin out here once.'

De Silva reached down for the torch under her seat and Barclay copied.

'What did it turn out to be?' Barclay asked.

'Well, it was a penguin,' Ste said, his voice flat, the car rumbling across the sand again. 'But, you know, a plastic one. Something from the fairground we think. We've had all kinds wash up here in the past.'

'I'm not sure that's a snow drift,' de Silva said, shining her light out into the black. 'Stop the car.'

It skidded to a stop, wet sand slapping against the window in dark clots.

De Silva opened the door and was out on the beach, the full beam of her torch reaching far into the distance. She started to run, convinced by what she'd seen just seconds ago. Behind her, she could hear Barclay's voice, lost somewhere in the wind that galloped down Southport beach. 'De Silva, wait!'

She could hear the engine then, getting louder, closer. Lights shone on the ground ahead of her. Barclay's sharp breath behind her, the sound of his feet on wet sand.

She stopped dead then. Looked left and right. She'd seen it, she was sure of it. A lumpy thing that looked like it didn't belong. Barclay caught up, a torch in his hand, and their beams crossed.

'Bloody hell, de Silva,' he breathed. 'Didn't think you had that in you.'

'I've been practising,' she said. 'I was sure that I—'

Barclay's light fell on it then. That same heap of black and white de Silva was convinced she'd seen from the car. 'Jesus…' he said. He had his phone out but shoved it back in his pocket. 'No signal.'

De Silva reached for her radio once more. The one she'd worn on her holster every day since that dreadful night at Rainford Lane school, where Lamond had attacked them both and almost succeeded in killing them. 'This is DCI de Silva,' she said. 'I need you to place a call for an ambulance.'

'BC7568 receiving. Yes, yes on ambulance request. Over.'

The black and white mound was just a hundred or so feet from the edge of the pier. Hair darkened by seawater, matted and spread around the woman's head almost like a dark halo. The torchlight on her pale skin made it shine like the inside of a shell which had been eaten out by seagulls.

But there, in the middle of the torchlight, barefoot and in a threadbare slip or nightgown, caked in blood and sand, was the person they suspected of being the baby's mother. As they approached, it became clear to de Silva what they were dealing with.

'God, Barclay,' de Silva whispered. 'She can't be more than thirteen years old.'

She knelt down, cold and wet spreading through the knees of her jeans. She put her fingers to the girl's neck and held her own breath.

Four

The corridors of Southport and Formby District Hospital were colder than it was outside, like the very bricks were made from ice. A patchwork of old brown and orange vinyl tiles, leftovers from the 1970s probably, led Barclay past single-pane glass windows and up a sloped corridor to the intensive care department.

In the ward, each patient slept in beds with tubes emanating from their bodies. A nurse checked a bag of clear fluids on an IV pole next to the bed of the girl they'd found. She was bound in several thick blankets, only her head and neck exposed. Now that her hair was dry, Barclay could see it was a mousy brown.

The nurse made some notes on a clipboard then slotted it back into the holder at the foot of the bed. Barclay spoke softly, quietly, though he doubted any of the other four patients could hear him. 'How is she doing?' He held up his warrant card, and the nurse's expression softened.

Barclay clocked the name badge, faded and worn. *Doreen*. A simple gold cross on a thin chain hung around her neck. Right then, Barclay decided that Doreen had been in this job for years, decades even. Her hair was greying around the temples, and her brown eyes were lined from laughter, or crying, and on her face, she wore the crumpled look of concern.

'She's seriously unwell,' Doreen said finally, with a faint hint of an Irish accent. She patted the girl's feet gently, now warm under the thick lemon-yellow blankets. 'The doctor has examined her.' Here, Doreen took a breath. Whether to stall what she needed to say next, Barclay couldn't be sure. 'Shall I ask her to come and speak with you?'

'Is she available?'

'I can check.'

Doreen excused herself and for the first time, Barclay studied the girl in front of him. There were bruises across her face, a moody watercolour in shades of blues and purples and yellows. He knew what that meant without any doctor having to tell him. Experience had taught Barclay that bruises turn yellow-green five to ten days after the trauma has occurred. He found himself wondering whether the girl had had other bruises. Ones that had already faded. Or, grimly, ones that might never fade.

'I'm sorry,' Doreen said as she approached the bed. 'The doctor isn't available. She's with another patient. But she's asked me to go through things with you as best I can. Would that be okay? Or you could wait for Doctor Clements? I just don't know how long she'll be.'

I don't have the time to wait, he thought. 'I trust you,' he said. 'You know, I read once that patients can hear people around them when they're in this state. Is there somewhere we can talk privately?'

Doreen smiled and said, 'Come this way, Detective.'

Barclay followed her out onto the main corridor of the ward and noticed that the shade of teal scrubs on her trousers was slightly darker than her top. Probably an imperceptible difference to the casual onlooker, and maybe to Doreen herself. Her trainers were all-black Nikes, which squeaked when she turned sharply into a little side room. Her perfume smelled like a summer in the 1990s and early 2000s, bright and citrus.

CK1 by Calvin Klein, he thought. He hadn't smelled that in such a long time. Not since his teenage years in school when he'd first discovered aftershaves and wet-look hair gel. For a while, it had been his signature scent.

'Take a seat,' Doreen said as she sat down. 'We're waiting for a private room to become available, but once there is one, she'll be moved in there. Do you have news on who she is yet?'

'No, not yet.'

'I understand she was found in water?'

'Well, on the beach.'

'Right, I see.' Doreen leaned in, her elbows on her knees. 'Well, she's lucky.' She shook her head. 'Considering the alternative, I mean. God bless her. She has a fractured talus, her ankle there. Also, a fractured tibia, and you could see the bruising for yourself. Most of it, anyway.'

'Most of it?'

'Yes, it's quite extensive. She did have water in her lungs, which we've managed to clear. There's a bleed on her brain and she's scheduled for surgery in the morning,' she said. 'With injuries like hers though… it can make surgery more complicated. So, we'll keep her under for now and hopefully bring some of that swelling down, too.'

'Will she regain consciousness?'

'We can't say for sure,' she said. 'The bleed on her brain might have… Well… she might not be entirely herself even if she did regain consciousness.' Doreen opened her mouth to say something else but stopped herself. Her lips formed a hard line, and her eyes flitted to the ground then back to Barclay.

'I get the sense there's more you want to say.'

Doreen sat back in her chair. 'I've done this job for almost thirty years, you know, though I may not look it.' She chortled and Barclay smiled politely. 'We see all sorts of things pass through those doors, especially so during Covid times. I've seen women give birth after spending five hours stuck in a car wreck on the M55. I've helped to treat babies suffering from neonatal abstinence syndrome while their mothers talk to the wall about a new washing machine, high as kites. Had to call people on Skype to tell them their loved ones were no longer with us. Send their belongings back to their families in a plastic bag after they'd been quarantined.'

Doreen closed her eyes and Barclay wondered whether she was collecting her thoughts, or unsure about how to proceed.

He'd read somewhere that health professionals who had worked through the Covid pandemic were in the throes of PTSD, and that was something Barclay could relate to. 'But…?' he nudged, gently.

'That poor girl.' Doreen shook her head, her eyes slick as wet glass. 'I can't imagine what she went through to deliver that baby.'

'You're certain she gave birth then?'

Doreen nodded.

At least we know she's definitely the mother, Barclay thought.

'But,' Doreen began, 'there's evidence of… horrendous abuse.' She crossed herself and leaned forward again. 'Can I say something? But you have to understand this isn't the language the hospital would have me use. I'd never write this in her notes, and Dr Clements would probably have me sacked. I'll tell you my opinion if it's off the record?'

'We'll draw our own conclusions when we get the doctor's notes.' Barclay nodded. 'Go on.'

'What I saw during her examination… what I saw goes well beyond just childbirth, Detective. There was…' She trailed off and looked to the window, where another nurse hurried past, but peered in for a moment.

'You can tell me,' he said in a soft, comforting voice.

'Poor girl,' she said. 'They must have…' Doreen wiped away the tears that now tipped out of her eyes and down her cheeks, leaving pale scars in her foundation. 'They must have really wanted to hurt her. Really wanted her to suffer.'

Barclay put a hand on Doreen's knee, soft and reassuring, he hoped. 'I'm sorry you had to see that. It must have been difficult.' Barclay swallowed down his own experiences. The awful things he'd felt during his navy career and the brutality of killers like Lewis Lamond, the hatred and anger he'd taken out on his victims. On their bodies.

He knew what Doreen had seen because he had seen it himself. Had felt it. Had known it intimately in the showers aboard the HMS *Iron Duke* when blood ran down his legs and into the drain.

If only these horrible things that happen to us were as easy to wash away as blood, he thought.

'I'll be fine,' Doreen said. 'I'm being a silly beggar, sure I am. And besides, God is watching over that poor girl. I know He is.'

Barclay's fingernails dug into his palms. Some men feel like they can do whatever they want, whenever they want. Demand things of people they think are weaker. Inferior. Demand things of their bodies, their minds. And if they don't give them up willingly, they are taken by force. No doesn't mean no. To them, it's an alternative way of saying yes.

God may be watching her now, Barclay thought. *But where was He when she was suffering? And who is watching the animals that keep doing this to people?*

-

Barclay walked through the sliding doors of the hospital's main entrance and out into the cold early February morning, where the air stung his cheeks. Tufts of snow fell like tiny pigeon feathers when a flock is spooked, and it reminded Barclay of being at the Pier Head with Sarah, where she'd charge at pigeons until they took flight and circled until it was safe again.

Across the carpark, leaning against the driver-side door of her car, was de Silva on her phone. When she saw him, she hung up and headed over. 'How is she?'

'Couldn't see the doctor. A Dr Clements,' he said. 'But I spoke with a nurse who said... well, let's get back to the station. Clements might have sent her official notes over by then.'

'I've got that appointment to get to.' Her voice had a wobble to it, which Barclay decided sounded almost like she was about to become overwhelmed. 'Nothing to worry about and I'll be back this afternoon.'

'Okay.' He felt de Silva didn't want to tell him where she was going, and that was her right to do so. She wasn't answerable to him in any way.

He studied de Silva's face. Something had crumpled her brow into ridges, like sand when the tide has gone out. 'So, how is she?' she asked.

'Well we know for certain she gave birth recently,' he said. 'She's in a really bad way, de Silva. There are signs of extensive physical abuse.'

'Sexual?'

'Doreen, the nurse I spoke to, seemed to think so,' he said. 'But we won't know for certain until we get that report from the doctor.'

'This keeps happening, doesn't it?' De Silva looked up into Barclay's face, her eyes searching his for something Barclay was unsure of. 'I don't know what we can do to stop it. All these women and girls who get hurt, butchered, raped by men.' She paused, as though thinking what to say next. 'I feel like we're coming in too late. The damage is already done and we're just trying to Sellotape a picture together to understand who did it and why. Catch the bad guy when he's already done the bad stuff.'

'We can't see the future,' Barclay said. 'We don't know what's around the corner, because how can we? But we do piece it together because we have to. It's our job and we're good at it. We do it every day. And we do it because we have to hope that we make a difference. That we can make it before the bad guy hurts someone else.'

Barclay almost believed his own words. They felt hollow in his mouth, like they were echoes of things other people had thought or said. Things he was supposed to say and feel. He knew there was no conviction behind his words because, ultimately, de Silva was right. The law isn't set up to protect women and girls before something can happen. But did Barclay himself believe? He didn't know how to answer that question any more.

'You're right,' de Silva said.

'You get to your appointment, and I'll head back to the OCC, see if we can get a name of our girl in there.'

'I've got a name,' de Silva said.

'I left you in the carpark for ten minutes, de Silva…'

She held up her phone with a smile. 'That was Lawrence.'

'Any news on her detective exam results?'

'Nothing yet, but I know she'll have passed,' de Silva said. 'She'll be fine.'

Barclay knew the same. He liked Lawrence. Admired her. Saw a lot of his younger self in her. 'So, this name?'

'Beatrice Tredwell,' de Silva said. 'She went missing from a mental health facility in Manchester three weeks ago. Lawrence went through the missing persons, found a social media post someone had made, and sent it through. I was able to ID her. But, there's more…'

'Go on.'

'There was a storm the night she went missing. Caused a power outage,' de Silva said. 'They thought she was still sleeping, but found her door ajar. Anyway, they realised it wasn't her in the bed. Just a pillow made to look like she was sleep.'

'A bloody pillow! Jesus, does that trick actually work?' Barclay shook his head. 'We'll need an official ID. I'll ask Lawrence to get in touch with the family.'

'She's already working on getting in touch with the biological father now.' De Silva checked her watch and pulled open the car door. 'Look, I'm going to have to set off. But her mother's new husband… well, he's under suspicion of sexual assault. Beatrice accused him of a spate of attacks before she was checked into the facility.'

'Do you think it was him who took her? If she's accused him of abuse, and given what the nurse told me…' He trailed off. 'I'll get in touch with the mother then.'

'You can't.' De Silva climbed into her car and started the engine. The window wipers squeaked across the glass of the windscreen, and the radio hummed softly, some song that sounded the same as every other song on the radio these days.

'Why not?'

'Greater Manchester Police don't know where she is.'

Five

De Silva had lied to Barclay. There was no getting around that.

Ordinarily, she wouldn't, and she knew that he knew she would usually rearrange any personal appointments when a case of this magnitude presented itself. She was also aware that she was purposely vague with Barclay, and was certain he'd have picked up on it and had questions.

However, this wasn't an ordinary appointment. Even that morning, when they found the baby on the pier, the teenage girl on the beach, de Silva had it in her mind to cancel. The girl was alive, though. Barely, but she was in the best place, receiving care in hospital. There was work to do, she knew that. She reasoned with herself that Barclay knew what he was doing. And, as a detective chief inspector, she didn't need to be hands on all of the time. DSI Murphy had reminded her of that fact many times. That was her way, though. It was how she operated.

Barclay knows that, too.

She'd received the phone call just two days ago, when she had her head deep in her mum's paperwork. An old pension policy de Silva hadn't known anything about, from a curtain company her mother had apparently worked for in the 1970s on the corner of Long Lane, and some other smaller pots from previous employers which looked as though they'd been drained dry to cover her care.

De Silva's mobile phone had rung out. A call from a number she recognised all too well as HMP Hull. It would be his fourth attempt to reach her that week. She couldn't say why she'd answered that time. To hear a familiar voice even after everything he'd done? To see what he had to say for himself after these long months since his arrest? Perhaps to distract herself from the paperwork, from the worrying about how she and Laney would afford her mum's care going forward.

She had answered the phone, despite knowing there was a massive red flag waving right in her face. It was more than a professional conflict of interest due to the ongoing investigation. She was the lead investigator on the case where he was a perpetrator. This couldn't end well, she knew that. Still, she answered.

Now, as she was sitting in the waiting room of HMP Hull, after all of the other visitors were gathered into the main visitors' centre, de Silva was asked to step into a side room. She was searched, a little too rigorously she thought, and then led into another room where there was a table and two chairs, all bolted to the ground. A small rectangular window high up on the wall let in soft yellow light. A prison guard was standing inside the door.

O'Brien had never been a slender man, but as de Silva walked into that tiny room which smelled like bleach, she saw now that his time inside had taken several pounds from his frame. His neck had turned into loose, sagging skin, and his almost seventy years – the same age as her father would have been – had caught up with him.

'Sit down, sit down,' he said with a beaming smile, as though welcoming her for afternoon tea at The Ivy. His eyes were wide, taking all of her in. 'You're looking well, Win. Taking better care of yourself now. Ah, it's wonderful to see. Kath would be so proud.'

His wife. She'd died from cancer last year, and de Silva had always thought of her as a friend. But since O'Brien's arrest, the detective in her couldn't help but wonder what Kath had known, what she had let slide, and there was a guilt in even thinking that of a dead woman.

She'd seen so many criminals come through those interview rooms who had led double lives that their loved ones had known nothing about.

'You look ill,' de Silva said.

O'Brien looked down at the scratched and stained table. 'Well, I'm not at my healthiest, I'll say that. This place...'

In truth, de Silva was surprised he was still alive. In de Silva's experience, nonces had a way of finding themselves hurt or injured, clinging on to life in the hospital wing; because their beating, their murder, would be a badge of honour for most other inmates. De Silva had half expected a phone call from the prison to say that he'd been found hanged in his cell, like Lewis Lamond had been.

That monster had torn through Liverpool when he'd raped and murdered teenage girls two years ago. His particular psychological damage was made up of a mixture of his upbringing, a hostile neglectful mother, an absent father, and because he attended Rainford Lane School for Boys, where multitudes of little boys were subjected to horrendous attacks. The same school where O'Brien himself had abused young boys in the nineties, whose names he would never remember. Maybe Lamond himself was one of O'Brien's victims. It was the same school where de Silva's own husband, Ritchie, had been a pupil.

O'Brien had told her once, when he'd been arrested, that there would be a clean-up operation to follow. That the people behind the abuse at the school, behind an app that had been rife across the smart devices of young kids, would leave no stone unturned when they needed to protect themselves.

It was de Silva's belief that Lamond was killed before he got to speak out about something he may have known. Before he revealed any identities. Last year, when people connected to the school were turning up dead, Jacob Meeks, a man who had also attended Rainford Lane, was found murdered. Brutally butchered in his own flat.

And of course, her own Ritchie had...

Well, death seemed to follow those poor boys like it followed de Silva, and at the heart of it was O'Brien and his friends. The ones he'd never grass on.

'What do you want from me?' de Silva asked.

'You'll be pleased by the news reports, I'm sure,' he said, smiling. 'Jeremiah Sure. Another one bites the dust?'

'I don't feel that way, no,' she said. 'If there was any justice in the world, he'd answer for what he did in court.'

'He may not have even done anything; who can tell?'

'You can tell.' She restrained herself from an outburst, kept her voice low and even. 'You'd know if he was involved. If anyone else on that list we were given was involved. All those judges. GPs. Surgeons. Politicians. *You* can tell.'

O'Brien glared at her with eyes that, she was sure, had once been blue. Now they were dull and grey, with lined skin and dark circles around them. He looked like a spectre. 'How's your mum? Little Marie Brophy.' He laughed. 'She was a firecracker in her younger years, you know? Always giving your dad what-for when he stepped out of line. Probably where you get it from. Never afraid to speak your mind.'

'There are a few things on my mind right now if you'd like to hear them?'

He laughed again and held up his hands in mock surrender. 'Oh, please. Go ahead. Lash me with your judgement.'

'You deserve to be judged.'

'As do you,' O'Brien said. 'We all do. Every single person on the planet.'

De Silva eyed him, noticed how the grey tracksuit he wore hung loose from his body. 'Not every single person on this planet buggered countless schoolboys. You're a paedophile, Tom. You can't even tell me whether my own husband was one of your victims because there were so many of them.'

Behind her, the prison guard cleared his throat and she was sure she caught him utter 'Jesus' under his breath.

She went on, 'You tried to conceal evidence in the murder of Jacob Meeks, the man who was about to publish a book, a first-hand account of his experiences, and about his theories on this organisation you've tried to protect and—'

O'Brien put a hand up. 'Okay, enough.' He coughed repeatedly, and de Silva caught a wince.

He's in pain.

'You've got it all backwards,' he said. 'I'm not trying to protect them. Not now. I'd tell you, but you wouldn't listen, would you?'

'I've wanted to hear you tell me everything since I arrested you,' she spat out.

'And didn't that feel good?' He grinned at her; even his teeth seemed discoloured in this place.

In truth, it hadn't felt good. It had felt awful. 'So, are you ready to talk?'

He sighed, sat back in his chair and looked about himself, at the dank place he'd found himself in. 'What's become of us, Win? I didn't ask for the feelings I have,' he said. 'I didn't want to act on them.' He cocked his head. 'You're right that I couldn't tell you whether Ritchie was one of mine.'

That made her shudder.

O'Brien continued, 'Whether any of them were. That embarrasses me.'

That's the bit he's embarrassed about, she thought. She kept her eyes on him, allowing him to fill the silence between them.

'There were so many,' he said. 'They would come and go. They'd come in from... well, all over the place really. And that book, I took it because of what it said about your Ritchie. How he took the life of one of his abusers and buried the body out there in those woods.'

'You took that book because if I found what it said, I'd be able to connect all of the dots, leading right back to you,' she said, looking away from him, staring at the grimy prison wall. She doubted very much that anything O'Brien had done in his life was to protect anyone but himself. When her dad had died, she'd looked up to O'Brien. He'd become a sort of mentor, a father figure, to her. She'd respected him, like her father had done once. Loved him even.

She wanted to ask him. Needed to know, but couldn't bring herself to say the words. What would it change in her? What happy memories would it cost her if she were to know whether her own father had known of O'Brien's crimes? Sometimes, there's a bliss in not knowing.

O'Brien wiped at his mouth with the sleeve of his tracksuit top. 'Have you heard from him?'

'Who?'

'You know who I mean.'

She did. Crosby. The man she'd had an affair with when Ritchie had stopped wanting her. 'Just once,' she said. 'He's not attempted to make contact since.'

O'Brien seemed to consider her then, his eyes narrowed, his head cocked again. 'Does that hurt? The man you loved, who you cheated on the other man you loved with, now doesn't even want to know you. Does it hurt?'

De Silva got to her feet and turned toward the door, where the prison guard swung it open and she was about to step out.

'Wait.' O'Brien was on his feet. 'I still wanted to speak to you about something.'

'Put it in a letter. That way I can throw it in the bin. You've asked me to come here to play games. Nothing more.'

'It does hurt, doesn't it?' De Silva was sure she could see a smirk on his face, or something like it. 'Sure, you know what he is. A cold-blooded killer; a traumatised youth in a man's body living out some revenge fantasy. And despite it all, there's something still there, isn't there? You're left wondering: what were you to him? Just a quick fumble in the incident room when no one was watching? Or were you something more? Something lasting.'

'Fuck you.' She walked out of the door into the secondary room where she'd been searched earlier. As the prison guard was about to close the door, O'Brien cleared his throat.

'I'm dying,' he said.

De Silva looked to the guard, who shrugged, and she walked back inside to the table. The door closed and bolted behind her. She didn't want to care, didn't want to give a damn whether former-DSI O'Brien lived or died after the things he had done. She'd hardened herself to him. The love and fondness had been replaced by bitterness and anger. Disgust. Still, she was more than curious at his revelation.

She was standing on the opposite side of the table and O'Brien sat back down in his seat, looking exhausted. 'Of what?' she asked.

He shrugged in response and added, 'You and Kath, as much as you were on my back about smoking. Well, you were right in the end. I have a second scan coming up.'

Lung cancer.

'How long do you have?'

'Few months,' he said. 'But, you know, who knows? Could be weeks, could be years. Doctors are smart, but they're not Mystic Meg.'

'Is that all you wanted to tell me, because I have an incident room I need to get back to.'

'Work, work, work. Certainly changed your tune. I remember having your resignation on my desk not so long ago.' He smiled, but it was faded somehow. Like he didn't have the energy to make it believable. 'Please sit down, you're making me nervous.'

I'm *making* you *nervous*, she thought. She gripped the plastic chair. Social conditioning told her now was the time to say she was sorry to hear the sad news, but she couldn't. O'Brien had ruined lives. People were dead because of the things he and his friends did to those boys.

'Kath, God rest her soul, and I – we didn't have kids, as you know,' he said. He steepled his fingers in front of himself. 'We have no one to leave anything to. The house is paid for already. There are no debts, and we have some money stacked away.'

'I'm not looking after your affairs when you die, Tom,' de Silva said. 'We aren't friends, and you're not my—' She stopped herself. Her heart was beating so fast she wondered whether O'Brien could hear it from across the table. 'It's beyond inappropriate. The state can look after your stuff when you're gone if you've no family.'

'Oh, I have a lawyer who's taking care of all of that.' O'Brien waved a hand dismissively. 'It's not that I want you to look after my affairs, but more what to do with those affairs. Where the money goes when it's released, and when the house is sold.'

'Then you don't need me.'

'Take it.' O'Brien coughed, a long fit, and de Silva thought his lungs might pop up from his chest and out of his mouth. When he calmed, he dabbed at his mouth, at the tears in his eyes. 'I'd like you to have it all. Kath felt the same; I know she did. One of the last things she said to me was about looking after you.'

De Silva's legs felt weak and she pulled out the chair from under the table to sit down. 'No,' she said. 'Absolutely not.'

'Why not?'

'You know why.' She shook her head. 'You're all but a convicted child rapist. Your money is tainted. Everything you've done is.'

'I'm not convicted yet,' he said. 'Might not be convicted before I go, either.'

'I'm sure that's a done deal, Tom.' She bit her bottom lip, tried to shake away the disbelief at O'Brien's words. 'So, you want to leave me your money. The proceeds from your house. Why?'

'I have no one else to leave it to,' he said. 'For a while there, you were the closest thing Kath and I had to a daughter.' He took a breath, ragged and crackling. 'Kath loved you. I love you.'

De Silva felt tears prick at her eyes as O'Brien's words stung her skin like nettles. 'I feel nothing for you but shame,' she said.

'Embarrassment. Anger. Hate. Spite. I wish nothing for you but the very worst of what could possibly happen to you.'

'Oh no, Win, tell it to me straight,' he said, strained. Then, his voice turned soft and small and distant. 'But I understand.'

'This, what's happening to you now. It's the least of what you deserve,' she said. 'I hope your final hours are at least half of the agony you put those boys through. I hope you know pain in your last days like you've never felt before. And I hope that, if there is a hell, you relive your own death forever.'

'Win…'

But she couldn't stop herself now that she'd started. Everything she'd wanted to say but had kept ring-fenced by her professionalism was let loose between the walls of this tiny room in Hull. 'What you and friends did to those boys, to my Ritchie…' The emotion of it all swelled in her chest. 'You're the reason he killed himself. You're the reason Mike Crosby is the way that he is. You're the reason so many people are dead rather than facing the justice they deserve or living the life they should have been able to, free from it all. You're the reason I'm—'

'You're what? Come on, Win, let it out.' He reached over and touched her hand, and she snatched it away from him and stood up.

'I'm going now,' she said, her voice rich and thick with everything she felt. 'Don't contact me again, Tom. And when you go, when you draw that last stinking fucking breath, make sure you've told your solicitor not to contact me either. I want nothing from you.'

O'Brien nodded and looked down to the table, his shoulders slumped, and in that moment de Silva thought he looked defeated. Done. Resigned.

By the time she got back to her car, she was almost overwhelmed by it all. It rose in her like that old black tide she felt after Ritchie's death. O'Brien's offer, him mentioning how Kath had wanted to look after de Silva even in her final moments, his read on how she felt about Crosby, it had almost cut to the bone. She wanted to scream, to slam at her steering wheel and rage at her windscreen, but she couldn't. Wouldn't.

There was work to be done back in Liverpool and she needed to keep it together for Beatrice Tredwell, to swallow it all down and compress it into the pit of her stomach where the rest of the unresolved things lived.

As she started the car, she thought of how death seem to follow her around, a murmuration at the edges of her life that took people from her one by one until finally…

It comes for me.

Six

'Where the hell have you been?'

De Silva had only just parked her car in the OCC when she received the call from DSI Murphy, demanding to know her whereabouts, and asking de Silva to come to her office immediately.

'We've already had calls from the *Liverpool Journal* and national media.' Murphy was sitting behind her desk, her platinum blonde bob tied back into a tidy bun. De Silva noted the puffiness around her usually bright eyes. 'I need you to move fast on this one.'

'I'll move as fast as the evidence allows,' de Silva said. 'I'll pull the team off non-urgent cases.' She took a breath and said, 'They've been here since early hours, ma'am. Likely they'll be here after hours, too.'

She nodded. 'I'll approve any overtime. Just keep me updated. You'll loop in the Protecting Vulnerable People Unit?'

'Yes,' de Silva said. 'We have a full caseload. What shall we do with the rest of it?'

'Hand it off,' she said. 'All of it.'

De Silva's heart sank. 'Even the investigation into Rainford Lane School for Boys and The Woulds app?' The case that had haunted de Silva and her team for years now. The very case that led to the death of Jeremiah Sure, which the media, she knew, would somehow blame her for. The one that had reached into the heart of her home, into this very office before Murphy inhabited it, the one that had taken the middle finger on her right hand, and had almost ruined her.

Murphy looked down at her desk and sighed. 'We've not seen any movement on that. More's the pity.'

She thought of her Ritchie, of Crosby, the other man she'd loved – and of O'Brien. Before she'd seen him earlier that day, she couldn't even bear to think of him, let alone say his name out loud, and now he was dying.

Good riddance.

The truth was that de Silva hoped this new case, as awful as it was, would give her something else to focus on other than what happened last year. 'I'll let Investigator Ayris know we're stepping back for the time being,' she said. 'Keep him on side.'

'Exactly what I would have suggested,' Murphy said. 'Keeping the NCA close is a good idea.' She sounded mildly surprised and de Silva tried not to take offence. 'Though, to be honest, I'm not sure what Ayris is still doing here.'

Neither do I, de Silva thought.

De Silva nodded and stood. 'I'll get on with it. I was on my way to check on this footage we have from the witness who reported the… the body… when you called. I'll arrange for a briefing with the media for early tomorrow morning.'

'Keep me updated,' Murphy said. 'I think on this occasion, the chief constable should be involved with the briefing.' She took a breath and let it out quickly, like she was going to say something else but thought better of it. 'That's all,' she said.

De Silva left the office as her phone rang. Barclay. 'Hand off everything we have to other teams,' de Silva said.

'Jesus hell, de Silva. I had Murphy here breathing down my neck earlier about where you were. I didn't know what to say.'

'What did you say?'

'I said you were at an audition for the circus,' he said, sarcasm dripping down the line. 'I said you had a therapy appointment, the ones O'Brien mandated for your return.'

Barclay always had her back, she knew that. 'Did you hear what I said about handing things over?'

He sighed. 'Yeah, I heard. Even the Rainford Lane thing? The app?' There was an edge to his voice, something bordering frustration. 'De Silva, I found that app on my own daughter's tablet.'

'I've not forgotten.'

'I'm not handing that off for some other team to mess up.'

'We're parking it for now,' she said. 'Relax, we'll get back to it. But right now, we have a dead newborn and a seriously ill mother.'

'I know,' Barclay said. 'I know. I'm sorry.'

'It's fine,' she said. 'I'd feel the same if I found it on Bonnie's iPad.' In truth, she'd already checked Bonnie's devices and found nothing. She told Laney to check them at least once a week, though she wasn't sure that was advice that her sister had chosen to follow. 'Where did you set up?'

'Where do you think?' He snorted a laugh.

'I think the basement is almost traditional at this point, isn't it? I'm coming down now.'

'Right,' he said. 'Bye.'

'See you in a sec.' De Silva hung up and headed for the lift.

She thought of going straight up to see Ayris, but she wanted to get downstairs and see that footage. It was already almost six p.m. She'd been up and about for over fourteen hours already, but she was damned if she was going to let her team burn themselves out, too.

Ayris can keep.

The basement corridor was warmer than she remembered, and she noted that two new electric heaters had been installed on the wall. The door at the end of the hallway was ajar, and beyond, the room was bright and noisy.

As she stepped inside, everyone turned to her. For a split second, she felt like she was in one of those old Westerns where an outsider comes to the town's saloon. 'Come on, the lot of you, let's be having you. Back in bright and breezy though please, and who's doing the morning coffee run?'

'What about speaking to Mitch Whitley?' Barclay asked.

'We've got his initial statement,' she said. 'I want to read over it before I speak with him properly, so, Braxton, can you call him and ask him to make himself available here tomorrow mid-morning?'

Braxton nodded his big, bald head, which shone under the yellow fluorescent lights. 'Sure can.' He picked up his phone and started dialling.

'Good, then get home,' she said. 'Come on then.' She clapped her hands three times. 'Coats and handbags, gents, let's be having you. Lawrence, any news yet?'

Lawrence was shorter than all of them. Petite, de Silva would say, with dark eyes and hair to match. 'No,' she said. 'Not yet.'

'Well I'm sure it'll be good news when it comes,' de Silva said as Lawrence passed her out the door. 'O'Connor, take your wife out, will you? You were working late all last week on that Durairaj case. How is the old man anyway?'

'He'll live,' O'Connor said, running his fingers through his thinning hair. 'Be in hospital for a while though, and no luck on finding the attacker.'

De Silva tutted. 'Well, keep an eye on him, won't you, but not tonight. Eyes on the wife.'

O'Connor laughed. 'Oh, she will be pleased, I'm sure.'

De Silva waited until they were all gone before she turned to Barclay, who was standing with his arms crossed. The frown had added decades to his forehead. 'I'm not happy about leaving that case, de Silva,' he said.

'I've heard you and I agree, but we've got other things we need to focus on right now, haven't we? Did anyone have the presence of mind to request CCTV from nearby businesses?'

'I got O'Connor on it.' He sat down at his desk. 'Waiting for them to come back to us.'

De Silva pondered that, sat down too, and leaned back in her chair, stared up at the ceiling. She had been sitting down there so many times through her career, and sometimes on those late nights scouring over case notes and witness statements, the lights would go out and she'd be left in the eerie dark. She wasn't afraid of the dark generally, but there was something about basements. Something about *this* basement. She'd worked through so much down there that it almost felt haunted.

'Do you want to take a look at this footage?' Barclay asked. 'I uploaded it to our shared drive. Password protected after last year's hacking scandal.'

De Silva wheeled around to him on her chair as he pulled a blank pad and a Bic from a drawer under the desk, pen poised ready to make notes.

The video played. The open expanse of Southport beach, the tide just about splashing around the edge of the pier. Snow covered the parts of the beach where the seawater hadn't touched.

The drone camera was steadier than de Silva had expected. Clearer. She'd imagined some shaking, grainy footage where one pixel was indistinguishable from the next.

It flew over the edge of the pier and down the boardwalk, where the old pier train used to run from the arcade to the end and back again. It stopped suddenly, and de Silva could make out the roofs of buildings. The fast-food places, she assumed. It retraced its flight path and hovered over the edge of the pier, where she and Barclay had been standing just this morning.

There she was. Naked in the snow. The drone dropped down slowly, honing in on the baby. It was still. Unmoving. Not even its chest moved. De Silva wondered whether the baby had been dead for some time before the drone turned up, and swallowed whatever emotion threatened to claw its way out of her stomach.

De Silva rewound the footage. 'There she is. Look.' She rewound it again. The drone dropped down toward the body and as it was about halfway, de Silva paused the footage. 'There.' She pointed to the far right of the screen.

De Silva rewound the footage slowly until it became clearer. Beatrice Tredwell clung on to the railings, facing down over the choppy tide.

She took a look back at the baby and jumped.

'Jesus Christ,' de Silva said. 'What drove her to that?'

Barclay shifted in his seat. 'I don't know. That poor girl.'

De Silva couldn't decide whether he was talking about the baby or Beatrice, but didn't ask. She thought of The Woulds app case and how it would need to be sidelined again for a more immediate and pressing issue. She sighed and said, 'We need to talk to Rob Ayris from NCA,' she said. 'Let him know what's happening with The Woulds app case.'

'And I suppose you want me to do that?'

'You could speak to him tomorrow.' She shrugged. 'It's up to you.'

He rolled his eyes then looked at his watch. 'He might not even be here, probably left for the day already.'

'Well, like I said, it can wait until the morning if you'd prefer?'

'No, I'll be in late tomorrow. I want to head over to Stockport.'

'What for?'

'Beatrice's mother, Charlene Khan, has a sister living there,' he said. 'I want to have a chat with her, see if she knows where her sister is.'

'Can't you just ring her? Or get Greater Manchester Police to talk with her?'

'No,' he said. 'I want to do it myself.'

'Right then.' De Silva smiled, thinking how much like her Barclay was becoming. 'I suppose you'd best go and see Ayris and get yourself off home.'

Seven

Barclay made his way upstairs. Through the full-length windows, he could see the night was dark as sin, and the sky was grey. The blizzard that the weatherman had promised hung in the air like a threat.

He took one step at a time. If he took the lift up, he wouldn't have enough time to think about how to approach this conversation.

Since their awkward liaison last year, Barclay hadn't spent any time alone with National Crime Agency investigator Robert Ayris. When he did find himself in meetings or briefings with him, he'd kept his eyes focused on the table-top or his notepad or the presentation. He was sure de Silva had already picked up on the weird energy between the two of them.

How could she not?

With any luck, he wouldn't be in his office, and Barclay could at least say that he tried. His new favourite thing to do was to eat dinner, have the TV on low, and watch videos of cow hooves being trimmed and treated by Keepingcowsmoovin on Instagram. It had become his way to self-soothe. Some people watched those rug-cleaning videos, but they weren't for him. He liked the idea of something being discovered, of the poison being drawn out, of it being tended to by someone who cared.

Barclay thought this conversation could have been an email; but de Silva seemed insistent that it needed to be a face-to-face conversation. He believed then, more than ever, that de Silva knew something had happened between them. This was exactly the awkward type of encounter that she would find funny, he knew that.

Only she's not here to see it. He walked out from the stairwell and into the corridor that led to Ayris's office. 'This is a bloody joke,' he said, under his breath.

'Are you talking to yourself?' That familiar, warm voice, the Scottish accent just clinging on after years in the Big Smoke.

Barclay turned to see Ayris stepping out of his office, a leather satchel on his shoulder, and his big coat on over a fitted suit, brown suede shoes that Barclay knew would get ruined if it snowed any more. But by God, he was a handsome man. Beautiful, Barclay would say only to himself.

'No,' Barclay said. 'I was just coming to see you.'

'Ah right,' he said. 'I'll go back in.' Ayris chuckled to himself and pushed open his small office door, threw his bag down behind the desk and moved to the thermostat to turn on the heat. 'I'm not sure if I'm turning into a pussy having lived down south so long, or whether it's genuinely freezing.'

'Could be both.' Not even Barclay knew what he meant by that. He closed his eyes, wishing he could erase that moment from reality. 'De Silva sent me,' he said finally.

'Oh aye? Well, we both know you wouldn't come here of your own volition now, don't we?'

'Oh.'

'It's a joke,' Ayris said, his eyes sparkling.

'We're having to take a step back,' Barclay said.

'Could you close the door? Keep the heat in.'

Barclay closed the door and pressed his back up against it. 'From the case. The Woulds app. All of it. We've got something really urgent we've been put on.'

'The baby in the snow?'

'So you've heard about it then.'

Ayris nodded. 'Aye,' he said. 'Well, it's understandable this is put on the back burner. We've not seen any movement on it since we made those arrests.'

He was right. The child abuse at Rainford Lane School for Boys in the 1980s and 1990s led to some of the most brutal killings Merseyside had ever witnessed, when victim-turned-murderer Lewis Lamond spun his rage outward into the world. After weeks in incarceration, he was found hanged in his cell. Apparent suicide. *Apparent*.

At the time, neither Barclay nor de Silva knew that Lewis Lamond's murders would lead them down a rabbit hole of child abuse, violence and conspiracy, which led right into the very heart of Merseyside Police. To people they had once trusted. Into their own homes.

'It's not my decision,' Barclay said. He puffed out his chest, as though there was something he needed to prove; though, to himself or Ayris, he wasn't sure. 'Personally, I think rooting out an international sex trafficking cataloguing app is a hefty priority.'

Ayris nodded and sat down at his desk, gestured that Barclay should sit opposite. 'It's not an easy decision to make, is it? The abandonment and death of a baby versus the sexual exploitation of potentially thousands of children. I'd hate to be sitting in the chief constable's chair right now.'

Despite his better judgement, Barclay took a seat opposite Ayris. In taking a seat, he felt himself warm to the man again, like their history didn't matter, didn't count – not with everything else going on. 'It's temporary,' Barclay said. 'I'm eager to get back to it.'

Ayris nodded and folded his arms. 'There's something I need to tell you, too. I was going to wait until I had a chance to speak to the CC and the ACC, but you're here now.' There was something in Ayris's tone. A heaviness, a weariness.

'Go on…'

'The NCA are calling me back to London,' Ayris said. 'Immediately. I'm to pack up my things and head back tomorrow.'

'Oh.'

Silence.

Barclay stared at the desk between them, then asked, 'What does that mean for the case?'

'It's still open,' Ayris said. 'Active. But in truth, we've not seen sight nor sound of The Woulds app. Whatever it was... a catalogue, a user-tracking tool, a portal for these adults to... well, you know... It's vanished.'

I do know, he thought. 'So, is that it? The NCA are washing their hands of it? Like it never existed? Do I need to remind you that I found that thing on my own daughter's tablet?' An anger rose in his voice, thick and raw and full. 'Now you're telling me that, what? You just can't be arsed any more?'

'No, that's not what I'm telling you.' Ayris got to his feet, his voice stern but soft. 'The app has disappeared, Barclay. We can't find it anywhere in app stores, whether on the dark web or otherwise. I didn't say we've stopped looking. The only jump we've had in this case is from that bloody hacker woman last year. It's embarrassing.'

Barclay found it hard to look at Ayris. Whether it was because The Woulds had all but disappeared, that these men might get away with having abused children again, or whether it was the news of Ayris's leaving, Barclay couldn't tell. 'It's disappeared before though. Then re-emerged.'

'I don't think it'll come back now. Not as The Woulds anyway. That would be deeply stupid of them. No, it'll be called something else now. We might never—'

'Don't tell me that you might never find it,' Barclay said. 'I don't want to hear it. The case is being parked, you're moving back to London and kids are still getting hurt.'

Ayris put a hand on Barclay's arm, warm and soft, and to his own surprise, Barclay accepted the gesture. Felt comforted by it.

'Look,' Ayris said, 'I was here to find a connection between Lamond and the others, and this app.' Ayris took his hand away and sat straight. 'And you and de Silva did that for me. There's no reason for me to stay now that's done.' His eyes locked onto Barclay's. 'Is there?'

Barclay felt his stomach coil into knots like a writhing snake. Ayris's eyes were bright even under the gloomy office lights. 'No,' Barclay said. 'There's no reason.' He stood and opened the door, walked out into the cold corridor. 'I'll let de Silva know,' he said over his shoulder.

He turned toward the lifts before Ayris could say anything else. Something bubbled under the surface of his skin, something he knew he should feel deeply, but was subdued by his medication. He pressed the button for the lift and hoped it arrived before Ayris followed him out. Before whatever it was could show itself on his face. They'd spent just one night together, which Barclay could only remember in scraps, but what that night meant to him at the time had stayed with him.

More than just sex. It was comfort. Compassion. A kind of symbiosis.

No, Barclay told himself. *I was seeking validation, and he gave it.* In the moments where Barclay had been sober that night, he'd felt needed. The way Nick hadn't needed him in a long time. He hated himself for that weakness.

Barclay pressed the ground floor button and the lift doors slid shut.

In the midst of a separation from Nick, Ayris was what Barclay needed. Validation, in truth, is what Barclay always sought in his life. Whether it was sexually, in a relationship, or at work.

He thought of his time aboard the HMS *Iron Duke*. How he didn't make a report right away. He wanted to give the benefit of the doubt. And then, when it started to happen again and he had to defend himself, he had no option but to admit the truth.

He wasn't sure what Ayris meant to him. Whether, in fact, he meant anything at all – whether the idea of someone paying attention to him, understanding him, wanting him, was the thing that meant something. That meant, ultimately, he was needed even for those few hours they spent together.

The lift doors opened on the ground floor with a ping.

Eight

It was just a wall. Decades and weather had aged it so much that some of the brick had crumbled. Ivy had invaded it, had stabbed through the cement and buried its roots deep into it. That wouldn't stop him or Terry from getting over it though. In truth, the ivy was a help to them rather than a hindrance. It gave them something to grip, footholds to use, and in its aged thickness, their weight was nothing to it. Still, they went over it one at a time.

He landed in snow first; the bits and pieces they'd packed jangled lightly in his backpack. He stopped still in case someone had heard and knew he'd have to remember to cover his tracks. Terry came over second, landing as though he was made of nothing.

It would be an easy job, especially in the snow. The garden was mostly shadows and dark, and a sliver of the crescent moon lit the evergreens and naked tree branches in a silver-blue.

What the owner of Elm Cottage didn't know was that it had taken them just three days to track her down. What she also didn't know was that for the last two weeks, he and Terry had were standing in this exact spot next to a sapling and watched from the shadows. Terry had told him it was a young plum tree, that he'd seen one once and wished they'd had one in their garden when they were kids. What Mrs Christine Jones didn't know was that last night, he and Terry had got closer than they'd ever got before. Right up to her windows.

They had watched her move through the kitchen into a dining room in a pale blue dressing gown, her hair in tight curlers and wrapped up in a net. They knew that she liked to make herself some hot milk before bed. They knew that she used the same cup each night, a white one with pink and blue flowers on it.

She was old and the decades since they had last seen her hadn't been kind to her face. It was lined terribly, and still she smoked, even at her age. They knew that because there was an empty flowerpot near the back door, filled halfway with water, and butts floated on the surface like dead fish. When she got into bed, they would listen as she spent twenty minutes coughing.

Mrs Jones had had a dog, but Terry had seen to that. The yapping little thing would give the game away as soon as they stepped inside the house. It had to go. But he couldn't do that himself. He wouldn't. But Terry… well, he would do anything it took. Once they'd arrived too early and heard her calling the dog in from the garden. Princess, she'd called it.

'Like a fucking imbecile,' Terry had said, his voice a scratching whisper. They'd waited until she'd let the thing out for a wee, and while she was boiling her milk, Terry had taken it over the wall. God knows what Terry had done with it. He didn't want to ask.

Last night, Mrs Jones had cried at the kitchen table, her gnarled old hands shaking as she sipped her hot milk, steam fogging her glasses. He had smiled when he recognised that look on her face. Her twisted, downturned mouth, her scrunched-up pink eyes. It was agony. Pain. Torture.

It was something he and Terry were all too familiar with.

To him it was right that Mrs Jones now felt that way. It was just. It was something she deserved to experience, and he wished that, in the time since they had last set eyes on her, her life had been full of it.

Her last few minutes would certainly feel that way for her.

The kitchen light went out and they made their move. Slinking out of the shadows, they moved across the crazy-paving path toward a barren border, which he imagined would be full and bright in spring, and reached the back door.

He stepped back, watched as an upstairs light turned off, and then they waited. All he could hear in the dark was the sound of his own breath, could see it curling around itself in the cold air. The tall old trees that flanked the north side of the garden shushed as if willing Christine Jones to sleep.

'Hurry up.' Terry's voice rasped, impatient and excited.

They waited there for another hour before Terry got to work.

The back door had a pin tumbler lock, and their reconnaissance these last few weeks had meant that they had come prepared. He passed the backpack to Terry, who took out the bump key and the hard rubber hammer. The latter was the same size as one of those old toffee hammers and just as tough. They had tested it on their own front door, so they were certain they didn't have to take the chance of bringing a metal one.

Terry inserted the bump key into the lock, softly so it made no sound, and not all the way. Just shy of being fully seated. Terry held it in his left hand and turned to the right, just enough pressure, and passed the small hammer to his brother.

He tapped the end of the key lightly, just like they'd practised. The hard rubber hammer barely making a sound, while his brother kept that turning pressure consistent. With each bump of the hammer, the key turned even more. He knew that inside the lock the pins were jumping one by one, and pretty soon they'd be inside.

They had waited years for this moment, but Terry's patience was beginning to wear thin. Finally, a click. Terry turned the handle and the door opened without a single sound.

He closed the door behind them, softly. He slipped out of his shoes, but Terry didn't bother. He took out a pan from the cupboard, filled it with water from the tap and put it on the hob to boil.

Upstairs, Mrs Jones coughed.

Soon, he thought, *she'll try to scream*.

Nine

Stockport

12 February

Harwich Close was made up of just ten houses, brown brick and huddled close together. It wasn't too dissimilar to where Barclay grew up in Skelmersdale. Tragically overlooked and dramatically underfunded by governments – Tory and Labour alike – who couldn't care less about the people that lived in these houses, who walked these streets, and paid their bills and council tax.

The council had attempted to make the area a bit prettier with small patches of unkempt grass, which were marked by tyres, and snowfall had settled in the crevices.

He bumped the two left tyres onto the kerb at the entrance to the close and headed toward the first house on the left, careful as he crossed the icy patch of path. An open porch hung over a brown wooden door, the varnish peeling and bubbled. A simple brass knocker hung below three small windows in the shape of an arch, and Barclay tapped it softly.

The door flew open to a woman in grey leggings and an oversized jumper, misshapen and bobbled, the colour of pale blue spring skies. Her hair was tied up in what Nick would call a get-shit-done-bun, and her glasses were small and rimless on a long, thin face. 'Can I help yuh?' she said; her voice was soft, but the raised-lip sneer gave her true feelings away.

'Mrs Bullock?' Barclay asked. 'Annie Bullock?'

'Listen, don't come knocking on my door asking who's who.' She took a step out of the door onto the path, and Barclay stepped back. 'Knocking like you're a bleedin' bailiff. Who are you and what do you want?'

Barclay took out his warrant card and showed it to her. 'Detective Sergeant Ben Barclay,' he said.

She leaned in closer to the warrant card and squinted, despite her glasses. 'Merseyside Police? You're a long way from home, son.' She looked around the close quickly, as though hoping no one had looked through their discoloured office blinds or net curtains. 'What do you want?'

'I'm looking for your sister, Charlene Khan.'

'Not spoken to her in months, wouldn't know where she was.' Annie turned back and stepped inside her house, hand on the door ready to close it in Barclay's face.

'It's important that we find her… are you Annie Bullock?'

She nodded and folded her arms. 'I am.'

'It's really important that I find Mrs Khan,' he said.

Annie put her hand out to stop him from talking and in a hushed tone she added, 'We don't call her Khan around here. Not any more.'

'Not any more? Why would you call her anything "around here" if you've not seen her in months?'

'It's fine, Annie, I'll speak with him.' Another woman at the door, who could have been Annie's twin if she wasn't at least six inches shorter with darker hair. 'Have you found her?' She looked dreadful. Her hair was a greasy mess that hung in tangles above her shoulders, her eyes red and puffy, dark circles formed on the bags under them. 'Have you found my Bea?'

'Could I come inside, Mrs Kh— Charlene?'

Annie looked over at her sister, a frown on her already lined face, and Charlene nodded. 'I think you best had, cock.'

The hallway was carpeted in something Barclay recognised from his own childhood, the deep warmth of red velvet cake, with yellow-gold floral motifs all over it. It had been well-worn, a sign that it had been in place for years. Not threadbare, but in need of a good carpet shampoo. The walls were embossed white wallpaper, like square tiles with more flowers inside. Parts of it looked nicotine-yellow, but that could have been the light.

He followed Charlene through to the living room, which was decorated completely differently to the hall. Perhaps Annie was decorating in stages. Smooth white walls with large prints on, deep blues and golds. On one feature wall, painted hipster-grey, hung a large gold ornate mirror, the rectangular kind that Barclay had seen hundreds of times in hundreds of homes. In the corner, a large TV that rivalled the one in his own living room.

He heard the front door shut and the letter box clatter, and Charlene gestured that Barclay should sit down. 'You've found her, haven't you? She's dead, isn't she?'

He felt the presence of Annie at the living room door, her eyes on him. He turned to look at her, then back to Charlene. 'Maybe we could talk alone?'

'Ey you, this is my bleedin' house! I'll decide where I stand.'

'Annie, please...' Charlene said, tears in her eyes now.

Annie huffed and as she disappeared somewhere, Barclay heard her muttering, 'I'll sit in here out the way, like a mute.'

'Sorry,' Charlene said. 'She can be a bit... much.'

'Don't you apologise on my behalf!' Annie's voice was as loud as though she were still in the living room, and Charlene got up and closed the living room door.

'We've been trying to trace you, Mrs Khan,' he said. 'We sent officers from Greater Manchester Police to your home, and—'

'I couldn't take it any more,' she said. 'The journalists at the door, the there's-that-poor-cow looks from people. I had to get away for a bit.'

Barclay understood. 'Mrs Khan, we have found Beatrice,' he said. 'She's alive, but she's—'

Charlene sobbed, relief crumpled her face and she found balance on the arm of the comfortable-looking fabric armchair she'd been sitting on. 'Oh, thank God.' Tears fell in streams, and a weight seemed to shift from her back and shoulders. 'Where?'

'She was found on Southport beach.'

'Southport?' Her eyes wide, spittle flying from her lips. 'What was she doing there?'

'We don't know yet,' Barclay said. 'We were hoping you could tell us. Do you have any family in that area? Any friends?'

'No.'

'Does Beatrice?'

'No. Look, when can I see her? Will you be bringing her home or taking her back to Allerton House? Not that they should have anything to do with her now after all of this.'

'Mrs Khan, please sit down.'

She complied.

'Could you tell me more about how she ended up in Allerton House?'

Charlene sighed, wiping at her tears. 'God, it's never ending, is it?' The new-found strength in her back and shoulders seemed to dissolve as she slumped again. 'She made herself sick. Saying all kinds of things about my husband.'

'Did you believe her?'

'No,' Charlene said. 'He was a good man. A decent person, but after the things she said about him… well, that was the marriage over.'

'And that's why she ended up in Allerton House?'

'She'd make herself sick,' she said. 'Not like anorexia or anything, but she'd sit in that room and wind herself up for hours. She'd slam the doors, punch the walls. She broke her finger once. The final straw was when I found her blending tin foil into the mashed potato I was making for dinner.'

Jesus, Barclay thought. He was no doctor, but he knew that didn't sound good. It was clear that Beatrice had become a danger to others, and to herself. 'I won't lie to you, Mrs Khan, your daughter is very sick,' Barclay said. 'We won't be able to move her from the hospital in Southport, but I can take you there when I go back to Merseyside, if I can clear it with the ICU doctor.'

'ICU? What the hell's happened to her?' She wiped away tears with the sleeve of her top, and Barclay reached into his pocket for a packet of tissues and handed them to her.

'We're not sure,' he said. It was best that he didn't tell Charlene the particulars of her daughter's condition. The doctors could do a much better job, he was sure, and they'd be able to answer any questions she had. 'We know that she's seriously ill and she's unconscious. I have to ask, Mrs Khan—'

'Please don't call me that.' She dabbed her face with a tissue and handed the packet back to Barclay. 'He left as soon as the going got tough. Though, I can't blame him I suppose. Everyone made his life a living hell. I loved him. He loved me. And now he's gone.'

Barclay wondered whether Charlene held any resentment for that loss.

'She wasn't always like this,' Charlene said. 'She was happy once. When she was younger. She'd always be smiling and laughing. Good at home, brilliant at school. Loved art. She'd paint the loveliest things. Sunsets and forests. Taught herself on the YouTube.'

Barclay found himself smiling. 'She's an artist,' he said.

'She could be,' she said, nodding. 'There was some art gallery she was in touch with for work experience. She was so excited.' Charlene smiled, looked up and out of the front window. Barclay thought that she looked hopeful, that all of this could one day be put behind them and Bea would be back to her old self.

'What changed?' Barclay asked.

'Her dad and me split up,' she said. 'It's all our fault, isn't it? I just want my little girl back to who she was. How she was. Before all of this… shite.'

He didn't want to tell her that Bea may never be her old self ever again. 'Mrs Kh… Charlene, there is something else I need to discuss with you.'

'The baby.' She nodded. 'I know. It became a bit obvious while she was in Allerton House. No hiding that.' She looked at him then, her eyes wide again, her face a picture of fear. 'Is the baby okay?'

Barclay let silence answer for him. He shook his head gently, and Charlene wailed. 'I'm so sorry,' he said.

Annie came in then and much to Barclay's surprise, she was crying too. The sisters held each other, and Annie repeated, 'It's fine. It's all right. Bea'll be fine.' Barclay felt like he was the only person in the room who was unsure whether Beatrice would be fine.

-

The hospital staff ushered Charlene Khan through to the ICU, and Barclay told her that he would wait outside until she was done. Through the frosted window of the ICU, he could see the shape of her reach her daughter's bed, could hear her cry out.

'Can't imagine what she's going through.' De Silva's voice from somewhere behind him.

He didn't turn to look at her but watched Charlene's shape as she seemed to cave in on herself. Barclay could imagine it. He pictured walking into an ICU and seeing his little girl there, his darling Sarah, hooked up to life-support machines.

'Yeah,' he said, finally. He turned to her. 'What're you doing here?'

'Wanted to come and see how she was,' de Silva said. 'How did the mother take it?'

An odd question to ask, but Barclay knew where de Silva's brain was going with it. 'Like any parent with a missing kid, I'd imagine,' he said. 'Have you been in to see her?'

De Silva nodded. 'No change,' she said. 'But with her mum here now, well, who knows. They say they can still hear your voice, even when they're unconscious, don't they?'

Barclay wondered who *they* were but nodded his agreement. He'd had a similar thought earlier. 'How did the press conference go?'

'Same old,' she said. 'We put out a request for any information. The chief constable did most of the talking. One thing I did notice though. Remember Joel Matthews?'

'Unfortunately, yes.' Barclay had grown to hate that man and thought of him as 'The Rat'.

'Not seen him around in months,' de Silva said. 'The *Liverpool Journal* sent someone else. A young woman, couldn't have been more than twenty-five.'

Maybe he's dead, Barclay thought. He chastised himself instantly. *You can't say things like that about people.*

'Hopefully something terrible has happened to him and we'll never see him again,' de Silva said.

But she can.

'Fancy a brew?' Barclay asked. 'I could do with something hot and strong.'

'Yeah,' she said, 'and a lift back the OCC would be good, too. I got a lift off O'Connor. He's up here visiting that Durairaj fella, letting him know the case is being handed off to another team.' They turned and headed down the corridor.

'That's good of him.'

'Any excuse to get out of actual work, that one,' de Silva said. 'So… can I drive?'

'You're not insured on my car, so no.'

'I'm comprehensive, I'll have you know.'

'Which only covers a third party when driving someone else's car.'

'Come on, Barclay. I'll get us back to the OCC in no time.'

'No.'

Ten

The last flakes of snow flew from Barclay's bonnet and into the air behind them as they hurtled down the Formby Bypass toward Thornton. De Silva turned off the wipers and turned down the heating to twenty-four degrees. It was too hot for Barclay, and he desperately wanted to roll down his window.

'My God, this thing can really go,' de Silva said. 'I had no idea with the way you drive.'

Barclay secretly seethed and kept his *fuck you* to himself.

They'd called ahead and asked Braxton and the others to chase up the CCTV from around the pier, and hopefully by the time they got back to the OCC, the team would have found something. Then de Silva had called someone at Greater Manchester Police, some guy she used to work with called Collins, and set up a call about the Beatrice Tredwell disappearance his team had been working on.

There were times when Barclay questioned his choices in life, and this last twenty-four hours were some of those moments. He'd been witness to some of the worst crimes committed against young girls throughout his career, and this was no different. Girls who had their whole lives ahead of them, either snuffed out or changed irrevocably by men. He wondered when, or if, that would ever change.

He thought of Sarah, that precious little life he vowed to protect, and wondered how far any parent can keep their child safe from the horrors that swirl around them like falling snow. Like Charlene with Beatrice.

But these awful things didn't just happen to girls. He thought of his own life, his career in the navy, which was so promising to begin with. How he'd thrown it all away for the truth. His truth. He'd sat with that awful night for days before he decided to do anything about it – he could still taste the sweet, stale stink of whiskey in his mouth. In his sleep, he could hear the grunting, the whispered, 'It's okay. Shh, it's okay. It's just a bit of fun.' Barclay hadn't found it fun.

Then, afterward, when it was over and he got into the shower, the hot water stung as it reached him down there. As the water washed over him, he heard the last words Jonathan Jackson spoke to him. They were so soft, so gentle, they felt like mist. He'd said, 'We're still friends, aren't we?'

Jackson didn't wait for an answer, and Barclay didn't have one to give.

'You all right?' Glancing between Barclay and the road, de Silva's eyebrow was arched.

'I'm fine.'

'Tell your face then, it might have forgotten.'

Barclay rolled his eyes. 'I think I need another coffee,' he said. 'Still feel half asleep.' He knew she'd be able to tell that he was lying. She was good at that. Observant. Sharp.

-

The OCC seemed busier than normal, like a hive of bees working and thrumming. Barclay and de Silva found their way to a private conference suite off the first-floor corridor and sat down. Barclay took out his phone, found the meeting invitation in his diary and typed the conference ID into the keypad on the desk.

The screen said *Waiting for others to join…*

A man appeared on the screen, his fringe swooping low above bushy eyebrows, the thin face and shoulders of a marathon runner. 'De Silva,' he said, an air of affection and familiarity. His accent was Scouse, and even though he knew they'd worked together, it still took Barclay aback for some reason. Liverpool and Manchester were less than forty miles from each other, but sometimes they felt worlds apart. A division brought on by football rivalry and exacerbated by subsequent hooliganism. *In reality*, Barclay thought, *the cities and their people have more in common than not.*

'Ed.' De Silva nodded, her smile tight. 'Sorry, DCI Collins now, isn't it.'

'Well, you know, I learned from the best.' Then his smile dropped, his shoulders seemed to tense. 'Sorry, I wasn't thinking.'

'About what?'

Collins took so long to answer that Barclay thought the internet had dropped. 'O'Brien,' he said, finally.

'Well, he *was* the best at the time, Collins,' de Silva said, her voice even. 'He just turned out to be a nonce, too.'

Collins bit at the nail on his thumb and nodded. 'So, you want to know about Allerton House?'

'Yes,' de Silva said. 'We know that's where Beatrice Tredwell was at the time of her disappearance.'

'Yeah, that's right,' he said.

Barclay took out the notepad from the inside pocket of his jacket and pulled the pen from the wire spirals at the top. 'How long had she been there?' he asked.

'Oh, good morning.' Collins made a point of it, inclined his head slightly to the right. 'I'm DCI Collins.'

'I'm sorry,' Barclay said. 'I'm DS Barclay; I work with DCI de Silva.'

'Well now we're over the niceties…' de Silva said impatiently.

'She was in the Allerton House psychiatric facility for six months,' Collins said. 'This was her second visit. The first time was a year ago, and she spent four months there. It specialises in psychiatric care for teenage and young-adult girls… er, women.'

'Just females?' Barclay asked, scribbling.

'That's what I said, yes.' Collins rubbed at his forehead. 'It's managed by a Doctor Spearritt and a small staff.'

'And Beatrice,' de Silva said. 'What can you tell us about her?'

Collins picked up an iPad from his desk and scanned it. 'Preferred to be called Bea. Her parents are divorced. Her mother married a man named Azad Khan not too long after the split. And that,' he said, 'is where things get a little… weird.'

Weirder, Barclay thought. 'You mean the accusations Bea made against Azad Khan?'

'This one does his homework well,' Collins said to de Silva with a chuckle. 'Good for you, lad.'

Barclay's chest and face burned with the shame of Collins's statement. All too easily embarrassed when it came to the topic of his ability to do his job well, he looked down at his notepad.

'Khan professed his innocence, of course. They all do,' he said. 'We had to release him though. Lack of evidence, but the investigation is still ongoing. In the choice between her daughter and her new husband, I guess Bea's mum definitely made a decision. Bea was shipped off to Allerton House, and Khan moved back in for a while. He moved out shortly after.'

'According to her mother, Bea became a danger to herself and to the Khans,' Barclay added. 'It sounded like she needed to be in that facility. I'm not sure it was as easy a choice as you're making out.'

'What happened to Khan?' De Silva leaned in, but cast a glance to Barclay, probably making sure he was taking notes.

'We'd been called out to his address a few times. Vigilantes taking justice into their own hands. He's been attacked, his property damaged; people have even broken into his home in the middle of the night. Tore up his house and made him watch.' Collins sighed. 'He's moved to south Manchester now.'

De Silva cleared her throat. 'So, back to Allerton House,' she said. 'This Doctor Spearritt, did he know she was pregnant when they took her in?'

'He said he didn't know at the time,' Collins said.

'Was there not a medical performed upon intake at the facility?'

'It's a psychiatric facility, as I said. But no, there was no medical check beforehand. Not that I know of anyway.'

Barclay made a note of that.

'Spearritt,' de Silva said. 'What did you think of him?'

'A bit weird, if I'm honest. This weird, jittery energy like he'd had too much coffee. Know what I mean? Like he had to constantly move or fidget.'

'Nervousness?' Barclay offered. 'I think having the police sniffing around your psychiatric facility following the disappearance of a patient is a nerve-inducing prospect.'

De Silva shot Barclay a quick, sharp look, then said, 'How did she get out, Ed? Do we know?'

'I have the security guard on duty's statement here, I'll send you a copy, but in essence, it was blamed on a power outage caused by a rainstorm. Internet, CCTV, security doors all went down. The backup generator didn't kick in. By time the security manager, a Marcus Blakeman, got back from the basement where he was checking the fuse board, he found Bea's room door open and her missing.'

De Silva pushed back from the desk and sighed as she sat back into her chair. 'No CCTV. No witnesses. Nothing.'

Collins said, 'Look, I'm sorry it's not much. We checked on Khan and he had an alibi for the night of Bea's disappearance, corroborated by CCTV and witnesses at the pub he was at.'

'I didn't see any statement from Khan in what you sent over,' de Silva said.

'I didn't want to waste your time.' Ed smiled. 'There's nothing in there, but I can send it over if it'll help?'

'No, it's fine,' de Silva said.

'Khan's of Middle Eastern descent, is he?' Barclay asked.

'Yes, he is,' Collins said. 'His parents are from Pakistan, but Azad himself was born here. You know what the public are like, they hear a rumour and a name like that, and well, you know... All hearsay. Everyone gets angry, real quick. The public see people with a name like Khan involved in something like this, and even if he's innocent the racists win. Riots, hatred all over social media, lunatic extremists voting Reform while pointing fingers at, and wanting saving from, extremists.'

'Well,' Barclay said, 'however you look at this, Bea was pregnant and now she isn't. Now we can take some DNA samples from the baby and prove Khan's guilt or innocence either way.'

Eleven

The slow, awkward monotony of police investigation had always gotten to de Silva. The hurdles. The red tape. The quagmire of paperwork and countless procedures and protocols dulled her usually keen mind. These past two years had driven de Silva almost to the ground, where she'd thought of quitting altogether more than once.

But it was moments like this one that made her remember who she was, and why she chose policework as her profession. It was more than just admiration for what her father did for decades; it was in her as much as it had been in him.

'DCI de Silva.' A voice snapped her out of her own mind, and she was thankful for it. As the lift door opened and Barclay gripped it so that it wouldn't go without her, DS Hugh Arlow approached, looking dishevelled, a broad smile on his face. 'Morning,' he said, not looking at Barclay. 'Could I have a word?'

'Of course.' She looked to Barclay. 'One second.' De Silva followed Arlow further down the corridor away from the lift, and out of Barclay's earshot, she noticed. 'Everything okay?' In truth, de Silva hadn't ever really taken to Arlow. He had a reputation for being a bit… out there, to say the least. Not weird or anything, just an acquired taste.

Arlow used to be a handsome man, de Silva was sure of it. Now he didn't seem to have his hair cut with any regularity, and his skin often looked ashen. Flaky. He was from Warrington, but he'd lived in Liverpool for years; he moved to Old Swan to be with his girlfriend, and they married the following year.

'What can I do for you?'

'Well, I know you've got your hands full down here,' he said. 'But a case came in, and as we've still not replaced DI Prendergast, I thought I'd pick it up.'

Prendergast had been a hard man to replace. She'd imagined Barclay for the position once, had even mentioned it to O'Brien, but he'd said it was too soon. It would cause unwanted conversation about the unfairness of it. Then, when they'd managed to get along without a replacement, the thought of a new DI seemed to vanish. She needed to get back onto that, despite what Murphy said about the state of the budget.

'Is it a big case?' de Silva asked. 'And you won't be working on your own, I assume?'

'Well, no,' he said. 'I was thinking I could work with Laila and Meera.'

De Silva stared at him. She knew the names but couldn't quite place them. 'Yeah,' she said. 'Okay.'

'DCs Laila Yates and Meera Patel,' he said with a grin.

'Yes, I knew that, thank you,' she lied. 'What's the case?'

'An elderly woman was found dead in her home last night,' he said. 'There was a house fire, but preliminary checks indicate there may have been a stabbing.'

'Jesus, it's getting bad out there isn't it?'

'Worst it's ever been, I think,' he said.

'I'd feel better if you were close by rather than up there in CID.' De Silva thought on it for a moment. 'You can work downstairs in one of the other rooms,' she said, pointing.

'In the basement?' The disdain on his face was clear.

'You get used to it,' she said, her turn to grin now. 'I'd just feel better if you were close by, given it's a potential murder case. I can make sure you're not doing stupid hours and getting home on time for your wife.'

'You don't need to worry about that,' he said. 'Sophie and I split up. We're divorcing.'

Suddenly, Arlow's appearance made sense to her, and she felt bad for judging him on it. 'I am sorry to hear that, Arlow. Are you sure you're okay to be at work? Do you need time off?'

'I'm fine,' he said. 'I think it's been coming for quite some time, and we both recognise that now.'

'Well, either way, I'm sorry. It can't be easy splitting up after so long together.'

He shrugged. 'You get used to it.'

'You can speak to me if you need to,' she said. 'Or, there are lots of employee support programmes I can give you—'

'I'll be fine, thanks,' he said.

The corridor suddenly felt small, like the walls were drawing in, making this whole exchange even more awkward than it needed to be. 'So...' de Silva said. 'I'll leave you to it, but contact Emma Carey, the pathologist. See if she can fit a preliminary examination in tomorrow.'

'Yes, I was thinking the same,' he said.

'Good,' she said, and meant it. She hadn't spent much time with Arlow, and if she wanted to have a cohesive Major Incidents team, she'd have to start getting to know the broader CID teams too. 'I'm in the next room if you need anything,' she said as she turned away and headed back to the lifts and a waiting Barclay.

'What was all that about?' Barclay asked.

'Just a new case,' she said. 'He can handle it. When did you say Mitch Whitley is coming in?'

Barclay looked at his watch. 'I'll give him a call to nudge him on.'

The lift doors opened just slightly then jammed. De Silva looked to Barclay, and he glared back. He pressed the *Door open* button. Nothing. He gripped the door and pushed it back, a vein in his neck tensing.

'This is all we need,' de Silva said. 'I can't be stuck in a lift with you, Barclay, I just can't.'

Barclay gripped the door with two hands and pulled at it. Finally, it gave way, and he stepped out. The doors were about to close again, but Barclay gripped them and de Silva slid out. As Barclay let go, they closed instantly.

'Report that to maintenance,' she said.

'Yeah, I'll get on it.' As they walked toward the incident room, he pulled out his phone and dialled a number. He was efficient, she'd give him that.

They walked through into the incident room, where everyone stopped talking. Their eyes turned to Barclay and de Silva. Braxton was on his feet, a whiteboard marker in hand, about to write something on the evidence board. 'Morning, boss,' he said.

'Okay listen up,' de Silva said.

'Sorry, before we start…' Harris said. 'The fingerprints that the SOCOs recovered. We found a match.'

'What?' De Silva knew the team could go at it when they set their mind to it, but having a match in such a short amount of time was brilliant even for them. 'Oh well,' she said, 'enlighten us.'

'Two sets of prints were lifted from the board removed from the entrance to the pier,' Harris said, his mouth lined from years of smoking. 'Both belonging to two young… er, reprobates from Southport. The database pinged them straight away.'

'Their sheet includes breaking and entering, shoplifting. Some typical ASBO stuff,' Lawrence said. 'But nothing much more than that.'

'Do we think the prints are old?' Barclay asked.

'No,' Braxton said, 'Scientific Support confirmed they were fresh prints, so they actioned them immediately.' He cleared his throat. 'We've asked Albert Road nick to bring them in for questioning.'

'No,' de Silva said. 'I'd rather we did it. Harris, head down to Southport now. Call O'Connor on the way; he's already up there at the hospital. Call the station, and if they've already brought them in, ask them not to go any further until you arrive.'

Harris was on his feet, stuffing his arms into his duffle coat sleeves.

It wasn't that she doubted the capabilities of anyone at Albert Road, but she needed to be able to review the interview straight away. Get the answers she needed without having to wait on someone else who had other priorities than her team.

Barclay approached her from behind. A hand on her shoulder, he whispered, 'Mitch Whitley is here.'

She nodded. 'Could you have someone wait with him in Interview Two. I want to take one last look at the footage before I speak with him.'

'No worries.' Barclay walked out into the corridor on his phone.

'Lawrence, with me.' She grabbed her laptop and heard Lawrence clamber for her own things; knowing her it would probably be a pen, a pad and her jacket just in case.

'Er, boss,' Braxton said, 'we just got some CCTV footage from the amusement arcade on the promenade. You want to see it now?'

'Of course,' she said.

He loaded it up on his screen and the rest of the incident room gathered around, Lawrence with her notebook and pen. Braxton skipped the footage on, until a black car came into shot.

The passenger side door flew open. The car skidded; though the footage had no volume, de Silva could almost hear the screech. A bundle fell out of the passenger seat onto the path.

'That's her, isn't it?' Lawrence asked.

De Silva leaned in closer. Her eyes fixed on the person as they collected themselves and got to their feet. The driver of the black car, a sports utility vehicle, got out and approached her. It was definitely a man, but with a cap on, she couldn't make out his face. Then another car came into shot. A light-coloured one, but she couldn't tell for sure in the green hues of the night-vision camera. The light car stopped. The driver got out, and then the driver of the black car climbed back into their own vehicle and sped off, smoke rising from the back wheels.

The girl, Beatrice, bent double in pain, turned down toward the pier. The driver of the light car followed her a short way, but remained in shot as he, yes it was a he, de Silva decided, got back into his car and pulled away.

'He just left her,' de Silva said. Her mind raced with the possibilities of what she saw. 'Could you send this to Ludlow in the VEU? We need the footage enhanced. I want to know if we can get a reg on the SVU, and I want faces if we can. A stretch, I know, but ask anyway. And that light-coloured car… I want to know make, model, reg.'

'I'll see what they can do.'

De Silva knew the Visual Evidence Unit were stretched, their budget and team both cut in the last round of cost-saving measures, another glorious Tory decision which had implications those in Number 10 could never quite fathom.

'You ready, Lawrence?'

'Yes, boss,' she said, though she couldn't take her eyes from the screen.

De Silva got it. She understood that seeing a member of the public just leaving a girl in clear distress was shocking. Disturbing. But de Silva knew that Lawrence would come to understand, this type of thing happened all the time.

-

Conference Room 6 was at the end of a long corridor, painted a light shade of grey. De Silva stopped at a small window at the end, where the weak winter sun shone, the colour of diluted orange cordial. Down there, the roads were slick and wet and bright, but the clouds leaned in on the city, grey and gloaming, even so early in the day.

Winter here has a way of making the days feel like some sort of forever-dusk, she thought. *And there'll be more snow soon; the roads will be carnage.*

She peeled her eyes away from the window as more flakes of snow drifted against the glass, as though desperate to come inside. As she walked into the conference room, she wondered what it would be like to be covered in snow. To fall asleep there, to be buried in it, and to see nothing but frozen white. Forever.

Sometimes, out of nowhere, her mind had wired itself to indulge in these morbid curiosities. The therapist had confirmed that this was normal, that as long as there was no direct threat to herself or anyone around her, de Silva was okay.

She flicked on the TV and plugged her laptop into the docking station on the table. Lawrence sat down beside her, and while she logged in, de Silva said, 'How are you feeling about it? Getting your results I mean.'

Lawrence shrugged. 'I did my best,' she said. 'That's all I could have done, so if I don't pass, I can try again.'

'Good way of looking it.'

'But I'm also bricking it, if I'm honest.'

De Silva snickered. 'I remember that feeling.'

Her dad had still been alive when de Silva put in for her detective exam. He'd already taken a desk job by then, nearing medical retirement due to his deteriorating health. One night, she'd gone around for dinner, and he'd said, 'You're not yourself, girl. What's up?'

'Just stressing myself out,' she'd admitted. 'Expecting my results any day now.'

He'd put a hand on her shoulder and looked her in the eye. 'You're the smartest one in this family. Definitely smarter than your poor mam; she doesn't know her arse from her elbow most days, God love her.'

' 'ey you, you cheeky bleeder!' She'd slapped him on the arm with a wet tea towel she'd used to dry the pans before she sat down to eat her own meal. They'd all laughed. God, even Laney had laughed.

'What I'm saying is, love, you'll be fine.' He tucked into his sausage and mash and with a mouthful of dinner said, 'Trust me.'

She had trusted him, and when the results came in, her career had changed forever.

'From what I've seen,' de Silva said to Lawrence, 'You'll make a great detective. It's hard work, but you've been putting in the hours to get that experience you need, and it makes all the difference. I know you'll do it.'

Lawrence flushed. 'Thank you.'

De Silva turned back to her laptop and loaded up the drone footage Whitley had submitted. She played it once through. The drone moved over the beach in a straight line, turned back on itself, and completed the pattern until it finally reached the pier.

She smiled to herself. Knew she'd caught it and turned her laptop to Lawrence. 'Tell me what you see.' De Silva started the footage again.

Lawrence leaned in closer. 'He's moving the drone up and down the beach.' She shrugged. 'He said that he was trying to film the snow coming in from over the sea, didn't he, so this tracks.'

'That's what he said, yes,' de Silva said. 'But there's only a few seconds of footage looking out to the storm clouds.' She paused the footage as the drone camera caught the edge of the pier. 'So, what are you seeing?'

'The beach,' Lawrence said. 'The sand.' It dawned on her. Her eyes flicked to de Silva, then back to the screen. She started the footage again. 'He wasn't recording the sea or the snow at all.'

See, de Silva thought. *You'll make a good detective.*

Twelve

Mitch Whitley fidgeted in his seat, a chubby man with a pink face and a receding hairline he hoped was hidden by a black Montirex cap. But Barclay wasn't fooled. He'd seen this look on so many gym bros, who were all unwilling to admit the truth that they were losing their hair.

'How long are you gonna keep me waitin'?' Whitley said, a wobble in his voice. 'I've got stuff to do today.'

Barclay watched him carefully and shrugged. 'You know how it is.' Whitley's nervousness was clear in the way he bit his bottom lip, in the way he pulled at his fingers, each in turn, until they cracked. People were always nervous when speaking to the police, especially sitting in an interview room for this long. But given Whitley's career history as a police officer, Barclay assumed he would be more resilient.

Barclay checked his watch again. It had been thirty minutes since he'd brought Whitley through, and it was unlike de Silva not to keep him in the loop if she'd been pulled into something else.

'She'll be along shortly,' Barclay said, and not for the first time. 'Do you want a coffee? Or something to calm your nerves? Tea?'

'I'm not nervous.' The man looked at his hands, then tucked them under the table. 'I'm fine.'

He didn't seem fine. If anything, he seemed like there was something very wrong. It was in his eyes, that kind of rabbit-in-the-headlights stare Barclay had seen so many times. The look of someone who knows something is about to happen and their whole world will fall apart as a result.

Another half hour passed before the interview room door opened gently, and de Silva came in with her laptop in hand. 'Sorry,' she said, closing the door behind her. 'I'm sorry I kept you waiting.'

'Do I need a lawyer for this?' Whitley asked.

De Silva sat down and smiled. Barclay knew it then: she'd found something. She loved this part. Knowing she knew and watching them trying to work out what she knew, filled de Silva with a joy she could never express, and it excited Barclay to watch. As she put her laptop on the table, Barclay noticed a few sheets of paper turned face-down.

'Well, we're just having a chat about what you've been up to, and what your footage found,' she said. 'Do you feel like you need a lawyer for a chat?'

'That depends what you're going to ask, I suppose.'

'Why would it depend on that?' she asked.

Whitley shrugged, his fingers clicking again under the table. 'I don't know,' he said. 'Never been questioned by the police before.'

'I see,' de Silva said. 'But you've been this side of the table before. You know it's just a chat.'

'I know it's *never* just a chat.'

De Silva's grin had all but disappeared, replaced now by a straight mouth and a creased brow. She meant business.

'We can pause now if you like, Mr Whitley,' Barclay said. 'You can call your lawyer, and you can wait in here until they arrive?'

'No,' he said. 'No, let's just get on with it.'

'Well, I'm DCI Winifred de Silva, and I'm sure Barclay's already introduced himself.'

Whitley nodded.

'So, you used to be in Merseyside Police before you jibbed us for the highs of social media?'

He blinked at her. 'What does that have to do with anything?'

'Just making conversation.'

'Well, that's none of your business,' he said, puffing out his chest.

She stared at him, cocked her head, and waited.

Whitley groaned. 'Social media was slow at first, but I got a following and the income is pretty steady now,' he explained. 'Will that do?'

'That's great, I'm pleased for you.' There was something in de Silva's tone that told Barclay she was anything but pleased for him. 'And your police career,' she added. 'Work on anything big that I might have heard of?'

Where was she going with this? Barclay's mind buzzed and he leaned in closer to the table, eyes drifting from her to Whitley and back again.

'I was a PC,' he said. 'We didn't get anything juicy. That went to you lot.'

De Silva nodded. 'I see. I read that you were a constable with us for just a few years before leaving to begin your career as a social media personality. *It's Whitley, Mitch.*'

'It's a play on the Britney Spears—'

'I was never a fan. What made you leave?'

'I don't see what this has to do with anything.'

'You had aspirations of working on the Protecting Vulnerable People Unit,' she said. 'With former-DCI Mike Crosby.'

Barclay's jaw tightened at even the mention of that man's name. He glanced at her, her face flushed red, and then back to Whitley.

'You were friends with Crosby, weren't you? Saw him socially?' She was probing him, nudging him into a corner he might never get out of.

'We knew each other,' he said. 'Isn't that what colleagues do? See each other socially?' Whitley clasped his hands together and rolled his thumbs over each other. 'Besides, didn't you?'

She seemed to ignore his jibe and pressed on, 'When Mike Crosby resigned, you resigned the following day.'

'Where are you going with this?'

'Do the names Joanna McKenzie and Layton Cullen mean anything to you?'

Fuck, Barclay thought. *Fuck, fuck, fuck.*

'Yes.'

'Would you like to elaborate?'

'I want my lawyer,' he said. 'Now.'

De Silva turned one of the pieces of paper over. 'This is a conflict of interest form Merseyside Police asked every officer to complete a few years ago,' she said.

Barclay remembered that form. He himself had nothing to declare, but it had made some officers nervous. He dared not think of the reasons why.

Whitley peered at the paper.

'This here is an updated version you were asked to complete by HR. You printed your name and signed this declaration here on 28 June 2021. In the box that asks whether you have any personal relationships outside of work with any other officer, regardless of rank, you entered one name. Can you read it out?'

Whitley leaned back in his chair, wouldn't look at the paper in front of him again. He trembled, Barclay could see that from across the table, and as Whitley's bottom lip wobbled, Barclay wondered whether there would be tears. 'I'm sitting here asking myself.' Whitley paused here, looked de Silva dead in the eye. 'Whose name you wrote on your form.'

'We all make bad decisions, Mr Whitley,' she said. 'Why don't you start telling me about yours?' She drew in a breath, not waiting for him to respond. 'I think we should go on record now,' she said. 'You can call your lawyer, and I can have someone stay with you in here until they arrive.'

-

It took an hour for Whitley's lawyer to arrive at the OCC, and Barclay checked his watch regularly. He was having Sarah for dinner and a sleep-over tonight, and he didn't want to be late. He had just two more hours before he had to set off and pick her up.

When the lawyer did finally arrive, she looked as though she'd come straight from lunch with friends. Her hair bounced beyond her shoulders in a curly blow; she had loose-fitting jeans as seemed to be the style these days.

She bustled past Barclay and into the interview room. 'Mitch, are you okay?'

He nodded, his face paler than Barclay had ever seen any man look. De Silva didn't take her eyes off him as she watched the interaction between Whitley and his lawyer.

'I'm DCI de Silva—'

'I'd like some time with my client,' the lawyer said, already heading back toward the door.

De Silva stood and put her hand out. 'I'm DCI de Silva,' she said again.

The lawyer expelled air through her nostrils, clearly exasperated. 'Lynch,' she said. 'Kit Lynch.'

'And this is DS Barclay,' de Silva said. 'Now that we've extended each other some professional courtesy, please, take all the time you need.' Lynch nodded and led Whitley out into the corridor. As he passed, de Silva caught his eye and said low enough so that just Whitley and Barclay could hear it, 'You'll need it.' She winked.

A few minutes later, Whitley bundled back in the room behind his lawyer, head down, like a chastised school child who'd been caught doing something naughty. Lynch hadn't even taken a seat down before she said, 'Are you arresting my client on suspicion of something?'

Barclay waited for de Silva to sit down next to him. 'No,' he said.

'Then we're leaving.'

'We haven't finished our questions just yet,' de Silva said. She looked directly at Whitley. 'There's a dead child here, another child seriously ill in hospital; why would you not *want* to help?'

'My client is saddened by the loss of life,' Lynch said. 'Make no doubt of it. He found the child himself. Called the police. Jesus, he *was* police. But from my understanding, your questioning seems to have been about his career with Merseyside Police and not this sad set of circumstances.'

'There are a few things I'd like to talk to you about,' de Silva said directly to Whitley. 'Just questions. I *can* caution you,' she said.

'Is that necessary?' Lynch asked.

'That depends on your client.'

Whitley looked to Lynch, his face mottled pink, and she shook her head. Whitley pulled at the middle finger on his right hand. 'What about?'

'Mitch…' Lynch said, her voice low, a warning.

'The name you entered on your conflict of interest form,' she said. 'Can you read it?' She slid the page across to him.

'Joanna McKenzie,' he said without looking at it.

'Detective Constable Joanna McKenzie,' de Silva corrected him. 'What was your relationship to her?'

'We were… involved.'

'Sexually?'

'And dating, yes,' he said. 'So what? I declared it. She did, too. Or said she was going to.'

'She did,' de Silva said, sliding another conflict of interest form toward him. 'DC McKenzie died in a road traffic accident two years ago, didn't she?'

'She did.' He glared at the table, his bottom lip pouting, but Barclay wasn't buying the sad ex-lover act.

'And you were in the car with her at the time of the accident,' de Silva added.

'I was…' He glanced at his lawyer.

'Can you cut to the chase?' Lynch asked, impatiently.

'DC Joanna McKenzie was one of the lead investigators in the discovery of a body found at Formby woods,' de Silva said. 'A case that former-DSI O'Brien assigned them to.'

'What's your point?' Lynch again, nostrils flaring.

'A case that Mr Whitley here was heavily involved in during his time as a constable with Merseyside Police.'

'What exactly is your insinuation?' Lynch's tone firm, her voice filling the room.

De Silva ignored the lawyer, and said to Whitley, 'You were also keen to become involved with the Protecting Vulnerable People Unit under former-DCI Crosby's leadership.'

Whitley pulled so hard on his finger his knuckle clicked loudly in the room, and he closed his eyes, as though the act of cracking his fingers like an angsty teenager gave him some sort of relief.

'I was seconded to his team for a bit before the Formby woods case,' he said. 'It means nothing. I just worked with him.' He looked at de Silva then, his eyes round and almost black, and to Barclay they looked like pig eyes. Snuffling around in filth and never knowing that they're about to be slaughtered. 'It's not like I was fucking him.'

De Silva's hand tensed so much her knuckles turned white. She held her breath and sat back in her chair, put her hands under the desk, where Barclay was sure they were still bunched in anger.

'Why are you asking these questions?' Lynch asked. 'Get to the events on the pier or we're walking.'

'What were you looking for on Southport beach, Mr Whitley?' de Silva asked, finally.

'Don't answer that,' Lynch advised. 'This interview is over. Mr Whitley, you need to come with me now.'

'I started this investigation for you,' Whitley said. 'I called the police. If it weren't for me, you'd have found that baby weeks down the line. Months maybe, with it being closed off to the public. Birds would have—'

'Mitch!' Lynch's voice rang in the warm air between them all.

Whitley was on his feet again, 'Good luck with your investigation, Detectives.' As he passed de Silva, he whispered, 'You'll need it,' and winked.

De Silva smiled. 'I'm coming for you, Mr Whitley.'

'I'll make a note of that comment, DCI de Silva,' Lynch said.

'Please do.'

Whitley followed his lawyer out into the corridor, where a uniformed officer led them out toward the reception area. Barclay closed the interview room door behind them and turned to de Silva. 'You can't goad a witness like that, de Silva. Come on.'

'I'm telling you, he's involved in this,' she said. She swooped up her laptop. 'His girlfriend who was investigating Bob Brendan's death out there in Formby woods is no coincidence. I can feel it in my bones.'

Bob Brendan. That name. Again and again. He was the head at Rainford Lane School for Boys in the nineties. The head and the leader of an organised child sex and exploitation ring which operated out of the school's basement.

'That's good for you and your bones. But in terms of facts, in terms of evidence, we have nothing.'

'Detectives detect, Barclay.' She pulled open the door, the cold air from the corridor rushed in and Barclay shivered.

They were about to leave the room as Lawrence blocked their way, almost sending de Silva's laptop crashing to the floor. 'I'm sorry!' Lawrence said, her voice high, eyes panicked.

'It's fine,' Barclay said. 'De Silva's always in someone's way. What's up?'

'Two things,' Lawrence said. 'The first is that Harris and O'Connor have finished with the kids who removed the boarding from the entrance to the pier. Harris knew you'd want to speak to them yourselves. They're just down the corridor.'

'Thank you, Lawrence,' de Silva said, moving around her into the corridor.

'What was the other thing?' Barclay asked.

'We had a call from the officers at Southport hospital.'

'Is Beatrice awake?' de Silva asked, hope thick in her voice.

'No.' Lawrence shook her head. 'It's her dad,' she said. 'He's there now, kicking off. Said he wants her transferred closer to home, not taking no for an answer.'

'Has he seen Beatrice yet?' Barclay grabbed his jacket from the back of the chair.

'No,' Lawrence said. 'The doctors won't let him in. That's the problem.'

De Silva looked to Barclay. 'Could you…?'

Barclay looked at his watch. *There's time.* 'I'm on it,' he said. 'Lawrence, up for a drive?'

-

Barclay and Lawrence walked across the carpark in silence. The light dusting of snow softened the sound of their footfalls to a dull thud, and in the air, their breath slipped out of their mouths in tendrils, twisting in the cold air.

The main reception doors slid open, and a curtain of hot air blew down on them. Not quite strong enough to rid their bones of the cold, but still a welcome change.

Then, his voice boomed through the waiting room; some patients had rose from their seats and moved to a quieter part of the room. A security officer was nearby talking into his radio, while two uniformed officers were standing in front of the shouting man, listening. Letting him blow off the steam.

Barclay spotted Charlene trying to get in between Lee and a second security officer, but he kept pushing her aside. The security officer seemed to recognise Barclay and waved him over.

'And who the fuck's this now?' His Manchester accent was thick and nasal.

'Lee, just leave it will you, you're making a holy show of yourself,' Charlene said.

'*I'm* making a show of *myself*!' Lee screamed. 'I'm not the one who married a fucking...' He stopped himself as he eyed Barclay up and down. 'I want my daughter away from you and out of this hospital.'

Barclay's eyebrow arched. 'I'm Detective Sergeant Barclay, Mr Tredwell. If you'd like to keep your voice down, I'm sure we can find somewhere quieter to talk things through.'

Lee put his hand on Barclay's shoulder, and Barclay eyed it coolly. 'You do us a favour and fetch us the doctor,' he said. Then, his face turned red, and he shouted, 'So I can get my fucking daughter out of this place.'

'Lee!' Charlene said, pulling on his arm. She looked to Barclay and Lawrence and said, 'I'm so sorry about this.'

Barclay took hold of Lee's hand and removed it from his shoulder. 'People here are sick, Mr Tredwell. The rest are just doing their jobs. Now, I'm not your personal assistant, and I'm not a fucking dog, so I won't be fetching anything. Either you quiet down and come with me, or you'll spend the rest of the day in a cell down Albert Road nick, you prick. I mean pick.'

Barclay turned away from him without waiting for his reply, and walked across to the receptionist, a round-faced man in his late fifties, wearing a hospital-branded blue fleece. Barclay asked him if they had a private room where he could speak to Mr Tredwell, and he was pointed down the corridor to the right.

When Barclay turned back to Lee, his face was shades of pink and red, his eyes bloodshot. 'Mr Tredwell?'

Tredwell, even taller than Barclay and with a shaved head he thought had gone out of style in the early 2000s, followed him down a corridor to a small room. Barclay opened the door and let Lawrence and Tredwell enter first. 'Take a seat. Lee, is it?' Charlene scooted in as Barclay was about to shut the door.

'Do you mind if she stays?' Barclay asked.

Tredwell nodded. 'I don't care what she does,' he said. 'But yeah, you can call me Lee.' He lingered around the four chairs and the table, pacing.

'This is PC Lawrence. She's working with us on the case involving your daughter.'

'Well, I want to see her. Now.'

'We get it,' Lawrence said. 'But you have to understand that we need to protect your daughter. Right now, we don't know what happened to her, where she's been since she disappeared, or how…'

Barclay saw the panic on Lawrence's face, the open mouth, the wild eyes. She was about to talk about the pregnancy, about the baby, Barclay knew that, but she'd second-guessed herself. Had panicked, wondering how much Tredwell knew. How much he *should* know at this stage.

Good, Barclay thought. *She's thinking right.*

'How what?' Tredwell asked.

'How all of this happened,' Barclay interjected. 'How she's been missing for three weeks, and nobody saw her.'

Lee turned to Charlene. 'I told you not to put her in that place. You and that husband of yours.' Finally, he sat down. 'There was nothing wrong with her; it was all that Aladdin or whatever he's called.'

'It's Azad!' Charlene shouted.

'Mr Tredwell,' Barclay said, sitting down. 'I'm going to warn you just once about making racist comments, do you hear me? We can have a chat about your feelings, but I won't tolerate blatant racism, do you understand me?'

'You and Mr Khan didn't get on?' Lawrence asked.

Tredwell clenched his fists. 'I knew there was something off about him when I met him. And now look. My Bea's in hospital and he's walking around scot-free after what he did to her.'

'He didn't do anything!' Charlene shouted. 'He moved away after everything that happened with her. I don't know why she said the things she said, but Azad never touched her.'

'Well I think he did,' Lee said, his face crimson and wet. 'All fucking nonces aren't they, them lot? Killers, rapists. We don't know who the fuck we're letting in the country.'

Barclay felt a ball of anger form hard and burning inside his chest and knew that Lee Tredwell voted Reform. 'That's your final warning, Mr Tredwell. Any more and I'll instruct hospital staff to not let you see your daughter at all. And while we're discussing it, Mr Khan was born and raised in Oldham,' he said.

'When Bea started saying this and that about him touching her…' Tredwell shook his head. 'Well, I went round there didn't I. Put my hands on him to see how he liked it.'

'So, it was Bea who told you that Mr Khan was having an inappropriate sexual relationship with her?' Lawrence asked.

'He wasn't!' Charlene chipped in.

'Mrs Khan, it might be easier if you stepped outside,' Lawrence said.

'Look, can I see my daughter or what? I'm her fucking dad after all.'

Barclay didn't take his eyes from Tredwell, but said, 'Lawrence, could you check with Bea's doctor to make sure that Lee can have a supervised visit with a security officer? Charlene, I'll come and see you before I go.'

There was a rage in Tredwell that Barclay didn't trust. He didn't want that around Bea while she was healing, but that, ultimately, was not his choice. He didn't know her, hadn't even spoken to her, but somehow, he felt protective of her.

He thought of Sarah.

Lawrence was up and on her feet without saying a word, Charlene with her, and they left the room.

Something inside Barclay told him there was more to this whole thing. Maybe it was in the way Tredwell seemed so agitated – but then how would Barclay himself act if Sarah was lying in a hospital bed? Perhaps he was still hyper-sensitive from the interview with Mitch Whitley. And there was all of *that* to deal with.

He studied Tredwell's broad, red face, lined from years of smoking or from working outside in the elements. Maybe both. Even though it was short, Barclay could see silver and white coming through in those tiny strands of hair. If he let it grow out, he'd probably look much older. 'Who do you think took your daughter?'

'If I knew that, you'd have found their body by now.' Tredwell's voice was low, almost a growl.

'The doctor said Mr Tredwell can visit his daughter, but only for ten minutes.' Lawrence's voice from the door.

Barclay smiled at Tredwell. 'There you are. We'll leave you to it, but your visit will be supervised and short.' Tredwell was about to speak, but Barclay was on his feet and said, 'It's for Bea's protection, Mr Tredwell. It's what we all want, isn't it? For her to be safe. Finally.' Silence then. 'Lawrence, will you escort Mr Tredwell?'

Tredwell nodded and got to his feet, followed Lawrence out to the corridor.

Barclay couldn't shake the feeling he'd had while speaking to Tredwell, that niggle he'd begun to hone. There was something wrong there, and he wished he could put his finger on it. As he walked out of the main entrance into the carpark for fresh air, he sifted through the whole thing.

Bea had accused the new husband of abuse, and then she was placed in a psychiatric facility at the request of her mother. Khan was arrested and later cleared. Greater Manchester Police had nothing to go on.

'I'm sorry about him.' Charlene's voice from beside him. 'He's never changed, not since I met him. Always been a bit of a twat.'

'You can say that again,' Barclay said. 'You all right getting home?'

'I brought the car today,' she said. 'Well, Annie's car.'

'Bit of a journey coming back and forth every day, isn't it?'

'No choice really,' she said. 'Can't afford a hotel, so there's not much else I can do.'

'I can speak to the hospital,' Barclay said. 'I'm sure they could sort something for you. For Bea's sake.'

'That's nice of you,' she said. She looked down at the ground, her face scrunching into a wrinkled mess. 'Is she going to be okay, do you think? What's happened to her, I… I can't imagine the pain she went through. If I hadn't have put her in Allerton House, she'd have been safe at home instead of…' Tears slid down her tired face.

'Charlene, she wasn't happy at home. She needed help.'

Charlene nodded. 'No, you're right. The only time she's ever happy is when she's with that soft shite in there. God knows why, but she looks up to him. Loves him.'

Barclay didn't know what else to say to her. 'I'd best be setting off,' he said finally. 'You drive safely.'

'Do you have kids?'

Barclay didn't want to discuss Sarah at work, but Charlene was in pain. Any comfort he could bring her, any tiny touch of humanity he could give, would be worth it. 'I have a daughter.'

'That's lovely,' she said. 'You keep her safe.' She took her keys from her pocket and pressed a button on the fob and somewhere the hazard lights of a car blinked twice. 'I'd best be setting off, too. I'll see you.'

'You too,' he said. 'And make sure you're getting some rest.'

Charlene trundled off to her car and pulled away, her tail-lights disappearing into the dark. Barclay took in a deep breath and let it go. This case was getting messier at each turn, and he knew that tonight might be the last time he would see Sarah properly for a few weeks. He dreaded having that conversation with Nick but somehow, he had to make it all work, and somewhere an engine roared to life. Something sporty.

Headlights ahead shone bright.

He covered his eyes as he walked across the carpark and couldn't make out the car or its colour.

The engine revved.

Barclay started to jog toward it.

The headlights turned to full beams and blasted through the dark, almost blinding him.

The engine revved again.

Tyres gripped the gritted carpark with a sound like crunching glass.

The headlights seemed brighter now. Closer.

Barclay felt it hit him like the blow of a mallet. The stink of burned rubber in the air, the smell of diesel.

His skull cracked into the cold ground.

Then, as the February night settled in around him, Barclay's world was black.

Thirteen

De Silva had been on a run. The cold air had raked at her lungs, stung her face and made her lips dry. This was only the third run in the last two weeks she'd managed to fit in, but she was determined to get back into the habit. Running helped her think. Focus.

There was a small fishing lake right near her house, and around that a decent path, which only puddled when the rain was excessive. The snow had been trampled and flattened, turned black by dog walkers out for fresh air.

As she ran, she thought of the interview with the two young scallies whose prints they'd found at the pier.

'Please, honest, you've got to believe me,' the youngest one had told de Silva. 'Me and Ty, we got there when the drone was already there. Tried lashin' stones at it, then the fella turned up out of nowhere, sweatin' like a fat pig. He offered us fifty quid each,' Leo said. 'To just get out of there. Say nothin', know what I mean? But, listen, my sister's just had a baby, and I wouldn't like to know it was left like that. We told him to ring the plod, er, you lot, and he wouldn't at first. We told him we would, and so he did. Watched him do it like, but he told us to get out of there. In case you lot picked us up for wreckin' tha' door.'

De Silva could believe what she had heard from the lad, but still it wasn't solid enough to pin anything on Whitley. An ex-bobby's word against the word of two young tearaways? No one would believe them over Whitley. Still, she couldn't help but ask: was Whitley really stupid enough to trust young lads who'd do and say anything for fifty quid? Besides, there was a reason that Whitley didn't want to call the police at the time; but now he was lawyered up, she needed more to go on to bring him in.

Alongside all of this and what was happening with Beatrice Tredwell, an elderly woman had been found at her home following a house fire. And on top of that, she needed to look into the death of Joanna McKenzie and the disappearance of Layton Cullen.

She completed five circuits of the small lake before heading off down the main road toward Amber Mews and her warm home. Thankfully, she'd had the presence of mind to turn on the heating before she'd left.

She'd not yet eaten, but ordering a take-away to undo all of the good she'd just done on her run felt like the right thing to do. She ordered it quickly on the app and turned the shower on.

Later, she was sitting in the office she'd made for herself that overlooked the untidy back garden. Come spring, she'd need to get someone out there to tackle the weeds, mow back the grass and maybe plant something that added some colour. Some much-needed vibrance to the space.

She pictured herself sitting outside at a garden table she didn't have, on a chair she didn't yet own. She'd be reading the newspaper or sipping coffee, looking at plants and flowers she liked the look of but would never learn the names. That dream of spring seemed so far away.

She logged into her work laptop, connected the VPN via the Microsoft app on her phone, and typed in the name: *Whitley, Mitchel.* De Silva didn't believe in coincidences as a rule, and any link between Bea's reappearance and Bob Brendan's death was too much of a chance to pass unquestioned.

Whitley had joined the force five years prior to him leaving and had expressed a clear interest in working with the Protecting Vulnerable People Unit, which DCI Mike Crosby led at the time. There was nothing in his file. No commendations, no reprimands. He was, de Silva decided, a man who came in and did his job. Still, she couldn't shake the unsettling feeling that some of that job was working with the PVPU under Crosby. She wondered whether she was seeing connections where there weren't any, or whether her keenly honed intuition was right.

She shook her head and groaned, typed another name into the PNC search screen: *McKenzie, Joanna.* The photo from her file loaded and de Silva couldn't help but think she was way out of Mitch Whitley's league.

We can't help who we fall in love with, she thought.

The autopsy report read like that of any other RTA victim she'd ever read. Skull fractures, severe traumatic brain injuries, facial and basilar skull fractures. The latter resulted in spinal fluid leakage. There were also multiple rib fractures. Likely cause of death was due to C1-C4 spinal injuries causing respiratory arrest.

'Jesus...' de Silva said to herself. The vehicles hit front-on, off-set, meaning the driver's side took the brunt of the collision. She hoped that McKenzie hadn't suffered, that her injuries meant any pain was over quickly.

She clicked out of the post-mortem and into the police report. The other vehicle was a black Audi with blacked-out windows. The car had been reported stolen that same day by the owner. The driver, who must have been seriously injured themselves, was never found. When police arrived on the scene, the car was empty.

That's weird, she thought. *To just step away from an accident like that. Still, Whitley himself got off with a broken arm and a fractured cheekbone.*

She wanted to know who to contact if she needed more information about the post-mortem, so de Silva clicked back into that report. Neither Carey nor Brennan were listed, their usual signatures not there at the bottom of the report. Instead, the pathologist was listed as Dr Francesca Watson, who de Silva had never heard of before.

De Silva picked up her phone and made a note of the name in the Notes app, along with the post-mortem date: Monday 22 August 2022.

Just a week after we found the body in the woods, she thought. And one week after de Silva's whole world fell apart when she'd discovered Ritchie's body hanging from the banister.

She thought about giving Carey or Brennan a call, to understand why they hadn't looked after McKenzie's post-mortem, but it was already so late. She'd do it in the morning.

De Silva felt her eyes getting heavy and turned her head slightly until her neck clicked. She needed to get some sleep, and in the morning, she'd call Brennan and Carey.

The call came as she laid her head down on the pillow. The woman on the end of the line introduced herself as Doreen, a nurse from Southport hospital, who had a Northern Irish accent. 'I'm sorry,' she said. 'Your friend, uh colleague, Ben Barclay? He asked me to call you.'

'What's happened?' De Silva heard the rush of her own blood coursing around her head, thrumming in her ears, as she sat up in bed. 'Is he okay?'

'Sure, he's going to be fine,' Doreen said. 'A car hit him and sped off.'

'Hit him? Are you sure he's all right? Did they catch the bastard?'

'He's fine, Detective,' she said with a slight chuckle. 'He's gone on home just now. His husband came to collect him.'

De Silva wanted to hang up the phone and call Barclay straight away; she'd feel better once she heard his voice and knew he was safe. 'Thank you for calling,' de Silva said.

'Oh, erm…'

Something in Doreen's tone told de Silva to stay on the line. 'Are you all right? Is there something else?'

'I don't know how to say this,' she said, her voice wobbling. 'Usually, Dr Clements would make this call herself, but she's tied up with patients. She's been on shift since yesterday afternoon. God love her.'

'Doreen, isn't it?' de Silva asked. 'Just tell me. Or I can come down to the hospital right now.'

'I think you may want to come down anyway,' Doreen said. 'We're all heartbroken here.'

'About what?' De Silva was beginning to lose patience. 'What's happened?'

'After your friend left,' Doreen said, almost whispering into the phone, 'Beatrice Tredwell passed away.'

'I'm on my way.'

Fourteen

Nick fussed. Fluttered about, unable to sit still. First it was a blanket, then an extra cushion, then pacing in front of the TV checking when the Chinese take-away would deliver the food.

Barclay was in pain. It was late and he wanted to go to bed, but his stomach growled, and his head felt light. Despite the pain, the hospital said there was nothing broken. Just bruising and, in Nick's defence, the biggest graze Barclay had ever seen. From his hip all the way to his underarm. And that cut on his head… well, Barclay was glad he couldn't see it.

They hadn't managed to stop the car before it screeched off out of the carpark, and before Barclay's head cracked against the tarmac, he didn't have a chance to make a note of the reg.

Sarah had nuzzled in next to him, fast asleep in the nook of his arm. She'd been happy with a spicy sausage pasta bake which Barclay had left over in the fridge. Shortly after she was flat out, cuddling Mingo.

'This is taking forever,' Nick said. He put his phone into his pocket. 'It's bloody late.'

'You can go if you like,' Barclay said. 'I can answer the door.'

'You just want the crispy chilli beef to yourself.' Nick smiled and sat on the couch, Sarah between them. 'I'm not soft.'

'I'm sorry if you had plans tonight,' Barclay whispered and kissed the top of Sarah's head. 'And I can't thank you enough for cancelling if you did; for bringing her over.'

'Ben, she'd be crushed if she didn't get to see you tonight,' Nick said. 'She loves coming here.'

Something shifted its weight inside Barclay's chest. An unusual mix of love, pride and something else. A regret. Loss. Remorse. He and Nick hadn't spent this long in each other's company in a while, and it felt good. Easy. Familiar. Like something he'd mislaid and almost forgotten about.

'I worry about you,' Nick said, softly. 'Your line of work is dangerous. This type of thing happens a lot.'

'Not as often as you'd think.'

'Often enough,' Nick said. 'It wasn't too long ago that me and Sarah had to go into hiding. Also, not that long ago you were involved in a bloody shoot-out in the Lake District.'

'It wasn't a shoot-out.' Barclay laughed, then hissed at the pain in his ribs. 'You make it sound like the Wild West.'

'Not far off.'

'You need to behave yourself,' Barclay said. 'We're not even together any more and we're still having this conversation.'

Nick looked down at his shoes, then around the room, and Barclay wondered whether he was trying to distract himself from the sting in Barclay's words. He reached over and touched Nick's hand. His skin was soft and warm, and Barclay wished those hands still touched him.

'I didn't mean it the way that sounded,' Barclay said. 'I just mean… this is my job, you know? You don't need to worry about me any more.'

Nick prodded Barclay in the side and he winced. 'Don't I? This must be imaginary then, mustn't it?'

'No, it's very real,' Barclay said. 'Jesus that hurts.'

'I worry, Ben,' Nick said. 'Just like you worry about her. Like I know you still worry about me.'

Barclay didn't know what to say. He hadn't expected this conversation at all. Hadn't expected Nick to bring Sarah, hadn't expected him to order a meal for them to eat together. Hadn't expected to feel how he felt. Of course he still cared about Nick, his soon-to-be ex-husband. They'd been together for years, had known each other longer than that, and those feelings don't just disappear overnight.

He hoped that they'd never go. That, in twenty years' time when they'd both moved on, he'd still feel this love for Nick. This need to know that he's okay, that he's safe.

'Why don't I put her to bed?' Nick stood and scooped Sarah up into his arms. 'I can sleep in the spare room with her. Get up early and get her off to school. I should have taken Stefan up on his offer, really.'

'What offer?'

'He said he'd look after her tonight while I came to help you out.'

'That's nice of him,' Barclay said, trying to sound as though he meant it. In truth, he'd never taken to Nick's boss at the gallery. Couldn't put his finger on it. 'But she's fine here. *I'm* fine.'

'Well, it's just that I've had to take her to the gallery a few times,' Nick said. 'When you were busy with work. She likes him and he likes her which I'm even more surprised at. I didn't know that he has a niece too, about the same age. We're taking them both to a soft play place tomorrow.'

Barclay hoped that Nick would ask him to go with them, but the invitation didn't come. 'I've not ironed her any clothes for the morning,' Barclay said, changing the subject.

'I'll do it first thing.'

Barclay nodded. 'You don't have to, you know?'

'Shut up.' Nick walked away, their sleeping daughter in his arms, and Barclay sat in the quiet of his living room. He could smell Nick's cologne in the room, warm, soft and gentle. Like vanilla pods and ice cream and honey.

His nighttime cologne, Barclay thought and laughed to himself. Nick was the only person Barclay knew who had a signature evening-at-home scent. He missed climbing into bed, and falling asleep next to him, and waking up with Nick's smell pressed into their pillows.

When Nick returned, Sarah fast asleep in her bed, the food finally arrived. Nick brought it out into the living room on plates, and they talked about the old days. Before Sarah, before they were married, when their lives were centred around getting to know each other. They laughed about those early holidays to Gran Canaria or Corfu, when they were skint and stayed in three-star all-inclusive hotels an hour's bus ride from the beach.

None of that had mattered to them. They'd had each other, and that was all they'd needed. Or wanted. When the laughs died down, Barclay's mind wandered to the inevitable: where it had all gone wrong. When they'd looked at each other and that love, that excitement, that need for one another, had gone.

In truth, for Barclay, it had never gone. He loved Nick now like he'd loved him on those cheap-as-chips holidays abroad. Adored him just as much as the day they got married at St George's Hall and they'd had their reception in the Palm House at Sefton Park with close friends and family.

Nick put down his fork, chewed the crispy chilli beef slowly, and said, 'You know, Sarah made this fingerpainting at school,' he said. 'It was for a project about what she wishes for the most, or what she wants the most, I can't remember which. But she painted all of us. On the beach. Together. It's in my office at work, but I'll bring it to show you.'

'I'd like that,' Barclay said. 'I, er… I wish things could be different with us.'

'Come on now,' Nick said and looked away at the TV, even though it was switched off. Just a black, blank screen reflecting the pair of them sitting next to each other. 'We're past this, aren't we? You've moved on.'

'I haven't moved on.'

'That NCA fella would beg to differ, I bet.'

Ouch. 'I've had to work with him, Nick. But he's gone now. Or going,' he said. 'But what happened between me and him… well, it's nothing like what we had.' Barclay tried to swallow, to force the food down his dry throat. 'Have you?'

'Slept with an NCA investigator? No.'

Barclay ignored the quip. 'Moved on, I mean.'

Nick forked some beef into his mouth and chewed slowly. Barclay wondered whether he was buying himself some time. 'No,' he said. 'Well, Stefan has suggested that we—'

'I knew it!' Was it this all along? That Barclay had always known that Stefan secretly wanted his husband? 'Bloody Stefan of all people.'

'Yes, Stefan. What's wrong with that?'

'Well, he's a bit...'

'A bit what?'

'Gay.'

'You're a bit bloody gay.' Nick laughed and threw a forkful of rice at Barclay, who laughed, then winced and held his side. 'What a weird thing to say.'

'You know what I mean. Camp.'

'He's not camp,' Nick said. 'He's just a bit... flamboyant. Haven't we transcended "camp" now anyway? Labels and all of that?'

'Not these days, no. There seem to be more labels than ever. I still don't know what an otter is, and I'm not sure I want to find out.'

'You're not one,' Nick said. 'So I wouldn't give it too much thought.'

'What am I?'

'Erm...'

'Besides stunningly handsome, I mean. What am I?'

'Conceited.' Nick shook his head, unable to hide his smile. The one that Barclay had missed so much and in that moment, he knew that Nick was feeling the same way: he was enjoying himself.

'So what did you say?' Barclay asked as Nick looked puzzled. 'To Stefan.'

'I said no.' He took a forkful of rice into his mouth. 'We're friends, and besides... he's not my type.'

When Nick had finished eating and Barclay had picked at the mound that remained on his plate, Nick tidied everything away and as Barclay heard him turning on the dishwasher, he got to his feet.

'I'm going to turn in,' Barclay said. 'I'm sorry.'

'It's fine. It's late.' He looked at his watch. 'Or early, depending how you look at it.'

'Are you okay to lock up?'

'Sure.' Nick lingered for a moment. 'Look, why don't you take the morning off? Come the soft play centre with me—'

'And Stefan.'

Nick grinned. 'Yes, and Stefan. And little Indiana,' he said.

'I dunno...'

'You can barely walk without wincing,' Nick said. 'You can't exactly chase down any bad guys, can you?'

'I could ask de Silva,' he said. 'It's a bit late to be ringing her now, but I'll go round in the morning.'

Nick nodded. 'Okay. Well, Sarah would love you to come. I'd love for you to come.'

Between sleep, Barclay heard the shower running. Heard the handle of his bedroom door turn. Felt Nick's small, slender frame climb into the bed beside him and as Barclay turned to him, their lips finding each other in the dark, he forgot about the pain.

Later, when Nick fell asleep, Barclay lay awake staring at the ceiling. He'd lost count of the amount of times he'd wished that he could wake up to Nick in his bed. That they would somehow reconcile, despite everything.

Despite my work, he thought. *Despite how hard things were. Despite Ayris and Stefan.*

What did this mean? Was it just sex? A moment of weakness brought on by Nick's perception that Barclay was, in some way, in need of comfort and familiarity? A pity fuck?

But it didn't feel like fucking. It felt... different. Like the early days of their relationship, where they took their time together. Sensual almost.

His phone lit up and he leaned across to grab it, felt the pull and burn from the graze on his side and the sting of his bruised ribs. A message from Lawrence said that she'd checked the hospital's ANPR on the carpark. It had been non-operational at the time Barclay was mowed down. There was nothing to go on.

It's a warning, he told himself. *Someone doesn't want us on this case.*

Fifteen

13 February

The hospital carpark was almost deserted in the early hours of the morning. The small Accident and Emergency department still rumbled with life, the grumble of ambulance engines, and the swirl of the lights. De Silva climbed into her car as flecks of snow blew onto her windscreen. The yellow lights of the carpark gave it an otherworldly feel: like the nighttime was lit, like it was fire.

The nurse who had called de Silva had met her at the entrance to the hospital, and took her into a small room which was accessible only by Doreen's security pass. Her eyes were red and she wiped at her nose with a ragged tissue which de Silva guessed she'd had hold of for hours.

'We'd high hopes for her,' Doreen said, her Irish accent stronger now that de Silva was sitting across from her. 'We all prayed she'd pull through after… well, after what happened with that wee baby.'

De Silva had felt the same. In her private moments, she had hoped that they would get some answers about what had happened to Beatrice that night. How she'd disappeared from a secure unit in Manchester. *And*, de Silva thought, *whether any of the rumours about her stepfather were true.*

Dr Clements hadn't arrived by the time de Silva needed to head off home, to finally get some sleep before the long day ahead. At least, that was the plan. Her watch told her it was seven minutes past six. Even if she went home now, she'd only have time for a half hour's sleep before she had to get up again. She needed to shower at least, to change into clean clothes and brush her teeth.

Doreen had returned to apologise for Dr Clements, and had told de Silva that ultimately, multiple things had contributed toward Bea's death. Hypothermia, damage to her internal organs caused by broken bones, blood loss from childbirth without medical intervention.

The post-mortem would tell them more, and de Silva hoped there would be a quick turnaround.

De Silva found her car where she'd left it, tucked away near the entrance under a tree. She put the heating on straight away and sat there while the freezing air from the vents turned breath-warm and she rubbed her hands together. She'd thought about calling Barclay to check in on him, but decided it was far too early.

The clock on the dashboard shone green. Twenty past six.

She'd promised herself that she would go and visit her mum at the home, but now that would have to wait. This case was getting more complicated by the hour, and after meeting with O'Brien, she couldn't afford to take another break during work hours. Murphy was watching her.

Yeah, well fuck Murphy. If I'm late, I'm late.

As she drove toward Liverpool, careful on the roads where snow was banked at the sides, grey and black, she called the home to see if she could pop in out of hours as a special favour. She didn't care if her mum was sleeping. Didn't care if she spent the entire time just watching her breathe. De Silva just wanted to see her. It had been days. *I'll stay for just ten minutes*, she promised herself, and the night manager.

The place smelled like it always had done, of stewed meat and vegetables, and it hung in the air, thick and invisible, but always present. Her mum's bedroom door was open, just a bit, and in a tiny shaft of light from the corridor, de Silva could make out her aging mother's grey hair.

She'd been dark when she was younger, like Laney, and she'd loved her hair. If younger Marie Brophy was able to see old Marie Brophy, it would break her heart. But that's the thing about getting old: you're not old until you are. You remember everything until you forget.

De Silva crept in, closed the door back to its original position and sat on a comfortable armchair, wrapped a blanket around herself and watched her mum.

'Are you an angel, girl?' Her mum's voice was quiet, almost a creaking whisper, rasping like she needed a drink. 'Come to take me away, have you? To my Carl?'

De Silva shifted in her seat. It looked as though her mum's eyes were still closed, but who knew. 'It's me, Mum,' de Silva said. 'It's Win.'

There was a time when de Silva could say her own name, and her mum would know her. Or, when Marie's face would light up at the sight of her eldest daughter. Those days were gone. Each time de Silva visited now, it was as though her mum was meeting a stranger. Someone she hadn't given birth to or raised.

'Win?' Marie croaked. 'Win what? Not that Postcode Lottery shite, I never play it.'

'No, that's my name. Win,' she said. 'Winifred.'

'Ah, that's a lovely name. You know, my mam was called Winnie. I always liked the name. Sounds nice, doesn't it, girl?'

'It does,' de Silva said. 'I remember your mum. And your auntie Elaine.' They were the namesakes of de Silva and Laney. Two mad old women who were always together and outlived their husbands by decades, based solely on a diet of real ale and pork scratchings, or so de Silva's memories of them had her believe. Maybe that was because the only time she saw them was at the pub or family functions.

'Auntie Elaine used to have a barge on the canal, you know?'

'I know,' de Silva said. 'I remember that she made jumpers out of wool she bought from farmers there. Scarfs. Socks.'

Marie sat up in her bed, slowly and on weak arms. 'Oh they didn't half scratch. They were bleedin' awful things, but we had to wear them,' she said. 'They were presents.' She took a long breath, as though contemplating the state of the world, and continued on: 'My mam used to say Auntie Elaine would have all kinds back on that bloody boat. Men, you know? Oh she loved men and men loved her. She was so glamourous with all that red hair. Movie-star looks and those big bright red lips, and when she would sing… oh my, she had the voice of Boy George.'

De Silva tried not to laugh. She had seen Elaine's photographs in the family albums but had to admit she'd never heard her sing. When de Silva and Laney were kids, Marie would dig them out and they'd go through them one by one. She would tell her daughters every family story there was to tell. How one of their uncles had gone off to war and was buried in France, his name engraved on a wall in Ver-sur-Mer. How she'd had a younger brother named Edward who'd died at three months old. He'd been buried in Bootle Cemetery, but none of the other family were and she didn't know why.

'One time Auntie Elaine found out a man she was seeing was married. She hung his undies up on a wire coat hanger at the back of the boat like a flag. Shouted his name all up and down the Leeds-Liverpool, had a scrap with his wife when she came to collect them.' Marie laughed, which turned to coughing and spluttering.

'Oh, Mum.' De Silva moved to her, perched on the edge of her bed, felt the sheets slip over the rubber-topped mattress. 'I wish there was something we could do.' Marie said nothing. Maybe she didn't know what to say. Maybe she didn't know what was happening. 'I'm going to go and let you get back to sleep.' She kissed the top of Marie's head. 'I'm sorry I woke you up.'

She helped Marie to lie back down again, to find a comfortable position, and pulled the duvet up over her. The room was hot, the central heating humming out boiling air, but Marie had started to feel the cold more and more, especially this winter.

'Good night, God bless,' de Silva said, kissing her mum's forehead. She walked out into the corridor and looked back in one last time.

'You didn't answer my question, girl.'

'What's that?'

'Are you an angel come to take me away? I've been waiting.'

'No, I'm not,' de Silva said. 'And if you see any knocking about, you tell them to do one, won't you? You're not going anywhere.'

She could hear a snore rattle at the back of her mother's throat as de Silva headed down the corridor. *Already asleep.* She walked out into the reception area, waved to the night manager near the front desk, and made her way out to the car.

There's an awful thing that happens when you watch someone wasting away. Becoming someone other than who they were. Losing their memories, their mind, the thing that made them who they were. Each time you visit, there's a change, and the heart you've tried so hard to keep together cracks just a little bit more. Another piece of it falls away like flaking paint from a damp wall.

-

De Silva was barely out of the shower and dressed when the doorbell rang. She left the kettle to boil and let Barclay in. 'I hope you're not coming to the office today,' she said by way of hello.

De Silva looked him up and down, her eyebrow arched. He looked dishevelled, his eyes puffy as though he'd not slept, and even though he beamed at her, she could tell it was forced. She gestured that he should follow her through to the kitchen. 'You look like shit, Barclay; what're you playing at?'

'Says you. Have you even moisturised this month?'

'You're lucky I've even had a shower.'

'Haven't washed your hair though, have you? I can smell the chip fat from here.'

'I'll demote you in a minute.' She shook her head, grinning.

'I was at the hospital last night,' de Silva said, searching the cupboards for that take-away cup she'd spent fifteen quid on from the Starbucks drive-through. The one with the spill-proof lid. She was certain she'd seen it somewhere.

'What for?' Barclay's face creased into concern. 'You okay?'

'I'm fine,' she said. 'But Bea isn't.'

'What?'

'She died, Barclay.' She stopped her search and looked at him. 'They're not entirely sure how, but they think there were a lot of contributing factors.' She resumed her search. 'I suppose we'll have to wait for the post-mortem results.'

'Her mum's going to be devastated,' Barclay said, sitting down on a stool at the breakfast bar.

'Yeah, and her dad'll be on the warpath,' de Silva added. 'And how're you feeling?'

'A bit sore, but I'll be fine,' he said. 'The car barely touched me. The tarmac did most of the damage.' He lifted up his loose-fitting white T-shirt to show her a bandage that already had evidence of seepage from his wounds.

She hissed. 'I think you should be at home resting. Did you get a reg? And what're you doing wearing white with a cut like that?'

'No. No reg. The ANPR at the hospital carpark wasn't working.' He looked down at the ground. 'If I didn't know better, I'd think it was more than coincidence and... God, de Silva, what're you looking for? Let me help.'

'This bloody cup I had. Or, I was sure I had. I'm in a rush. Murphy wants a meeting this morning. Feels like every morning at the minute. She's riding my back worse than ever.' De Silva rolled her eyes, grabbed the cup she'd been hunting for from behind a bag of washing machine pods, and rinsed it out. She flipped the kettle on to boil again and turned to look at him. 'Are you sure you're up for this today? It's going to be a busy one.'

'When isn't it?'

'I know what you're going to say…' She poured the hot water into her travel mug. 'You're worried this black car has something to do with the case, given the CCTV footage from the amusements place at the pier?'

'No,' he said. 'It's a completely different type of car.'

'Bea's dad? You said he was a bit of a dickhead, didn't you. What does he drive?'

'I'm not sure,' he said. 'The least of our worries right now, isn't it?'

'Oh yes, a detective sergeant on a high-profile case gets knocked down by an unidentifiable car outside a hospital where a very poorly young woman has been taken, and of course – it's the least of our worries.' She shook her head and laughed. 'We'll talk about it later, after my meeting.'

'Well, that's what I wanted to talk to you about,' Barclay said. 'I wondered if I could take the morning off. Nick's going to this play centre thing with Sarah, and she was pretty worried about me last night and I—'

'It's fine,' she said. 'Take the day.'

'No, I'll be back after lunch.'

'I said take the day.' De Silva took a sip of the instant coffee and spat it back out into the sink. 'That's rank. Remind me to get some good coffee at some point.'

'You've not used Bisto by accident have you?'

'I'm tired, but I'm not that tired.'

'Because one time I used Bisto.'

'It's not bloody Bisto.' She threw the cup into the sink, promised herself she'd sort it out later. 'I'd best get going. Get myself a nice coffee on the way.'

Sixteen

The thought of spending time with his family seemed like a good idea, even though Barclay still didn't really know exactly where he and Nick stood. Their relationship, to him, was a bit of an enigma. A puzzle. A Rubik's cube he wasn't sure either of them had the patience to resolve.

But the reality of walking into an indoor soft play was a completely different thing. Kids screamed from almost every corner, ran past chasing each other, jumped into ball pits and scrambled out, red shining balls spilling out over the side.

'He's over there, look,' Nick said. 'He's already got us a table.' Nick worked through the charging kids like it was second nature, while Barclay, who had hold of Sarah, clung tighter to her. She struggled to be put down and ran straight toward the waiting, open arms of Stefan.

'You should have cancelled him,' Barclay said.

'We'd already made the arrangements,' Nick whispered through a smile. 'So behave yourself.' Stefan took Sarah by the hand and headed over to them both. His niece, Indiana, walked at his side, her dark hair in fat ringlets that seemed somewhat old-fashioned, but what did Barclay know? 'Hello, Stefan.' Nick kissed Stefan on both cheeks. 'You remember Ben, don't you?'

'How could I forget?' Stefan offered Barclay his hand, the way a royal would, as though Barclay should kiss it. There was a ring with a pearl set in it on his little finger, and he wore an extravagant, long scarf, silk maybe, in swirling shades of blue. Whatever it was made from, it definitely wasn't made for the winter.

Barclay ignored it and smiled, stiffly, then looked to Nick. 'I'll get us some drinks.'

'I'd have a Prosecco, but it's hot drinks only,' Stefan said, laughing at his own joke.

I didn't ask, Barclay thought. 'So, do you want a hot drink then?'

'A tea,' he said. 'If they only have PG Tips, I'd rather tap water.'

Barclay nodded and walked toward the bar. Sarah ran past him with Indiana and, hand in hand, they headed for the climbing apparatus, her little red ribbons bouncing and shining as she ran. She'd be lost in there for hours, and she'd sleep on the way home. Wake up starving and desperate for something to eat later.

Barclay was pleased to find that the tea was indeed PG Tips and so placed a tap water down on the table in front of Stefan. Nick looked up at him, horror etched on his face. 'He's very literal, your fellow, isn't he?' Stefan said, moving the water to the other side of the table and getting up to go to the counter himself.

Barclay sat, passed Nick his latte, and sipped his own black coffee. Nick smacked him on the leg, one sharp, hard thwack. 'If you're going to behave like this, then go home,' Nick said.

'Behave like what?'

'You know exactly like what,' Nick said. 'Why are you being like this? I said no to dating Stefan, and that's that. So if you're being like this out of jealousy, you're also being massively misguided. Or are you so ashamed of your sexuality that you think any camp or effeminate man is beneath you? Less than you?' He took a breath and a sip of his latte; the foam settled on his top lip. 'Look, Stefan and I arranged to have a nice day with Sarah and Indiana. You're here because I thought it would be nice for Sarah. So be nice or leg it, Ben. I mean it.'

Barclay took all of Nick's words on the chin, and each one felt like a blow. He stood up and went over to the counter, put his hand on Stefan's shoulder. 'Look, I'm sorry,' he said.

'Well, it's not that I'm above tap water,' Stefan said. 'I'm just not convinced of what's in it these days.'

'Right,' Barclay said. He didn't really know how to interact with Stefan. They were worlds apart, galaxies even, but still he had to try. 'Well, I'll get you whatever you want. Like I say, I'm sorry. It's been a difficult week.'

'Well, you're in luck, this beautiful young girl has told me they have some Earl Grey.' He beamed at the spotty teenager behind the counter. 'Are they individually wrapped teabags?'

'Yeah,' she said, as though she begrudged the breath never mind the word itself.

'And do you have lemon rather than milk?'

'Lemon?' the teenager asked. 'It's tea, mate.'

Barclay had to agree with her.

'So, no lemon?'

'No,' she said. 'We've got milk.' She threw a few small, sealed milk pods onto the tray with the stainless-steel pot of hot water, the teabags and a cup.

'Well, that's a start,' Stefan said. 'He shall be paying.'

The teenager nodded, offered the card machine to Barclay to tap his phone, and Stefan sauntered off with his steaming pot and individually wrapped Earl Grey teabags. Barclay paid for the tea, rolled his eyes at the girl, who curled her lip at him.

'And where are the little darlings?' Stefan asked, looking over at the play area.

'They're up there.' Nick pointed to the top, where Sarah and Indiana played with a little blond boy in dungarees. He looked to Barclay then and said, 'Thank you,' and kissed him on the cheek. Barclay felt himself flush. Nick had that effect on him. Always had done, and probably always would.

He wasn't sure if they could overcome what had happened to them, whether they could find their way back to being together – to being a solid family unit – but right then he didn't care. He'd tolerate Stefan, he'd have fun with Sarah, he'd feel closer to his husband than he had in months and tomorrow he'd deal with work.

Today was not about dead things and missing girls; it was about family. It was about coming together.

Barclay watched Sarah come down the slide, which looked too steep for someone as small as she was, and Indiana came down after her. They both screamed and laughed, and he wondered whether this was the version of Sarah he had been missing out on. He wanted to go to her and sit behind her, like he had done before. In the early days, when they'd first adopted her. Where she'd held on tight to his hands and screamed with excitement and terror as they slid down, or if there was a dip in the rollercoaster in the little kids' section at Blackpool Pleasure Beach. He remembered thinking some of those rides were bloody scary. He told Nick, and himself, the only reason he screamed was to get into the spirit.

She ran over to him and gave him a hug and asked him to take her on the little bumper cars at the back. 'I love bumper cars,' he told her. 'They were my favourite thing when I was your age.'

'I don't think your dad would fit in them now though, babe,' Nick said, laughing.

'I'll say,' Stefan said under his breath then sipped his tea, but Barclay caught it.

'You have to take me too, Uncle Steffy,' Indiana said, grabbing Stefan's pinky finger and pulling him up and out of his seat.

'Come on, come on, come on!' Sarah dragged Barclay to the bumper cars. Surprisingly, they were big enough for both of them. Sarah was sitting in front, holding on to the steering wheel and Barclay was behind her, his hands next to hers. They looked so tiny. They *were* so tiny.

There was a countdown, then a far-too-loud klaxon, and all of the cars moved about like bees, zipping between, around, and at each other. Barclay gripped the steering wheel tight, Sarah's hands on top of his. He avoided an oncoming car, couldn't regain control of the wheel as it crashed into the red painted tyres that marked the edge of the area. Sarah cried out.

Barclay looked down at her, at a split in the knee of her leggings where blood formed in a thin slice. She cried out at first and as Barclay picked her up she said, 'It doesn't hurt, I want to go back!' She screamed and raged and kicked out at Barclay when he said no. 'I hate you!' she roared and slapped his face hard. It stung and Barclay felt tears form in his eyes.

He'd never seen her like this before. And even though it was just a cut knee, an accident, he wanted to get it seen to. He'd seen too much hurt recently and he could speak to her about her behaviour afterward. The bumper cars zipped around him as he tottered toward the exit, his daughter screaming at him in his arms.

Stefan watched on, his car stopped still, mouth ajar. Barclay felt him watching. Judging.

Nick took her in his arms and said, 'Come on, let's get this cleaned up.' He whisked her off to the toilets and Barclay could still hear her rage from the table.

Stefan and Indiana joined them back at the table. 'That was quite something,' Stefan said. 'Her reaction I mean.'

Barclay shrugged. 'Kids.' Maybe he'd overreacted. Maybe he should have let her continue, despite the cut. That was the thing about parenting: there were no hard and fast rules. Everything was guesswork, looking back afterward and deciding whether what you did, said or reacted to was the best thing.

Indiana ran off after the little boy in dungarees, and Barclay found himself alone at the table with the man he felt so uncomfortable around. The clamorous chaos of children happened all around them. Barclay felt Stefan's eyes on him again. 'You know,' he said. 'I was worried about Nick when you left.'

'You make it sound like I just walked out,' Barclay retorted, not looking at Stefan.

'Didn't you?'

'Whatever happened, or happens, between me and Nick, is none of your business. It's nobody's business, Stefan.' He chuckled slightly to keep his tone friendly, but inside his blood roiled.

'Happens?' Stefan turned his white mug around on the table. 'You sound hopeful.'

Yeah, and I bet you'd love to know why I feel hopeful.

'Sleeping together again doesn't heal a marriage,' he said. 'It just means you're both men with needs.'

'What is your problem, Stefan?'

'*My* problem?' Stefan laughed, a sneering thing. 'It's you who has the problem with me, Ben. You always have done and you always will. If you want to know the truth of how I feel, I don't think you could ever handle how close Nick and I are.'

'And I don't think you could handle the fact that Nick is married,' Barclay said. 'To me.'

There was a quiet then. Barclay watched the kids playing and Stefan sipped his Earl Grey. 'I just feel that Nick deserves someone who matches his heart, his effort. Someone who shows up for him fully.'

Barclay could have thrown Stefan's tea all over him or swung for him. 'And you think that's you, do you?'

'Look at you.' Stefan leaned in closer, his voice low and hissing. 'So afraid that I have designs on your husband. Your soon-to-be *ex*-husband.'

'Nick told me you asked him out, Stefan, so don't try to gaslight me with my own feelings,' Barclay said, matching Stefan's hushed tone. 'I know exactly what you're doing, I know exactly why you're here, even if Nick doesn't.'

'There we are.' Nick's voice now. 'All done, and do you have something to say to Daddy?'

Sarah wrapped her arms around Ben and he held her tight. 'I'm sorry, Daddy,' she said.

'It's fine, sweetheart; I'm sorry too.'

'Are you ready to go and find Indiana again?' Stefan asked. 'She's up there with the child who looks like he's from *The Little House on the Prairie*.'

'What's that?' Sarah asked.

'Pay no mind to this silly old man,' Nick said, kissing his daughter's cheek. 'Go and have another half hour and then we'll get some lunch.' Nick adjusted the red ribbons in Sarah's pigtails, then spun her around toward the soft play. She ran off toward Indiana again but stopped first to throw herself into the ball pit.

Barclay leaned over to Nick and whispered, 'I'm sorry about that. I think I overreacted.'

'You don't need to apologise for parenting, Ben,' Nick said. 'She's your daughter too.' He put his hand on Barclay's and squeezed. 'I'd have done the same thing. She's just a kid. She's going to get into scrapes, cut herself, come home with bruises. You can't wrap her in cotton wool. We both just need to relax.'

Barclay knew that. He was just… God, he didn't even know what he was doing. It was his job to protect her, to make sure she was safe and happy. 'I'm sorry, I just panicked when I saw the blood I think.'

Nick squeezed Barclay's hand again. 'It's just a cut.'

He was right, Barclay knew that. He nodded and decided he'd say no more about it. He fell silent, one arm slung over the back of his chair as he listened to Stefan and Nick's conversation about a new artist they wanted to showcase at the gallery. Stefan's voice was loud over the din of children playing, his hand gestures animated. Barclay tracked Sarah and Indiana on the top tier of the play area, which seemed impossibly high for kids so young, as they vanished into the padded mouth of a tunnel with a clown's face.

The air smelled like coffee, fried chips and hot plastic, and Barclay couldn't wait to get some fresh air. He caught Sarah's red ribbons up top, a bright flare in the chaos of kids clambering past her. She gripped on to some netting and crossed carefully, Indiana behind her, shrieking with laughter, as the boy in blue dungarees chased them.

Barclay smiled.

Moments later, Indiana emerged from the soft play and darted to their table, her face wet, dark hair clinging to it. 'Need a drink,' she said. Stefan handed her an unopened bottle of blackcurrant juice and she drank it all down.

'Tell Sarah she needs to come and have a drink, too,' Nick said.

Indiana nodded, drank in gulps and threw the bottle back on the table before bounding away back to the play area.

Barclay was still watching her go, climbing up some padded stairs to the first floor when a ripple of movement caught his eye from the left. A clown dressed in bright colours, honking on a bulb horn, danced around in shoes far too big. He tripped over himself and forward-rolled into the play centre. He gave a high-pitched laugh that Barclay found only a little terrifying.

Suddenly, circus-style music played over the speakers, and the kids came swarming out of the soft play like ants to a lump of sugar. Barclay scanned the group quickly. Indiana. A boy in a pirate hat that Barclay hadn't seen before. The other boy in the blue dungarees. But there was no sign of Sarah. No flash of her red ribbons.

'Nick,' Barclay said, but the two kept talking about work. 'Nick,' he said again. 'Where's Sarah?'

Nick stood up, scanning the three floors of the soft play apparatus, but they seemed empty. Barclay got to his feet and moved closer to the group of kids that had come to watch the clown dance and roll around the floor. They screamed and laughed at him as he fell and pulled long balloons out of his pockets.

Maybe she's gone the long way around, Barclay thought, expecting her to pop up any second. Behind him, he could hear Nick calling Sarah's name. Barclay looked back, but she wasn't there with him, and Nick was following Barclay now.

Barclay circled the climbing area, checking every exit, each tunnel that led from a slide or a higher level. Standing on tip-toes, he to peered into the higher, netted platforms. No Sarah.

His face burned hot. His stomach flipped and tied itself into knots. The noise pressed in all around him. The children yelling, the loud circus music, the toot of the clown's bulb horn.

He passed a *Staff only* sign, climbing up the foam-covered stairs and onto the second tier. He moved across the nets and through the plastic clown tunnels. Nothing. He looked down at Nick, who was watching from below. 'She's not here,' he shouted over the music, his voice tight.

He climbed back down, and as he did, Barclay saw a staff member wheeling crates of juice through a service door which had been propped open by a few boxes of fizzy drink. For a moment, the dancing clown obscured his view, but he made his way to it. The corridor beyond the door curved away and out of sight.

'Can I help you?' The girl from the till came from the corridor.

'My daughter,' he said. 'We can't find her.'

'No kids can leave without an adult,' the girl said, almost rolling her eyes. 'If you're still here, she is.'

He felt like screaming at the girl. 'How many exits are there?'

'Just the front exit.'

'And back there?' Barclay asked.

'It's staff only back there.'

'And how many fucking kids care that it's staff only? Get me your manager right now.'

Nick caught up to him, touched the small of his back. 'Ben, where is she?' There was panic in his voice now; the shrill edge of it was apparent.

Barclay turned and scanned the main entrance. A staff member buzzed out families with kids and let others in through the other gate. In this tide of coming and going, Sarah could be halfway across the carpark before anyone had even noticed.

He turned back to the girl from the counter. 'Why're you still standing there? My kid is missing; get me your manager now!'

She huffed and walked off, heading back down the corridor she came from. As his eyes followed her, they fell on the red fire alarm on the wall. He imagined the siren, the lights, the music cut dead. He imagined parents grabbing their things, their children, and heading outside. He imagined a member of staff marshalling everyone from inside into a designated safe zone where a headcount would be completed.

His mind raced with the things he had seen and heard throughout his career. The kids that go missing. The ones that turn up harmed or worse… *No*, he told himself, *no one would take a detective's kid. She's here. She has to be here somewhere.*

She knew not to go anywhere with strangers. She knew that because they'd had that talk with her after they'd found The Woulds app on her tablet. She'd understood. Hadn't she?

Barclay lifted his hand and smashed it against the plastic safety covering of the fire alarm.

Seventeen

De Silva drove across to see Dr Carey after lunch, a cream cheese bagel in a tiny brown bag from the deli on Gaskill Road. She'd eaten it on the drive and as she'd climbed out of the car, she'd found a blob of cream cheese on her black padded coat. It'd have to go into the wash that night, but there was nothing she could do about it then.

Carey met her at the roadside next to Greenbank Park, two take-away coffees in long white cups. De Silva grinned, could have kissed the woman. 'You've no idea how much I need this,' she said. 'Thank you!'

'A black Americano, if I remembered correctly.'

'That's the one,' she said. 'I owe you one.'

'Pretty sure you owe me more than one by now, Win.' Carey laughed, took a sip of her own drink and de Silva could smell the too-sweet caramel syrup from where she was standing. 'Should we have a little walk around the park?'

'I do need to get some steps in before heading back,' she said. 'I've not got long though.'

'Don't worry, neither do I.'

They walked down the busy street toward the black iron fencing that penned in one of the few remaining green spaces in this part of the city. Since the city lost its World Heritage status, the entire place felt like a building site. De Silva hated to think of her beloved small city becoming a never-ending construction, something that never seemed truly finished, like Manchester.

Greenbank was a small park with a café and restaurant alongside a pond in the centre and flanked by trees on the far side. It would be dark in a few hours, and the park would empty out. Everyone returning to their homes, removing their winter layers and turning on their fires or central heating.

'So,' de Silva said, hoping Carey would pick up the conversation. When she didn't, de Silva pressed on. 'Why here? Bit of a way away from your office, isn't it?'

'I'm sick of the sight of that office, to be honest,' Carey said. 'I arrive when it's dark, I leave when it's dark, and the SAD lamp doesn't help.'

De Silva understood that. There weren't even windows in her basement incident room. 'I just wanted to talk to you about the Joanna McKenzie post-mortem.'

'Yes, I got your email.' They passed the busy Watering Can restaurant and the play area and curved around the edge of the lake. 'I remember the case coming in,' she said.

'I'm just trying to understand why you didn't do the post-mortem,' she said. 'I spoke with Grindon already and he was busy with something else.'

Carey gestured to an old black bench, which had seen better days, covered in white bird shit. They perched on the end, where it seemed less likely to stain their clothes. 'She was young, wasn't she?'

'Almost thirty,' de Silva said, sitting down, feeling the cold already pervade her thick coat. 'No age at all.'

'I was geared up to perform the post-mortem,' she said. 'Report my findings to the Coroner's Office.'

'So what changed?'

'I don't know how or why, but they brought in someone else. The Dr Francesca Walton you mentioned in your email.'

'Do you know her?'

'No,' Carey said. 'Well, not really. I've seen her speak at a few events. She doesn't work for the Coroner's Office. She's always worked in the private sector, as far as I know.'

'Is it normal that someone from outside would come in to perform a post-mortem like this?'

Carey shook her head, played with her earlobe with her free hand. 'No, I've never known it. Not even when a local pathologist is unavailable. If that were the case, they'd bring in someone from another authority.'

'But you were available.'

'I was.'

'There's something else I can't quite understand,' de Silva said. 'From what I read in the report, McKenzie's death was a result of her injuries. So why the post-mortem?'

Carey smiled. 'Because a senior investigating officer from Merseyside Police would have had to have declared the death suspicious in order to warrant a PM, you mean?'

'That's exactly what I mean, yeah.'

'Well, that's the question, isn't it?' Carey's free hand became animated as she spoke. 'Which senior officer made that decision and why? Mechanical failure? Criminal activity related to the death? And if so…'

'Why then ask for someone outside of Merseyside to perform the PM?' De Silva finished Carey's sentence, knowing their minds were racing down the same track toward the same questions. 'I think I need to exhume her body, Carey.'

'Woah, Win, slow down!'

'If there's something to find, we might still be able to find it,' de Silva said. 'That's the royal "we" by the way. Obviously, I mean *you*.'

'McKenzie's been in the ground for over two years now,' Carey said. 'It's not as easy as exhuming the body and finding potential new evidence. There may not be much of her left.'

'I have to try,' de Silva said. 'If I feel that there's something off about all of this, I have to try, don't I?'

'Feelings aren't evidence,' Carey said, standing and gesturing that de Silva should follow her around the lake. 'You should know that better than anyone. And you're going to need evidence to get the coroner to agree to an exhumation. There's a lot of factors for them to consider there. McKenzie's family being one of those factors. And don't forget you might put some noses out of joint at work. Whoever requested the original post-mortem certainly!'

De Silva didn't care whose nose was out of joint, as long as the truth came out. 'I'll deal with all of that.'

'Jesus, Win,' Carey said. 'I know I'm wasting my breath saying this to you.'

'You know me so well.' De Silva chuckled, threw the dregs of her black coffee into a bin as she passed. 'I'll speak with a few people at work first, don't worry. I'll give the coroner just enough doubt that he won't be able to say no to me.'

'*She*,' Carey corrected her. 'Patsy Sayward. She's not known for being backwards in coming forwards. Whatever that means. What does this have to do with your current case?' Carey asked. 'I'm just awaiting some test results back on the baby, by the way. Hopefully today or tomorrow.'

'I wish I could tell you, Carey, I really do.' De Silva knew she couldn't discuss the case with someone outside the police. She'd known Carey for years, had worked with her on multiple occasions, but even still… it was best that some information was kept to the incident room. 'Maybe when I'm a bit closer.'

'Closer to what?'

'The truth.'

-

'You want to do what?' Murphy's eyes had gone wide, but the rest of her face didn't move. Frozen by Botox, de Silva had assumed. Everyone was at it these days; maybe she needed to give it a whirl herself.

'I know,' de Silva said. 'I know it's a bit unorthodox, ma'am, but—'

'You want to exhume the body of a detective constable who died in a car accident two years ago, and for what? You *feel* it might be connected to your current case? I think we're way beyond unorthodox right now, Win. Come on. The budget alone would be—'

'I don't give a shit about budgets,' de Silva spat out. 'There's a bigger picture here, I'm telling you.'

'What are you basing that on? The fact that Mitch Whitley, who found that poor baby and called the police, was dating the poor DC who lost her life?'

'Well, it's more than that,' de Silva said. 'She and another DC were investigating the death of Bob Brendan, the headmaster of Rainford Lane School for Boys, when she had her accident.'

'De Silva…' Murphy shook her head. 'Win… come on, look at this from my perspective. You've got nothing to go on other than some coincidence and circumstance. I can't take that to the ACC and expect him to sign off additional budget for an exhumation.'

De Silva rolled eyes, almost groaned. 'I know,' she said. 'I know.'

Murphy stood up, collected her phone from her desk and slid it into her pocket. 'I have a meeting with the ACC and the chief constable right now,' she said. 'Get me some evidence I can present to them, and I'll suggest that we exhume DC McKenzie's body.'

'I've got the team on it,' she said. She followed Murphy out of her office, and the silence on the way to the lifts was awkward. De Silva was thankful when Murphy decided to take the stairs up to the next floor. She wasn't one for small talk; she'd always felt trapped by it, under pressure to say something that sounded casual and unrehearsed. She'd sooner just not say anything.

The incident room felt flat. The death of anyone during an active case was difficult to comprehend. It's something she could never get used to, and in the rock-bottom lull in morale, she knew the team were feeling it, too. The discovery of the baby was bad enough, but then to lose Bea…

The only thing de Silva and the team could do now was to find out what had happened to both of them.

De Silva glanced at her watch, almost five. 'All right then, let's see what you've got,' she said. 'Lawrence?'

'Dr Francesca Watson has retired,' Lawrence said, getting to her feet, scribbling down her findings on the evidence board, the dry-wipe marker squeaking in blue ink as she wrote. 'Two years ago. She lives in North Wales with her husband, and she has early-onset dementia.'

De Silva flinched. She wouldn't wish that awful condition on anyone. 'That's terrible,' she found herself saying. In all of the years that her mum had been in a home, she'd never spoken about it at work. She was sure that her team knew, of course, but it was just something that went unspoken. She never mentioned it, and they never asked.

'I couldn't think of anything worse,' O'Connor said, looking down and shaking his head.

'Do we know who requested the post-mortem in the first place?'

'I'm sorry, boss, no,' Lawrence said. 'There's no record of it anywhere. But we did find the name of the company who Watson worked for.'

'Go on,' de Silva said.

'It's a company called UK Lab Solutions,' she said.

'Anyone there we can speak to?'

'Unfortunately, the company is defunct,' Lawrence said, writing on the board again. 'Last year, funding was withdrawn and the business was closed down.'

'Funding?' de Silva asked. This whole thing was becoming more and more confusing. Privately funded companies performing post-mortems that should have been conducted through the local authority by a Coroner's Office pathologist. *This has to mean something*, de Silva told herself.

'UK Lab Solutions was owned by a holdings company,' Lawrence said. 'Holdings companies have shares in lots of businesses. It's how they make their money. This one, T & K Holdings, has investments in other businesses right across the country. From prisons to cybersecurity. I even found some connections with the European Space Agency.'

'Jesus Christ,' Braxton said.

'Is there anyone at T & K Holdings we can speak to?'

'Next on my list,' Lawrence said with a smile.

'Tomorrow's list,' de Silva said. 'That's great work, Lawrence. Thank you.'

Braxton cleared his throat and spoke up. 'I'm sorry, boss, I don't mean to question you on this at all. But what does all this have to do with Bea Tredwell?'

That's the question that de Silva needed the answer to herself. 'I don't know,' she said, honestly. 'I'm not sure it's connected at all just yet. We have some time to look into this as a potential connection while we await the DNA results of Bea's baby. I'm assuming it'll be tomorrow now, but Carey is on it.'

Braxton nodded, though de Silva recognised doubt when she saw it. It was right there in his arched eyebrows, the creased brow, the slightly open mouth.

'Okay,' de Silva said. 'Arlow, Patel, Yates. Any update on the elderly lady?'

'Quite a bit,' Arlow said, standing and taking the blue marker from Lawrence. 'We know that her name is Christine Jones. And we've had confirmation that she suffered quite a vicious attack prior to the fire being started.' He wrote that down on the board. 'She was stabbed multiple times on her chest, neck and her face.'

'We had those findings already,' de Silva said.

'Yes, but they were confirmed,' Patel said. 'We got the report from Grindon today.'

De Silva nodded. *Go on.*

'But there's something else,' Yates said. She looked to de Silva then looked down at the floor. 'She was the former deputy head teacher at Rainford Lane School for Boys.'

De Silva's stomach dropped. Her breath caught in her throat, and her heart thump-thumped harder beneath her ribcage. She knew she'd heard that name somewhere before. Finally, she swallowed and took a breath. 'Are you—'

De Silva's phone rang out in the quiet of the incident room. She took it from her pocket and found Murphy was calling. She stepped outside into the corridor before answering it. 'Ma'am?'

'Win, are you still in the office?'

'Yeah, we're just wrapping up for the day.' Even as she said it, de Silva knew she wouldn't be leaving the incident room for another few hours. Not now.

'I've just been with the chief constable and the ACC,' Murphy said. 'I'm afraid I don't know how to tell you this.'

'Tell me what?'

'It's Sarah Barclay,' Murphy said. 'She's missing.'

Eighteen

Life is sometimes broken up into moments, like chapters in a novel, like the scene selection function on an old DVD. As de Silva crossed the cordon onto Otterspool Promenade, she tried to remember that fifty-two per cent of missing children were found within eight hours. Seventy-nine per cent were found within twenty-four hours. But that didn't take away the sheer panic of that space and time where they had completely vanished.

All of the guilt, the upset, the frustration. The tears and the agony. It had a way of scarring parents, in de Silva's experience. It would stay with them. It would stay with Barclay and Nick. It would forever be that time they'd almost lost Sarah. Or that time she went missing. It would haunt them, make them cling tighter to her. Or, to the memory of her.

No, de Silva told herself, *don't let that negative thinking in. Dark thoughts breed dark outcomes.*

The open expanse of the promenade was mostly grass, covered then by banks of snow, which turned red and blue under the turning lights of squad cars. The tinny chatter of police radios, the thrum of helicopter rotor blades, somewhere high in the black sky. She didn't look up for it but searched the gathered crowds for Barclay's face. But the face she found wasn't his. Her eyes locked with DSI Murphy's.

She tried not to think about why the helicopter was out in full force tonight, but the whisper of snow had it grounded when it came to Bea Tredwell. *Still*, she reasoned with herself, *maybe the forecasted snow is over and done with?*

'De Silva!' Murphy's crisp accent came across the icy fields, and her voice seemed almost flattened by the fallen snow. They walked toward each other.

'Where is he?' de Silva asked.

'I'll take you to him.' Murphy nodded, an indication that de Silva should follow her.

'Who's in charge, PVPU?'

'Yes,' Murphy said, her feet crunching as they crossed a field of snow. 'Detective Inspector Cordelia Lavery will be leading the investigation.'

A DI has already been assigned, de Silva thought. That meant the feeling was that wherever Sarah was, it wasn't anywhere near here. 'Right.' She knew Lavery. She was a good bobby, but in all honesty, de Silva had never taken to her. She had a sharp mouth, cutting sometimes, and she'd always felt that Lavery lacked the tact and warmth of someone who should work on PVPU.

Her mind shifted to Mike Crosby. He had seemed warm and caring once. In the old days, before he'd lost his mind and tried to have her killed, she was sure that he had been good-natured. Loving. Maybe that was all a lie, too.

Opposite the play centre, sitting on the backseat of a squad car, half-in and half-out, was Barclay. He had a blanket wrapped around his shoulders and his trainers looked soaked. Behind him was Nick, bundled in a big coat that must have been Barclay's judging by the size of it. As she approached, another man de Silva didn't know or recognise got out of the far side back door.

'Is there any news?' the man asked. He had hold of a little dark-haired girl, whose eyes drifted open and closed as he moved.

They all looked exhausted.

De Silva ignored the man and was thankful when Barclay had spotted her and got out of the car, dropping the blanket to the ground. 'Ben,' she said, putting her arms around him as best she could. 'We'll find her. Lavery's a good detective, and our PVPU team are second to none.' It felt odd to have said that last part, given what they both knew about Mike Crosby, but he was just one bad apple among a cartload of good ones.

Barclay's eyes looked pink and raw, as though he was holding it all in. 'I was there,' he said. 'I should have been watching more closely.'

'Look, you were in a safe setting,' de Silva said. 'You're supposed to be able to let your kids run free in those places. That's the point.'

Nick clambered out of the car behind Barclay. 'We were all there. None of us saw what happened.' Tears streamed down his flushed cheeks, and his chin wobbled. He shook and held the woollen coat tighter to him.

She didn't know what to say to Nick. Perhaps she didn't possess the tact and warmth of someone who worked on PVPU, either. Good job she didn't work on that team. She looked to Barclay and lowered her voice slightly. 'Have they checked the CCTV from the premises?'

Barclay shrugged. 'I… I don't know,' he said. 'I didn't ask. I should have asked.'

'I'm on it,' de Silva said, putting a hand on his forearm. 'Just stay here and stay warm. I'll be back in a second.'

'We just weren't watching for one second, and…' Nick broke down into tears and Barclay held him close. But there was something else there, something unspoken, something in the way that Barclay looked at the man de Silva didn't know. Something in the way Barclay's square jaw flexed.

'I'll be back in a second,' de Silva repeated. She turned to Murphy and took her aside. 'Where is Lavery?'

'She's over there.' Murphy pointed to the railings overlooking the Mersey as it curved inland and on toward Warrington and Manchester.

De Silva crossed the snow-caked frozen grass, heard it creak beneath her feet as she went. DI Cordelia Lavery was alone at the railings overlooking the river, and de Silva couldn't help but think she should be right in the middle of it all, instead of here alone. She should be combing those bushes and woods for any sign of Sarah. But then she never did have a good reputation for working with others, something de Silva could appreciate. Still, she was unrelenting in her application of procedures and protocols, and de Silva had once heard Mike Crosby describe her as 'a fucking jeb end, but a bloody good bobby'.

Lavery's long, black ponytail swung in the wind bounding down the Mersey basin as de Silva called to her. 'DI Lavery!'

The woman turned, her eyes searching the freezing landscape until they settled on de Silva. 'I was wondering how long it would take before you showed up,' she said.

'Good evening to you, too,' de Silva said, mostly to herself, and hoped her words were lost on the wind. 'What do we know so far? What happened here?'

'I'll be submitting a report on my early findings to DSI Murphy in the next few hours,' she said.

'This is a colleague, Lavery. A friend,' de Silva said, her voice hard with defence and authority. 'So cut the shit and watch who you're speaking to.'

Lavery glared for longer than de Silva felt necessary, but finally she pulled out her phone, covered in yellow and pink Post-it notes. 'The girl's fathers, Nick and Ben Barclay, brought her here for a—'

'Her name is Sarah.'

'Yes, I know.'

'So use it,' de Silva spat back at her, only mild annoyance icing her voice now. 'I shouldn't have to tell someone of your rank and in your team that. Surely.'

Lavery unstuck the Post-its from the back of her phone and placed them on the front. 'Nick Barclay, Ben Barclay and their friend, Stefan Preston, were at the soft play centre over there.' As she spoke, she moved Post-its from the front to the back of her phone. Some weird system only she knew the rules to, de Silva assumed. 'They'd been inside for less than an hour. She was reported missing around 12:30 p.m. today. We've been combing the area ever since then. But…'

De Silva was taking it all in and understood. In February, the dark settles quickly in Merseyside. Even by four p.m., the sky would have been turning dark, and Liverpool would dim in the winter gloom. De Silva checked her watch. It was after six and Sarah had been missing for well over five hours already.

'I'm assuming you've checked CCTV footage from the soft play centre and completed a full search of the facility?'

'Yes and yes,' Lavery said. 'I know what I'm doing, de Silva.'

'I wish that gave me some comfort,' de Silva said. 'That's not me questioning your skills, Lavery. I'm just concerned about Sarah.' *And Nick and Barclay*, she thought. 'Did the CCTV show anything?'

'It's with our VEU for enhancements, but… well, I'm afraid it does appear to show Sarah Barclay leaving the premises at 12:13 p.m.'

'You what?' De Silva's voice boomed in the open expanse. 'On her own? Aren't there protocols in place for that?'

'She wasn't alone,' Lavery said.

De Silva felt the night turn colder; the saturation of the darkness turned that little bit blacker. Her forehead began to ache as the weight of Lavery's words settled around her. Sarah hadn't walked out of the play centre and got lost somewhere. She was taken out of there.

With purpose.

With intent.

De Silva shuddered to think of what that intent might be. 'Do we have a face? Any distinguishing features? Anything?'

'As I said, VEU are on it,' Lavery replied. 'But from what I could see, I doubt we'll make out a face. A hoody and a cap. That's it.'

'And is there CCTV outside? Does the site itself have a carpark?'

'No,' she said. 'There are parking spaces further back toward the entrance to the promenade, but in front of the play centre, there's just a stretch of road. There are lamp posts there but no CCTV other than the exterior of the building.'

'And?'

'He turns left with her, off in the direction of a secondary carpark which is only sometimes accessible by road. There's a gate there. Today it was locked. He heads toward the second carpark and out of sight. We're working on locating any other CCTV in the area.'

De Silva nodded. 'How much do they know?'

'I haven't updated them yet, and they refuse to go home until I can come and see them.'

'Would you want to go home?'

Lavery didn't answer.

'And you've questioned everyone that was there? The staff, too?'

'The play centre was busy, but uniform teams collected witness statements, yes,' Lavery went on, her breath pluming in front of her face. 'Nobody remembers seeing her or the person who took her.'

'Okay, so what's next?'

'We continue to search this place,' Lavery said. 'It's huge, but we had the helicopter signed off, so that should make things a little easier. We have people on the ground, on foot, searching through the woods over there in case. We have drones in the air already.'

De Silva couldn't help but think what the *in case* was. In case he'd left her there, alive or dead? She felt bile in her throat. De Silva approached the railings to steady herself and looked down at the river. 'And what if she's down there?'

'It's not easy to walk down there right now,' Lavery said. 'We've searched with the helicopter and found nothing, but I do plan on having Underwater Search drafted in when it's safe to do so… I'm sorry, are you taking over this case?'

'No,' she said.

'Right, well I think I'm done answering your questions for now.' Lavery put her phone, Post-its and all, back in her pocket. 'I'm very busy.'

'I told you before to watch who you're speaking to,' de Silva said, her voice a low grumbled warning. 'Now, I'll go and see if I can get Nick and Barclay to head home.'

Lavery nodded. 'We have their statements and I'll be in touch.'

De Silva understood Barclay's need to be there, to be around the vicinity, but de Silva also recognised how difficult things could be with the parent of a missing child hanging around. Especially a bobby. Especially a bobby like Barclay.

'Lavery,' de Silva said. 'This is important to me. Important to Barclay.'

'I know,' she said. 'I'll find her.'

De Silva crossed the field and headed back toward the pulsing lights of the carpark where Nick and Barclay eagerly waited for news. Any news. The night was cold, and de Silva shivered under her black puffer coat.

De Silva convinced Nick and Barclay to head home, and their friend had agreed to go with them once his sister had collected his niece. He said that he wanted to keep an eye on them and make sure they were okay. She'd reminded Barclay that there would be media attention the next day, that Lavery would have to initiate a briefing with the media, and she'd ask Nick and Barclay to be there.

She wondered whether Barclay felt what she herself felt. The team had searched Otterspool Promenade and the surrounding areas for over five hours. Nothing. The helicopter had detected nothing. There were no witnesses. Lavery had ordered uniformed officers to do door-to-door on the houses on the far side of the promenade, but de Silva knew. She knew, and she hoped she didn't have to spell it out for Barclay.

As time wears on, the likelihood that we'll find Sarah alive wanes.

Nineteen

Leah was standing in her back garden with a cigarette in her hand. Even though she'd stopped smoking, she liked to stand in the garden just holding one. Smelling the acrid stink as the paper burned down to the nub, and the grey ash fell to the floor. But tonight, she took a pull of it. She'd promised herself she would stop when Scar came home. That's what she liked to be called. Scar, not Scarlet.

Scar fits, Leah thought. *That's all that's left of her now.*

There are things no one talks about when horrors have happened to your child. She tried not to dwell on it, but she hardly slept these days and as she lay staring at the ceiling, all Leah could do was think about it. Think about the things the police had told her, the things Scar wouldn't. Or couldn't. Think and hold a cigarette between her fingers.

Scar had gotten worse since Jay left. Leah didn't even know where he was any more. Child support arrived in her account on the twenty-seventh of every month, but beyond that… nothing. It came from a bank account she didn't recognise, so she assumed he'd set up his own one at some point and stopped using the joint account altogether.

She'd had to take on some extra shifts at the call centre in Aintree, which meant more time away from home, but there was no real choice. They had to live, had to pay the bills and Scar needed things. Needed therapy. The NHS took too long. Underfunded by the thundercunts in Downing Street, over-stretched by waitlists since Covid, and Scar needed help right then.

The security light above the door went out, plunging the garden into near pitch black. Leah waved her hands above her head until the motion sensor kicked in and the light came back on.

In the time since she'd been home – and Leah was glad to have her home, make no mistake – Scar had been distant. Outside of herself, almost. Like the happy home they'd once shared had become a haunted house. Scar had self-harmed in the bathroom, bit her nails down to the quick while sitting at the top of the stairs, had stopped talking completely and had taken to going out walking in the middle of the night. She'd come back in the early hours, soaked to the bone if it was raining or with cut feet if she forgot her shoes.

In truth, Leah was at her wits' end, and that was why she'd begun smoking again. They'd offered to take Scar to rest. That's what they said, wasn't it? That it was rest she needed, as though all of her troubles were brought on by exhaustion.

She put the ciggie out, rubbed it against the brick wall, then threw the end of it into an old terracotta pot that had seen better days. It once grew lavender and she'd watched the bees come for it, but now the only things sprouting were the burned, old ciggie stumps, with a red ring from lipstick or gloss the colour of tulip petals.

As she closed the back door and turned the key to lock it, the front door clattered. *No, not again*, Leah thought as she marched through to the front of the house. The door clattered against its frame and she pulled it open to step outside. The street was dark, and nothing moved. Somewhere in the distance, she could hear someone singing that Phil Collins song about the air tonight. It sounded mournful, like most solo singers do when they let rip on the way back home from a night out.

'Scar!' she shouted as she walked down the path to the metal gate, wide open onto the street. She looked up and down but there was nothing and no one about. *She must have moved quickly*, she thought.

Leah closed the gate, shaking her head, resigning herself to the fact that this could be her life forever now. Wondering where her daughter was, worrying about how to keep her safe from harm, and knowing that the harm had already been done. Scar had left childhood at the age of just seven when she disappeared for those three weeks. The police had found her phone. Found that bloody app on it she'd seen warnings about on social media since. The Woulds they'd called it. Those warnings had come too late to help Scar, to help Leah. She had seen a story about it on *Granada Tonight* just the other day, warning parents.

After that, Scar was not allowed a phone or an iPad. Now the police had no idea where that app came from. The Woulds had ruined Scar's life, torn apart Leah and Jay's marriage and then just disappeared, as though it were salt dissolving in water.

Leah closed the front door after her and thought she'd heard something out in the kitchen. 'Scar?' She bounded through toward the hallway. 'You better not be in that fridge after not eating your tea.'

No reply. No one in the kitchen.

She ran up the stairs, her knees creaking. She knew what to expect already. An empty bed. The clothes she'd had on that day missing. Her favourite backpack. The small leather black one they'd got from Greatie Market after the police brought her home. They'd found her wandering down the M62 toward Liverpool, near one of the Warrington junctions.

When she pushed open Scar's bedroom door, there she was in her bed. The black hoody she'd had on that day strewn on the floor next to the battered old Converse she insisted on keeping. Despite the new ones – identical in every way – sitting, unboxed, in her wardrobe.

She was relieved. *Maybe things are changing. Finally*, she thought. For the first time in weeks, she smiled, wishing and hoping that this was the start of something. She crept across the creaking floorboards and sat on the edge of the bed. As she leaned over to kiss her daughter's cheek, she realised it.

Scar's body wasn't solid. It was soft, like—

Leah pulled back the covers. Her daughter's pillows had been positioned so that, if Leah peeked in before bed, she'd think Scarlet was asleep.

She's gone.

She looked down at the clothes on the floor. Before bed, Scar had put on the silk-type striped pyjamas Leah had bought from the big Tesco in Litherland, but they were nowhere to be found now.

Leah thought of the front door. She could convince herself that she'd just popped down to the shop, but she hardly ever went out any more. Or that she'd gone to a friend's house. But there weren't friends any more. They'd stopped knocking for her. She wondered whether, like Leah, the friends didn't recognise Scar, whether she was far too changed by what had happened to her.

She walked to the bedroom window and opened the blinds, looked out into the dark night. Through the window, a sharp icy breeze crept through like a ghost on the wind, moaning at the window frame.

Scar, she wanted to scream, *for fuck's sake, where are you?*

Twenty

14 February

The midwinter night scratched its way slowly toward dawn, one that Barclay wished was some distance off yet. If it was still dark outside, it meant that time hadn't moved on too quickly, that there was still a chance they'd find Sarah. But, if the sun came up and she was still missing, Barclay felt that that was somehow a loss. As though finding her was a race against the rising of the sun.

Barclay was standing by the window, the curtains pulled back, and the night turned the glass into a black mirror. Across the street a lamp post burned white light and in the glass of the window, he caught sight of himself. Yesterday's clothes creased. His jaw tight, clenched. *They'll find her*, he told himself over and over. He had to tell himself that, but the detective in him knew the grim truth.

He turned his back on himself.

Usually, Valentine's Day was filled with love and laughter in this house. Cards and gifts and hugs and kisses. All of that was gone now.

All of that was gone long before this, Barclay corrected himself.

Nick was sitting on the couch, staring at the glow of the open-flame fireplace, hands clasped between his knees, knuckles white as bone. His face was blank, expressionless, a look Barclay hadn't seen on Nick's features before. Shock, maybe. Barclay wondered for just a second whether what Nick felt was guilt. That was something they could share.

Stefan hovered near the armchair on the back wall, still holding his jacket as though he was unsure if he should sit down or leave. He hadn't spoken since his sister had collected Indiana, and Barclay wished he *would* leave and never come back. He felt that if Stefan hadn't been there, then none of this would have happened. But that was useless. A silly trick his brain played on him in hopes of laying blame somewhere.

A voice murmured from the kitchen, where the family liaison officer talked quietly on her phone, her clipped tone at odds with the soft domestic hum of the boiling kettle. She'd introduced herself as DC Char Mackintosh, and insisted they were to call her Char, not Charlotte. Barclay knew of her but had never spoken to her before. She'd already made them numerous cups of tea, and if Barclay saw another milky brew, he'd go insane.

He chewed the inside of his cheek and picked at the skin around his right thumb. It stung as the skin peeled back, revealing fresher, pinker skin beneath. The young skin, not ready to face the world yet. He used to do that all the time as a kid. A kind of coping mechanism he'd found for himself during those school days where his friends turned against him, called him a queer. Called him a faggot. When his dad left and started a new family. When his mum's hatred of his dad turned to apathy for Barclay.

Something hot bubbled in his stomach, eager and urgent as anger, and for a moment he thought he'd be sick. There was nothing in him to bring up, other than the cups of tea Char had made him. The stillness of the early hours seemed to have crept into the quiet of the living room, where each of them stared, cold and unmoving as statues.

But Barclay wondered whether right then, he should be frantic. Whether rage should be boiling through his veins. The medication which had served him so well now meant that everything he knew he should feel, needed to feel, wasn't there. *No*, he thought, *not completely absent. But way down there. Somewhere deep.*

He began to spiral, mentally lashing himself for not feeling his emotions keenly. Sharply. He ached for them: the grief and frustration at Sarah's being missing, even the self-punishment of guilt for allowing this to happen.

How could this happen? Sarah knew not to walk off on her own. And how could Lavery not have come and given them an update already?

He looked down at his phone. There was nothing from Lavery or de Silva and he wondered what they were doing. Still out there searching for her? Reviewing evidence back at the OCC? Interviewing witnesses? No, that would be silly. The one thing that he knew for sure was that Murphy wouldn't let de Silva anywhere near this. It was a conflict of interest at least.

A conflict of interest, he thought. *She's just a little girl, not an interest.*

'Did you see anything?' Barclay said, his voice low but sharp. 'Either of you.' He'd asked these questions numerous times. He wasn't sure if he was even asking them to confirm what they had or hadn't seen, or whether he wanted to play the scene out again in his own head.

Nick didn't answer. He stared at the fire, as though it might give him the answer he needed.

Barclay slumped onto the sofa next to his husband and took hold of his hand. This wasn't about blame. It wasn't about making someone feel bad. It was about finding the truth. Finding Sarah. Finding her before she got hurt. 'I just don't know how,' Barclay said, his voice thickening with emotion. 'How did she just *disappear*? The play centre is supposed to be safe. And Otterspool isn't the wilderness. It's busy. Dog walkers, families, bikes. She knows not to go off with people.'

'Ben, we were all distracted,' Stefan interjected. 'We thought she was safe.'

'*Thought?*' Barclay stood now, incensed that Stefan had even spoken. 'We shouldn't have *thought* she was safe! We should have made sure. We're her fucking parents!' His voice rose, a booming thing in the once quiet living room.

'Everything all right in here?' Char was at the living room door, leaning on the frame. Barclay nodded at her. 'I've got the kettle on, but maybe you should try to get some rest.' She disappeared again.

Rest, Barclay thought. He had given that advice to the parents of missing children many times through his career. To friends and family and lovers of those lost.

'This was an accident,' Stefan said.

'Why are you even here?' Barclay's voice a low hiss. 'Other than wanting to be with my husband, why are you here?'

'Stop it, Ben,' Nick said, his voice small and far away. He looked up at Barclay, his eyes slick like wet glass. 'This isn't his fault. It's ours. We should have known where she was at all times.' He cried and didn't bother to wipe his face. 'It was like… one minute she was there, and then she wasn't.' His voice cracked and he buried his head in his hands and sobbed.

Barclay folded his arms, as though by sheer will, he could keep himself together. But he relented and held his husband close, felt his hot tears soak into his T-shirt. Silence fell in the living room again, broken only by the clink of a teaspoon from the kitchen and the crackle of the open fire. The normalcy felt almost obscene to Barclay.

Only God knew where Sarah was. Whether she was warm and safe, or cold and frightened. And they were sitting in the living room drinking tea and waiting. Her guardians. Her protectors. They'd failed her.

'And Indiana saw nothing?' Barclay asked, looking to Stefan.

'You know she didn't,' Stefan said. 'She said Sarah was playing with that little kid in the dungarees. The police spoke with her and she has to go to make an official statement tomorrow.'

Stefan sank into the armchair finally, neither of them met each other's eyes, and Char brought in four teas on a tray Barclay didn't even know Nick had.

'Have you had an update?' Barclay asked.

‘DI Lavery is on her way around to speak to you now,’ Char said. ‘There’s nothing to worry about, she just wants to give you an update.’

‘Can’t you just give us it?’ Nick asked, his eyes wide and full, like a dog begging for scraps.

‘I think it’s best we wait for Cordelia,’ Char said. ‘Anything could change between the time I spoke to her and when she arrives. She’ll be just a few minutes.’ She said no more, lifted a tea for herself from the tray and left. Barclay watched as steam rose and curled out of the other three mugs and imagined the tea going cold.

The doorbell rang what felt like an eternity later, where Barclay had questioned everything: his relationship with Nick, Nick’s friendship with Stefan and even his own moral compass.

DI Lavery was standing in the gloom of the open door, lit only by the warm yellow of two lamps. One on a radiator cover, and the other, a standing lamp on the opposite side. Her face was grave. That’s what they say isn’t it, when a person looks solemn. Grim. Defeated. Grave.

‘Well?’ Barclay asked. ‘Did you find her?’ He had to ask, but in reality, Sarah would have been there with Lavery if they’d managed to find her. *Unless…* He imagined her cold as the metal slab she lay on. Alone. In the morgue. His detective brain went there without apology, and he attempted to summon that professional distance he’d begun to hone these last few years.

‘No,’ Lavery said. She didn’t take her eyes from Barclay. ‘Could we sit down? I have to run through a few things with you.’

Nick turned first and Stefan followed him in, his hands on Nick’s shoulders, squeezing. Lavery stepped inside. ‘You can be straight with me,’ Barclay said. ‘If you…’

‘I’m not even thinking that,’ she said. Barclay felt like a *yet* had been omitted from her sentence. ‘Let’s take a seat.’ Lavery led the way into the living room, and Barclay felt the cold of the night stream off her as she passed. It made him shiver.

In the living room, Nick watched Lavery and waited as she sat, his eyes brimming again, ready to break down. Stefan's beady eyes flicked from Lavery to Nick and back again. They reminded Barclay of the eyes of a rodent, dark in the living room, reflecting only the orange of the fire.

Barclay took a seat next to Nick, put his arm around his slender shoulders and pulled him in tight. Lavery cleared her throat. 'You understand that the questions I'm about to ask may be difficult to answer,' she said, her tone icy and distant. 'But they are necessary. I have your statements from earlier, so I know the circumstances of Sarah's disappearance. But now I need to know what has happened here.'

'Here?' Nick asked.

'At home,' she said.

Barclay felt a lump form in his throat. This was the part where his and Nick's marriage would be looked at forensically, like a piece of evidence. 'Is this necessary?' he asked.

'Yes, it is.' She took a breath, drew a pack of Post-its and a pen from her pocket. She clicked the nib out.

Barclay looked to Stefan, watching. 'Do you need to be in here for this?'

'Ben…' Nick's voice was soft, and he didn't look at Barclay as he spoke.

'I'll give you some space.' Stefan left the room, and they heard him whispering to Char beyond the closed door.

'What is your relationship like?' Lavery said, jumping right in.

'With Sarah?' Nick asked.

'With each other.'

Nick looked to Barclay then. Those eyes, the shining blue looked dull now, altered by the redness of anger, of pain, of upset. Guilt. 'We, er…'

'We've been separated,' Barclay said. 'Sarah has been splitting her time between both of our houses.'

'Did she find that difficult? The living situation I mean.'

'She liked having two rooms,' Nick said. 'Two houses. Two sets of clothes and toys.'

'And before you split, had you been arguing?'

The closeness of this line of questioning felt raw and sharp. Like a dissection. 'No more than any other couple, I suppose. We had some difficulties, but we never let Sarah hear about that. She never heard raised voices if that's what you're asking.'

'Was there any violence in your relationship with each other? Physical? Sexual?'

'What sort of a question is that?' Barclay gripped hold of Nick even tighter, afraid he might jump up and throw DI Lavery out of the house.

'No!' Nick said. 'Nothing like that. We loved each other… love each other, I think. We just couldn't find a way to make it work. But recently, we've…'

'You've what?'

'We've been… well, working things out, I suppose.' Nick looked at Barclay, who nodded. 'We're keen that Sarah doesn't think that this is normal. I think we'd wait to see how things worked out before we even considered telling her, before there was any moving of houses.'

Lavery nodded, scribbling on her Post-it, then replacing it with another. 'Were there any arguments with Sarah lately?'

'No,' Barclay said.

'Well, there was something at the soft play today,' Nick said. 'But it was nothing.'

'What happened at the soft play today?'

Barclay tutted, becoming increasingly impatient. She should be out there scouring all of Merseyside looking for their daughter, not sitting here half-accusatory of them. 'It was nothing,' Barclay said through gritted teeth. 'We were on a ride. She had an accident and I made her leave the ride, and she wasn't happy about it.' *She told me she hated me*, he thought.

'I see.' She scribbled more notes, placing her Post-it on the back of her phone. 'Did anyone else know that you'd be at the play centre today?'

Barclay looked to Nick. 'No,' Nick said. 'Just the three of us.'

'The three of you as in you, your husband and your friend Stefan?'

'That's right,' Nick said. 'His sister will have known, too. Indiana, his niece, came with us.'

'How long have you known Stefan?'

'What?' Nick almost laughed. 'I've known him for years. I work with him.'

'Where is that?'

'At a gallery in town,' Nick said. 'The Grey Room.'

'You've worked there how long?'

'Originally I was there for over ten years,' Nick said. 'Then when we adopted Sarah, I took time off. I went back last year.'

Lavery replenished a new Post-it again. 'Does Sarah have anything with GPS on it? An AirTag in a pocket maybe? Something like that?'

'No,' Barclay said. Barclay remembered they'd found Sarah's coat on the back of one of their chairs, red like her ribbons. He had meant to talk to Nick about getting an AirTag, but worried that his fatherly concerns over Sarah were going too far, whether they were creeping into paranoia. He wished he'd had that conversation now.

'Can you think of anyone that Sarah might have left with?'

'No,' Barclay said. 'We had that talk with her multiple times. I know the school talk about it, too.'

Lavery nodded. 'Does she have a tablet? Smart device?'

'She has a tablet, yes,' Nick said. 'She didn't have it with her today, if that's what you mean. We limit her screen time. We have done since last year.'

'I see,' Lavery said. 'What happened last year?'

'Well, she has two,' Barclay added. 'One here and one at mine. Sometimes she'd forget it and there'd be hell to pay. So we decided to—'

'What happened last year?' Lavery repeated her question, more pointed.

'We, er… there was an app on it,' Barclay said.

'What was the app called?'

Barclay hesitated, felt the words bend and snap in his throat like branches of dying trees.

Pen poised, Lavery glared up at him from her Post-its. 'I don't need to remind you, DS Barclay, any information could be invaluable.'

'The app was called The Woulds,' Barclay said.

Lavery's eyebrows arched high over her eyes; she stared at Barclay as though waiting for him to react. She glanced to Nick and back again. 'I see,' she said. 'Has Sarah ever mentioned speaking to someone online?'

'No,' Nick said. 'We watch what apps she's using now.'

'Right.' Lavery put her Post-its away. 'Where does she use the tablet?'

'What?'

'Here at home? At school?'

'She uses it here,' Nick said. 'At Ben's house too, like he said. She's not allowed it at school, so she wouldn't ever take it with her. If we go to our parents' houses, she has it then too.' Nick's eyes flicked to the ceiling, as though thinking. 'Sometimes I have to take her to work and she has it then.'

'I see,' Lavery said. 'And are you sure she's not been using apps that give people direct access to her via messaging or something similar? A lot of these kids' games are like that now.'

'We're sure,' Barclay said. 'We check her tablets every night.'

'Both of them?'

'Yes,' Barclay said.

Lavery nodded. 'Okay,' she said. 'I'll need you to give me those tablets. Just to rule them out through our digital forensic teams. I'll take the one that's here with me now, and Barclay, if you could provide the one at your home as soon as you can.

Now, I'm going to share some information with you that might be difficult to hear.'

'Oh God!' Nick sobbed again, his cries wringing out of him.

Here it was. The thing he felt in his bones, in the fibre of his being. He didn't want to believe it. He looked at his watch. She'd been gone for well over fourteen hours. The statistical likelihood of her being found alive was dwindling.

'Just tell us,' Nick said, panic widening his eyes. 'What's going on?'

Silence. The crackling of the open fire. The scrape of a chair on tiles from the kitchen. The kettle grumbling to life.

'Given what you've told me and your certainty that Sarah wouldn't leave with someone she doesn't know...' She trailed off, her eyes on Barclay.

He knew then. He knew exactly what Lavery was thinking. If she didn't leave with a stranger, then more than likely, she left with someone she'd already met.

Lavery took a breath and said, 'We have footage of someone leaving the play centre with Sarah.'

Twenty-One

De Silva had managed just a few hours' sleep, even though she was exhausted from the lack of downtime yesterday. As the sun came up and turned the winter sky rust-red and gold, her thoughts turned to Barclay and Nick. She was sitting at the dining table, a mug in her hand, and stared out at the sky. Murphy had kept her in the loop, but she was under strict instructions to stay out of the investigation. The last she'd heard was in the early hours, that Lavery had gone to speak with Nick and Barclay.

In the end, she'd moved herself, showered and set off for the OCC. Murphy had called her as she was pulling into the carpark, insisted she joined her in her office immediately.

Murphy's office smelled like vanilla, but it felt thick on de Silva's chest, and made her cough. She spotted a plug-in air freshener on the far wall and fought the urge to turn the intensity switch down, to open one of the security windows just a crack and stood in front of Murphy's desk.

Murphy was at her computer, and in the corner, next to an old-fashioned filing cabinet with a spider plant on top of it, stood the assistant chief constable, Nathan Pryce. He was a man of averages – average height, average weight, average looks, though his face was severely lined, so much so he reminded de Silva of a raisin. His mousy brown hair was thin, and there had been rumours that he'd had a hair transplant in Turkey. Clearly it hadn't taken. He wore round glasses that were an odd match for his already round head, so they looked impossibly small on his face.

'Please, sit down,' Murphy said. Usually, she was a picture of health and appeared well put-together, as though waking up and looking perfect was as effortless as breathing. But not today. 'I'm sure you're familiar with ACC Pryce?'

De Silva nodded. 'Good morning, sir.'

He said nothing.

'Good.' Murphy's eyes were puffy, so much so that they looked swollen, her hair wasn't as carefully styled as it usually was, and de Silva was absolutely certain that she was wearing the same crisp white shirt as the day before.

She looks like half-boiled shite, de Silva thought.

'Thank you for coming in this morning,' Pryce said. He had one of those voices that sounded as though he was straining to speak. Like he had laryngitis and speaking was a maximum-effort activity.

It was unusual for the ACC to be seen outside of his office, a meeting room or in front of the cameras. In truth, de Silva couldn't remember the last time she'd seen him when she wasn't passing him in the corridor.

'There's a lot going on it seems,' Murphy said. 'Your investigation into Beatrice Tredwell's disappearance and reappearance. A woman found murdered and burned in her own home.'

'Yes, I'm aware,' de Silva said. *And Sarah*, she thought. But that wasn't her case. It was Lavery's.

'And now you believe there to be a possible link between the death of DC McKenzie and the disappearance of DC Cullen, who had previously investigated the Bob Brendan case.' Murphy spoke as though she were reading a list of de Silva's wrongdoings. 'What exactly do you think that link is?'

'I'm not sure yet,' de Silva answered, honestly. 'But it may require me to exhume the body of DC McKenzie.'

'I thought you'd been joking,' Pryce said to Murphy. He eyed de Silva and sneered. 'Have you any idea how much exhumations cost? You'd need a writ from the High Court!'

'No,' she said. 'But I've a good idea of the cost of not knowing the truth about a loved one's death. I imagine

McKenzie's family would feel the same, if not the chief constable.'

'We'll talk about that as and when any evidence arises, de Silva,' Murphy said. 'But that's not why I asked you here this morning.'

'Then why did you?'

Silence. What was going on here? De Silva's mind raced ahead of itself, examining the possible eventualities of this conversation.

Murphy cleared her throat. 'Does the name Scarlet Putney mean anything to you?'

De Silva's skin turned cold. 'Yes,' she said. 'It does.'

-

After meeting with Murphy and the ACC, de Silva needed to get out and get some fresh air before the rest of the team arrived. She called Lavery and asked for an update, which she had reluctantly given. The update was that there was no news to give. VEU were still working on the CCTV footage.

By the time she'd settled herself at her desk with a hot coffee and an almond croissant, and logged onto the PNC to access the Scarlet Putney case notes, Braxton ambled in. He looked dishevelled and dreadful. Still, de Silva was thankful that he'd at least combed his hair – what was left of it – and brushed his teeth. Sprayed some deodorant and a little aftershave. He smelled like her dad. Like his aftershave came from one of those white bottles with a little blue boat on it.

'Morning,' he said, his voice low and gloomy. He sat down at his desk with a take-away coffee in hand. He sipped at it. 'Is there any news on Sarah?'

De Silva shook her head. 'Nothing new yet,' she said. 'Braxton, can I talk you through what I'm thinking?'

His face said, *At this hour?*, but he nodded eventually. 'Yeah, go 'ead.'

'We have Beatrice Tredwell taken from a secure mental health facility,' she said. 'Sarah vanishes from the play centre at Otterspool, and I've just been in a meeting with Murphy.'

'About what?'

'Do you remember the name Scarlet Putney?'

He cocked his head as though clawing through the filing cabinet of his memories. 'No,' he said. 'Should I?'

'She wasn't one of our cases,' de Silva said, sliding her laptop across to him. 'Her disappearance was investigated by Mike Crosby's team in PVPU. She disappeared for three weeks when she was seven years old. Turned up again walking down the M62 toward Liverpool half naked. Well, last night she disappeared from the home she shares with her mum.'

'Jesus,' Braxton said, closing the laptop lid. 'I don't know how much more of this I can take hearing about. It's constant.'

De Silva had to agree. This type of story was becoming all too common, especially for her team. And now it had ripped itself into Barclay's own family. 'Her phone was found when she disappeared the first time,' de Silva said. 'This was a few years back, so it wasn't immediately flagged until we started looking into things.'

'Sorry, I'm confused,' Braxton said. 'Looking into what?'

De Silva took a deep breath. 'She had The Woulds app on her phone.'

Braxton's eyes went wide. 'So we have Scarlet Putney, who was a known user of the app, and little Sarah Barclay, who we know had the app on her tablet.'

'That's right.'

'And we have the death of Christine Jones recently, who used to work at Rainford Lane School for Boys,' Braxton said, nodding, as though things were beginning to come into focus for him.

'Yeah.'

'And you don't believe in coincidences.'

De Silva shook her head.

'So, now we have to find out whether Beatrice Tredwell ever used that godforsaken app, don't we?'

'I think that's our next best step,' de Silva said.

'So, are you thinking Scarlet was *taken* from her home?' Braxton asked. 'Do you need me to speak with her mum?'

'I'd love that, Braxton,' she said. 'It's like you can read my mind. Could you track down her father, too.'

'Yes, I'll get right on it.'

The others filtered into the incident room, their group chatter instantly dying off, and de Silva wondered if they sensed something in the air of the room. Something physical that they'd been able to detect.

'I think we need to go back to the start of all of this.' De Silva stood and walked across to the evidence boards. 'Let's put McKenzie aside for a minute.' She looked up at the boards, shining white under the fluorescent lights. It was all there, but nothing was tied together. She scrubbed it all away with the eraser and started writing it all up again. 'Beatrice Tredwell wasn't supposed to escape from whoever had her in that car that night at Southport,' she said. 'But she did. If the driver of that second car hadn't have shown up, then God knows where Bea would be now. Would we have even known about it?'

Silence in the room.

'Okay, look I know this is messy. I know there's a lot to sort through. We're short-staffed with McLachlan and Barclay out, and we were already thin on the ground. I know that.'

Silence again. She was certain they were all feeling the burden of even more cuts to police budgets.

'How did we get on tracking down the drivers of the cars from the CCTV footage at Southport pier?' she asked. 'Any leads?'

'Yeah,' Harris said, reading from a small notepad. 'We couldn't get a registration on the car Beatrice got out of,' he said. 'The angle is all wrong, but we're still chasing up other footage from different angles, so I'm hopeful.'

'And the other car?' Barclay asked.

'Now there we did have a hit. It belongs to a Mr Warren Childs,' he said. 'We called him yesterday afternoon to ask him to come in for an official interview today. But when I spoke to him, he said he was on his way back home from a concert he'd attended in London that night.'

'And he drove home the same night?' Lawrence asked.

'Who was playing?' Braxton asked.

'Bryan Adams.' Harris turned to Braxton with a smile. 'Cracking voice. Bloody love me some—'

'Back to Mr Childs,' de Silva said.

'I've called him in for a chat today as I said,' Harris said. 'From what he said on the phone though, he got a good look at the driver of the other car.'

'Description?' de Silva asked.

'Yeah.' Harris got up, moved to the evidence board and picked up a dry-wipe marker, began writing as he spoke. 'Five foot seven inches, or thereabouts, dressed in a dark tracksuit, it didn't appear to be branded. His trainers were all-black, too, no brand discerned.' He narrowed his eyes at the pad, clearly finding it difficult to read his own handwriting. 'Dark skin, he says. Possibly of Asian descent.'

'Of course,' O'Connor said.

'Oi,' Braxton warned. 'Watch yourself.'

'Anything else?' de Silva asked, glad that Braxton had said something to quell those particular prejudices. She knew she'd have to take O'Connor aside, put him in his place, remind him that his duty was to the victims; and with a sinking feeling, she knew how that conversation would go. There was a rising hatred of people who weren't straight, white men across the country, and she was sorry to see that it had pervaded her team. The UK was slipping more toward the right, more toward racism, sexism, homophobia and intolerance. *Well*, she thought, *not on my team.*

'Not so far, no.' Harris sat back down, threw his notepad on the table.

'I want you to stay with that one, Harris.'

'Yes, boss,' Harris said.

'Braxton, I know you said you'd speak with Leah Putney, but could you assist Harris.' It wasn't a question. She turned to Lawrence and said, 'Could you call Leah Putney and ask her to pop in for a chat? Give me a few minutes and I'll fill you in on that case.'

'Yeah, course,' Lawrence said.

'Good.' De Silva was pacing now, biting the inside of her cheek as she thought. 'O'Connor, will you assist Lawrence?'

'Sure will.'

'Arlow, have you managed to speak to any friends or family of Christine Jones?'

'No,' Arlow said, simply. 'Because there are none. No next of kin. Her neighbours said she kept herself to herself. She smiled in the street but never stopped for a chat. We're working on finding friends, but… seems like she hardly left the house.'

'I see.'

'But there is something else…' he said.

'Go on.'

'Patel?' Arlow gestured toward Patel, who moved to the evidence board and picked up the dry-wipe pen.

'Yates and me put the particulars of Jones's murder into the PNC,' Patel said.

De Silva stopped pacing and stared at Patel.

She wrote on the board. *Sharp force trauma to the majority of victim's body. Fire at the property. Scalding on the victim's body prior to death, as though burned with hot water or a heated implement.*

Yates got to his feet then. 'And we got a hit.'

'A few hits,' Patel added.

'There was a similar incident in Devon in 2011,' Yates said.

Devon, de Silva thought. *Is that…*

'Another in Derby in 2002,' Patel said.

'Christine Jones was known to have worked at Rainford Lane School for Boys,' de Silva said. 'We also know that before and during his visits to Rainford Lane, Jeremiah Sure owned and operated a summer camp for disadvantaged kids in Devon. I need to know if they are connected. And I need to know who died in Derby in 2002.'

'We're on it,' Patel said.

'There was one more hit on the PNC, boss,' Arlow said. 'One right on the border of Merseyside and Lancashire. It's a toss-up as to who would usually respond to a call like that.'

'And was it us or West Lancs?'

'West Lancs initially.'

'Initially?'

Arlow opened the backpack on his desk and pulled out an iPad, quickly logged in. 'This is a map showing the site of the murder and the house fire. The place is called Foxglove Farm, and the year was 1999,' Arlow said.

The others had gathered around him now, eagerly staring down at the small screen.

'So?' Braxton asked, leaning in to look.

'What else do you see?' Arlow zoomed in on the map slightly.

De Silva took the iPad from Arlow, moved the map around with her finger. As she was about to zoom in, she saw it. The Rainford Bypass running nearby. The stick-thin, jagged road of Rainford Lane forking off the busy road and up toward a square box marked with a name.

Rainford Lane School for Boys.

All these recent events were a part of something bigger; de Silva was certain of that. 'Braxton, could you contact Rob Ayris from the National Crime Agency? Tell him what we've got so far, and we'd appreciate some help.'

'I'm on it,' Braxton said, heading off to his desk.

'Er, de Silva,' Arlow said. 'I know more about Foxglove. If you want to hear it.'

'You've got that right, Arlow, I do want to hear it.'

'Could we step outside?'

'Yeah,' she said, following him out into the corridor, and Arlow closed the door behind them. 'What is it?'

'The couple at Foxglove Farm were called the Simmonses,' Arlow said. 'We found that pretty easy.' He grinned, then thought better of it. 'We found a police report.'

'They had a criminal record?' de Silva asked.

'No, nothing like that,' Yates said. 'They called the police following a situation at their farm back in 1996. Three years before their deaths.'

'What kind of situation?' *Come on*, de Silva thought. *Out with it.*

'West Lancs Police were called to the farm following a young lad who turned up in the middle of the night,' Arlow said, keeping eye contact with her. 'According to the report, the lad didn't speak, or wouldn't speak, but that he showed signs of... well, there were bruises. Cuts. Marks up his arms and on his neck.'

'Okay...' She thought of the images they'd found in the photo album in O'Brien's loft last year. The torture. The violence. All inflicted on those tiny bodies. She felt sick.

'The Simmonses guessed where he'd come from,' Arlow said.

She nodded. 'Rainford Lane School for Boys,' she said. 'Right, and what did they do with him? Did the officers bring him into the station?'

'No,' Arlow said. 'By the time West Lancs arrived, the school's head, a Mr Robert Brendan, had already been to collect him and take him back to school. Claimed the bruises were from in-fighting and sports, and that it would be handled. Boys will be boys and all that.'

'And all of this is in the report?'

'Yes,' he said.

'So what're you thinking?' de Silva asked, searching Arlow's face for answers.

'They were a young couple. Quiet. Had kids of their own,' Arlow said. 'They went to church on Sundays and on religious holidays, their neighbours liked them. Hardworking. There was some debt there, but which farmers aren't in debt, am I right?'

'Can we cut to the chase?' de Silva asked, stopping short of tapping her foot.

'Well…' Arlow continued. 'This report was the only thing that tied them to the police. Otherwise, they kept themselves to themselves. Quiet, as I said.'

'So…'

'If I had to hazard a guess,' he said, 'and it would be a guess at this point… I'd say their murder was definitely a targeted attack.'

'Based on the violence of it, I'd agree,' de Silva said. 'It does feel personal. What're you thinking?'

'I'm thinking about the boy from Rainford Lane that they sent back to that place,' Arlow said.

'Three years later?' de Silva asked, though she supposed she'd heard stranger things, especially in the last few years. 'If it was the kid from the school, why would he wait all that time before taking his revenge?'

'Maybe he had to wait for something,' Arlow said. 'Like the school to close down permanently following Robert Brendan's death?'

'I understand your thinking,' she said. 'Does the police report mention the name of the boy concerned?'

'No,' Yates said. 'But West Lancs did something interesting.'

'Go on…'

'The farm was on the border, neither their jurisdiction nor ours, but they responded. The school, however, was definitely on our patch. So, they made a recommendation that Merseyside Police go out and visit the school. Robert Brendan said everything had been dealt with and there would be no more instances of running away from any student. The officer asked to see the boy, and the report said he seemed in good health and positive. Even apologised for causing the Simmonses any upset and wasting police time.'

'Two sets of officers spoke to that boy from two different police forces and neither one of them got the poor lad's name, am I getting this right?'

'Er, yes,' Arlow said. She was sure she caught his right eye twitching. 'Well, about that…' Arlow handed de Silva the file. 'He was a DC back then,' he said.

De Silva looked down at the reporting officers' names at the bottom of the sheet. *DC Carl Brophy*.

Dad.

Twenty-Two

The house was still. Not the comforting kind of still. Not the relaxing, tranquil kind you're thankful for at the end of a hard day's graft. The other kind. The eerie kind. A stillness that is *too* quiet.

Sarah's bedroom was neat and tidy, the way Nick would have it. Barclay was standing near the window, looking out at the front garden below, clinging on to Mingo, the small stuffed penguin they'd got her during a trip to Chester Zoo four years ago. It felt soft in his hands, tiny and fraying at the edges. Soon, the stitching would come away, and everything inside would come out, Barclay was convinced of that.

On her desk, just the right size for her, was a colouring book. A half-finished image of a house on a hill, in scratchy pencil, all done in colours no house would ever be. Black and purple and green. Like a bruise.

'I feel like we're doing nothing.' Nick's voice from behind Barclay. He didn't turn to his husband.

'Has Stefan gone?'

'He has,' Nick said.

Barclay nodded. 'Well, we're doing nothing because that's what's expected from us,' he said. 'We should wait here in case she comes home, or in case someone calls.'

'What do you mean "someone"?'

'Someone who's found her, or seen her, or...' He couldn't finish that sentence and wished he hadn't started.

'Has her?'

Yes, Barclay thought.

Nick went to him then, threw his arms around Barclay's back. Barclay could feel the hot tears through his T-shirt again. 'I don't want to think of her like that, Ben,' Nick said.

Barclay turned, pulled his husband closer to him. 'I know,' he said. He didn't want to think of that either, but the detective in him knew that the longer this went on, these were the conversations they'd need to have.

'You should have told me,' Nick said. He drew back, wiped away his tears, anger flashing on his face, red. 'You should have fucking told me there was more to this app, Ben!'

'You know I couldn't ever win with you, could I?'

'What are you talking about?'

'We broke up because you were sick of me bringing work home—'

'We broke up,' Nick screamed, 'because a killer sent you threats about our daughter. We had to run and hide in a fucking hotel, Ben!'

Barclay looked at the grey carpet, fluffy and in need of hoovering. 'That's not… I know that… You were on at me all the time about bringing work home. So I stopped talking to you about it.'

'You found that app on our daughter's tablet just a few months ago, and you didn't think I'd want to hear that these girls from the news have been using this app too?'

'Not using. Used. It's all in the past,' Barclay said. 'The app disappeared. It's gone.'

'There's a girl on the news now who has connections to it, Ben.'

'How was I supposed to know she'd gone missing? I've been here with you! Besides, we don't know if there is a connection now, and the girl's thirteen.'

'She was seven when she went missing!'

Feet out on the landing. The groan of the same floorboard that Nick had moaned at Barclay for months to have fixed. Char in the doorway to Sarah's bedroom, another brew in her hand.

'Come on, you two,' she said, a warm and professional smile on her face. 'This is the fault of neither of you. You need to stick together now, not tear each other apart over who said this and who said that. If there are things you need to get off your chest, you do it now, and then you move on united.'

'I just can't get my head around how...' Barclay said, and Nick moved away from him. 'How she vanished.'

'We've gone over this...'

'I know we have.' Barclay sat down on the edge of Sarah's bed and even then, he was almost the same height as Nick. 'But how? How did she disappear? How did we not notice a person taking her out of that place? Why didn't she shout out for one of us?'

'Go on...' Char said. 'That's a good start.'

'You blame me, don't you?' Nick asked.

Barclay's jaw clenched. 'No,' he said finally. 'I was there, too. But you two were deep in conversation.'

'So what?' Nick howled. 'We work together! And what were you distracted by? The fact that you weren't at work in that grotty little basement, or the fact that I was talking to Stefan and not you?' Nick's face was red, coloured by fury. 'You haven't even fucking cried, Ben! Over your own daughter!'

A knife to Barclay's heart. He felt winded by his husband's words, like his legs would give way at any moment. 'I...' He couldn't manage to form a sentence.

Nick's eyes and mouth wide, he put a hand to his head. 'God, what are we even doing? At each other's throats!' He moved to embrace Barclay, who side-stepped the gesture.

Ultimately Char was right, they had to be there for each other in whatever way they could. But right then, Barclay couldn't think of anything worse than Nick holding him. Not after what he'd said. 'Have you heard from Lavery?' he asked Char.

'Not yet.'

'What is she doing? Has she started searches back up in and around Otterspool?'

'She has, yes.'

'Right then.' He moved to the bedroom door and stepped out onto the landing. 'I'm going to go and help the search party.'

'I don't think that's a good idea,' Char said, moving out of Barclay's way.

'Nobody asked,' Barclay said.

'I can't just sit here either,' Nick said. 'I want to come.'

'And what if she comes home and we're not here?'

Nick nodded. 'I'll ask Mum and Dad round.'

Barclay pressed Mingo into Nick's chest, and he took hold of the stuffed toy and squeezed it. 'I won't be long.'

'I'm going to advise you both to stay put,' Char said. 'You know yourself, Ben, having family around on an investigation like this could cause more harm than good.'

'Not everyone's family is a detective,' Barclay said, leaving the room. 'I'm not sitting around here and waiting for someone to tell me they can't find her.'

'Keep your phone on,' Char called after him.

Barclay's steering wheel felt like a ring of ice as he gripped it and pushed the start button. The engine moaned and strained as he reversed slightly to move around Char's Ford Mondeo.

It would take around twenty minutes to get to Otterspool prom if the traffic was light, but realistically, Barclay knew that after twenty hours…

He found de Silva's number on the car's touchscreen and pressed call. 'Hi,' he said simply.

'Are you okay?' De Silva sounded almost out of breath. 'I'm just on my way to an interview,' she said.

'Oh.'

'Are you okay? Sounds like you're driving; where are you going?'

'Otterspool,' he said.

'Barclay…' It was the tone he'd expected. The warm but what-are-you-doing one. 'Have you even let Lavery know you're heading down?'

'I sat in that house all night waiting for a call that didn't come, de Silva. I can't sit there any more.'

'No, I get it,' de Silva said, her breathing normal again. 'But I think you should stay home. It's what we'd tell anyone.'

'So I've heard.'

'It's practice because it's what's best, Barclay,' she said. 'Come on, you know that.' She took a sip of something, and he imagined her drinking steaming black coffee.

'I know someone took her,' he said, his voice wobbling and soft. 'But what if they… what if they dumped her?'

'We don't know anything for certain yet, Barclay,' she said. 'But Lavery is capable. She's a bit of a twat, but she's capable. Has she given you an update?'

'We had a chat,' he said. 'We spoke about The Woulds app, about the possibility all of this is connected. But she's not ready to go down that route yet.'

'Well, I've checked in on her through Murphy,' de Silva said. 'She's doing everything right. Search parties. CCTV checks, doorbell and home security footage, traffic cams, social media posts. I know why you're concerned about The Woulds app. But Sarah isn't a troubled teenage girl.'

'Neither was Scarlet Putney the first time,' he said.

'Look, you don't want to jump to any—'

'Don't say "conclusions",' Barclay interrupted, strength in his voice now. 'She didn't just evaporate. Someone took her, whether they'd planned it or it was a spur of the moment thing… they'd watched her. They chose that time to take her. While we were distracted.'

'I know,' she said. 'I don't think Lavery is ignoring the link, Barclay. I really don't. I can speak with her and see what her team's working on if you like? Or better yet, tell her to keep you in the loop?'

'I'll call her, don't worry.'

'Look, just be careful out there,' she said. 'It's light out for now, but it'll start turning dark in a few hours. Stay with the main search party and don't go off alone. If you find something, you call Lavery first then you call me, okay?'

'Okay,' he said. 'Look I'm going to go; I'm nearly there.'

'I don't like the idea of you being out there, Barclay,' she said. 'Not in the state you're in. You're upset. Distracted. You could hurt yourself. Get someone else hurt. Miss something that's right in front of you.'

'Yeah,' Barclay said. 'And there's enough of that going around already.' He wound down the window, dragged the box of anti-depressants from his coat pocket and threw them out onto the road.

Twenty-Three

De Silva needed to step outside for some fresh air. Not that the smell of warm engines and exhaust fumes was in any way comforting. Barclay had hyper-focused on being able to find Sarah himself, and she knew that there was no talking him into staying at home.

She needed to check in on Lavery, make sure she was aware of Barclay's plans first and foremost. The last thing they needed was Barclay obstructing the investigation or, even worse, destroying evidence by inserting himself when he wasn't wanted or needed. She'd give Lavery the heads-up in a second; she just needed a moment to decompress from the weight and pressure of the incident room.

She'd sent Braxton out to search through the Putney residence for any clue as to where Scarlet may have gone, and the rest of the team had their tasks. What did that leave de Silva herself with? An aching guilt for not being able to move quicker, to have saved Bea Tredwell's life, that there were no protections in place for people like Scarlet Putney. That the truth about McKenzie would be put on the back burner yet again.

If there was anything she was certain of, it was that Mitch Whitley knew something about Bea's reappearance, and she was sure that he knew more than he was letting on about the death of DC McKenzie. She'd need to speak to him again. Something informal this time, try to coax some small element of the truth out of him, then maybe she'd have enough to make an arrest. Enough to make an official request to have McKenzie's remains exhumed.

'You okay?' Braxton's voice from behind her.

'God, I thought you'd left already?'

'I was just grabbing a brew for the drive,' Braxton said. 'Besides, I called ahead. Scientific Support aren't quite finished with the Putney residence yet. Everything all right?'

She sighed. Braxton wasn't normally the person she'd go to and share her thoughts with. But it wasn't as though she could pick up the phone and offload to Barclay. 'I can't shake the feeling,' she said. 'This is all connected. I know it. I can feel it in my gut.'

'Through the app? I think you're right,' he said. 'You know how it is, boss. A gut feeling is good, but without actual evidence, you might just need a shit.'

De Silva laughed in spite of herself and a silence fell between them. 'You're right,' she said. 'Let's see what the team can pull together. It could be something, or it could be coincidences.'

'Which you don't believe in.'

'And that's the killer, Braxton,' she said with a smile. 'I don't believe in them because coincidences are rare, in my experience.'

She bit at the skin on the side of her thumb, where she'd picked away at it.

'What else are you thinking?'

'That the only three people who might know what's going on here are sat in prison cells,' she said. 'One I can't stand to look at, the other has refused to see me multiple times and the third one I have absolutely no rapport with at all.' She held up her hand. 'Unless you class taking my finger as the basis of building a witness/bobby relationship?'

Braxton laughed now. 'Well, it's different now, isn't it? You're at a point where you can compel Crosby to meet you. Whether he'd actually open up to you is another matter.'

'And so that just leaves O'Brien.' She avoided telling Braxton that she'd already met with him just the other day. 'I remember when Barclay and me were interviewing him when we made the arrest. He said something about a clean-up operation. That these people behind the app, behind Rainford Lane, would start to cover their tracks. What if that is this?'

Braxton shook his head. 'Nah,' he said. 'Can't be.' He leaned against the railing that overlooked the carpark. 'A missing kid. One dead. A dead baby. Then Sarah… How is any of that clean? How is any of that organised? And how does that relate to the murders Arlow is looking into? If these people have half the power O'Brien seemed to suggest they had, then none of this reads like something they'd have any part in,' he went on. 'This is messy. Sloppy.'

De Silva nodded. Braxton had to be right. Letting one girl slip out of a car, heavily pregnant, and taking another from her own home was too disorganised for a serious child sex trafficking ring to be involved in. Especially as they'd remained undetected for decades. They'd lingered around in the dark, wet, grim parts of the world, like mould around a filthy plug hole. 'You're right,' she said.

'It has been known, boss.' He chuckled. 'Look, we don't know how all of this is connected, or even if it is, but that's why we're here.'

'I bet Mitch Whitley knows how all of this is connected,' she said.

Braxton shrugged.

'I need to speak to him again, Braxton,' she said. 'Will you come with me when you're back?'

'Of course,' he said. 'What are you going to do?'

The realisation came to her like a train hurtling through a tunnel: loud, wind sucking at her clothes and skin, trying to drag her toward the body of it. 'Braxton…' she said, her voice wobbling. 'What if Bea Tredwell's death wasn't natural causes?'

'Go on…'

'What if O'Brien is right and this *is* a clean-up operation? Wouldn't they want Bea out of the way? Permanently!'

'You could be on to something, boss.'

She turned back toward the entrance of the OCC. 'I'll meet you back here in a few hours.'

'Where are you going?'

'To chase Carey and Grindon to sort the Bea Tredwell post-mortem,' she said. 'Then I'm going to see an old friend.'

-

O'Brien had laughed at her, then took a coughing fit between sips of what must have been room-temperature tap water. 'You think… they're worried about… things being messy?'

De Silva sat in silence and watched him heave until he finally calmed down, until the coughing stopped, and he wiped the hand that had covered his mouth on his grey tracksuit bottoms. If she checked, would there be blood there? Is that how advanced his condition was?

That was nothing to do with her. Not the reason she was there. She'd told him last time that he deserved to be ill, but she knew that wasn't true. Nobody deserves sickness; no one earns cancer karmically.

'In an interview with us last year, you used the term "clean-up operation",' de Silva said. 'The likes of which we've never seen before, so you said.'

'I did.' He coughed again, and to de Silva it sounded wet. 'Well, maybe you're speaking to the wrong person. Are you forgetting you know someone who worked for them last year?'

'I've not forgotten,' she said. 'I don't understand it, but I've not forgotten.' She kept her eyes on him, because she knew if she looked away, O'Brien would recognise that small moment of weakness. He was speaking about Crosby, who had somehow got himself mixed up in working for the very people who destroyed his childhood. The same people who had wanted her dead. 'He won't see me.'

'Have you asked?' He smirked.

She had to look away then. O'Brien knew her better than she knew herself sometimes; and in that moment he knew that she would never have reached out to Mike Crosby. 'I can't.'

'Why not?'

She knew the emotions behind the reasons why, even if she didn't know the reasons themselves. But, she supposed, she was repulsed by him. Sickened. He had tried to kill her. Kill Barclay. He let his friend take her, take her finger; Billy was supposed to have killed her and left her out on the Cumbria Fells somewhere. All on the orders of the people behind The Woulds app, behind the abuse at Rainford Lane. She wouldn't pretend to understand Crosby's reasoning, probably couldn't even if she tried.

'Because you're scared to sit opposite him.'

'I've come for information.' De Silva looked at him again. 'I've got a therapist already, thanks.'

'How is that going?'

De Silva rolled her eyes. 'Are you going to keep this up? Are you going to tell me you could smell me coming and that I have cheap shoes and an expensive handbag? Just cut the shit, Tom. Do you know anything or not?'

'The cutting wit of Winifred de Silva, everyone.' O'Brien clapped his hands together slowly. 'Just like your mother.'

De Silva leaned in. 'What can you tell me about Mitch Whitley? He was a PC at the time of Bob Brendan's body being discovered. He was in a relationship with one of the detectives you put on that case. Joanna McKenzie. She died shortly after.'

'A car accident, yes I remember,' O'Brien said. 'A necessary thing, I'm afraid.'

'Necessary how?' This was it. Her heart thundered in her chest. 'Tell me about it.' She glared at him. 'And why you failed to mention she was dead when I asked you about this last year.'

'You know, maybe you should take me in,' he said. 'Record the conversation for old times' sake. I'm not sure I'll make it to the trial.'

De Silva studied his face then, a stony expression, eyes that seemed grey where they should have been white. Maybe he had the truth of it then; maybe he wouldn't make it to next week never mind to trial. 'Just tell me,' she said.

'I knew that body belonged to Bob Brendan,' he said. He cleared his throat and for a moment de Silva thought it would turn into another coughing fit, but it didn't.

'How did you know?'

'A feeling,' he said. 'Deep down here.' He put his right hand over his stomach. 'I couldn't have *known*, not for certain. Not until you and Barclay were put back on the case. How is he by the way? All that trouble with that husband of his, I hope they're happy now. And his little Sarah.'

De Silva's stomach flipped at the mention of Barclay's daughter. It would have been on the news by now, and O'Brien would have seen it in the common room, maybe. Were his words heavy with some sort of insinuation, or had she imagined it? From what she knew of O'Brien, he wasn't into little girls; but who knew for certain?

'So, you had a feeling it was Bob…' she urged him on, shutting down any conversation around Barclay.

He shook his head. 'Always wanting to get straight to it. No one takes the time to just *talk* any more.'

'I'd rather not be here any longer than I have to be.'

'I have that scan in a few weeks' time; do you remember me telling you?'

'I don't,' she said. 'And, Tom, right now I don't really care.'

Silence. He looked down at the table, at the hands that looked to de Silva like they had aged; they were thinner, paler, lined. She wondered whether he felt the same about them, whether he was marking the passage of time, or his final weeks, by the lines etched into his hands.

'I need to be clear about what you're telling me right now, Tom,' she said. 'You said that McKenzie's accident was a necessity. What did you mean by that?'

O'Brien drew in a breath that rattled somewhere at the back of his throat, and said, 'I had to put someone on the case,' he said. 'Those two were the greenest pair of detectives I could find. Thought it was their big break.' He laughed, his eyes distant as though watching a TV on the wall behind her. 'They connected the dots. Of course they did. Not as green as I thought.' He chuckled again. 'Still, I had to be sure it was Bob before I could tell... anyone.'

'The men behind The Woulds app you mean?' De Silva asked. 'So you had a direct way to contact them then?'

He pursed his lips and looked over to the prison guard standing near the door. 'I did,' he said. 'I do. But I doubt they'd take my call now.'

'Because you shared information?'

'A dying man is still a threat to them for as long as he has breath in his body,' O'Brien said. 'You see, I knew Bob had broken his arm. I was there when he did it. It was a camping trip at a friend's place. We'd take some of the local lads out for... well, to get them away from home.'

Something writhed in her stomach. Uncurling. Unfolding. For a moment, she thought she'd be sick. Then, it clicked in her mind, like the corner piece of a jigsaw. 'You took them down to Jeremiah Sure's summer camp in Devon,' she said. 'So why did McKenzie need to die?'

'Crosby was on their payroll long before last year's events,' he said. 'He assigned one of his men to get close to McKenzie.'

'Mitch Whitley.'

O'Brien nodded. 'She had no intention of toeing the line, burying evidence I'd just as soon never got out. I'd completely misread her. I thought, you know, a lovely-looking young woman in the early stages of her career would want to do as she was told.'

'Pretty doesn't mean pliable, Tom,' she said. 'You thought you could control her and she showed you otherwise. I suppose when you're used to dealing with scum you have low expectations of others, and your low expectations meant you got blindsided by someone doing the right thing.' She took a moment to watch his face, those heavy lids over his darkening eyes. 'Or trying to.'

He glared at her.

'And DC Cullen,' de Silva said. 'Where is he? Dead, too?'

'I don't know where he is,' he said. 'He disappeared the same night as McKenzie's accident. And that's the truth. They found his medical records and had them matched. I tried to hide it all, but in the end I couldn't. They were good at what they did.'

'And what happened next?'

'I...'

'You what?'

He seemed to look around her. Past her.

'Tom,' she said. 'What did you do?'

'I let *them* know,' he said, still looking at the wall behind her. 'Next thing I know, Cullen is missing and McKenzie dies in a car accident.'

'Was Mitch Whitley involved? Was Mike Crosby?'

'Hmm?' He paused, rubbed at his temple. 'Yes.'

De Silva knew she couldn't trust the word of someone who had lied to her so much in the past, had concealed the awful things he'd done for decades. 'Did he know about you and Rainford Lane? My dad?' The question floated in the air between them like motes of dust. 'Did he know about any of it?'

O'Brien stared again, almost as though he was looking through her. His eyes like grey glass. Then he blinked, and whatever he had pictured, remembered or imagined seemed to disappear. 'Bob Brendan broke his arm coming off the climbing wall.'

'I asked you about my dad,' de Silva pressed, leaning forward.

'We knew Bob had disappeared back in '97.' His lips curled back from his teeth, almost a sneer. 'I knew someone had gotten to him. I told the others... we should lay low for a while. Then the staff started to leave. Funding seemed to dry up. The school closed. Then thirty years later that body shows up in the woods.'

'Did my dad *know*?' On that last word, she slammed the table hard.

That stare again, this time he leaned to his left and seemed to look behind her. She turned back, a chill sliding across her shoulders, but there was nothing there.

He touched his hand to his head and winced. 'I have a headache, and I thought…' He trailed off, looking down at his hands again.

'Thought what?' Something was wrong; she could feel it in her bones. Something in the room had changed. Something in *him* had changed.

He hadn't seemed to hear her.

'Tom, was my dad involved in any of this, or did he have knowledge of it?'

He looked at her, placed a hand to his head, and moaned. 'I'm sorry…' When he looked at her again, shapeless words came from his mouth, just sounds on a rasping breath.

'Tom?'

The left side of his face seemed to slip, shifting like a mudslide.

She turned to the prison guard and yelled, 'Get a medic in here now.' She was on her feet as O'Brien slid from his chair and hit the floor, his eyes scrunched tightly together.

My God, she thought. *My God, he's going to die.*

De Silva arrived back at the OCC after dark. She still hadn't called Lavery for an update. On the drive back, her mind had swirled from her visit with O'Brien. She felt exhausted by their meeting. Weakened somehow, as though speaking with him had pulled all of the energy out of her.

She'd sat in the incident room raking over the events of the day for an hour before Braxton started calling and asking where she was. As she stood and headed to meet Braxton outside, she felt the pull of shame and guilt. She'd left a sick man, a potentially dying man, all alone in a hospital he didn't know.

She tried to reason with herself. Told herself that she didn't owe O'Brien anything, but no matter how many times she repeated it, the shame didn't go away.

'Finally!' Braxton said when she exited the main doors of the OCC.

'I'm sorry,' she said. 'I'll fill you in in the car on the way to Whitley's. I think I have enough to get McKenzie's body exhumed.'

'What? Really?'

'I'll call Murphy on the way to Southport,' she said. 'Get the ball rolling. You ready then?'

She called Murphy on the way to the car, who said she'd need to clear an exhumation of McKenzie's body. 'But O'Brien's admission, though unofficial and marred by his subsequent ill health, is a hindrance. Let's see what happens.' She hung up without saying goodbye as usual.

As they reversed out of the carpark bay, de Silva's phone rang. Carey calling. 'Evening,' de Silva said. 'You're working late.'

'I've been working late all week,' she said. 'I wanted to triple check these results I have for Bea Tredwell's baby.'

'Triple check?' De Silva glanced at Braxton, who shrugged. 'Why?'

'I found something very interesting.'

De Silva could imagine Carey now, talking with her hands, even though she was on the phone. 'I'm not good with suspense.'

'There was evidence of homozygosity,' she said, quickly.

'Homo what?'

'I'll spare you the science part, but what I'll say is that incestuous relationships can expose recessive alleles through increasing homozygosity.'

'That's sparing me the science part is it?' She laughed. 'What are you telling me, Carey?'

'That, based on these results, and I *have* triple checked them…' Here she took a breath. 'The baby Beatrice Tredwell gave birth to was fathered by someone in her family.'

Twenty-Four

DI Lavery was standing at Nick's front door with a tablet under her arm when Barclay went to answer the doorbell. He'd got back to the house, freezing, long after the sun had set. It was pitch black outside, and the snow fell from the sky in tiny, light flakes.

'I may have some news,' Lavery said, stepping inside and passing him into the kitchen.

Nick was sitting with his elbows on the table, chin resting on open palms that partially covered his face. He got to his feet when Lavery entered and Char instinctively moved to the kettle to boil some water. Lavery took a seat, and Barclay hovered near the door.

'What is it?' Nick asked. 'What's going on?' His voice was high, airy and urgent.

'I've been waiting to get enhancements back from VEU before showing this to you,' she said. 'They've enhanced the footage as much as they're able.'

'VEU?' Nick asked.

'Visual Evidence Unit,' Barclay said. 'They handle CCTV, enhancements, all of that.' He looked to Lavery. 'Footage of what?'

'We're also still awaiting some footage from the carparks in the surrounding area,' she said.

'What's the hold-up?' Barclay asked.

'I won't bore you with the details,' she said, 'but basically the carpark cameras are operated and monitored by a third-party company. We've been waiting for them to pull their finger out of their arse.'

'Show us what you've got.' Nick moved so that he was sitting next to Lavery, and Barclay joined them. He was standing with his arms folded behind Lavery and stared down at the screen. He braced himself.

Lavery pressed play. The scene was chaotic. Kids darted about, screaming, laughing; parents were shouting at their kids to come and eat or to have a drink.

'There,' Lavery said.

Though Barclay couldn't make out faces, his heart contracted when he saw Sarah walking hand in hand with someone dressed in activewear. Not uncommon for any dad to be wearing. A cap covered his head and his face. Just as he was about to lead Sarah out of the security gate, with a wave to the girl who let him out, Sarah turned back.

Barclay reached down with a shaking hand and paused the footage. 'She's looking back for us,' he said. 'She's looking for us and we didn't even notice,' he said. He stepped away from the table and the screen, covered his eyes and tried to stop them twitching with tiredness. *She looked back because we hadn't noticed*, Barclay thought.

'What did he tell her to make her go with him?' Nick asked. 'What did he say? Because she knows stranger danger and all of that. Especially after what happened with that Lewis fucking Lamond at her school!'

'Do either of you recognise this man?' Lavery asked. 'The clothes he's wearing, perhaps?'

'No,' Barclay said.

'No, I don't think so,' Nick said. 'People dress so alike, don't they? Especially in gym stuff.'

Barclay hadn't seen his daughter in two days, and then there she was on the screen in front of him. He wished he could reach in and take her, make her safe, hold her close to him.

'But there she is.' Nick covered his mouth, and his shoulders shook. 'My little girl.' He looked up at Barclay. 'Where is she, Ben?'

'Is that it?' Barclay asked, his throat dry, his voice cracking. 'Is there any other footage from other locations inside? Do they not have things like that for insurance purposes?'

'I'm afraid not,' Lavery said. 'The cameras over the actual play area had apparently malfunctioned. They didn't know that until they tried to access the footage from the cameras.' She paused, looked them both in the eye. 'I know that's incredibly frustrating. But like I said, we're awaiting footage from the surrounding areas, which my team are working on. But there's one thing we know for sure now.'

'That she was taken,' Barclay said, finishing her thought for her.

Nick jumped up and clung to Barclay. 'Someone has her,' he screamed. 'Someone has our little girl, Ben!'

In his heart, he had already guessed as much, but there was always that hope. There, in front of that screen, those hopes evaporated into nothing. He would never find Sarah in the woods. They'd never receive a phone call from a neighbour who had found Sarah wandering around the streets and taken her in.

Someone had taken her. They'd taken her with purpose. And all the while, Barclay and Nick were sitting just metres away, oblivious.

'So now that we know,' Barclay said. 'What's your plan?'

'We ramp up the social media posts,' she said. 'I've already had that organised with our public relations team. I'd like to do a press conference first thing tomorrow morning. I'll need you both there.'

'I don't know if I can do that,' Nick said, his hands shaking, bottom lip wobbling.

'You can,' Barclay said. 'Because we have to. These are important. We get to show pictures. Someone might recognise her. They might have seen something without realising they'd seen something.'

'Look,' Lavery said. 'I'll be in touch via Char here with the details when I have them. Just do your best to get some rest. There's work to do now. My team are on it. I'm hoping we'll have some news really soon. But this is a positive step, though it might not seem it. We know now what happened, whereas before this video we were guessing.'

Barclay understood the sentiment, though he was unsure he appreciated it. Though it was an update in the case, it was a blow to it as well. If whoever took Sarah wanted to hold her for ransom, they'd have been in touch by now. He knew that. He knew DI Lavery knew that.

She stood and nodded to them both. 'I'll be in touch,' she repeated, leaving the kitchen.

I'll be in touch; the words repeated in Barclay's head. As though Lavery were discussing an application for a loan or a missing cat. He went out into the hallway when the door closed behind Lavery and pulled his arms into his big coat, the woollen one he had come to love.

'Where are you going?' Nick asked.

Barclay pushed his wet feet into his soggy trainers, and they squeaked as he moved. 'I can't sit here, Nick,' he said. 'I'm going out to clear my head.'

'But you're all right getting off and leaving me to sit here, aren't you? Bloody hell, Ben, I need you here. With me.' Nick burst into tears. From tiredness. From heartache. From the repeated pattern that had always been their relationship. Nick at home, Barclay at work. 'Our daughter is missing, I'm climbing the walls in here, and you're off on your own like…'

'Like what?'

'Like what's going on right here doesn't matter!' Nick screamed. 'You think you can swan in and swan out again without a care in the fucking world. You think you're only ever answerable to yourself, but that's not how relationships work. It's not how a marriage works.'

'I don't think that.' Why couldn't Nick see that everything Barclay did was for him and Sarah, for the betterment of their little family? 'I think that I have to try to do something,' he said, choking back tears he feared would come. 'That's who I am. It's what I do. God, Nick, I love the bones of both of you, but I can't pretend I'm someone I'm not.'

'And I can?'

'No!' Barclay moved closer to him, wanted to hug his husband but resisted. 'You can be who you are, and I can be who I am. And, if I'm being honest with you, us being who we are led you to make the decision that we shouldn't be together any more.'

'Yeah, well maybe I was right the first time.' Nick's voice was low then, a growl, something ferocious and vicious.

Barclay nodded. Finally, there it was. The truth at the heart of their relationship that they'd tried so hard to ignore. Their recent closeness, the night spent in Barclay's bed. It was a dream. A nice idea. It was sex and it was comfort and familiarity. He was stupid to believe that he and Nick could work.

Barclay headed out of the front door, slamming it behind him. Nick shouted something after him; it sounded like a wail, and Barclay ignored it. He stopped still on the drive and thought about grabbing the door by its letter box and slamming it again. Over and over and over until it fell off its hinges. Until it lay on the floor and he could kick the glass right out of it. Until it was smashed and destroyed and completely useless.

Twenty-Five

'I know you've just got home,' de Silva was saying into her phone. 'I know, and I'm sorry, O'Connor. I wouldn't ask if this wasn't urgent.' She had to check Whitley out. Without any legal cause to bring him in again, other than the suspicious variation of his account versus the young tearaways', she'd have to find something.

'Go on then…' O'Connor said. 'But you can explain it again to my wife; she already thinks I don't like being at home.'

'If you get your shoes on and comb your hair right now, I'll pay for you both to have a dinner on me somewhere nice.'

'I'll hold you to that, boss. Who am I after?'

'Lee Tredwell,' de Silva said. 'I know it's in Manchester; I just don't want GMP to make the arrest. I want to do it ourselves. Let me know when you've arrived at his house and I'll call GMP out of courtesy. You make the arrest and bring him back here. Take a squad car and a few on-duty PCs with you, won't you?'

'What's he done?'

De Silva explained as she listened to the moans and grunts as O'Connor got himself ready again and huffed as he got into his car.

'Jesus Christ,' he said. She heard the engine of his car cough and splutter. 'Bloody thing. So what're we thinking then? That all of this about Azad Khan was a smoke screen?'

'That's exactly what I'm thinking,' de Silva said. 'Look, I'll have to go. Let me know as soon as you've made the arrest, won't you?'

'Will do, boss.' She heard the click of his seatbelt. 'Ring you later.' He hung up.

They waited outside the house on Gloucester Road for over an hour. The lights were off, the place was in darkness, but it wasn't even eight p.m. Braxton was sitting next to de Silva, glancing up from his phone to the dark house occasionally. They'd parked just down the street from it, and, between the long drive that curved toward the house and the tall old oaks surrounding it, they couldn't make out much.

They'd driven past earlier, but there was no vehicle on the driveway, and no indication that anyone was home. De Silva did spot a garage attached to the house and felt the urgent pull to check it out. *You're a DCI*, she told herself. *You don't go snooping around garages after dark.*

She'd always been hands-on. She couldn't help it; it was a part of who she was. There was an office assigned to her in the OCC, but she never used it as she preferred to sit with everyone else. Wherever the action was. Last she'd checked, her office had turned into a dumping ground of broken or unused equipment.

Story of my life.

Right then, she wanted nothing more than to go home. She was tired, exhausted from the early start, from her interaction with O'Brien, but there was something about Mitch Whitley that didn't sit right with her. He had been in a relationship with a detective who'd died whilst investigating a case connected to Rainford Lane School; he was friends with Mike Crosby; and the teenage boys who'd torn off the wooden access door to the pier had told a slightly different story to Whitley's.

'Doesn't look like there's anything doing…' Braxton said at her side; he whispered but breathed heavy through his mouth. He flicked through the day's *Liverpool Journal* he'd brought with him until he found the sports pages at the back.

'You know,' she said, 'you didn't have to come. He's not home, clearly, and I just wanted to check the place out. See where he lives.'

'The last time we heard that from you, boss, you ended up in a shoot-out in Cumbria, and the time before that—'

'Yeah, okay, Braxton.' She tried to keep the smile from her face. 'I get it.'

'Well, I'm just saying.'

'Well don't "just say" anything.'

'Yes, ma'am.' He didn't look up from the paper.

De Silva gnashed her teeth. 'Are you trying to piss me off?'

'Yes, ma'am.'

'Well, it's working,' she said. 'Just keep quiet and for God's sake, Braxton, breathe through your bloody nose.'

Ultimately, de Silva knew that Braxton was right. There'd been no signs of movement from inside the house. No comings or goings, but still something tugged at her. She was ready to leave but couldn't. 'How's McLachlan getting on?' she offered, by way of conversation.

'I don't think he'll be back for a good bit yet.'

'Oh?'

'Pneumonia's really taking its toll on him,' Braxton said, folding the paper up onto his knee. 'Turns out he's not been using the heating in his flat.' Braxton shook his head. 'Cost of living and all that.'

'He makes a good wage, doesn't he?'

'Depends what you mean by "good", doesn't it? He doesn't earn as much as the fat cats setting the tariffs, if that's what you're asking. None of us do.' He paused, looked out of the window up at Whitley's massive house. 'Well, maybe *he* does.' He arched his thumb toward the house. 'You know, money will be the reason he left the police for social media.'

'Surely he's not earning that much from flying drones over Merseyside and posting stuff on the internet?'

'Well, it's what people like. Seamless, streaming images over some nice relaxing music before bed. Maybe even some ASMR.'

She stared at him then, felt her mouth open. 'Is that like S&M?'

Braxton put on a feminine voice and asked, 'Are you okay, hun?' Chuckled to himself and then returned to his own deep timbre. 'De Silva, where've you been? It's all ASMR and ex-boyfriend revenge poems these days. Everyone's got a platform, their own channel; and everyone thinks their voice is important. They all need a good fucking slap if you ask me.'

'I didn't,' she said. 'So, is McLachlan going to be okay, do you think?'

Braxton let out a sigh. 'He'll be all right, so the doctors say. Just a process, isn't it? Recovery, I mean.'

'I'll have to go and see him,' she said. 'When all of this settles.'

'He'd like that, I think.' A long pause. 'Well, of course, I blame the Covid jabs.'

'Oh no, I'm not talking to you about this again.' De Silva cut the conversation dead.

'Well, if it suits you to keep your head buried in the sand, then so be it…'

If she heard his mouth-breathing or he started talking about how the death of Princess Diana was actually an assassination orchestrated by MI5, she would go insane. 'I'm going up to the house.'

She was out on the street before Braxton said a word. She tapped on the window and mouthed to him, 'Stay here.'

The night air was frigid, not a lung-raking coldness, but something else. The sky was a solid mass of grey, threatening yet more snow. A gritter whizzed past and rock salt clattered against the side of her car. It pelted her shins and boots.

When the way was clear, she crossed the road and walked up the drive. She stopped in her tracks at the realisation that a floodlight could blast her with cold white light at any moment. If a light came on, she'd go to the door and knock, think of something to say on the fly, and so she pressed on regardless. By time she reached the front door, there was no night-splitting blast, but a small, blinking red light from security cameras. One above the front door, and one on each corner of the façade.

He could be watching right now, she thought to herself and shivered.

She peered through the front windows into a sitting room. No TV, but old green Chesterfield armchairs, similar to what her nan had in the nineties. The wallpaper wasn't tatty, but not modern either. Floral patterns in shades she couldn't pick out in the dark.

De Silva wondered whether the lack of warmth, the absence of modern taste, meant that there was no woman in Whitley's life. Maybe the house was left to him in the will of a grandparent or mother. Maybe he bought it this way and couldn't be bothered to modernise it.

Or couldn't afford to.

A big house for a police officer's salary, she knew that much at least. But, she supposed, Whitley wasn't police any more. Maybe he'd bought it with money from his social media channels and didn't know what to do with it once he had it.

She took one last look through the window, at the closed door at the back of the room, where a sliver of light crept through the crack at the bottom. *If there are lights on, someone's usually home.*

Snow fell softly and silently. Huge flakes clung to the tight curls of her auburn hair as she crept around the side of the house, through a wooden gate which had been left slightly ajar. It didn't creak when she pushed it and she was thankful for that small mercy.

She reasoned with the professional police officer that sat somewhere at the back of her brain, judging her for entering property without permission or reasonable cause. *I'm just looking*, she told herself. Even as she tried to calm the inner critic, she knew that just looking never ended well. Not for her.

A rectangular patch of light fell onto a crazy paving patio and edged onto an overgrown lawn, from a light that was on in the back of the house and blasted through the window. De Silva dropped down, took out her phone and opened the camera app. She turned off the flash option, then pressed record and pushed her phone camera up to the edge of the window. She turned it left and right slightly then brought it back to her.

She pressed play to watch the video she'd just recorded. The sudden change in light meant the camera had taken a moment to adjust, as though waking up to summer sun, needing to rub sleep out of its eyes. Then, de Silva saw it.

The oven door was dropped open; yellow light came out from inside it. The big light hanging over the kitchen table was switched on. Mitch Whitley was sitting there, dripping as though he'd just stepped out from a shower. By the way his shoulders shook, she could tell that he was crying. As the footage took in the room, she saw tape at the edge of the windows and under the door that led into the other side of the house. A half-arsed job to cover the cracks, with gaps everywhere.

Now why would he—

Tape. Cracks. Open oven.

She jumped to her feet, her phone in her hand, already dialling numbers. She tried the French doors, but they were locked. Whitley looked at her. His eyes were red and swollen, and he blinked, as though uncertain of who or what he was seeing.

'Go away!' he shouted, slobber at his lips, spittle flying. 'I'm sorry, I'm sorry, I'm sorry.' He shook that big head of his.

A tinny voice from the phone, '999, what's your emergency?'

'This is DCI Winifred de Silva with Merseyside Police. I need an ambulance and fire services to 16 Gloucester Road. Now!' She hung up, dropped her phone into her coat pocket. 'Mitch, whatever has happened… whatever is going on, I can help you.'

'There's no helping me now.' He wiped at his wet face.

She needed to get him outside into the fresh air. With the door open, the gas would escape. She could talk him down then move in and switch it off. 'Just open the door, Mitch. We can talk about it.'

Whitley took a silver lighter from his pocket. Liquid dripped from his nose onto the table, which de Silva now noticed was slick too.

She took a step away from the door and called, 'BRAXTON! Braxton!' She took out her phone to call him as she heard the car door slam, and Braxton's voice call something.

She tried the door again, hoping that by sheer will of mind, she'd be able to open it. 'Come on, Mitch. You're one of us. Once a bobby, always a bobby. We can sort this.'

'We can't,' he called to her through his tears. 'I *had* to do it, and I'm sorry.'

She turned, scrabbled around the patio in the dark for something, anything, to break a window. There was an old stone plant pot, square and covered with moss and filth. It was heavy, but she could lift it. She wondered whether hitting the glass could somehow cause a spark. She didn't know, but she had to try. She threw the planter at the glass, but she over-estimated her ability to throw, and it slammed into the patio beneath the doors, shattering into pieces.

Fuck!

Braxton came around the corner of the house, telescopic baton ready. 'De Silva, what the fu—'

'Call emergency services back. Find out how long they're going to be.' She turned back to the French doors and tried to kick them. The glass rattled in the white uPVC frame. She tried again. Nothing. She grabbed Braxton's baton from him and tried that, but there was no effect.

It happened slowly.

Whitley sparked the lighter, but it didn't catch.

The baton hit the window once more. Nothing.

Whitley tried the lighter again.

Nothing happened.

De Silva swung the baton at the glass door.

No effect.

Braxton on his phone, talking loudly to the emergency services about an ETA.

Whitley sparked the lighter again.

The kitchen split open in a bright bloom of yellow light. The windows shattered outward, de Silva fell back onto the overgrown lawn and then there was a silence. Braxton's face came into view. His mouth moved but de Silva couldn't hear what he was saying.

A ringing in her ears, she sat up as smoke billowed up from the kitchen windows like black storm clouds through broken teeth, and it drifted into the night sky and the snow. Somewhere under the ringing, she could hear Braxton, faint and far away.

She got to her feet, and he steadied her, phone still in his hand. In front of her the kitchen was decimated, a burning mess. Something moved in the fire. A solid mass in the wild flames. Then the sounds of the world became solid again. The screech of birds. A car alarm blaring. The rise and fall of sirens somewhere in the distance. Braxton's voice asking her if she was okay. And the screams.

The screams.

He burst out of the kitchen, his skin scorched and on fire, smoke lifting from him like steam after a hot bath, but black. The stink of burning meat. De Silva ran toward him, pulling off her coat and tackling him to the lawn. She smothered the flames with her black padded coat, and as the lights of the emergency services shone into the dark, Whitley's screams subsided and his eyes closed.

For all of the terrible things de Silva had seen throughout her career, the charred, sizzling face of Mitch Whitley after that fire would stay with her forever.

Twenty-Six

He had lost count of how many times he and Terry had walked by the house on Harcourt Street. Always at night, and always when the lights in every other home were out. In that darkness, they felt free enough to scope it out. They'd climbed over the back wall multiple times, not needing to speak to co-operate. Their movements seemed synchronised, rehearsed somehow over the years they'd spent together. They were brothers after all.

On this night, the house looked sadder than it had done. Colder in some way. Even at Christmas, just weeks ago, there had been no lights in the windows. No decorated tree in the living room with presents underneath it, wrapped and waiting for Christmas morning.

He had told Terry why that would be the case.

It was the husband's fault.

Once, they'd watched her walking up the street alone, Aldi shopping bags stuffed full, the plastic handles stretching under the weight of whatever was inside. She looked beaten. Worn out. The police had found her daughter, but that didn't matter. It was too late, Terry had decided. The damage was already done.

There would be headlines in the morning, and that was Terry's favourite part. It would hit nationally when they realised there was a pattern. He wondered how long it would take the police to link everything together. Terry said once, 'You can't have faith in the bizzies.' His voice rasped like a rusty tool. 'They don't know their twit from their twat.'

Terry always knew the truth of things. Always seemed to have the answers.

The lock on the alleyway gate had been broken for weeks, and he wondered whether anyone had bothered to report it to the council or whether people didn't care. It was just where they kept their bins. Where rats and urban foxes roamed in the dark. Where domestic cats sat on the tops of red brick walls watching, their eyes shining in the night.

Third from the end on the left was the garden of the house they were interested in. They'd noticed a few times the last two weeks that she had left the downstairs window open just a crack. One of those large fire windows meant for speedy evacuations in case of an emergency. They'd thought about using it countless times.

'No,' Terry croaked. 'Now isn't the time.'

He'd been right of course.

It came as a surprise really. They'd been lying in bed staring at the ceiling, listening to the traffic outside when Terry's voice seemed to come from nowhere. He couldn't see his brother's face, it was so dark in the room. 'I think tonight's the night,' he said. 'Can you feel it?'

In truth, he couldn't feel it but said that he did. For some reason, Terry was able to feel when the time was right. He had this undeniable pull to go to them and make them hurt.

He was up and ready in five minutes, but Terry was standing there already dressed and waiting. He always worked so fast.

That night, as they crept over the wall silent as those alley cats, he saw the window ajar again. He wondered at how she hadn't noticed. How she hadn't felt the draught creeping in like death.

'She's thick,' Terry had said. 'Thick as pig shit.'

He had always thought that saying was a peculiar one and wondered how thick pig shit actually was. He pushed the thought aside, knowing that Terry hated when he had this type of question.

'You're always distracted,' Terry had told him once. 'Always thinking about mad stuff, when you should have your eye on the ball.'

Even in saying that, Terry had inadvertently distracted him. How do you have your eye on a ball? *It doesn't matter*, he told himself. *Focus.*

'Focus,' Terry said, as though reading his mind.

'I am,' he said, pulling open the window with gloved fingers. Once inside, he shivered. The room was frigid. Terry went straight through to the kitchen and he followed him, watching as he put a pan of water on the stove and lit the hob.

A plastic carrier bag hung from the handle of the back door. A makeshift bin filled with potato peelings and ends of carrots. He wondered whether she'd made some sort of stew, and his stomach grumbled.

A sound from upstairs. Footsteps, or maybe there was another window open up there too, and something had blown off a shelf. Turning down the flame under the water, he and Terry listened. Nothing.

It wasn't loud enough to be something falling, he thought. There it was again, the sound like a floorboard croaking underfoot. *She's awake.*

Outside, two cats yowled, and he wondered whether they were going to fight. He liked seeing cats fight. Fangs. Claws. Fur flying. It excited him to see neither of them backing down, and he wished he had that passion, that determination, when he was a kid. When Terry was, too.

These old houses, he reasoned with himself, *they make noises. Especially in winter.*

The water on the hob bubbled and spilled over the edge of the pan and then they heard her voice, thick with sleep. 'Who the bloody hell are you?' That poor girl's haggard mother was standing in the living room door.

Terry lifted the pan before anything more could be said, and raced through to the living room; he flung it at her. She clawed for her face, screaming from the agony of it. *Now*, he thought, *now we can get down to business.*

She couldn't open her eyes, and he was grateful for that. As she fell to her knees, he wondered whether she wished there had been someone there to save her. Well, those wishes would go unanswered and the consequences for the things she had done would, finally, find her.

He drew the knife from his jacket pocket and put a hand over her mouth.

'This is what you deserve,' Terry's voice croaked in the dark, icy living room. 'Isn't it what she deserves, Rob?'

Twenty-Seven

The room where Merseyside Police held press conferences was a large open space in the headquarters on Cazneau Street. Seats were set out in rows which reminded Barclay of church pews. Only the congregation that would file in today were those who'd come to worship the very worst of the world. The horrors. The missing people, and the dead.

Barclay was standing on the slightly raised platform in front of a table with a white cloth over it, emblazoned with the Merseyside Police constabulary insignia. He'd once held that as a symbol of his freedom from his own past, as a talisman of his hope for the future. A symbol of all of the things he could do to right the wrongs in society. He'd overcome so much to get there, to become a detective, that he'd naively thought this was it. No more could happen to him because he'd made it.

He'd been wrong.

There are no neat happy endings like in the movies. The character's story doesn't end when they overcome a terrible experience in the navy. The terrible, haunting night aboard the HMS *Iron Duke*, and the subsequent investigation. It doesn't end when that character becomes a person whose job it is to help and protect others.

Things continue. Life is tidy, then it's messy, then it's falling down around our ears. There is consistency in life only its inconsistency. There are no true endings. *Not until we're dead*, he thought. *And even then…*

Lawrence came in the door at the far end, where later, eager journalists and photographers would buzz in, desperate to get a glimpse at the grieving parents. The anguished detective whose life had turned sideways. They'd salivate over it, keen to get back to the office with their copy and their photographs.

He wanted to protect Nick from that, from seeing his own tissue-burned face on the news, in the papers and online. But that was an impossibility now.

Lawrence strolled to the front row and stopped there, looking up at him. He stepped down from the platform and sat on the chair next to hers. 'I'm so sorry about Sarah,' she said. 'I can't imagine what you're going through.'

'No, I can't really imagine it myself.' He slumped into a seat and Lawrence sat next to him. He wasn't sure what he was feeling. He couldn't seem to collect his thoughts and knew then that it was his own fault. The doctor had warned him not to come off his tablets in this way. That he should wean himself off slowly. Now, that was too late. 'She sent you, didn't she?'

'I was coming anyway,' Lawrence said. 'But she's been a bit caught up. Not sure if you've seen the news this morning, but Mitch Whitley blew up his house last night.'

'Oh.' He knew that he should care. That he should find some modicum of interest for Lawrence and for Whitley, but in truth he felt like there was nothing inside him. No compassion. No zest. No need to know the truths of anything other than where his daughter was and who had taken her.

'She was there,' Lawrence added.

Barclay's eyes went wide as he turned in his chair to look at her. 'She what?'

'She and Braxton went out to chat to him,' Lawrence explained. 'Found him in his kitchen, doused in petrol they think, gas coming out of the open oven and off the hob. He's… well it doesn't look good.'

'That woman,' Barclay said, shaking his head. 'If she's not losing a finger or getting hit on the head by a serial murderer, she's out getting herself blown up.'

Lawrence smiled, but Barclay felt it was more to be polite than finding him funny. He got it. This was not a space for laughter. 'How are you feeling?' she asked him.

'Like I want to collapse,' he said. 'No, like I've already collapsed in on myself.' There was more to it. He couldn't tell her about the void he felt swirling around itself inside him, or how the tears he kept inside were burning behind his eyes, how his stomach grumbled and complained, and he couldn't remember when he'd last eaten.

She took his hand in hers, squeezed it tight. She felt warm and Barclay appreciated that about her. She must have thought better of it because she removed her hand and clasped them together on her lap. 'How is your husband?'

'Nick's a wreck,' he said. 'We fell out and I stayed at mine last night.'

Lawrence shrugged. 'These things happen when there's pressure,' she said. 'You'll be all right. But you need each other now. That's something you should both remember.'

'I know we do,' Barclay said, misplaced annoyance in his voice.

'Oh, I'm sorry,' Lawrence said, shaking her head, brow creased. 'I didn't mean—'

Barclay sighed, letting the annoyance drain from him. 'I know you didn't.'

Lawrence looked at her watch. 'I should get going,' she said. 'But I'll be back there when the briefing starts.' She nodded to the space behind the pull-up banners with the Merseyside Police insignia. 'The boss told me to tell you this: she knows that you know the score, but to let Lavery take the questions, or the chief constable; I heard she's coming down, too.'

The door opened behind them, and they both turned to see Lavery walking up between the aisles.

'She scares the life out of me,' Lawrence whispered. 'I heard some of the lads saying that if you look her in the eye, she'll turn you to stone.'

He chuckled. 'That's wicked.'

'We'll be letting the media in in around five minutes, Ben,' Lavery said when she reached them. 'We'll bring you and Nick in with Chief Constable Bradshaw when they're all settled. Does that sound okay?'

None of this sounded okay. He'd prefer to be at home with Sarah, or chipping away at the case in the incident room. 'Got it,' he said.

'So, I'm going to have to ask you to vacate the room.' Lavery's face was as dispassionate as ever, never giving away whatever she was feeling or thinking. 'And I know I said as quickly as possible on this, but I really am going to need you to provide Sarah's second tablet to us. Today.'

Barclay nodded and heaved himself to his feet with a groan and a pop of his left knee. 'I don't know if I can do this,' he said quietly to Lawrence, his heart hammering at his ribcage. His whole body ached. It felt heavy and useless and clumsy. His eyes itched from lack of sleep, and his mind felt like a mass of wet cotton wool. Thick. Unmanageable. Disorganised.

'You have to do it,' Lawrence said softly. 'I'll come find you later.' She put her hand on his elbow. 'You'll both be fine,' she said. 'Just remember you're doing this to find Sarah.' She flashed him that broad smile of hers before she turned to leave.

Just the sound of Sarah's name made Barclay's chest throb, a hum of emotions colliding like birds in an aviary. Hope. Regret. Guilt. Pride. Disgust. And, the thing that made them all unified and cohesive, the thing that made them all solid was one thing.

Rage.

When he lay on his own bed last night, fully dressed and on top of the covers, he wished that could feel it fully. It was there, of course, but it was quiet. This person who had taken his daughter was a faceless, shapeless man. Barclay didn't know the man's eye colour, his skin tone, the shape of his nose. He didn't know the man's name or where he came from.

So, his rage turned to those he did know. To Nick and Stefan and himself for not taking the care to keep an eye on her. *She's just a little girl*, Barclay told himself. He knew that thinking this way was pointless. Blame didn't lie with Nick or with Stefan, or himself. It lay in the shadow of the man that took Sarah.

Twenty-Eight

De Silva had called O'Connor from the waiting room of the accident and emergency department of Southport hospital last night. She'd felt fine, but she knew that Murphy would be breathing down her back if she didn't at least get checked out by a doctor. She'd begun to feel that these corridors and these walls were her second home.

As she sat and waited hours to be assessed, she knew that somewhere else in that building, Mitch Whitley fought for his life. Far from the chest-rattling coughs of the old man in the thin wax jacket, the bleeding forehead of the kid now asleep on his dad's lap, the poor red-faced baby feeding at his mother's breast, a doctor or surgeon looked down on what was left of Whitley's face.

She'd got herself a full-fat Coca-Cola from the vending machine that only accepted card payments. Operating it was like some challenge from *The Crystal Maze*, but she got there in the end. She took a few sips and finally the shaking of her hands, the light-headedness, the jangling of her entire body began to subside, and she took her phone out of her pocket.

'Bloody hell, boss,' O'Connor said. 'Braxton's just been filling us in.'

'Are you all right, boss?' Harris's voice.

'You're on speaker phone,' O'Connor said.

'I'm all right,' she said. 'Just a bit achy. Nothing a good spa day wouldn't sort out.' She turned her neck until it cracked, and she felt some pressure across her shoulders release. 'I missed your calls earlier,' she said. 'Was it about Tredwell?'

'It was,' he said. 'We've got him. He's been in custody for a good few hours, though.'

She looked at her watch. Pretty soon they'd have to let him go or charge him. 'Yeah, I know,' she said. 'I'm sorry, there's not much I can do. I'll be here for another hour or so at least, I think. I'll get a taxi back to the OCC.'

'I could come and get you,' Braxton said.

'No,' she said. 'I'll get a taxi.' She winced at a pain in her back as she breathed, remembered she'd been thrown to the ground with a force and heat like she'd never felt before. 'I'm wondering if someone has been talking about this case,' she said. 'Or the exhumation request has somehow become common knowledge, and that's why Whitley did what he did tonight? He's afraid we'll find out what happened to DC McKenzie.' She waited for someone to jump in and profess their innocence, but nobody did. 'If it's not one of you lot blathering all over the shop, the only other person who knew about it was Murphy, and whoever she had to speak to about it.'

'Jesus,' O'Connor said. 'Another leak. It's like PC Maloret all over again.'

'Let's hope it's not,' she said. 'I'll speak to Murphy. But Whitley could have done what he did for some other reason, but it feels pretty fucking coincidental, and I—'

'Don't believe in coincidences,' many voices came down the line at once. She had to smile at that.

'Winifred de Silva, please,' a voice boomed over the waiting room from a short woman in a nurse's uniform. 'Winifred de Silva!'

'Look, I'm going in,' de Silva said. 'I'll call you when I can.' She was up on her feet, approaching the nurse with a slight limp in her right leg. 'Speak to Murphy.'

'One more thing before you go, sorry.' Arlow's voice, high and rapid.

'Quickly.' She put her index finger up to the not-so-patient nurse and mouthed, 'One minute.'

'It's Charlene Khan, boss,' Arlow said.

'What about her?'

'Well, she's been found dead.'

De Silva hadn't expected this. The cold tone of Arlow's delivery of the news almost made her shiver. Bea Tredwell dead. Her baby daughter dead. Her father arrested on suspicion of being the baby's father. Now the mother was dead, too. 'How?'

'That's it, boss.' She was sure she heard Arlow's awkward snigger. 'She was stabbed multiple times to her face, neck and chest. Then her house was set on fire.'

'Like Christine Jones,' de Silva said, her mind whirring.

'And like the couple at the farm in the nineties,' Arlow added.

'Get on the phone to Greater Manchester Police, Arlow,' she said. 'Speak with DCI Collins and tell him I've asked you to call. We need to get to the bottom of this, and my thinking is that this whole thing is connected.'

'Winifred de Silva,' the nurse called again, looking straight at de Silva.

'I have to go.' She hung up. 'I'm sorry,' she said to the nurse. 'Work's crazy.'

'Yeah, don't I know it.' She led de Silva through a set of double doors.

De Silva was seen to and released within twenty minutes. Just some cuts and bruises to her face, neck and hands, but nothing that wouldn't heal. Some bruising to the ribs, too. Not much they could do for that.

She called a local private hire taxi and managed to get back to the OCC in under an hour, despite the old man's exceptionally slow driving. *He'd give Barclay a run for his money in that regard*, she thought to herself. She'd called ahead and asked someone to make her a coffee and make sure it was a hot one.

By the time she'd checked in on the incident room, grabbed her coffee and made her way to the interview suite, the black coffee had already gone cold. She decided that that felt right; that her cold drink suited the tone of the past few days.

The thing about interviewing potential suspects is that very rarely do they lay everything out for you. They hardly ever tell the truth, and they *never* give you the full picture.

She'd had Braxton bring in a tray with a sandwich, some crisps and a hot drink. And as they waited for him to be brought in, Braxton struggled to find comfort in the old, hard chair next to her. He fidgeted so much he reminded de Silva of Bonnie during a long drive somewhere. Impatient and expectant. 'Will you sit still!' de Silva said, finally.

He was so close that she could smell that his deodorant couldn't quite mask the fact that he hadn't managed to shower. A uniformed officer escorted Tredwell in, pushed him into a seat and walked back out into the corridor.

'These are for you, Lee,' de Silva said. 'I'm sorry it's taken me so long to get here. I've been caught up. But I'm here now.'

Lee Tredwell ignored her, didn't even look at her, his face pale as he scoffed down an all-day-breakfast sandwich and slurped a milky coffee.

De Silva had already decided not to tell Lee about the death of his ex-wife just yet. She needed him focused. She needed honest answers to her questions, and any distraction would be an excuse for him not to talk about what he had done to Bea that resulted in her giving birth to his baby.

She was certain that all of this led back to Lee himself. He was somehow mixed up in all of this, in Bea's disappearance, probably the death of his ex-wife somehow. She wondered whether all of this led back to that app that had dogged her career for years now. The Woulds. He knew something about it, she was certain. More than all of that, she needed to see if there was any remorse in him, any sense of the magnitude of what he had done to his own daughter.

Lee finished eating and swallowed the last of his coffee. He seemed calmer than he had done previously. Less agitated. De Silva started in the usual way, telling him their interview would be recorded, to confirm his name and whether he understood why he was being held and interviewed. He answered her quickly, as though this was all some inconvenience to him.

'Why don't you start telling me about your relationship with your daughter, Beatrice?' de Silva asked.

'You what?'

'When did your feelings toward her change?'

His face seemed to tighten, his eyes narrow. 'You must be mad,' he hissed. 'I told you lot. That thing her mother is married to… it's him…'

'What makes you think it was him?'

'Because Bea said it was.'

'Shall I tell you what I think?' De Silva didn't wait for him to reply. 'I think Beatrice desperately wanted to talk to someone about the abuse she was enduring. The only way she could talk about it and not implicate her dad, implicate you, was to blame it on someone else. So, when Azad Khan came along…'

'Are you calling her a liar?' He sneered at her, his face flushed red. 'She's fucking dead and you're calling her a bastard liar.'

'No,' she said. 'I'm not. I think she blamed it on someone else to cover for a father who told her that he loved her. Who groomed her. What age was she?'

'You're trying to push me into confessing something I've not done,' he said. 'She was my daughter. I'm not some filthy fucking nonce.'

'What age was she when you first instigated a sexual relationship with her?'

Braxton shifted in his seat beside her, as though struggling to find a comfortable position again.

'She's. My. Fucking. Daughter,' Lee spat out. 'I would never!'

'Did you sneak into her room in the middle of the night when your wife was sleeping? Is that how it started?'

'What the fuck is going on here?' He leaned back on his chair, folded his arms. 'You drag me out of work and not to a Manchester station, but all the way here.'

'That's because this is our investigation,' de Silva said.

'So, if I called Manchester police now, they'd know exactly where I was and why I was here?'

'Are you sure you don't want your legal representative here?' Braxton asked, the first time he'd spoken since Lee was brought in.

'I've done nothing wrong!' he shouted. He closed his eyes, breathed deep, calming himself. 'Where are you getting this from? Has her mum been down your ear, turning it all round on me?'

'We know you've had a sexual relationship with your daughter, Mr Tredwell, because the baby she delivered is yours.'

His mouth opened, ready to speak, but it seemed as though the words wouldn't come. He looked away, his eyes on the wall to de Silva's right. 'No...'

'Yes,' de Silva said.

'She is my daughter,' he said. 'I would never do that to her. I love her.'

'I'm sure that's what you told Beatrice as well.'

'You're not listening,' he said. 'What makes you think the baby was mine?'

'We have documented forensic evidence,' she said. 'Our pathologist ran DNA samples of the baby, which showed homozygosity... long strings of identical genes.'

'So?'

'So, a child is usually born with two versions of genes, called alleles. When the child is born of parents that aren't related by blood.' De Silva watched him. There was something on his face that she couldn't quite place. His brow hung low over his eyes, and de Silva thought he looked almost Neanderthal. 'This type of anomaly is detected in children born of incest.'

Lee's jaw clenched. His neck and cheeks flushed. 'I'm not that child's dad and I've never interfered with my daughter.'

'Mr Tredwell, the forensic analysis doesn't lie,' she said. 'The evidence is there. You're a blood relation. You had access to

Bea when you and Charlene were still together, and one-on-one access since the split with your ex-wife on the weekends you had your daughter staying over.'

'So… anyone who is a blood relative could have made this homo… homozyg…'

'Homozygosity,' Braxton interrupted.

'Homo-sy-goatity,' Lee repeated. 'Someone like an uncle?'

De Silva blinked. This was a question she'd asked Carey already because she needed to be certain that Lee was the father. However, Carey did say homozygosity can occur in a coupling from any blood relative. 'Yes,' she said. 'What are you saying?'

'I know this wasn't me,' he said. 'So I have to look outside. To the family.'

De Silva leaned in. 'Do you have a brother?'

He paused. 'No,' he said. 'Well, yeah I do.'

'What do you mean by that?' Braxton asked.

'He was inside until last year. We haven't seen each other or spoken in months. But Charlene has a brother. Just the one.'

'Why did you and your brother fall out?' Braxton asked.

'Just…' Lee scanned the ceiling tiles. 'I didn't want him around Bea.'

'Why?' De Silva's brow creased as she shifted in her seat. 'Why didn't you want your own brother around Bea?'

'He was…' Lee scratched at his arms, making them red. 'He was inside for attacking some people. He's… got a temper. Now look, I know what that sounds like, but he wouldn't do this to her. He loved her.'

De Silva nodded. 'Do you have a name for Charlene's brother?'

'To be honest, I thought he'd moved away,' he said. 'Scotland or something. That's where Charlene's family are from. Originally.'

'His name?'

'John,' he said. 'John Uxbridge.'

'Do you know where he lives?'

'Last I knew, he lived in Cheshire somewhere,' Lee said. 'As I said, I thought he'd moved to Scotland, but Bea told me he'd been around a lot more since I left. Best asking Charlene, though. Not sure how much help she'll be. He was always her blue eye.' Tredwell's hands were shaking. 'You think it was him then? He's done this to my Bea?'

'We'll look into it,' Braxton said. 'Now, your brother's address?'

Lee shrugged. 'No idea,' he said. 'He moves around and I've not spoken to him since he came out. He could be anywhere.'

'I'm assuming you know his name,' Braxton said.

'Peter,' Lee said.

'We'll look into him too,' de Silva said. 'Will you submit to a DNA test to rule yourself out?'

'Am I under arrest?' Lee asked.

'No,' de Silva said, looking to Braxton. There was no reason to arrest him, though his refusal would rouse de Silva's suspicions. Something to note for later. An informal interview was not grounds under the Police and Criminal Evidence Act to obtain a non-intimate DNA sample. Lee was well within his right to refuse.

'Then no,' he said. 'I don't trust you lot or that shower in Downing Street. You think I want my DNA experimented with in some lab? Probably cloning us.'

'You think anyone with that sort of power would clone you, Lee Tredwell from Manchester?' Braxton scoffed.

'Can I call that ex of mine of mine now? Tell her not to open her trap to her brother until all of this is straightened out,' he said.

'Mr Tredwell…' De Silva's pulse raced in her ears. She couldn't keep this from him, too. 'Do you know anyone who would want to hurt your ex-wife?'

'What? Why're you asking…' It dawned on his face then, his eyes round, his mouth open. 'What's happened?'

She didn't know how this would go. They'd been separated for years, but still they had been married. She could see on his face that his heart was already breaking; it was there in the quiver of his chin, in the pink flush of his cheeks, in the glassy eyes. Maybe she'd had Lee Tredwell all wrong. Maybe he wasn't the father of Bea's baby after all.

De Silva drew in a breath and started. 'I'm afraid I have some bad news, Lee,' she said. This was the part of the job she hated most. The part she had become all too familiar with recently.

Telling someone that their loved one is gone.

Twenty-Nine

Mitch Whitley's house still smelled like smoke. The acrid stink that stung at the back of de Silva's throat made her cough. The kitchen was a mess. The windows were blown out, the patio doors too. There was some structural damage to the brickwork there, and all of the kitchen units were scorched black.

De Silva had had no time to brief the rest of the team, and Murphy was calling her every half hour for updates. But the fire investigation officer had called her at midday and advised her the Whitley house was structurally sound if she wanted to take a look around.

Beneath de Silva's feet, pools of water splashed up the protective shoe coverings and drip-dripped onto her yellow hardhat the fire service had insisted she wore. 'If it's structurally safe, why do we need these?' she'd asked. The fire officer told her it was protocol, the FIO's orders, and she either wore it or left the premises.

De Silva had asked to speak with the FIO while she donned the regulation hardhat and steel-toe-cap boots and slipped the protective crime scene shoe coverings over them which she found stashed in the boot of her car. The cause of the explosion had been linked to a gas leak, though given de Silva's account of last night, the FIO suggested that it was clear the gas was leaked on purpose. It had since been switched off to the property completely, having caused some damage to neighbouring homes.

The FIO had suggested that precautionary scaffolding should be erected with immediate effect, and to their credit, she had seen scaffolding being dragged through to the back of the house when she'd arrived back from the hospital.

The FIO described the property as 'sparsely furnished' with 'a deteriorating quality of walls, floors and ceilings'. So, Mitch had bought this massive property in Southport and left it to rot? For what reason?

The FIO had mentioned that, according to the original plans for the house, there was a basement with an entrance to it under the stairs. It appeared to have been completely blocked off sometime in the past and was inaccessible.

Outside, the scaffolders were busy working on their rigging. A man drilled wooden boards over the blown-out windows, making the kitchen even gloomier than it had been.

A space heater was sitting in the corner of the kitchen, humming to itself as it turned the air hot and wet. It felt almost oppressive, like the air was alive, wrapping itself around de Silva, threatening to choke her.

'God, it looks bad,' de Silva said. She covered her mouth to cough, then added, 'They'll have to do a lot of work to be able to get it back on the market. Nice old house like this, it'll cost a fortune.'

'Yeah,' Braxton said absently from behind her. 'Are you sure you're okay to be at work, boss?'

'Oh, stop fussing, will you? I've already got a mother, thanks.'

Braxton stepped back into the front room, out from under the kitchen ceiling, where the only damage caused by the fire was the missing living room door and the charred doorframe. 'This place feels a bit… empty.'

'Is this not minimalist?'

'Minimalist is having a small number of things per room,' Braxton said. 'This is absentalist.'

'Is that a real thing?'

He shrugged. 'I've no idea. I'm sure Barclay would know.' He looked out of the bay window onto the large front garden, where old oak trees blocked the view of the road beyond.

'I think we should take a look upstairs,' de Silva said, joining him in the front room. 'He had to have slept somewhere surely. Did you read the FIO report?'

'I've not had a chance yet.'

'The FIO said there are three bedrooms and a small bathroom on the first floor. Two bedrooms and a larger family-sized bathroom on the second floor.'

'That's a lot of bedrooms,' Braxton said, following de Silva to the stairs. The carpet there had been pulled up sometime in the past, leaving behind exposed blonde wood and a gripper rod on each step.

De Silva headed up, the protective shoe coverings making a dull thud on the stairs.

Everything they needed was in that report, but she didn't have the energy to chastise Braxton for not having caught up on it. He'd spent the drive up here on his phone. Maybe he was like her. She was one of those people – the kind that needs to be in a space to fully immerse themselves into any given place, so they can come away with a better understanding. She wondered whether Braxton too was one of those people who would touch sculptures in the Bluecoat Gallery or to run his fingers along the brushstrokes of paintings in the Walker. The type of person who needed to touch to experience. The kind of person who broke the rules.

He followed her dutifully and said, 'I think we should call Scientific Support in.'

'Do you know how many people have been through here since last night?'

'Sixteen,' Braxton said. De Silva glared at him, and he shrugged. 'See, I did read something on the way here.'

'Right,' she said, surprised. 'And I thought you were on one of those smutty sites you visit.'

'That's slander.'

They reached the landing of the first floor, where four doors were varnished in the darkest brown de Silva had ever seen.

They seemed to suck the light out of the landing, turning the place murky. She pushed open the bathroom door with the toe of her boot.

Inside was an old salmon-pink suite with white tiles on the floor and up the side of the bath. The sink had been broken, probably years ago, judging from how the break had yellowed and become infested with black mould. The toilet had no seat, but the smell from it was horrendous. Worse than the smoke downstairs. Somewhere flies buzzed, and de Silva felt bile burn at the back of her throat.

'Well at least we know someone's been here,' de Silva said, her voice flat and dry. She turned away from the bathroom as Braxton slammed the door shut behind him. The stink came out on the backdraught, and Braxton retched. 'Do you want to wait outside, cupcake?'

'No,' he said, 'I'm fine.' A lie, de Silva knew. He looked dreadful, pale and clammy. 'Let's just… move on.'

De Silva pushed open one of the bedroom doors and inside, the wallpaper hung from the walls in damp strips, as though someone had started the job of putting it up then changed their minds. Except the green floral wallpaper looked ancient, faded by time and sunlight that would have blasted in through the windows if they weren't covered with thick, green velvet curtains.

The smell of mildew hit her and she wrinkled her nose, almost backed out of the room. On the near wall, five single mattresses had been stacked one on top of the other. Each stained yellow or brown. Or red.

In the far corner near the window, a single orange bucket. The cement-mixing kind de Silva's Ritchie used to have lying around the house. The kind he'd got from B&Q that time he did some repairs to the downstairs loo. Flies buzzed around it, and de Silva could only guess what was inside.

'I think I'd like you to call Scientific Support now,' de Silva said.

Thirty

Barclay had turned the heating on when he returned home from the press briefing. He'd shivered the whole way back, reeling from the flashing lights of cameras, the never-ending stream of questions from journalists.

'What were you doing when she vanished?' they'd asked. Or, 'Being a cop, should you not have been more alert?' and, 'Is this disappearance connected to Scarlet Putney?'

That's the question, Barclay thought.

As planned, Chief Constable Bradshaw had swooped in and answered any and all questions. Barclay and Nick had fumbled their way through a brief statement, where they spoke about how much they loved their daughter and wanted her back.

When they'd left, Nick had clung to Barclay and sobbed, but Barclay couldn't help but think they should have said more. Could have done more. Had they failed her? Would any of this even help?

In the car on the way back, Nick had insisted that he went to Barclay's house. 'I don't want be alone in that house,' he'd said. In truth, Barclay was still angry from their row the night before. Between Barclay leaving and seeing each other at the briefing, Nick hadn't tried to call, hadn't sent a text message, and Barclay had begun to convince himself that a little space from each other could be just what they needed.

They'd rattled around in Nick's house, the air stale and reeking of guilt, for two days. They had had no time alone. Either Char was there with her cups of fucking tea and encouraging rehearsed phrases which, Barclay was convinced, she'd used thousands of times; or de Silva would stop by, or Lavery, or even Stefan.

He'd called Nick in the car on the way back to Barclay's house, and told him all about how Indiana was traumatised by the events, how she'd clung to her stuffed lemur and cried herself to sleep. Barclay didn't care, and he knew that Nick was just going through the motions when he said, 'Oh that's so sad. Give her hugs from me.' His voice had been flat, almost cold.

That pissed Barclay off no end. That Stefan would ring in the middle of all of this and make it about his own experience, about his niece's suffering. That seemed just like Stefan though, or just like what Barclay knew of Stefan, which wasn't much he had to admit.

'You okay?' Nick asked, sitting next to Barclay on the sofa, handing him a hot cup of coffee.

'I just feel so useless,' Barclay said, taking the coffee and putting it down on the floor next to the couch. 'I'm not doing anything. I'm used to doing… something.'

'DI Lavery said she'd ring us if she heard anything,' he said. 'And Char is in constant contact with the team.'

'Nick, if someone took her for a ransom, we'd have heard by now.' He stood and paced. 'So why did they take her? What are they doing with her?'

The question he wanted to ask he didn't even dare say out loud, in case his words somehow became the truth: what are they doing *to* her?

'I just can't sit around here and wait to hear something,' Barclay said, running his hands across his close-cropped hair. 'I'm going insane.'

'I know what you mean.' Nick sat back on the couch, grabbed a cushion and held it close to him. 'I keep thinking of these scenarios. Like what she's doing, whether she's scared. When I manage to get some sleep, it's her face I see in the dark when I wake up.' His eyes welled up. 'Is she hurt? Is she crying? Is she calling for us? And why won't they bring her back…?'

'I know.' Barclay sat back down on the couch and together they cried. Beneath the shame, the guilt, the anger, there was a sense of frustration. The not knowing. The potential of never knowing, it weighed heavy on Barclay's mind.

For the first time, Barclay felt tears slip down his face, pulled from the well of something surging in his chest. When the crying was done, Nick leaned across the couch, took Barclay by the chin and kissed his cheek. 'Do you feel any better now?' he asked.

'Not really,' Barclay said.

'No, me neither.' He drank from his cold mug of coffee and tried to force a smile. 'Look, I shouldn't have said what I said yesterday,' Nick said. 'We shouldn't be at each other's throats. We should be supporting each other. Be there for each other.'

'I try to be, but you cut me down.' Barclay turned to face Nick, to look in those waterlogged blue eyes he'd fallen in love with. 'I don't know what's going on between us, Nick, but what I do know is that I can't carry on like this any more.'

'What do you mean?'

'We're done,' Barclay said. 'We were done that morning I got up and we both knew that I had to get out of the house. I did that for you, and it killed me. I left Sarah because you couldn't handle the work that I do.'

'There was more to it than that, Ben, and you know it.' His voice had risen; his eyes flashed.

'But this is what it always comes back to,' Barclay said, keeping his voice low, determined to quell an argument before it had the chance to ignite. 'To my work and how unhappy it makes you. How it affects *you*.'

Nick looked down at his cup, and Barclay wondered whether he was searching for something to say in his milky coffee.

'But I love it, Nick, and I'm sick of apologising to you for that.' Barclay stood and paced. 'What happened to you when Lewis Lamond sent those threats… well, I still feel guilty over that. Sick about it. But I couldn't and can't change what happened. It was my work that made sure you and Sarah were safe. It was my work that caught him and meant I could bring you both home.'

'It's your work that put us in a safe house in the first place.'

'No.' Barclay shook his head. 'No, it wasn't. It was the work of a man I was trying to track down. That was a result of *his* actions. Not mine. Not because I work for the police, but because he was sick and didn't want to be caught. But we caught him. I helped catch him.'

'I don't know what to say to you, Ben.' Nick shook his head, put the coffee down on the floor and stood up. 'I thought we were on the same page.'

'No,' he said. 'I don't think we ever were.' He hadn't planned this, hadn't rehearsed it, and the words felt like tiny blades even to him. He wondered what Nick felt. 'You thought we were on the same page because I was happy to continue to feel bad about what happened. Feel bad about the work I do and how uncomfortable it makes you.'

'That's not—'

'But it is,' he said. 'It's exactly right, and what you said yesterday was right. We should have left our previous arrangements in place and not got all caught up in each other's lives.'

'What are you saying?'

'My work makes you unhappy,' he said. 'But me pretending I'm not me is making me unhappy.'

'You're talking about this right now?' Nick's face flushed. 'While our daughter is missing?'

'Don't do that,' Barclay said. 'Don't make me out to be a villain again.'

Nick reached out and tried to pull Barclay close to him, but Barclay stood and stepped away from the couch. The hurt spread on Nick's face like blood in water, sudden and red.

'You should go,' he said. 'I'll be in touch if I hear anything about Sarah, and I'll expect you to do the same.'

A tear slid down Nick's face as he pulled on his coat. The sleeves too long for his arms. He'd always had a problem finding clothes that fitted his body. Barclay held everything in, barely breathed, until finally Nick picked up his car keys and left the house.

He needed to keep himself busy. If he sat down now, he'd cry and he'd lose hours to his guilt and rage. He could make himself useful by taking Sarah's second tablet to Lavery.

He found it tucked behind her pillow in her room, and as he tried to turn it on, he found its battery was dead. He found the charger in a drawer and took it down to the kitchen, which he flicked the kettle on to boil and plugged the charger into the tablet.

He wasn't sure how he felt any more. Confused. Lost. At boiling point ready to tip over. Maybe he shouldn't have said those things to Nick. Maybe he was throwing everything in his life away because of what was happening around him. A coping mechanism. Part of his pattern. *No*, he thought, *I'm not like that.*

His mind craved the quiet, longed for a peace he wasn't sure how to find. He reasoned with himself that what he had said, the insistence that their relationship was over, was the right and proper thing to do despite what was happening around him.

The tablet woke up. The screen filled with light and colour as though waking up from a long, much-needed sleep. As the kettle rumbled on toward boiling, he swiped up on the screen, felt the sticky remnants of something Sarah had had on her hands the last time she'd used it. He considered wiping it before he gave it to Lavery but thought better of it. She'd want it how it was, sticky screen and all.

He found the photographs app and started from the beginning. Pictures of her with Nick and Mingo, their faces creased with laughter and joy. Pictures of the park or them sitting at a restaurant table. The kettle bubbled in the quiet of the kitchen as his absence from these photographs screamed at him.

There was no wonder that Nick had felt so frustrated with him and his job. Maybe it was less about the work and more about the time Barclay needed to spend away from home because of it. He should call Nick and put it right.

He clicked out of the photographs app and vowed that when they found Sarah, he'd take countless photographs with her. But that was the wish of a father who hadn't been around when it mattered. The hope of a father who could only beg God for one last chance.

He swiped right to the games she used to play. The one with the mad birds that drove him crazy, the one she'd loved and laughed at and would play for hours before they'd limited her screen time.

Then he spotted it. An app he hadn't seen before.

An app icon with the figure 2 caught in a white spider's web on a black background.

The app name read: *In2Web*.

Thirty-One

Brennan's team moved in quickly and once again the Whitley house became the main focus for those who lived on Gloucester Road. De Silva had been thankful to get out of there, the smell had almost been unbearable, and as she watched Braxton taking deep breaths near the car, she knew Scientific Support could be hours inside.

She took out her phone and called Lawrence. 'Yes, boss, what can I do for you?' she asked, her voice bright and airy.

'Hi, Lawrence,' de Silva said, not caring to match Lawrence's positive energy. 'I need you to do me a favour.'

'Of course.'

'Could you call Allerton House, the place Bea Tredwell went missing from?' She didn't wait for a response. 'I need you to speak to Dr Spearritt, set up a meeting for' – she glanced down at her watch – 'two hours' time? I know it's short notice, and I know he'll have rounds. We can either do it over video call in two hours, or I'll go down there myself later today. His choice.' She didn't really have the time to go to Manchester later, not with everything going on. She'd also have to make Collins aware out of professional courtesy, and she didn't have the time for that either. De Silva was sure he knew about the fact that they'd taken Lee Tredwell into custody and was expecting a call.

'Anything else?'

'We'll be heading back to the OCC shortly,' she said. 'Was there any news on Charlene Khan's brother?'

'Still working on it, boss,' she said. 'We'll hopefully have more when you're back.'

'All right, thanks. Bye.' De Silva hung up and approached Braxton. 'What are you thinking?' She tilted her head up toward the house.

'Well,' he said. 'I doubt the man was collecting single mattresses to test the springs, was he?'

'No.' De Silva looked back toward the house. 'Whatever he was doing, it doesn't look good, does it?'

De Silva's phone rang out loud in her hand. She looked at the screen before answering. 'Brennan, don't tell me your team are done already?'

'You're going to want to suit up, de Silva.' Brennan's voice was muffled but the edge of urgency was unmistakeable. 'Get in here and meet me at the landing on the second floor.'

De Silva looked up toward the house. 'You got something for me?' She headed toward the drive, indicated that Braxton should follow her.

'You can say that again,' Brennan said.

-

The second-floor landing led off into two other rooms, both with the same almost-ebony-coloured doors. Brennan was sitting on a ladder that led up into the loft space. In de Silva's experience of lofts, those spaces above our homes where we hide the things we don't want to see, things never ended well. Last time she had been standing in a loft, she was attacked by O'Brien after she found a manuscript damning her husband for murder, and a collection of photographs taken at Rainford Lane School for Boys, which had damned O'Brien himself.

Brennan stood when he saw de Silva and Braxton approaching in their crime scene suits. He shook his head. 'We've photographed everything,' he said, his hands out in front of him, as though to placate her.

'Okay, let's take a look.' De Silva tried to side-step Brennan and get to the ladder.

'Just wait a second,' he said. 'I just want you to prepare yourself for what's up there.'

'I'm prepared,' she said. She didn't look over her shoulder, but added, 'Braxton, you prepared?'

'Yes, boss.'

'We're prepared, Brennan,' she said. 'Are you going to show us around or leave us to it?'

Brennan sighed and turned back to climb up the ladder. 'Come on then.' He climbed up slowly, methodically, a step at a time, and it made de Silva's blood boil. She wanted to get up there. Wanted to see what was so awful about what Whitley had been hiding.

The loft was a hive of activity. Brennan's team were a nest of bees who had moved in to escape the winter, and they'd busied themselves making this place their own.

'All right,' Brennan called out. 'Give us some space here. Take a break, back in fifteen.' The white suits filed down the only exit from the loft one by one, carrying kits and cameras.

There wasn't much headroom, but de Silva could stand up straight. Beside her, Braxton hunched to protect his head from colliding with any beams.

'Bit of a squeeze, isn't it?' he said, laughing. 'I'll be sound as long as there are no spider webs. I'll be down that ladder quicker than a rat up a drainpipe.'

'Let me adjust the lighting.' Brennan fiddled with the rig his team must have assembled and shone the clinical white light into every corner of the loft. Against the far sloped wall was a bank of computer monitors – ten in total. Next to them were what de Silva assumed were hard drives encased in five black shelving units, all with blinking green, yellow and red lights. One of the computer monitors was completely black except for a logo. The brown single-line outline of the head of what looked like a bear, and either side of it two green trees, the zigzag basic design reminding her of the Christmas cards Bonnie had made. With her heartbeat thrashing in her ears, her breath shaking, she stumbled over her own feet to reach the computer.

'Don't touch anything,' Brennan said quickly. 'We're not finished yet. But I knew you'd want to see.'

De Silva's mouth was dry, like parchment or dirt or something. 'Braxton, are you seeing this?'

'I'm seeing it,' he said at her side, his voice low and breathy. 'I thought there was no power to the house?'

'There isn't,' Brennan said. 'There must be a backup generator somewhere. I've not seen it. Or heard it.'

De Silva spun around to Brennan. 'I need your team finished with this equipment, Brennan. I need to get Digital Forensics in here going over all of this.'

'What if whatever's on there has been wiped?' Braxton asked. 'Or what if they can wipe it remotely right now?'

'Good thinking.' She bit her bottom lip. 'Call Holden. See if we can disconnect anything to stop remote access without doing any damage to whatever's on those hard drives.'

'I'm on it.' Braxton clambered down the ladder, and finally all de Silva could hear was her own breath.

'De Silva,' Brennan said, his voice clear and loud in the quiet space. 'That's not everything.'

'Jesus, Brennan, give a girl a minute will you.' She eyed the monitors, the winking hard drives, and her chest swelled with everything that had come before this moment. The many hours spent researching, performing background checks on everyone mentioned in the list provided to her by Breaker, and aside from that, all of the personal stuff. The heartache. Barclay's Nick and Sarah. O'Brien. Crosby. Her Ritchie.

The answers to that, the justice for all of it, could be contained right there on those hard drives in that loft space in Southport and the only reason she was standing there right then was because Mitch Whitley tried to end his life in the most violent way.

No, she thought, *no. The gas explosion wasn't about Mitch trying to kill himself. It was about him trying to cover up all of this* and *end his life.* If de Silva hadn't shown up when she did, hadn't been sitting outside of his property last night with Braxton, then more than likely all of this would have gone up with Whitley. With the house. Then there'd have been nothing. Just charred computer screens and burned hard drives.

She looked over at the monitor and that logo to the app she knew all too well. The bear. The two trees. It was the logo the Digital Forensics team had found when they discovered the app on Kelly Stack's phone, when they'd tracked it down to the dark web. Everything led back to this. To that app, and in turn, back to Rainford Lane School for Boys.

She thought of her husband. So desperate to escape his past that he hanged himself. Of Lewis Lamond, the teenage girl killer, a victim himself. Of Billy Thompson, rotting in a prison with Mike Crosby – also victims of the men that moved through the corridors of Rainford Lane in the dead of night like monsters hunting for victims. She thought of O'Brien. One of those monsters himself. One of the reasons all of this began. From the man in the woods, Bob Brendan, one of O'Brien's friends, to this very moment. There was an interconnectedness that de Silva couldn't help but marvel at. Couldn't help but be concerned by.

So many lives changed by that place, she thought. *Too many lives lost to it. To that app. To The Woulds.*

'De Silva.' Brennan's soft voice broke her from her reverie. 'You all right?'

Her eyes snapped into focus on his face, covered by protective gear, but she could still make out the furrowed brow. 'I'm all right,' she lied. 'You said there was something else?'

He nodded and moved to the back of the loft, to a panel that had been removed, but leaned back in its original place, where a sliver of light broke through, like daylight between bedroom curtains.

Brennan moved the panel aside, let the light spill in and through, and de Silva had to cover her eyes to peer in. 'Oh my God.' De Silva didn't speak to anyone in particular, and even so, her voice cracked. Behind the panel was a well-lit room.

A chair.

Soundproofing foam panels fixed to the walls.

A mattress.

A camera.

Two cameras. Three.

A shackle chained to the wall near the stained mattress. The air was still, and de Silva almost felt as though she was breathing something thick. Not quite water, but something else. Something hard that clumped at the back of her throat, solidified in her lungs.

It was a smell she recognised. It was death. As she closed her eyes, she could picture it all. A girl, young and pale and naked, clawing at the walls with dirty, bloodied fingernails, trying to escape. She sobbed and screamed and cried, but nobody heard her. She cried so much that it drained her of any energy.

The girl would sit on the chair or lie on the bed. Her ankle chained to the wall by the thick shackle, and men would watch her through the cameras. Did they watch her struggle to escape alone, or was someone else in here with her?

'Brennan, get your team all over this,' she said. 'Can you do it in an hour?'

'De Silva, come on! We have to be careful. Methodical. We need time. Something like this could take a week.'

She thought of the computer gear in the last room, looked at Brennan and said, 'We might not have time.' He frowned at her. 'I need you to check this room for any evidence that Sarah Barclay was in here.'

Thirty-Two

Speed limits didn't matter. Red lights were an inconvenience that Barclay didn't have time for. Pedestrians crossing the road at junctions without traffic lights were just an obstacle to dodge. Barclay was sure he'd receive several tickets through the post in the coming days and weeks, but he didn't care.

He felt Sarah's tablet next to him on the passenger seat, almost like it was pulsing. He'd had the presence of mind to wrap it up in a clear plastic bag to prevent any further contamination of evidence.

Evidence, he thought. The word had never frightened him before he'd found The Woulds app on his daughter's tablet last year, but now it filled him with a cold dread. And now In2Web was there. He knew this app and he knew what it meant. He just couldn't fathom how it had gotten there.

He skidded to a stop in the OCC carpark, and others either getting into or out of their vehicles stopped to stare at him as he grabbed the tablet and ran out of the car, slamming the door. He wasn't entirely sure he'd locked it as he raced up the steps to the reception doors.

He patted himself down, couldn't feel his swipe card in any pocket. The car. It must have been back in the car. He hammered on the glass windows that looked into the reception of the OCC, shouting to the officer behind the desk. 'DI Lavery,' he screamed. 'I need to speak to DI Lavery now!'

The officer ambled over to the security doors, which slid open as he approached. Barclay tried to dart past him, but the officer grabbed hold of him. 'Move, you soft cunt,' Barclay said.

'DS Barclay, if you'll calm down and take a seat, I'll call DI Lavery for you.'

'Move!' He shoved the man out of the way with minimal effort. Bounded to the security door that led off down one of the main corridors, but it wouldn't open. 'Open this door.'

The officer got to his feet again, walked over to Barclay calmly and in hushed tones said, 'I'd watch what you're doing, Barclay; you look bleeding hysterical.'

But he was hysterical. He was frantic. Almost manic. That was the point. 'I need to see Lavery now.'

'Fine,' the officer said. 'You take a seat, and I'll give her a call. You can't get through any of these doors without your pass. And if I let you in it's my job on the line, and I'm not willing to do that for anyone. I've got mouths to feed at home.'

That struck him. He got it. Matt Higgs, desk sergeant, had a family at home that he needed to take care of. They were his main focus, his reason for being here. Barclay put his hands up in surrender. 'All right,' he said. 'All right, I'll wait. Could you tell her that I have some evidence here.' He held up the clear plastic bag containing the tablet. 'She needs to see this now.'

'I'll let her know.' Higgs gestured toward one of the hard-backed plastic chairs in the waiting area. 'Please.'

Barclay reluctantly sat down, wishing that he'd brought his swipe card with him. It could be anywhere in the car. It could even be at home in a coat pocket. The quickest thing to do was to sit and wait for Lavery to arrive.

Within just a few seconds, Higgs sauntered across to Barclay. 'She's on her way to collect you, Barclay,' he said. He took a seat next to him. 'I heard about your daughter, and I'm very sorry. But Lavery's a good detective. She'll find her.'

Barclay wanted to scream that it had been three days and Lavery hadn't found anything other than some CCTV footage of a man they couldn't identify. He kept his mouth shut. The tension in his jaw made his teeth ache.

'Barclay.' De Silva was standing near the security door Barclay had tried to gain access to earlier. She tilted her head, a clear indication that he should follow her through. 'Thanks, Matt,' she said with a wave.

'Why did he call you?'

'He didn't,' de Silva said. 'Lavery's in my incident room, so when she got the call I said I'd come up myself. Look, you can't be here. The ACC spots you here, he'll go mad. Murphy, too!'

'I found something,' he said, handing her the tablet.

'Whose is this?'

'It's Sarah's tablet.'

'Ah yeah, Lavery said you were bringing this in,' de Silva said. 'Holden's team are working on the other one now.'

'It's the one we bought for when she's at mine,' he said. 'Tried to limit the amount of things we needed to carry between houses. To be honest, she took it back to Nick's that many times, it might not be the one I bought her at all.'

'Well, thanks for bringing it in,' she said. 'I've got a few things I need to sort out here, but how do you feel about me popping over later after work? I'll bring dinner. We can have—'

'De Silva, listen to me,' he said. 'Do you remember when Ayris talked to us last year. He said that The Woulds app was sold in a bundle with a VPN.'

'In to something…'

'In2Web,' he said, impatiently.

'That's it, yeah.'

'It's on this tablet.'

De Silva seemed to stop, as though she dared not even draw a breath. She knew what this meant as much as Barclay himself knew.

'It's them, isn't it?' he asked.

'We don't know that yet.'

'Come on, de Silva, it's usually you taking these leaps and me holding you back,' he said, his voice rising. 'We both know this is connected to The Woulds.'

'Barclay… I can't have this conversation with you. We're still looking into things. Lavery is still looking into this. I'll get her to come and see you.'

'You're not telling me something, and I know it.'

She turned away but he grabbed her arm. 'Barclay, I'm just going to get Lavery,' she said.

'De Silva…' His voice was soft and gentle now, wavering. 'It's Sarah. I need to know. Is this related to the disappearance of Scarlet Putney?'

'I can't…' She looked away from him.

'Please!' His voice boomed in the reception area, so much so that Matt looked up from his computer.

'Come with me.' She turned and walked down the corridor until she found an empty room. Inside was a desk, a single computer base and monitor with a thin layer of dust on it. The walls painted white. Inside felt clinical, devoid of any character or feeling or warmth.

He closed the door behind him and perched on the edge of the desk. De Silva rolled the office chair around to face him and sat down. She opened her mouth as though to speak but couldn't. It was as though the words wouldn't come.

He watched her and waited.

'You know that Scarlet Putney has gone missing,' she said. 'PVPU have found nothing. No evidence in her bedroom or the house that anyone was even there. Scarlet Putney hasn't spoken in years. She's essentially a mute. Her mum's distraught, and as you know… the first time she went missing, they found The Woulds app on her phone.'

'And this time?'

'Her phone wasn't at the house,' de Silva said. 'There's no evidence that anyone took her, Barclay; I want you to know that. She could have just as easily walked out of the house of her own accord. Maybe she took her phone with her.'

'Has it pinged on any masts?'

'No.'

'So, it's switched off then?'

'That's what PVPU are thinking, yes.'

'Doesn't that strike you as odd? A girl her age with her phone off? And what about Bea; did you find it on her phone?'

'We wouldn't, would we,' de Silva said, her voice grave. 'The app itself has disappeared; you know that.'

'And yet here's this VPN on my daughter's tablet,' he said. 'The VPN we know came with purchases of The Woulds app.'

'Leave it with me, Barclay,' she said. 'I'll get Holden's team on it now. They're already working on Bea's phone. Charlene Khan brought it in before she... well, before she died.'

'I want to come back to work,' he said.

'Not a chance, Barclay.'

'I can't sit at home.'

'And I can't have you sat in an incident room distracted by the disappearance of your daughter.' Each word was a bullet to Barclay. 'I'm sorry, but the answer's no. The best thing you can do is go home and wait to hear from me or Lavery. Understood?'

But that wasn't the best thing he could do. He could be out there, knocking on doors, asking questions. He could be searching.

'Barclay, I asked if you understand me.'

'Yes.' His bottom lip quivered. 'I understand.'

As he turned out of the security door, heard it swish shut behind him, he took out his phone and pressed Ayris's name again. Listened for the click and the answering machine message kicked in.

Where are you?

De Silva couldn't help him, Ayris was unavailable and he knew that Lavery played by the book. He'd have to take this into his own hands.

Thirty-Three

De Silva made the drop to Holden's team and asked him to prioritise any checks on the device. She wished he'd had a way to contact Breaker. She was convinced that although her methods may not be legal, her process would be a lot quicker than Holden's by-the-book team.

'De Silva, there's a queue,' Holden had said, scratching at his large belly that stretched the already strained material of his T-shirt. Some mad cartoon characters on it that de Silva didn't recognise.

'This is Sarah Barclay's tablet,' she said. 'Her *other* tablet.' She cut him off before he could say they already had her tablet. 'I need you to check them both. In the next few hours.'

'You're joking!'

'I'm not joking, no.'

She left Holden's open-plan office, and whispers from various workstations followed her out. She didn't care. It was her job to get what she needed to further the case along, and she'd be damned if she let some queue fuck up any chances of finding Sarah.

Actually, she reminded herself, *it's Lavery's job.* She'd keep her in the loop as soon as she was finished with Dr Spearritt.

She met Lawrence in the meeting room ten minutes later, after stopping to get them both some of the bad coffee from the break room on that floor. 'I've already joined the meeting,' Lawrence said with a broad smile and de Silva was sure she caught a twinkle in her eye. 'Saves us messing around. We've got a few minutes before Dr Spearritt is due to join us.'

De Silva handed her a coffee. 'Well put it on mute at least, and leave the camera off until he joins.'

Lawrence pulled up the floor plans on a tablet, then drew red crosses on the screen in marker, which de Silva assumed – and hoped – was water-based. 'There are cameras here, here and here.'

De Silva had read something about the CCTV network somewhere. She rifled through sheets of paper they'd printed off earlier. 'The external and internal CCTV cameras are on two separate networks,' she said. 'Why would that be? Collins didn't mention that to us when he spoke to me and Barclay, but here it all is. In his own notes.'

'Maybe one of the systems was older than the other?'

'Hmm.'

'Or maybe it's some security feature? That if the internal power goes out, at least the external is still active?'

'But if that's the case, wouldn't officers from GMP have seen Bea leaving Allerton House?'

'Yeah, you're right,' Lawrence said. 'I don't remember reading anything about missing footage from external cameras though.' She looked again at the floor plans, cross-referenced it with a paper in her hand. She took a blue marker and added in circles. 'There's a camera here at the gate, the only way in or out. One on each corner of the building itself. Two on the visitor carpark.'

'What about the staff carpark?'

'One sec.' She scoured the paper in front of her, leaning in as though that would help her to concentrate. 'According to the GMP report, there are no cameras on the staff carpark.'

'Is there a back entrance to the building?' De Silva leaned closer to the tablet in Lawrence's hands. 'There. Where does that lead to?'

Lawrence traced her finger. 'The, er, the staff carpark.'

'Well, isn't that an external camera there?' De Silva pointed at one of the crosses.

'No, it's an internal one, so it won't have recorded anything.'

'Did GMP draw any conclusions on how Bea left the building without being seen by staff?'

'They didn't.'

That piqued de Silva's interest. The lack of cameras leading out to the staff carpark was an obvious route. 'Do we have a complete list of all staff on duty that day?' she asked. 'Please tell me GMP did that much at least?'

'They did. I've got it here.' She handed the list to de Silva. 'All of them longstanding members of staff. Worked there for at least five years, all the way up to twenty-five years.'

She nodded. 'That doesn't mean they're not involved in this. Bea had to get out of her room somehow, didn't she?'

'I think you're right,' Lawrence said, staring at her tablet. 'A member of staff had to be involved in getting Beatrice out of her room and out of Allerton House. I think whoever led the investigation from GMP either didn't do a thorough enough job, or...' Lawrence trailed off, then lifted her eyes to look at de Silva.

De Silva wanted to finish that sentence for her but didn't. She thought of Collins, an old friend of hers. He moved over to GMP for promotion after de Silva got the available DCI position here in Merseyside. Collins had sent over the statements of each member of staff who was on duty that day and night, but there was nothing that seemed out of the ordinary. Sooner or later, she'd have to get her team down there to speak to those people again.

I wonder if—

'I know it might not be the time,' Lawrence said, breaking de Silva's thoughts. 'But I passed.'

'Lawrence, that's brilliant news,' de Silva said, putting a hand on Lawrence's shoulder. Finally, some joy in the world around her. 'We'll have to celebrate, won't we? Tonight maybe?'

'It doesn't feel right celebrating with all of this going on,' she said. 'Let's wait until Sarah's home. And if you don't mind, could you not say anything to anyone until after all of this?'

'Of course! But I can tell you now, they'll all be so excited for you.'

An image of an older man popped onto the big screen at the front of the room. Dr Spearritt had already pushed the glasses up on his nose three times in the few seconds he'd been on screen. His hair was silver, though not by design, de Silva guessed, and his lips were almost non-existent.

Lawrence scrambled for the button to unmute their mic, and de Silva chimed in straight away. 'Hello, Dr Spearritt. Thanks for joining us.'

'Oh, uh, hello there.' His accent wasn't a Manchester one, but it did have the soft edges of the north about it. 'I'm afraid I can't see you.'

'Oh, bloody hell.' Lawrence pressed the button on the device fixed to the desk. 'Can you see us now?'

'Uh, yes I can,' he said. 'Hi.'

Dr Spearritt had that nervous energy about him, which Collins had described. It reminded de Silva of the videos Bonnie watched on YouTube, where grown men and women pretend that they're anime characters doing and saying cringy things for likes.

'I'm sorry you have to look at our faces now, Dr Spearritt,' de Silva said, smiling to ease any tension. 'It's been a long few days for all of us and I'm sorry I'm only just getting to speak to you now.'

Spearritt smiled, his teeth grey and tombstone-like. 'Yes, uh, I can imagine. I was very sorry to hear about Beatrice,' he said. 'And her mother. I saw both stories on the news.' He pushed the glasses on his nose, even though they hadn't slipped. 'How can I help you? I told everything to that chap from Greater Manchester Police.'

'DCI Collins, was it?' de Silva asked. She nudged Lawrence, then nodded down at her tablet. She wiped away the marker, drew out a stylus, and took some notes.

'Yes, that was his name. So, uh, I'm afraid I'm not sure what else I could tell you.'

'I'm Detective Chief Inspector de Silva,' she said, eager to regain control of the conversation. 'This is… Police Constable Jayne Lawrence.'

'I would say it's a pleasure to meet you both,' he said. 'But, uh, under the circumstances, I'm afraid that's not true. And, as you'll know, I'm not permitted to speak with you about Beatrice's treatment here. Not without a court order, even though she's sadly no longer with us.'

'We understand,' de Silva said. 'This is just a conversation about the night she went missing.'

Spearritt took off his glasses and cleaned them with the open sleeve of his shirt. 'I understand.' He popped his glasses back on and checked his watch. 'I'm afraid I don't have much time, and as I say, everything should be in the statement I gave to DCI Collins.'

De Silva ignored him and pressed on. 'Just to confirm,' she said, 'all of the rooms are locked at night?'

'Yes, that's right.' Spearritt sighed, as though he was already bored of de Silva's questions. 'They are operated by swipe card security pads which only staff have.'

'Which staff?'

'I'm sorry?'

'Well, for example, is it a requirement that a maintenance person or cleaner has access to patient rooms with their security card?'

'We're exceptionally careful about who has access to our patients.' There was a forcefulness in Spearritt's voice then. A defensiveness. 'If someone who is not a doctor, nurse or orderly requires access, we grant them access temporarily.'

'Was anyone granted temporary access to Beatrice Tredwell's room on or around the day she went missing?' Lawrence asked, not taking her eyes from her notes.

'I can assure you that my security team are meticulous in their—'

De Silva cut him off. She didn't have time for this. 'Could you send us a list of everyone who had access to the patients' rooms on the day and for the week before Beatrice's disappearance, please?'

'Are you insinuating that a member of my staff had something to do with this? Greater Manchester Police were not so impertinent.' He pushed his glasses higher onto his bridge again. 'But then what could I expect from…' He trailed off.

'I think the end to your sentence there was "…from someone trying to do their job", Dr Spearritt, am I right?' De Silva knew exactly what Spearritt was getting at. She'd heard it all her life from people outside of Liverpool. You speak up, you're a loud Scouser; you call someone out, you're causing trouble.

'Well…' Dr Spearritt shook his head.

'We'd like an original copy though,' Lawrence said. 'Not the names imported into an Excel document. We want to see the original print-off or screen grab from your security system itself.'

De Silva was impressed. Seeing it that way meant nobody could tamper with the information as easily.

'Well, I…'

'We could come down to Allerton House and see it for ourselves if that's more convenient for you?' Lawrence asked.

'I can have Marcus, our security manager, sort that out for you immediately.' The camera wobbled slightly, and Spearritt's keyboard click-clacked as he typed. 'I've made the request now. You should have it shortly.'

'Now, about your other security measures,' de Silva said. Lawrence handed her the tablet, open to the floor plan; she could just about make out traces of the marker. 'You have a CCTV system which, as we know, went down on the night that this storm affected the power at Allerton House.'

'That is correct,' Spearritt said. 'The storm affected power here. Everything went down. Security doors, CCTV cameras, even the backup generator went down.'

'Except the external cameras remained active,' de Silva said.

She let that hang in the air. Spearritt stared at her, unmoving for the first time since the call began. De Silva stared back, cocked her head.

'I'm afraid I have to go shortly; I have rounds to complete and reports to write up,' Spearritt said. 'What is it you're getting at, Detective?'

'How did your external CCTV cameras remain active when the internal ones didn't?'

Spearritt shrugged. 'I'm afraid I don't know,' he said.

'Doesn't that strike you as strange?' de Silva asked.

'I wouldn't know whether that is strange or is not,' Spearritt said. 'I'm not an electrician or a security manager.'

De Silva nodded, certain Spearritt seemed more nervous than before. 'Did GMP ask for a copy of your external camera footage from that night?'

'They did,' he said. 'Eventually.'

'Eventually?'

'Yes, DCI Collins came back two days later to ask,' Spearritt said. 'As though it was…'

'As though it was what?' de Silva asked, already knowing what was coming.

'As though it was an afterthought,' Spearritt answered with a sigh. 'He took copies.'

'Lawrence, make a note to contact DCI Collins and ask for him to give us access to that footage,' de Silva said. 'Do you still have copies of the footage yourself?'

'I'm afraid the system recycles memory every seven days, meaning the footage from that night has already been deleted,' Spearritt said. 'Your colleague Collins has it. Are there any other questions, Detective? I really must be going.'

'I'll review the footage and those logs you promised us, and then I'll be in touch if we need anything else,' de Silva said. 'That's everything for now, thank you, Dr Spearritt.'

Spearritt nodded and left the meeting without saying goodbye.

'He seemed a bit nervous,' Lawrence said.

'A bit? He was like a box of frogs.'

'Do you think he knows more than he's letting on?'

'Well, we'll find out, won't we?' De Silva stood. 'Could you get in touch with Collins now? Let's get moving on this.'

'Are you expecting to find something?'

'I think we've taken what Collins and GMP have told us at face value, and after Bea's death, I'm not willing to take anything else for granted. I'm also going to need to see any internal CCTV footage from around the ICU on the day that Bea died; can you get that for me?'

'Yes,' she said. 'No problem, I'll ask the hospital security team for it. What're you looking for?'

'I'm not sure yet.'

Thirty-Four

'Now, here's what we know,' de Silva said, standing in front of her team. 'Computers were found in the home of Mitch Whitley, a former police constable who worked alongside Mike Crosby, the former DCI of the Protecting Vulnerable People Unit. He had a sexual relationship with Detective Constable McKenzie, who died in an RTA. Whitley was a passenger and survived the accident.'

'Any news on the exhumation?' Braxton asked.

'I'm coming to it.' De Silva put out a hand. *Hold on, Braxton. Let me finish.* 'The computers were taken in by Holden's team, and I've asked for hourly updates. I'm not tech-savvy. I don't know what is on those hard drives or how long it'll take for Digital Forensics to analyse them. Here's what I do know.' She paused, paced up and down, looking at the ground, trying to organise her thoughts. 'When Braxton and me entered the loft at Gloucester Road, one of the computers displayed a logo. One we're all too familiar with.'

'What was it?' Harris asked.

'It was two trees and a bear's head,' de Silva said. The team looked around at each other, murmurs of shock and disgust. 'The same logo as appeared on The Woulds app.'

O'Connor piped up. 'Fucking nonces, they're everywhere. I worked with Whitley for a bit. He seemed normal.'

They always do, de Silva thought. 'The Woulds app shares its name with a photo album found in the attic of former-DSI Thomas O'Brien. And, thanks to NCA intelligence, we know the app was a tool used by predators to have easy access to their victims. It was a database if you like. A catalogue, and a private social media platform run by these… people.'

'The Woulds though,' Lawrence said. 'Would what?'

'Co-operate,' de Silva said, her voice soft. 'I think.' De Silva felt a chill run across her shoulders. She thought of the children in that school, the ones in those photographs. The others who were affected by that app. And couldn't help but circle back to her own husband, a victim of that place.

'We know from the photo album we retrieved from O'Brien's property that these boys weren't just sexually assaulted,' de Silva went on. 'They were hurt. Some severely. Tortured.'

'So how does Beatrice fit into all of this?' Lawrence asked.

De Silva shook her head. 'We can't be one hundred per cent certain on that,' she answered. It was best to be honest, to be transparent about what was happening. She needed the team's buy-in, and this was the only way she knew how. 'Lawrence?'

'Oh.' Lawrence cleared her throat and stood. 'Right, de Silva and I had a conversation with Dr Spearritt from Allerton House earlier today. We requested CCTV footage from the premises and a list of those who had access to the patients' rooms.'

'Won't GMP have already sorted that?' Braxton again.

'Well, DC Wood from Collins's team got back to me ten minutes ago,' Lawrence said. 'The files containing the external camera footage from that night have been corrupted.'

'Corrupted?'

'In layman's terms,' O'Connor said, 'they're fucked. Useless.'

'Corrupted or destroyed?' Arlow asked.

Lawrence looked to de Silva, a glance that said, *Over to you.*

'I hate to even say this about a fellow officer, or another force,' de Silva said. 'We have reason to believe that Greater Manchester Police haven't been forthcoming with information or evidence obtained from Allerton House.'

'Fuckin' Collins,' O'Connor said. 'I never liked that self-serving little cunt. Thinks he's the big I-am because he was buddies with the ACC back in the day.'

'We don't know anything for certain yet,' de Silva said. 'I've already asked Murphy to speak with her contact at GMP to get access to any of Beatrice's personal devices. Bea's phone was destroyed during testing. Some tech malfunction.' She shook her head.

'That seems a bit suspicious, if you don't mind me saying, boss,' Harris said.

'I don't mind you saying,' de Silva said. 'I think you're right.'

'If all of this is connected, will they come back then?' O'Connor asked. 'The NCA?'

'I tried to call Ayris plenty of times, like you asked,' Braxton said. He winced. 'I get the feeling he's been avoiding my calls.'

De Silva had tried to call Ayris multiple times herself to fill him in on the recent updates. Something else she'd have to take to Murphy.

'What about Scarlet Putney?' Braxton asked.

'Lawrence?' de Silva said, inclining her head. She wanted to see whether Lawrence could deliver this information to the team, the way a detective would.

'Scarlet Putney is thirteen years old. She's being treated as a missing person and so PVPU will be handling the bulk of the investigation. We'll be looking at it because now we know there's a connection there with The Woulds app,' she said, eyes on her notes.

De Silva closed her eyes, felt the weight of her conversation about Scarlet with Murphy earlier pull down on her stomach. She felt sick. Like she could vomit on the carpet tiles of the incident room. Like she needed to sit down. Take all of it in herself first.

'Scarlet Putney disappeared at age seven and reappeared shortly after,' Lawrence said. 'She was found walking down the motorway near Warrington. She wouldn't talk. Psychologists concluded that she was suffering from trauma-induced amnesia. She'd been raped, that much was clear from physical evidence. Repeatedly. She exhibited signs of…'

Even as Lawrence said the words, de Silva felt like she would always be in the orbit of these horrendous types of crimes. Answerable to them. Pulled in by them until finally, maybe, she was destroyed by them. Torn apart by the gravity of each and every one of them.

'What happened to her was continual,' de Silva said. 'It happened again and again, and she was never allowed to heal. It was torture,' de Silva said, her voice cracking. 'When she was reported missing, her phone was found in a bus stop in Bickerstaffe. Miles away from where she lived. When Digital Forensics got a hold of it is when they found The Woulds.' She coughed to clear the anguish from her throat, thick and sticky.

'We spoke with her mum, Leah,' Harris jumped in, scratching his chin. 'We talked about all the stuff we already know. That Scarlet was reported missing for a period of time. That The Woulds app was found on her phone. Leah couldn't say how it got there.'

'What about her dad?' Braxton asked. 'What did you find out there?'

'Jamie Putney,' Harris said. 'An electrician, working on corporate contracts for a large-scale north-west-based firm. He travels a lot and has been away with work in Scotland, which we had corroborated by his employer, at the time Scarlet went missing. He's on his way home now to be with Leah, though the two are separated.'

'Separated why?' De Silva folded her arms, staring at Harris, taking every morsel of information in.

'Leah said that he didn't know how to cope with what happened to Scarlet,' Harris said, shaking his head. 'Couldn't handle it. He went away working more and more after she came back, and finally they just drifted apart.'

'So, what now?' Braxton asked.

'I've a few things I need to speak to Murphy about,' de Silva said. 'Braxton, we asked for a list of people who had swipe card access to Bea's room in the days leading up to her disappearance. Could you comb through it?'

'I'm on it,' Braxton said, rolling himself off toward his workstation.

De Silva nodded. 'Harris, your interview with the guy from Southport pier. The one who was there the night Bea jumped out of the car and escaped. Warren Childs, was it? How did it go?'

'That's him, yeah,' Harris said. 'Oh, he was all full of tears and regret.' He rolled his eyes. 'He thought they were having a domestic, thought she'd run off and decided to leave them to it. Said he had a breakdown when he read about her in the papers, saw her picture, you know?'

'Did his description of the man from the black car change at all?' de Silva asked.

'Not one bit,' O'Connor chimed in with a smirk.

'So much for conscientious citizenship,' de Silva said. She looked around the room. 'Right, Arlow...'

'Right, yes,' Arlow said, standing now too. He looked across to Patel and Yates and nodded.

'We spoke with the pathologist at the Greater Manchester Coroner's Office,' Patel said. 'He's completed some preliminary examinations but can't get to a proper post-mortem for a few days.' Patel grabbed notes from a desk nearby, stumbling over her words as she spoke. 'Charlene received nineteen stab wounds across her back and shoulders. Her chest. Her throat. Her face. He said it appeared to be a frenzied attack.'

'Anything else?' de Silva asked. 'There was evidence of pre-mortem scalding on the previous victims, wasn't there?'

'Yeah.' Yates spoke up for the first time. 'The pathologist's initial report said there was evidence of scalding across the victim's chest.'

Just like the others, she thought. 'All right, we need to start coming up with some answers on that one, the three of you.' She stepped to the board, scrubbed it all clean and wrote in the centre of it *Rainford Lane*. She drew a line from the centre and wrote *The Woulds*. Another that said *Scarlet Putney*, others for *O'Brien*, *Mike Crosby*, *DCs McKenzie and Cullen* and *Mitch Whitley*. More lines that led off to the far right for *Christine Jones*, *Charlene Khan*. 'This is all connected,' she said, the marker squeaking as she wrote. Finally, she wrote *Sarah Barclay*.

De Silva went on. 'Everyone on here has a link, or potential link, to The Woulds app or that school,' she said. 'We need to change focus now and find those links. Arlow, I want to know what caused the fires in each of these cases.' She pointed to the names on the board.

Arlow's phone rang out as he nodded to de Silva. 'Yes, boss, we're on it.'

'All right then, everyone, we've got work to do.' She clapped her hands twice. 'Let's get to it.' She knew this whole thing was connected. She just didn't know how Bea Tredwell and her poor baby were connected to it.

'We also looked into Lee Tredwell like you asked,' Yates said, her voice shaking. 'There's a few things you're going to want to hear.'

Thirty-Five

De Silva left the incident room after asking Harris to call Lee Tredwell to make himself available today. 'Whether we go to him or he comes here, I don't care,' she said. 'But we're getting to the bottom of this now.'

She had checked in with Murphy to raise her concerns about Collins. She hated doing it, but her investigation was suffering because of him. There was something about all of this, some reason why he was being unhelpful. In her experience evidence didn't become corrupt or damaged overnight. But more than that, she knew what this could lead to. She'd be a grass, and that type of stain isn't easily washed away.

'There's no decision yet on the exhumation of DC McKenzie's body,' Murphy had said. 'But I am getting somewhere. Give me until the end of the day.'

She'd left Murphy's office with every intention of going back to the incident room. The team were exhausted, working all hours and she knew they needed rest. They needed time away from their desks, and as the case swirled around her head, it began to swell.

She needed some fresh air.

De Silva found the OCC carpark to be almost empty except for a few staff cars she recognised – Harris's and O'Connor's – and a silver Honda she didn't. As she walked down the steps at the edge of the carpark, she wished she had a cigarette. She'd never smoked, not once in her life, but right then it felt like the thing to do. Smokers always said it relaxed them. Took the edge off. She could certainly do with that. These cases were all interconnected, and now at the centre of it was the little girl of a colleague. A friend.

The driver-side door of the Honda opened. 'Evening, Detective.' A voice she recognised, and a face she'd love to slap.

'Not today, Mr Matthews,' de Silva said. She turned away from him and walked up the steps to the entrance of the OCC. She hadn't seen him in around two years, and the *Liverpool Journal* had started sending a different reporter to briefings. She had assumed he'd been fired – though he should have been given the sack years ago.

'Can I have just a second,' he said. 'Er, please?'

She stopped dead in her tracks. Joel Matthews never said please, and she was sure she'd never heard him say thank you. She was also positive that he'd never used any manners for as long as he'd been on the payroll at the local rag.

She turned back to him and studied him. Matthews looked bedraggled. His short blond hair was a mess and in desperate need of a cut and style. His eyes looked swollen, probably from lack of sleep, and his clothes were creased. There'd been some sort of alien movement in recent years where people had stopped ironing their clothes, and that offended de Silva. She wasn't the tidiest, but she at least ironed her clothes.

'I don't have the time for this,' she said.

'Oh, I've heard,' he said. 'Missing girls, a dead baby, Beatrice Tredwell's mother found dead. And now little Sarah Barclay.'

'What?' She shook her head. 'No, I'm not even surprised you know. Pick that little nugget of info up from whatever sleazy cesspit you lot are a part of?'

He smiled, a sickly, smug thing. 'People like to talk.'

'Mr Matthews, if you've come here to gloat, then spare me. If you've got information, then share it,' she said. 'Otherwise, kindly do one.'

'I suppose you've already made the connections between the murder of Charlene Khan and Christine Jones, and that couple near St Helens in the nineties?'

'You know I can't discuss an active case with you,' de Silva said. 'I'd never discuss it with *you* at any point to be fair, not after what you did to Maloret.'

'Would it interest you to know that former-PC Maloret is pursuing a career in investigative journalism?'

That surprised de Silva. But, she supposed, Maloret had to find a career she could excel in. She'd have made a great officer, an asset to the team, if she hadn't been leaking information to Matthews for financial gain. Whether her mother's care bills were extortionate or not.

'What else do you know about it?' Matthews asked.

'I've already said that I—'

'Do you know who Christine Jones is?' he asked, interrupting her. 'Or was, as is more accurate now.'

De Silva studied him then. 'What do you know and who from?'

He tapped his nose. 'I can't reveal my sources, de Silva, you know that.' He sighed.

'I'm not at liberty to discuss anything with you, Mr Matthews.'

'Oh, cut the bullshit.'

'Watch your fucking mouth.'

Matthews leaned against his car, rubbed at his eyes, and for a moment de Silva was convinced there were tears there. He had caused her so much strife through the years, had targeted Maloret and bribed her into giving him information about the Lamond case. Then after that… he seemed to have disappeared.

'I've been a little… down on my luck,' he said. 'Thought I'd hit it big time going to a national. But they don't write how I write. They don't do things how I do things.'

'Oh, they don't coerce police officers at the start of their careers into giving you information in exchange for money? My heart bleeds for you.' De Silva knew there was an acidic venom in her voice. 'I have to go.'

'Christine Jones was the deputy head,' Matthews said. 'At Rainford Lane School for Boys.' He stood straight.

'You're not telling me anything I don't already know,' de Silva said.

'Then you'll know that she's right there in Meeks's manuscript. I've read it. She's right there in some of Lamond's earlier conversations with Merseyside Police. I've read them, too.'

'What do you want, Mr Matthews?'

'I want my life back,' he said. 'I want my career back to how it was.'

'I can't help you with that.'

'You can,' he said. 'All I want is an exclusive when you catch whoever is doing this.'

De Silva had the feeling that catching whoever did this would not be a simple task. More than that, the worst thing a detective can be is indebted to a journalist. 'There's nothing you could possibly offer me in return that would make me want to give you an exclusive.' She turned away from him and said, 'Bye, Mr Matthews.'

'I've been in contact with someone,' he said, shouting to her now. 'Someone who knows you and knows this case very well.'

'Who?'

'She calls herself Breaker.'

De Silva's breath caught in her throat. Breaker was the person who had leaked The Woulds databases to de Silva last year. She was the reason they had managed to arrest O'Brien and find the photo album brimming with evidence in his loft.

'Why?' de Silva asked. 'What does she want?'

'She says she has information,' Matthews said.

'About what?'

'Well, that's the thing,' Matthews said. 'She wanted me to come to you. Wants to set up a meeting. Face to face.'

'She already has my phone number.'

'She said that you'd say that.' Matthews approached her now, climbing the steps slowly. 'Breaker told me to tell you that she doesn't trust your phone lines, not your work phone, personal mobile or your home line. That's why she reached out to me.'

'And what do you get out of it?'

'That exclusive I so desperately need.'

De Silva thought about it. This could all be a load of bullshit and knowing Matthews it probably was. But she couldn't risk stepping back into that incident room knowing that she'd let a potential lead pass her by. No matter how dubious the source.

De Silva nodded. 'Set it up.'

'I'll be in touch.'

She turned away from him then, heard his car door close and the rattling of his battered silver Honda as he left the carpark. Her phone rang out as the OCC main entrance doors slid shut behind her. O'Connor calling. 'I'm on my way down now,' she said, by way of hello.

'Good,' O'Connor said. 'Tredwell's in the interview room.'

-

Lee Tredwell was sitting at the interview room table, fiddling with the drawstring on his tracksuit bottoms. 'About fucking time! Are you going to tell me what this is all about or what?' Tredwell asked, arms folded.

De Silva smiled as warmly as she could, but she despised this man. He was a liar, a fraud. 'In our last conversation, we spoke about the genetic evidence our pathologist found, suggesting that the baby Bea gave birth to was fathered by a blood relative,' de Silva said, determined to press on. Distraction being the thief of time.

'I remember you blamed it on me,' he said.

'At the time, you suggested that your ex-wife's brother may have some involvement. That he's the only male blood relative that could have possibly done it, given that your brother was in prison until recently, and you've not seen him since his release.' De Silva stared him down. He began to fidget.

'And have you found her brother?'

'We're having some trouble locating him,' O'Connor said.

'Yeah, I'll bet you are.'

O'Connor leaned in. 'What do you mean by that?'

Tredwell shrugged. 'He's a slippery little fuck,' he said. 'Always disappears and reappears whenever he feels like it. I got him a job in my place once. Kept fucking it up. Dunno why they kept him on.'

'You said that your brother was inside for attacking someone,' de Silva said.

'That's right,' Tredwell said. He tilted his chair, swinging on the back two legs.

'You didn't say he was inside for rape,' O'Connor chimed in.

Tredwell shook his head, his chair dropping onto all fours again. 'Look, Peter did what he did, and he's paid for it.'

De Silva was unsure rapists ever truly paid. The transaction of being inside for violence against women seemed woefully one-sided to de Silva. The lives of Peter Tredwell's victims would be forever altered, and what was the cost to Peter himself? Twelve years of his life with three square meals, a warm roof over his head and a high probability of re-offending.

'You told us he was released from prison last year,' de Silva said. 'And that you haven't seen him in months. In that time, your daughter becomes pregnant by someone with a familial connection and disappears from a secure psychiatric facility.'

'He wouldn't have done this,' Tredwell said. 'He loved Bea like a daughter. Besides, there's no way he could have broken into that place. He's thick as pig shit.'

'Tell us where he is, Lee,' de Silva said. 'What if he did do this to Bea? What if he's the reason she got hurt? What if he's that poor baby's father?'

'Ah fuck,' he said. 'Listen, I mean it... he wouldn't have done this. He wouldn't have touched her. He definitely wouldn't be involved in any of this. There's no point speaking to him; I know he wouldn't have.'

'I think when someone sexually attacks a woman, all bets are off, don't you?' de Silva asked. She knew that although he'd been arrested for a single count of sexual assault, around

84 per cent of rapes in the UK go unreported, a statistic that frightened her. Four in every five victims say nothing. She wondered how many of Peter's victims had kept quiet. 'I'm going to ask you again before I charge you with obstructing a police investigation, Lee. Give me his address.'

Thirty-Six

She had him. De Silva had an address from Lee, and she'd kept him in a cell for obstructing a police investigation. She'd let him go just as soon as they had hold of his brother. 'O'Connor, I want you to call ahead and speak to someone from Greater Manchester Police,' de Silva said as they watched Tredwell being escorted away from the interview room. 'Not Ed Collins, do you understand? We'll need some support to make the arrest. It could turn nasty.'

'Yes, boss,' he said.

'De Silva!' Murphy's voice from further down the corridor.

'Think that's my cue,' O'Connor said, scurrying off toward the lifts.

The two top buttons of Murphy's blouse were unfastened which was unusual for her. She had flushed cheeks and was slightly breathless, and de Silva presumed she'd taken the stairs down from her office. Her preferred method of getting around the station. In her hand was a white envelope, padded and thick.

'You looking for me, ma'am?'

'Yes,' she said. 'I've just got off the phone with DSI Little from Greater Manchester Police.'

'I'm not familiar, ma'am.'

Murphy waited until a uniformed officer passed them in the corridor and lowered her voice. 'DCI Ed Collins has been called in for internal review in his handling of the Beatrice Tredwell disappearance from the Allerton House facility.'

'Is that because of what I said?'

'No, I received the call from DSI Little before I'd had a chance to reach out to him myself about all of this. A detective constable raised the alarm after some… er… unusual methods of investigation on Collins's part.'

De Silva searched the woman's face. Maybe her cheeks weren't pink from the exertion of climbing the stairs after all. She'd known this was coming, felt it percolating in her gut. 'Ma'am, is there something you need to tell me?'

'I need you to understand that what I'm about to tell you is confidential in the extreme, Win,' she said. 'Do you understand me? If anyone finds out what I've told you, they'll track it right back to Little and he's my friend; it'll end both of our careers.'

'I won't say a word,' she said. 'You can trust me.'

De Silva knew that, even in saying those words, she'd never given Murphy any reason to trust her. To be fair to de Silva, Murphy hadn't ever given reason either.

'Upon investigation, Collins's bank account showed unusual activity.'

'Unusual how?' Her heart quickened. This was it. This was the reason GMP had been withholding information from her, had told her that evidence was damaged or destroyed.

Murphy pushed open one of the interview rooms; de Silva followed her in and closed the door behind them both. Murphy looked up to the corner of the room and de Silva knew she was checking the camera for a red light. They were only recording when there was a suspect in here.

'Unusual for a few reasons.' Murphy puffed up her cheeks and let out a long breath. 'There were large amounts paid directly into an account of his on the twenty-eighth of each month. The bank account was completely separate to the joint account he had with his wife. A different bank and everything.'

'Where was it coming from?'

'A company called T & K Holdings.'

De Silva's mind whirred into action. She knew that name. She'd heard it mentioned somewhere already. Where was it she'd—

Murphy pressed on. 'I looked into this as a favour to Little. T & K Holdings owns shares in all kinds of UK-based businesses. Haulage, imports and exports, contact centres, rail freight, cyber tech and security. God, they even hold shares in a private firm which manages prisons.'

'I know,' de Silva said.

'You know?' Murphy's shoulders seemed to tighten. 'How do you know?'

'I've come across T & K Holdings before.'

'When?'

'They owned, or funded, a laboratory solutions company.'

'And?'

'They were the ones who employed the pathologist who conducted the post-mortem on McKenzie,' de Silva said. 'Francesca Watson.'

De Silva couldn't guess what the hell was going on here and wished she could get in a room with Ed Collins and sort all of this out.

'This coupled with the things you've told me about the evidence they've been unable to provide… well, I don't know what Ed Collins was up to,' Murphy said. 'But I'm hoping that you can find out. I'm going to speak with the chief constable now to chase your request to exhume McKenzie's body, given this new lead.'

'Thank you, ma'am.'

'How are you doing downstairs?'

'We're busy, but we can handle it,' she said. That was a lie, she knew. She bit her bottom lip, determined now to reciprocate with Murphy like she'd never done before. 'To tell the truth, I'm struggling,' she said. 'Beatrice, Scarlet, Sarah. Whatever T & K Holdings has to do with this. The murders. And on top of that now I have to find Lee Tredwell's brother.'

'His brother?' Murphy sounded incredulous, her voice high. 'I thought he was in prison.'

De Silva's mum used to say, *Well, you know what thought did, don't you? Pissed himself and thought he was sweating.* She'd laugh like it was funniest thing on Earth, and de Silva would laugh with her, not really understanding what she meant. 'Yeah,' de Silva said. 'Well, he's out.'

'Do you need me to do anything?' Murphy asked. 'It's been a while since I've been out in the field, and to be honest with you, Win, I'm eager to get my teeth into something. Like the old days.'

'Woah, slow down, Xena,' de Silva said. Murphy sniggered. 'We think we found a possible link with Sarah's disappearance and The Woulds app. Digital Forensics are working on it, but I hope we'll have some answers soon.'

'I know it's personal for you, Win, but leave that case to Lavery,' Murphy said, her voice a warning. 'She's capable.'

'Is there any way that she'd consider staying close?' de Silva asked. 'As in, in my incident room? These cases are all connected; I'm convinced of it.'

'You know how she is, Win,' Murphy said. 'A territorial woman. But I don't think she's an idiot. She understands how important this is.'

'Thank you,' de Silva said, turning away.

'What will you do now?'

'I need to speak to the team,' she said. 'Morale's low down there.'

'Do you need me to come down and—'

'No, I've got it,' de Silva said. 'You just sort Lavery out and get me permission to exhume McKenzie's remains.'

'The footage Collins said was destroyed...'

'Yeah?'

'DSI Little found it,' she said. 'It's intact, so he says, and I've given you access to it via email.'

What the hell has Collins been up to? she wondered. 'Thank you,' she said finally.

'Here's a list of the companies associated with, owned or funded by T & K Holdings.' Murphy handed the envelope to de Silva, and she held it to her chest, nodded with a warm smile that she hoped Murphy read as a thank you, and left the interview room.

–

Downstairs, the energy in the incident room was flat, a heavy stillness interrupted only by the odd sigh, the clearing of a throat, and de Silva wondered whether everyone in that room could hear the ticking of her mind. A clock counting down the seconds to whatever horror was coming next.

Harris fiddled with the connection from the projector, struggled to get it into a port on the side of his laptop. Finally, he managed, and the image on the projector screen on the back wall blinked before it came into focus.

'And this is footage from where again?' Braxton asked.

'Allerton House the night of the storm,' de Silva said. 'It's the exterior, the staff carpark. The night Bea went missing.'

Harris pressed the play button.

'We were told there was no footage from the camera on the staff carpark,' Lawrence said, almost defensively as though she herself might have dropped the ball somewhere.

'Relax, Lawrence,' de Silva said. She couldn't yet confirm Collins's involvement in all of this, though it burned inside her.

There was no sound on the video, but de Silva could see rain falling in sheets; the sky at the top of the screen was grey, and wind shook the camera slightly, making the image wobble. The view was of the tiny staff carpark, where just five cars sat, being hammered by lashing rain. The angle was of the back of Allerton House.

'If there's more to this, skip it on,' de Silva said.

Harris skipped the footage on until the back door was flung open. Then, he stopped it, rewound it a little until he found the exact place, and pressed play. A man dressed in black and wearing a cap came out, carrying something on his shoulder. They all stepped closer. Not something, some*one*.

'That's her, isn't it?' O'Connor asked. 'That's Bea Tredwell.'

'Looks like it,' de Silva agreed.

They watched as the seemingly lifeless body was put into the back of a black van. De Silva had to squint to focus but could see no real detail. 'Rewind it a second,' she said. 'There, pause.' She stepped closer to the screen, felt the heat of the projector lights on her skin, dazzling her eyes. But she was certain. The baseball cap. It took her back to just a few days ago in the interview room.

'I need you to get a copy of this section to DI Lavery right now,' de Silva said. 'And I need you to get it upstairs to the Visual Evidence Unit for enhancement.'

Harris disconnected his laptop and was out the door. 'On it,' he said as he breezed past.

'Did we get anything else from GMP?' de Silva asked.

Braxton moved through some files on his computer. 'A statement from Azad Khan, which is interesting. Stating he always thought that Bea's dad was sexually abusive. He made that statement when he was questioned following Bea's allegations against him.'

'Something else DCI Collins didn't share with us,' de Silva said, scratching her chin. Ed Collins's involvement in all of this was blatant now. There was no denying it. The thing she needed to figure out now was whose payroll he was on.

De Silva looked around the room. Some answers were coming into focus. The truth taking shape and form, separating itself from lies, untruths, betrayals, but still the morale was so low. Despite everything with Barclay and Sarah, it was this team's job to carry on. It was what was expected of them. To solve the case. To bring justice to those who deserved it, and those who needed it.

De Silva wondered whether the personal cost of her work was too high a price for her to pay, and looking around at the others, she knew they felt the same.

She cleared her throat and stood up, moved to the centre of the room, where the evidence board containing their case notes so far waited behind her. Unsolved. 'We're several team members down. I know that,' she said. 'And Sarah Barclay feels personal. It does to me, too. But we have to keep the hope alive that we'll find Sarah, find Scarlet, with DI Lavery's help.'

'You know they call her Cordelia Ice Tits, don't you?' O'Connor said. 'Cold fish, that one.'

'She's the lead investigator into the disappearance of your colleague's daughter, O'Connor, so I'd do yourself a favour and swerve that shit,' de Silva said, staring him down. Her voice took on a commanding air, the one she used when she needed people to listen to her. And they did. O'Connor's face flushed pink. 'We have Peter Tredwell's address. Lawrence and I are heading out there with backup from GMP tonight. This case *is* moving forward.'

'Can I say something?' Braxton asked. 'I just feel like... with this whole case. It's constant. And, well, what's the point? We're always on the backfoot.'

'One step forward, three steps back,' O'Connor chimed in. 'Like we're fighting a losing battle.'

Silence fell in the incident room. Braxton and O'Connor were right. Continuing on now felt like a slog to de Silva, too. But it was important work, and besides, Scarlet and Sarah were still out there. So were the men who were doing this to kids across the country. And so was the killer who'd claimed the lives of Christine Jones, Charlene Khan and the Simmonses in the nineties.

'I hear you,' de Silva said. 'It's hard to carry on, isn't it? But we have to. That's why we're here. We can find Sarah, and Scarlet. We can bring them all to justice for the things they've done. Could bring a killer to justice. If this is all connected in the way we think it is, then these people... this app... it's destroyed so many lives already, and it will continue to destroy lives every day. Unless we do something about it.'

'Look at us!' Arlow said. 'We're a small team. Under-resourced, over-stretched. How can we do everything we need to do when the government force us to make cuts almost every month?'

'So then, what do we do, Arlow?' she asked, her voice raised slightly. 'Leave? Jack it all in because it's too much?' Her mind was beginning to clear itself, letting go of everything it had tried to work through these last few days.

'We can't pretend that we're not all struggling any more,' Arlow bit back. 'I'm sick of pretending that I'm not a human being too!'

'Arlow's right,' O'Connor chimed in. 'You look outside, and the people out there think we're scum. Think we're grasses. They think we don't do enough to protect them when they need it but won't give us the information we need to protect them. They think that we protect nonces and child killers. That some of us *are* nonces and child killers.'

Braxton said, 'And they're right, aren't they. O'Brien, Mike Crosby and now it looks like even Ed Collins was on the take. Just those three alone give every single one of us a bad name.'

She felt it then. A kind of disentanglement, like a pull in a jumper that would, if yanked, only get worse. 'Look, I get it,' de Silva said. 'I really do. But listen, we have people counting on us. The only thing we can do is carry on. That's the only choice.'

'Not for me it isn't.' O'Connor stood and headed for the door.

'Where are you going?'

'I'm not sure I can do this any more, boss,' he said. 'I think everyone in this room needs to ask themselves whether their heart's still in it, too. In the face of the odds stacked against us, what's the fucking point?' He left, the incident room door creaking on its hinges.

De Silva expected a doctor's sick note on her desk by mid-morning tomorrow. She cleared her throat. 'This is the job we wanted,' she said. 'We vowed to keep everyone safe.'

'But at a cost to ourselves,' Braxton said. 'To our own health.'

'Oh God, listen!' Her voice rose now. 'I'm exhausted. I'd love nothing more than to go home, or to walk out that door like O'Connor. But the truth is that I feel that the only choice here, the right thing to do, is to stay. Is to find Sarah. Find Scarlet. Solve these murders. Bring these bastards to justice.' She looked around at them, at their exhausted grey faces, their tired, dull eyes. 'I don't know about you, but I'm going to keep going. For Sarah. For Bea and Scarlet and for every victim of that fucking school and that bastard app.

'I won't stop until every single one of these people, the people behind The Woulds, the Rainford Lane predators, have got no place left to hide.'

Thirty-Seven

The intention was not to follow them. Not really. Barclay's mind was foggy, unfocused, since he'd thrown his medication away. The only thing that made sense to him was to find Sarah at any cost.

De Silva had instructed Barclay to go home and wait, but he couldn't. And after Ayris didn't answer his phone again, Barclay felt like he had no choice. As he pulled onto the M62 far enough back from de Silva's white Ford Kuga, he knew that he could turn back at any moment.

Exhaustion hit him with the weight of a sack of bricks. He turned his head until his neck click-clicked and crunched, releasing tension in his shoulders. His eyes felt heavy as the motorway lights passed him in hues of hazy orange. The cat's eyes fastened into the road like buttons holding it together winked at him as he sped on, keeping to the outside lane.

He knew that if de Silva saw him, she'd lose her shit. Force him to go back home. But if there was even just a whiff of a possibility that they had a lead on Sarah, then he had to know. But where was Lavery? He hadn't seen her when de Silva and Lawrence got into the car. He hadn't even seen her pristine BMW 5 Series outside the OCC. Maybe they were going to meet her.

They sped on down the motorway, and it became apparent to Barclay where they were headed when they passed the Warrington junctions and on toward Manchester. What were they going to Manchester for? His mind became crowded, like a horde of voices and thoughts all speaking at once. Charlene

Khan lived in Manchester, but she was dead. Lee Tredwell still lived there.

What was it? That he was so distraught by the death of his daughter that he kidnapped Sarah? *No, no, couldn't be*, he told himself. He was forgetting about the In2Web VPN app he'd found on Sarah's tablet. Who could have put it there, and why, he couldn't yet guess.

They pulled off the motorway about forty minutes later and drove down some main roads where the traffic was light. They pulled into a police station, though Barclay didn't have time to clock the name of it. He had to drive on or risk being seen. He pulled around the corner and stopped, U-turned and parked right on the junction, where it was likely he could get pulled by some busy-body bobby.

He could see the carpark of the station through some shrubs, saw de Silva and Lawrence climbing into the back of a police van, followed by some stern-faced constables. One of them stuck out especially, a grinning woman with short hair and broad shoulders. She looked like she played rugby, Barclay decided.

There's no turning back now, he told himself. Whatever they were up to was something big. He knew that de Silva couldn't ever tell him, so he'd have to find out himself. He'd have to see whatever this was play out in front of his face.

He heard the van doors slam, the engine roar as it came to life, and as it pulled out onto the main road, Barclay slipped in behind it. He didn't care if de Silva clocked him now; it didn't matter. They were too far into this to stop now.

Rows of old terrace houses zipped by, and Barclay kept his eyes on the road. They drove for what felt like hours, and all the while, Barclay's stomach grumbled. Nerves or hunger, he couldn't tell. Didn't care.

The police van came to a soft and slow stop on a quiet street, where redbrick houses flanked the road. Snow had been banked against the kerbs, piled high in varying shades of grey.

Barclay stopped and parked on the opposite side of the road, further back. He turned his headlights off and killed the engine immediately. He slid down behind the steering wheel as the side panels and back doors of the van opened and the team climbed out.

Last of all, de Silva and Lawrence jumped down. They'd taken off their big coats, and Barclay could clearly see their plain clothes harnesses, packed with PAVA, cuffs, a radio and a torch. Barclay knew that de Silva wore hers under her jacket or coat wherever she went now, since everything that happened with Lewis. Just like he did himself when he was on duty.

He peered over the top of his dashboard and ducked again as de Silva seemed to be staring right at his car. Did she know? Had she spotted him? He didn't care. He peeked again, and she crossed the street with the others toward an Asian mini-market. Already, people had come out of their houses to watch.

The uniformed officers were ahead, and Barclay climbed out of his car, closed the door gently so that it made no sound, and pressed the lock button on the key fob. His hazards flashed twice.

He jogged softly against the hedges of a garden to the edge where a recess in the road dipped inward to the entrance of the mini-market. Barclay could see now that there was a flat above it. He could hear de Silva's voice saying, 'Do you have trouble here a lot, Fairhurst?'

The tall, well-built woman spoke. 'Fights. Drunken singing inside and outside the flat. Loud music,' she said. 'People around here just want a quiet life, and they've got this tosser living upstairs.'

'Have you personally responded to any violence here?' Lawrence asked, her voice almost imperceptible.

Fairhurst nodded. 'Once,' she said. 'He'd been drinking, as usual, coked out of his eyeballs. Thought his girlfriend had been making eyes at another bloke down the local. He broke her jaw.'

'Christ,' de Silva said. 'How old was she?'

'Younger than him,' Fairhurst said. 'She was in her twenties, and he's well into his forties now. This was only last year. He said she fell down the stairs of the flat. She was that stoned, I doubt she felt a thing. In the end, she corroborated his story about the stairs, but...'

'But you didn't believe her.'

'Never,' Fairhurst said. 'You can tell someone who's been beaten, someone who's too scared to tell the truth a mile off. They've got that look, you know?'

'I do, yeah,' de Silva said.

Their voices were faint now and Barclay chanced a glance around the hedge and saw them heading toward a set of steps at the side of the shop. The uniformed officers, except for Fairhurst, had already gone up.

'Don't run!' A man's voice, loud as a thunderclap in the quiet street. 'Peter Tredwell! Stop him!'

Peter Tredwell. Barclay's mind raced. He needed to know what they were doing here, who Peter was, why he'd run from police, and why they'd needed a van's worth of backup. Something was going on, that much was obvious.

A thin, short man barrelled down the stairs, who looked to Barclay to be about three stone wet through. Somehow, he'd knocked Fairhurst onto her arse in the snow and ice. He turned back to look, took something from his pocket.

Crack.

Crack, crack.

The man was running out toward the road and the police van. Barclay jumped on top of him; something solid skittered onto the potholed tarmac. He turned the man over and looked at his scabby face. Red skin. Missing teeth. Peter swung out, his fist connecting with Barclay's jaw with a sickening crunch.

Barclay drew his hand back and brought it down full force onto the man's face, dazing him. His nose burst with hot, stinking blood and Barclay grabbed him by his threadbare coat and got him to his feet.

Barclay turned back toward the flat.

De Silva was on her knees, speaking into the radio fastened to her harness. Fairhurst was running toward Barclay and Peter, her cuffs at the ready.

The uniformed officers had come down the stairs, one holding his head, blood seeping through his fingers.

Fairhurst grabbed Peter, who was laughing at Barclay's side, his gums red and bleeding. Fairhurst said something to Barclay that he couldn't make out.

De Silva glanced back, searching for Peter, but her eyes landed on Barclay and held his gaze for a little longer than felt comfortable. She shook her head.

Lawrence was on the floor.

A crimson pool soaked into the grey-white snow.

Thirty-Eight

The sound of the siren was almost deafening. Two paramedics worked on Lawrence, with pads over the gunshot wound, a mask hissing oxygen into her lungs. But the blood soaked through the white bandages, and her chest barely moved despite the air.

De Silva hadn't even known where they were headed to, but she held on to Lawrence's hand. It felt cold, and de Silva tried to warm it. Tried to reassure Lawrence. This girl had her whole career in front of her, and de Silva was going to be damned if she lost another member of her team tonight.

The heart monitor let out a long, monotonous drone. The output screen showed a flat, green line. The paramedics shoved de Silva out of the way and began compressing Lawrence's chest. The blood continued to soak through the bandages and pool on the indentations of Lawrence's body.

They tried. Kept trying. But as the ambulance hurtled on toward whichever hospital they were heading for, Lawrence's body gave up.

De Silva had called Fairhurst from the Manchester Royal Infirmary and asked for a lift. They'd barely spoken on the journey back to the station, and de Silva could smell Lawrence's blood on herself. She quickly ran to the changing rooms where she was photographed and someone from the GMP forensics team took scrapings of dried blood. She dropped her clothing into evidence bags. *Evidence*, she thought. *The thing that kept Lawrence alive is just evidence now.*

Later, she scrubbed at her body under the hot stream of a shower. Blood swirled around the drain and slid down de Silva's body in little rivulets. The blood had seeped into every line in her hands, under her nails, and she was sure, somehow, it was in her hair. She dried herself and changed into a pair of trousers that were just a little too tight, and a faded black shirt that was too big on her. Still, she was clean.

Now, as she was standing outside of the interview room at Greater Manchester Police HQ, she tried to summon her strength. Her determination. The grit she needed to continue.

De Silva had called Murphy, had promised she would update the team on Lawrence's death personally when she got back from Manchester. That she'd go and visit Lawrence's mum and dad just as soon as she was finished with Peter Tredwell.

'Are you all right to do this?' Veronica Fairhurst asked.

De Silva didn't answer.

'Do you need me in there?'

'I'd like that,' she said. 'Thank you.'

'What about him?' Fairhurst cocked her head toward a side room.

'Him,' de Silva said, turning into the side room. 'I don't know what I'm going to do with.'

Barclay was sitting at the table, staring at it like a chastised school child. He looked up at them as they entered, got to his feet. 'De Silva, I—'

De Silva put her hand up and winced; the very sound of his voice grated on her in that moment. He'd been stupid. Reckless. 'You followed us,' she said. 'All the way from Liverpool?'

Barclay nodded.

'Why? And give me the short answer, Barclay.'

'I thought you had a lead on Sarah.'

De Silva nodded. 'Okay,' she said. 'Well, we don't. You know that I'd love nothing more than to find Sarah for you, but Lavery is leading that investigation.' She stared him down and he turned away from her, his face flushed. 'You were thoughtless.

You should have called me. You inserted yourself into a police operation. You're on leave and you're a civilian during that time. You acted rashly.'

'I know, I—'

'Shut up and listen to me, Barclay, before I really lose my temper.' She took in a few deep breaths through her nose before she continued. 'PC Fairhurst here took custody of the man we were looking for from a civilian man who was passing by at the time. That civilian heard gunshots and in an act of—' Barclay tried to speak, but de Silva pushed on, railroading his efforts. 'In an act of heroism, he tackled the armed man to the ground. In the commotion, he disappeared before we could get a full statement. Isn't that right, Fairhurst?'

'That's right, yeah,' Fairhurst said, her voice soft and sympathetic as she studied Barclay's face.

'DS Benjamin Barclay has been at his home in Liverpool tonight,' de Silva said. 'He had mashed potato and sausages for tea, and he watched the *News at 10* before going to bed.' De Silva opened the door, and a cold breeze blew in from the corridor. 'Good night,' she said.

Barclay headed toward the door. 'Lawrence,' he said. 'Is she…?'

De Silva shook her head, felt a thick swell in her throat and her voice trembled as she said, 'I'll speak to you in the morning.'

Barclay walked out into the corridor, and she heard his footsteps slowly fade away. If she knew Barclay like she thought she knew him, he'd be beating himself up and that was the last thing she wanted for him. Not now. Maybe she'd call him on the way home.

'Okay,' de Silva said, finally. 'Let's get this over with.'

They walked out into the corridor. 'DCI de Silva.' A voice she recognised from their earlier phone call as DSI Little's.

'I'll be inside,' Fairhurst said, excusing herself.

Little approached, his face grave, his hand outstretched to greet her. De Silva accepted it. 'DSI Little,' he said. 'Graeme Little.'

'It's nice to meet you in person, sir,' she said.

'I'm very sorry to hear...'

'Thank you,' de Silva said quickly, looking down to the ground then back to his face. 'Veronica Fairhurst was excellent. Does she have any plans for CID or a major incidents team?'

'Now don't you come sailing down the Mersey thinking you can steal my officers, de Silva,' Little said, playfully. 'Shannon, er DSI Murphy, told me all about you. A pain in her arse, she said, but a brilliant detective nonetheless.'

'Oh I don't know about that,' de Silva said. She felt anything other than brilliant. Things were falling apart, but still, they were one step closer to finding the truth of what happened to Bea.

'Humble too,' he said with a jolly laugh that made de Silva smile. She liked him. He was a breath of fresh air. Nothing like the stiff, stony exterior of DSI Shannon Murphy. Though, she supposed, even that was beginning to crumble. 'I want to thank you and your team for your input on these goings-on with DCI Collins,' he said, his voice almost a whisper. 'If it weren't for your intel and the integrity of one of our own detectives, we'd not have known he'd been withholding evidence. Burying it. I know my team have sent everything over now.'

'Yeah,' she said. 'Thank you for that; we're working through it.'

'Well, I'll be in the observation suite. No pressure.' He clapped her on the shoulder and walked off.

Right then, she thought. *No time like the present.*

She pushed open the door to the interview room. Fairhurst was already sitting, she and Peter Tredwell stared at each other and neither one broke as de Silva walked into the room. She wondered what the winner got.

De Silva sat down, opened the casefile on the table, pressed record on the device fixed to the wall. 'The date is 17 February 2024. The time is now 23:15.' Realising the lateness of the day, she felt the weight of what was still left to do like stones pressing down on her chest. 'This interview is with Peter Thomas Tredwell of Longsight, Manchester. Present are DCI Winifred de Silva of Merseyside Police and PC Veronica Fairhurst of Greater Manchester Police.'

She took a breath here and looked up at Peter, whose eyes only just left Fairhurst's face. He sneered as he looked at her, his teeth brown and rotting in his head. There was a staleness to his breath, as though he hadn't brushed in days.

'Mr Tredwell—'

'Mr Tredwell's my old man,' Peter said. 'And I don't like to be reminded of that cunt. The name's Peter.'

'Peter,' de Silva corrected herself. 'Do you know why you're here?'

'Yeah,' he said. He leaned into the microphone system on the wall, and affected a stiff, posh accent. 'For the benefit of the tape, Peter Tredwell knows why he's here.' He chuckled to himself, pleased with his little joke.

'We arrested you on suspicion of having sexual relationships with a person under the age of sixteen.' De Silva took a breath, steadying herself and her voice. 'Upon attendance at your address, you attempted to abscond the scene, and in doing so you shot and killed PC Jayne Lawrence of Merseyside Police with an illegal firearm.'

'Now that was an accident,' Tredwell said.

De Silva replayed the scene in her head. Tredwell had turned back and purposefully fired at all three of them standing there. That was no accident by any stretch of the imagination. 'We came to your property tonight to—'

'Oh, I know, I know!' Tredwell said, already bored of this interview. 'I knew I shouldn't have bought her that drink,' he said with a laugh. 'Hard to tell these days; everyone has a bald twat, don't they? I mean… do you?'

'Watch yourself, Tredwell,' Fairhurst said.

De Silva saw an opportunity and jumped right on it. 'Yes, maybe you shouldn't have bought her a drink,' de Silva said. 'At what point did she confess her actual age?'

'Afterward,' he said. 'After she'd sucked a line off me dick.' He laughed, his breath stinking in the air between them.

'For the benefit of the tape, could you confirm her name,' de Silva said.

He leaned in again. 'Oh, I don't know.' He waved his hand, dismissively. 'Lacy. Macy. Could have been Princess Di for all I care.'

'She was just sex to you?' de Silva asked.

'That's all they ever are,' he said. 'You think they want more from me?' He pointed at his own face, painfully thin, and de Silva wondered if he was, or had been, addicted to heroin. 'They want free drinks, and I want to fuck.'

'But you can't remember her name?' Fairhurst asked.

Peter sighed. 'God, he's no fun, is he?' He stared at Fairhurst again. 'Miserable. Your poor wife, she must be begging for a bit of decent cock.'

'I'm a female police officer,' Fairhurst said, her face stone.

'Well, there's a shocker, mate,' Tredwell said. 'Wouldn't have taken you for having yourself a twat bone. You one of those trans lot?'

'Her name,' de Silva said, bringing the conversation back on track.

'For God's sake,' Tredwell said. He leaned his head back and covered his face. 'Amelia, I'm sure it was.'

'Last name?' De Silva took out a small pad from her pocket.

'Now *that* I don't know,' he said. 'We weren't exactly down the registry office, get me?'

'Where did you meet her?' she asked, taking a pen from the inside pocket of her blazer. 'You mentioned buying her a drink. So, was it a pub?'

'The George and Green Dragon,' he said. 'Only place I go.'

De Silva scribbled that down quickly. 'And how old did Amelia say she was after you'd had sexual intercourse?'

He shrugged. 'Can't remember exactly what she said,' he said. 'I remember being shocked, but it was done and dusted by then. I'd already shot my load and asked her to get out.'

'But she was underage?' Fairhurst again.

'Yeah,' Peter said. 'But that's not my fault, is it? She was in The George drinking, and you've got to be eighteen to be served, haven't you? So, why would I think otherwise?'

'She must have looked significantly younger than you, Peter,' de Silva said, incredulous. 'If she was underage, you'd have been able to tell there was a definite age gap between you both.'

'Girls where I'm from, well they're not exactly known for make-up and eyelashes,' he said. 'They're all a bit rough. Know what I'm saying?'

'Right,' de Silva said. 'And what about your niece, Beatrice?'

Peter swallowed, sat back in his chair; his long arms hung by his sides, blue veins bulging. No track marks, de Silva noted. 'What about her?'

'Did you even know that she went missing, Peter?' de Silva asked. 'She was seriously unwell as a result of horrendous injuries.'

He leaned in, his usual antagonistic sneer vanished. 'She what?'

'She passed away, Peter.' De Silva stared at him as she said that. If she wasn't mistaken, his eyes seemed to haze over, as though his mind was elsewhere. 'Where have you been, Peter?' de Silva asked. 'She died two days ago.'

'Oh my God,' he said. 'She's a good girl.'

'Peter.' De Silva leaned in as close as she could without vomiting at Peter's breath. 'Were you aware that Bea was pregnant?'

'No,' he said. 'I didn't know that. That mother of hers, she keeps me away. How's our kid? Not surprised he didn't call. Must be beside himself.'

'We haven't come to ask you about Amelia,' de Silva said, 'but we will look into it.'

He bit his bottom lip so hard it turned white. 'What the fuck do you want then?'

'Beatrice's baby was found to have genetic abnormalities, which are common in children conceived through incest.' De

Silva watched his face carefully, waiting for any sign. His left eye twitched, the corner of his mouth lifted just slightly, before he ran his hand down his face, as though slipping on a mask. *Got you*, she thought. *He knows something.*

'How old was she when you first became sexually attracted to her?' de Silva pressed.

'Are you fucking mad?' Peter shouted. 'I'd never touch someone her age. Not knowingly before you start!'

'How old was she when you first convinced her to have sexual intercourse with you?' de Silva kept on.

'Are you not listening?'

'How did you feel when she told you she was pregnant?'

Peter looked at Fairhurst. 'Is she a fucking lunatic?'

'Answer her questions, Peter,' Fairhurst said, unflinching.

'Peter,' de Silva said. 'When you were brought into the custody suite, we asked you for a DNA swab, which you declined at the time.'

'You are fucking mad, clearly,' he said with a laugh. 'As if I'm giving you lot my DNA.'

'Well, according to Greater Manchester Police records, we already have your DNA profile,' de Silva said, her face neutral. 'It's on file from when you raped Pauletta Yin.'

'So what?'

'So, we can match that DNA sample to Bea's baby,' Fairhurst said. 'It's just a matter of time. So how about you save us all some time and effort and start telling us what happened.'

Peter's face turned the colour of ash.

'Where's your smart mouth now?' Fairhurst added, so low that de Silva doubted the recording would catch it clearly. Fairhurst cleared her throat and said, 'Would you like us to contact your legal counsel now?'

'Everyone makes mistakes,' Peter said; his voice sounded distant. Tears slipped down his face in torrents that he didn't wipe away.

'What kind of mistakes are you talking about, Peter?' de Silva asked.

'I...' He could barely speak as the tears tripped him. '...I did like her,' he said, finally. 'In *that* way. God knows I tried not to. I didn't want to, I swear. But there's something in me.' He pointed to his head. 'There's something rotten in me that makes me...'

'Did you have sexual intercourse with Bea Tredwell?' de Silva asked, keen to get this confession crystal clear for the recording.

'I...' Peter closed his eyes and swallowed something thick that clicked at the back of his throat. 'It was an accident really,' he said. 'I was minding her while her mum and dad were out. Years ago. She came out of the shower, and—'

'How old was she at the time?' Fairhurst asked.

'Seven,' he said.

It was de Silva's turn to close her eyes then. It reminded her of those times after a hard drinking session, when the room would spin and vomit would burn the back of her throat. She'd swallow it down and close her eyes until the room stopped tilting. Bea was just seven years old when her own uncle instigated a sexual relationship with her. De Silva didn't know whether to vomit or cry.

'What happened after that night?' Fairhurst asked, casting a quick glance to de Silva.

'She didn't want to be around me,' he said. 'Charlene kept her away from me, but when their marriage ended, I saw more of her. Lee was always around mine. Always leaving her with me. And I...' He was crying again.

'You groomed her,' de Silva said. 'Didn't you? You convinced her that what you were doing to her was normal.'

'I *loved* her,' he said. 'I know how that sounds, but I did. All the others, I couldn't stand them. But Bea... I loved her. But then things got out of hand...'

'What do you mean?' de Silva asked. 'How did things get out of hand?'

'I...' He paused, wiping at her face.

'Peter!' de Silva exploded. 'What happened?'

'I... shared her.'

'Oh fuck...' Fairhurst said, putting a hand to her mouth, rubbing at her chin.

'I found other people like me. Other men who loved girls the way I love Bea.'

'How did you find them?' de Silva asked, sitting back. There was no need to take notes now at all. It would all be there on the tape.

'Online,' he said. 'The dark web is full of that type of thing.'

'You know how to access the dark web?' de Silva asked.

'It's not a secret,' Peter said, shaking his head. 'Anyone can access the dark web easily.'

'So, these people you met online...' De Silva was determined to keep this conversation on track. She felt a weight in the pit of her stomach again. Peter Tredwell shared Bea with others. That poor girl, doing whatever she was told for the love of her uncle. She had no clue that what was happening to her didn't come from love, no matter what Peter told her. De Silva couldn't help but think of her own niece, Bonnie, how she'd destroy anyone that tried to hurt her. That she would protect her until her dying breath.

'Peter,' de Silva said. 'Have you ever heard of an app called The Woulds?'

'No,' he said. 'Should I?'

'It wasn't the method through which you met these other... people?'

'No.'

'When you say that you "shared her", can you elaborate?' De Silva's stomach lurched at the thought of it.

Peter sobbed again, covering his red face.

'I know this is difficult,' she said. Her voice was flat, even and professional, as though she heard this type of thing every day. She wanted to scream at him. Slap him. Punch him until he was a pile of sludge.

'A group wanted to meet up with us,' he said. 'Men. With their daughters, nieces, girls they knew. Things got rough. Things got out of hand and we left. I felt so bad. I apologised to her, I cried, I begged her to forgive me. She was bleeding, and I felt…' He took a breath and held it in his chest before letting it go in a dry sob. 'Few weeks later, we found out she was pregnant.'

De Silva's fury intensified. These little mind games Peter had played with his own niece were unforgiveable. 'What happened then?' she asked.

Peter shook his head. 'They wouldn't leave me alone,' he said. 'Leave *us* alone. They turned up at my flat, threatened me, said if I didn't introduce Bea to some of their mates, they'd make my life hell.'

'Can you tell us their names?' Fairhurst asked.

Peter sneered. 'You don't share bloody names at these things; are you mad?'

Fairhurst persisted. 'What did they look like?'

Although she appreciated where Fairhurst was going with this, de Silva needed to cut to the chase. 'You said they threatened to make your life hell. How?'

He paused, staring at de Silva. 'They had pictures,' he said. 'Videos. They weren't bluffing, either; they showed me.'

'Images of what? The time you'd spent with them?'

'Yeah,' he said, crying again. 'Of me and Bea. Me *with* Bea. I wanted to take her away; I wanted to take Bea somewhere safe, somewhere where nobody knew us. I told her to keep the baby a secret until we figured everything out, but her mum put her in that fucking place and, well, you know what happened.'

'Did your brother know anything about these threats?'

'No,' he said, looking at the table.

'Did you have anything to do with Bea's disappearance from Allerton House Mental Health Facility?' Fairhurst asked.

'No!' He was a snivelling wreck. 'It has to have been them, doesn't it? The people who threatened me.'

'What gives you that impression, Mr Tredwell?' Fairhurst asked.

'It's Peter!'

'Peter, please calm down,' de Silva said. 'What gives you the impression that it could be the people you met that night that took Bea from Allerton House?'

'They were relentless,' he said. 'Determined. They weren't taking no for an answer. Of course I knew she went missing,' he said. 'Our kid told me all about it. I felt sick. He was a wreck. Panicking.'

Finally, they were getting there. Peter knew more than he was letting on, and now it was all coming out of him. Every sordid, terrible detail. His eyes were glassy and distant, as though focusing on something far away. 'Did you tell him you had suspicions about who had taken her?'

'I spoke to him about it,' Peter said, staring at the wall beyond de Silva and Fairhurst.

'Did you tell him everything? About that night with those men?' de Silva asked.

'I didn't need to tell him.'

'What do you mean?' They were losing him quickly, his eyes glassy; his body seemed too relaxed, almost limp. He was giving up, de Silva could see that, and at any moment, he'd shut down. 'Peter, what do you mean you didn't need to tell him?'

'Well...' Peter's voice was soft, almost whimsical. 'I didn't need to tell him about that night because he was there.' He took a ragged breath, a smoker's inhalation. 'He was with us.'

'Interview terminated at 23:47 p.m.,' de Silva said, standing. She went out to the door, Veronica behind her, Peter sitting at the table, sobbing into his hands. 'Could you escort Peter back to the custody suite, and can you get him some legal counsel? He's going to need it.'

Veronica nodded and turned back into the interview room, taking Peter by the elbow. 'Come on,' she said. 'With me.'

When Fairhurst came back, they slumped into the chairs in the interview room. 'Fucking hell, Fairhurst,' she said. 'That poor girl.'

Fairhurst shook her head, staring at the table-top. 'I can't imagine what she must have gone through that night,' she said. 'She must have been so frightened.'

De Silva's phone rang out from her pocket. Harris again. 'I'm sorry, Harris, I meant to call you back.'

'Did you check your email?' he said. 'The picture I sent you.'

'One second.' She put him on loudspeaker and navigated to her email app. She opened the email from Harris and waited for the picture he'd attached to load on the screen.

'It's an image of the man from the CCTV at the back of Allerton House,' Harris said. 'VEU were able to enhance it, but they're still working on getting a reg from the van.'

The image loaded.

De Silva's heart thud-thudded in quick succession.

'Fuck,' she said. 'Fuck!'

Fairhurst frowned. 'Everything okay?'

Harris chimed in, his voice urgent. 'It's our old friend, isn't it? It's Mitch Whitley.'

Thirty-Nine

In the end, you have to make a choice. Do you let people get away with what they've done, or do you make them pay? Do you become your own karma, your own means of destruction?

He pondered these things while he showered, Terry next to him but not too close because that would be gay. He couldn't feel Terry's breath on his neck or hear the shower water dripping from his nose and… bits.

'Rob,' Terry said, his voice grinding like rusted gears. 'We have to go.'

Rob didn't want to go. He knew that this time, things would be harder. They'd have more work to do. It could all end messily for them, when there was still so much work to do. Rob rubbed soap into his skin, over scars the colour of fish flesh. White and meaty. Burns. The sharp edges of things that had cut into him as punishment.

Punishment, he thought. *Punishment is a stop on the road to redemption. That or discipline.* He wasn't quite sure which. In their deaths, he supposed, they'd never find redemption. Never be able to absolve themselves of the things that they'd done; just like Rob and Terry would never be able to absolve themselves of the things they'd allowed to happen.

'No matter how much we punish them all,' Terry concluded, as though reading Rob's mind. 'Get yourself dried and dressed. We need to go. Now.'

Rob switched off the shower, and the cold seemed to attack his skin instantly. He dried himself carefully, behind his ears, in between his toes and all between his legs, itself scarred white.

He tried not to think of those nights during the day. Those were the hours where he had to be a normal person. Where he had to do his job, pay the bills, sit in his office all day and pretend he cared about everything going on around him. Terry only left his room at nighttime, when the sun went down. Sometimes he'd show up when the world became a little too overwhelming for Rob. Terry had always been his brother's saviour. His protector.

They dressed together. Everything in black, right down to their underwear and socks from Primark. Not a thing on them would reflect any light tonight. They shoved balaclavas into their pockets and made their way out of the rented house with its damp walls and bare floors.

The roads were dreadful, and Rob had to drive the small van slowly. Even though he was convinced they had a slow puncture, Terry wouldn't let him stop to check the pressure. 'No,' he'd said. 'We get in, get it done and get out again.' He'd check the tyre pressure first thing.

Rob parked the van a half mile away from the house. It was best to be safe. He'd ordered tasers and stun guns from the dark web and they'd arrived quickly in unmarked boxes. They bounced in Rob's backpack, clacking against the casing of the one-thousand-lumen torch he'd found online easily. No VPN required, but he'd used one anyway.

The back of the house was well lit. The mother, the newspapers had called her Leah, was sitting on the back doorstep smoking a cigarette and looking up at the sky. There was nothing to see up there, banks of looming grey clouds in the nighttime blue. Another woman was standing next to her, also smoking, and the big light in the kitchen cast their shadows long on the patio.

From the roof of a neighbour's shed, Rob could smell the acrid stink, could see the smoke lifting from the burned orange ends of cigarettes, pluming out of their mouths and noses and drifting upward to the sky.

It reminded Rob of dead things floating to Heaven. Of the spirits, the souls, they were taught about in school well before Rainford Lane was even a thought in his mind. A nightmare to be endured. A terror that would, inevitably, follow them throughout the course of their lives.

Neither of them were watching.

Neither of them were prepared.

Above the back door was a white security light, which turned on and off intermittently as the woman with Leah shifted her weight. Attached was a camera. *Interesting*, Rob thought. People had taken home security seriously in recent years, given the rise of inexpensive smart devices which monitored their every move and made them feel safe.

He smiled when he thought of what the police would see when they analysed the footage from the camera. Beside him, Terry chuckled too.

They moved silently from the roof of the shed, back down to the ground. The neighbour's house was in complete darkness, and no security light betrayed their position.

The plan was simple, and it seemed to happen so quickly. Rob was up and over the fence before the woman next to Leah had even turned. He fired the stun gun at her, the wires extending out until they connected with her, piercing through her clothes. She was down on the ground convulsing, and Rob kept hold of the button. Seeing her face contort and twitch thrilled him so much. He felt himself get hard. She deserved it just as much as Leah Putney did. They both deserved whatever they got next.

Rob moved quickly, pulled the taser from his jacket pocket and pressed it into Leah's chest as she stood, throwing her cigarette onto the floor. It fizzed and popped and lit up, and her eyes went wide and wild. Her knees gave way and her whole body caved in. Her head narrowly missed the step she'd been sitting on. Any closer, and this whole thing would have been over. Next to Rob's foot, Leah Putney's cigarette smouldered and smoked.

Terry swooped in then with rope from the backpack.

There would be no help for either of them.

Not tonight.

Forty

18 February

De Silva arrived home in the early hours of the morning, when the snow began to drift down from dark, heavy skies. Her eyes stung from tears she'd had to hold back since she was sitting next to Lawrence in that ambulance.

The house was freezing when she got inside, and so she got into bed fully dressed in those borrowed clothes. She didn't even bother to even brush her teeth and pulled the covers up over her head. In that sanctuary, she allowed the tears to come. For Beatrice Tredwell and the awful things that had happened to her. For Barclay and Nick and Sarah. For Scarlet Putney. For Lawrence and her family.

On her way back from Manchester earlier, she'd driven to the address listed in Lawrence's emergency contacts. Her parents' home where Lawrence still lived, according to her personnel file.

As she was standing outside their front door earlier that night, a security light had flickered and came to life as fresh flecks of snow had begun to fall. Her breath misted in front of her, and somewhere inside she heard feet on the stairs, the hall light came on and the door opened just a crack. De Silva was glad to hear the rattle of a security chain. A dark eye and an arched feminine eyebrow appeared in the crack. They were Lawrence's own eyes, and de Silva felt her stomach lurch.

'Hello,' she said, her voice low and soft. 'My name is Win de Silva; I'm—'

The door closed, the chain rattled and it opened again, revealing a short, thin woman in a fluffy white dressing gown. 'I know who you are,' the woman said. She had so much of Lawrence about her that it hurt de Silva to look at her. 'Our Jayne doesn't shut up about you.' She peered past de Silva. 'If you're looking for her, she's at work. Well, you'd know that I suppose. So, what's—'

De Silva's words lodged in her throat like stones. 'There was… a situation at work.'

'Oh God.' Diane shook her head, tears streaming down her cheeks instantly. In de Silva's experience, mothers of hurt children always knew when something was wrong. 'Oh God, no. Tony!' Her voice was loud and shrill in the quiet dark of the early hours. She turned to the stairs. 'Tony, get up! It's our Jayne!'

A tumble and then feet moving above them, hurriedly.

'Where is she? Is she hurt?' Diane asked.

'I'm really sorry,' de Silva said.

'Where is she? We'll go there right now.' She turned back to the stairs. 'Tony, get your shoes and bring the car keys down.' Tony, the dad, a giant in comparison to his wife and daughter, appeared at Diane's side.

'Mr and Mrs Lawrence, it breaks my heart to have to tell you this…'

Diane gripped her husband's arms, whether for comfort or stability, de Silva couldn't say. Her screams echoed in the street, and bedroom lights came on from everywhere.

She had stayed with them for over an hour before she finally left. There was nothing more she could do. Nothing more she could say. Knowing that their daughter gave her life in the line of duty would mean nothing to them right then. That was something they'd come to understand later on, if they wanted to know the grim circumstances that led to her death. And, more than likely, they would want to know every detail eventually.

De Silva offered her personal phone number to them and left the couple to their grief. She passed a neighbour on the driveway, in a paisley dressing gown. 'What's going on in there?' she asked de Silva. 'Is everything all right? Di, are you okay?'

'I'd give them some time,' de Silva said, simply, and headed for her car. As she drove off, she wondered whether leaving was callous. Cold. Unfeeling. When her Ritchie had died, she wanted nothing more than for everyone to leave her alone to wallow in her own grief. Her own guilt.

Not everyone is like you.

Still, she reasoned with herself that she would call to check on them after she'd at least attempted to get some sleep.

In the dark absence of dreams, she heard a phone ringing. Felt something buzzing through her entire body like a pneumatic drill in her head and chest. Her eyes opened in stages, as though her brain was firing itself up ready to be awake once more, to face the next set of horrors that would, inevitably, be in store for DCI Winifred de Silva.

Her hand reached out to her bedside table, almost muscle memory, and gripped the shaking, solid shell of her phone. She pressed the screen and put it to her ear, let her eyes close again. 'Hello?' No reply. 'Hello?' The thing was still ringing in her hands. When she looked at the screen, she saw that it was her alarm sounding. It was nine thirty in the morning. She didn't remember setting the alarm, especially not for a time after she was due in the office.

She turned it off and dragged herself from the warm safety of her duvet and into the bathroom. She turned on the shower and began to undress as the room filled with steam. There was something in the act of undressing from clothes you'd slept in, as though you were removing layers of filth and grime, that felt therapeutic. She hoped that when she stepped out of the shower, she'd feel renewed. Regenerated and able to continue with the day.

As she stepped under the hot streaming water, she thought of Mitch Whitley's house, the hard drives there and the logo of The Woulds app on the monitor. She thought of the gunfire she'd heard so close to her own face, of the warm, red mist that filled the air. She thought of Bea and the horrors she must have endured at the hands of her own uncle and father, if Peter's testimony was to be believed.

She thought of Scarlet Putney, still missing. She needed answers, and she needed them all quickly. She thought of Sarah, and whether the same awful things that had happened to Bea were happening to them both right at that moment.

Finally, she thought of Jayne Lawrence. A young up-and-coming officer with years, decades even, ahead of her. The passionate, capable young woman who'd met her end at the hands of a child rapist. Lawrence was dead and pretty soon they'd have to bury her. They'd have to mourn her, and that was something de Silva struggled with.

Her immediate reaction was to push everyone away, distance herself from others, to go into herself and really study that grief. Look at it from every angle, get to know its many faces. But this time, she decided, she would have to try something new. Though, what that was and what that looked like, she had no idea.

She could have stayed there under that water for hours. It was hot, too hot really, and turned her skin red. She lathered a two-in-one shampoo and conditioner into her scalp, which she knew was no good for her hair, and rubbed cherry-scented liquid soap into her pale skin. Later, she would dry her hair. She'd make a coffee and take it to work with her. She'd stop off for some food, get some for the team too.

Her day would continue like nothing had ever happened. And that, de Silva knew, was the thing that bothered her the most. Life going on in spite of Lawrence's absence.

She knew that morale would be even lower than it had been in that incident room. But the team would need to be around people who understood what it was to lose a fellow officer, one of their own. They'd talk and then they'd have to pick up where they'd left off yesterday – in the black hole of this entire case. The interconnectedness of it, like spiderwebs in an old attic. With trapped prey wrapped in shrouds of webbing, the monster at its heart watching. Waiting. Ready to pounce.

She wondered what the face of that monster might look like. The terrible, clawing thing at the centre of it all, the thing that had birthed itself in the basement of Rainford Lane School for Boys, where this whole thing had started.

The Woulds back then was a collection of photographs. Child porn. Torture. They were the kids that would co-operate, the ones that wouldn't fight back or cause a fuss. Over the years, that idea took on fresh horrors as technology advanced. It had probably been a chat room at some point in the dial-up days of the internet, before finally becoming a social media app in the 2020s.

Cataloguing and tracking thousands of children. Subjecting them to grooming gangs, to predators who wanted to hurt them. Taking them away from their families and their homes and their nice warm beds, throwing them down into a world only few see, and even fewer ever return from.

She turned off the shower and dried herself, thought about calling Barclay but hoped that he was still asleep in his bed. Despite the state of their relationship, she hoped that he was in bed with his husband, and that they were holding each other.

That's what she hoped for Barclay. But for herself, she could only wish to catch the people who were behind this whole thing.

–

The roads had been cleared of snow again, but traffic flowed slowly through the city like columns of a funeral procession. Slow. Deliberate. Mournful. She hadn't put the radio on, hadn't connected her phone to the car's Bluetooth. Everything other than snail's pace and silence felt absurd.

And in the end, she didn't feel like stopping for food. Though her stomach gurgled and complained, she didn't feel hungry.

She pushed open the office door and found Braxton sitting at his desk. He stood up when de Silva entered, his eyes puffed and red as open wounds. At least he'd managed to change his clothes. 'What are you doing here so early?'

'Been here a few hours,' he said. 'If I stayed at home and looked at those four walls for another hour, I'd go insane.' He shook his head. 'How're you feeling?'

'I don't know,' she said with an honesty that surprised her. 'I feel… almost numb. But underneath that, something is bubbling away.' She had expected the whole team not to turn in, and she'd have understood. She also knew that there was a torture in being alone, in thinking, in reenacting traumatic events over and over. De Silva knew that all too well.

Her mobile phone rang – Murphy. She rolled her eyes. 'I'll be back shortly,' she said. 'I want to get through some stuff this morning, and there's a lot I need to update you on.'

De Silva answered her phone as she was on her way to the lift. 'I'm on my way, ma'am,' she said. She changed her mind and took the stairs up to Murphy's office, all the better to compose herself.

Murphy's office felt gloomy, and beyond the broad windows, the sky reflected that feeling as banks of black clouds loomed over Speke. De Silva was glad to find that Murphy was alone this time. That ACC Nathan Pryce wasn't standing at her back like some ghoul. Perhaps he was still in bed, completely unaware, or unfazed, by the death of Jayne Lawrence.

Murphy stood straight away and moved around the desk to greet her. There was an awkward moment where de Silva panicked, thinking Murphy would hug her. But she didn't. 'Would you like a drink?'

'A coffee would be great,' she said.

Murphy walked back around the desk, to the old-fashioned filing cabinet with the spider plant on top. 'Oh, for God's sake,

Win, I don't mean a coffee.' She pulled out a bottle of Burnt Faith Kentucky Smoke and two glasses from the top drawer, which clinked as she put them down on the desk. She poured with shaking hands, right to the brim of the glass. 'Fuck knows I need one myself.' She slugged it down and poured herself another.

De Silva stared at the brown liquid in the glass. Felt the urgent pull to drink it, to grab the bottle and swallow the whole thing. But that wasn't her any more. She had come past that. Still, that was not a conversation she was willing to have with Murphy. She picked up her glass and drank it in one go, felt its glow spread from her throat across her chest. 'Is this why you wanted to see me?' she asked, putting her glass down to be refilled. 'To get me drunk on duty?' She gulped another glass.

'No,' Murphy said, polishing off a third, and putting bottle and glasses away in the top drawer again. She sat down, made sure her blouse was safely tucked into her trousers, felt for any bumps or stray hairs in her perfect platinum bob, and cleared her throat. 'Collins was charged early hours this morning,' Murphy said. 'He's sought legal representation from a firm called Masters, Chandler and Prinz.'

'I know that name.' De Silva scraped through the cluttered, dusty papers in her mind, searching for something with that name on it.

'You should,' Murphy said, moving back to the filing cabinet and filling another glass. 'It's where Thomas O'Brien's lawyer worked.'

Burt Reeves, de Silva thought. During initial questioning after his arrest, O'Brien had indicated that Reeves himself was involved in all of this. He'd gone on the run, or so they'd thought. They'd not seen sight nor sound of him since that day in the interview room. *No*, she thought. *That's not where I know that name from.*

'That's also the firm that represented Mitch Whitley,' de Silva said. She made a mental note to look into that.

'Yes, well,' Murphy said. 'There's plenty to investigate. Especially given that Masters, Chandler and Prinz receive regular payments from T & K Holdings.'

'What?'

'T & K Holdings,' Murphy said, pouring herself another glass. Any more and de Silva would have to drive Murphy home. 'They offer donations to various charitable causes. Masters, Chandler and Prinz offer pro-bono services for clients who couldn't ordinarily afford their services. But someone has to pay, I suppose.'

De Silva's mind whirred and her head ached. She felt sick and dizzy and lost. This was a mire that she felt she may never find a way out of.

'I'm afraid I have some more bad news.' Murphy put the bottle away again and locked the filing cabinet with a key she put into her desk drawer.

De Silva sighed, unsure how much more bad news she could possibly take. Her life in recent years seemed to be a cycle of bad news, a repeated pattern. 'Go on…'

'I'm afraid Leah Putney was found early hours this morning,' she said.

'Found?'

'By Merseyside Fire and Rescue. Neighbours called police around two a.m. after they'd heard sounds of screaming from the property. There were no units available to attend, and by three a.m. the same neighbour called the fire service when they saw smoke billowing out of an upstairs front window.'

'Another fire,' de Silva said, looking away, the brandy buzzing in her mind. She wanted to ask for another; she wanted to slope off to the pub and drown her sorrows in something strong and sweet. *Focus*, she told herself. 'The previous victim where there was a fire showed signs of being stabbed,' she said. 'Is that the case here?'

'I don't know,' she said. 'The body has been transferred to the City Area Coroner. I suggest you make a few calls. There was another victim. A family liaison officer had been staying with Ms Putney. DC Chloe O'Meara. Did you know her?'

De Silva stared at the desk, at the small ring of condensation her glass had left on the polished wood. 'Not well, no.' *Not at all*, she thought.

'What are you thinking, Detective?'

'Honestly? I'm… I'm at a loss.'

'Where are the team?'

'On their way in I hope.' De Silva stood.

'You hope?'

'They lost one of their own last night,' de Silva said. 'I'd be surprised if they turned in at all.'

Murphy nodded. 'And Lee Tredwell?'

'I'll be charging him this morning,' de Silva said. 'We still have him in custody, but his brother's account of what happened is pretty damning.'

'That's good,' Murphy said. 'At least a small portion of justice for Beatrice.' She coughed to clear her throat. 'I do have some good news,' she said. 'Your exhumation request has been approved. It will take place this afternoon.'

That *was* good news. 'Thank you,' she said. De Silva stood up. 'Thanks for the drink, ma'am.' De Silva left the office without being excused, without waiting to see if Murphy had anything else left to say.

–

The incident room was packed when de Silva entered. She'd been reading the preliminary report on the Putney murder on her way down. She'd read that Brennan's team were all over it already.

There was a sombreness to the space, and, to de Silva, it seemed to have made the place darker. She felt a swell of pride in her chest that the team had come in, all except for O'Connor. She'd have to call him. Even Lavery was there, stone-faced. She could tell just by looking at Harris's red eyes that he'd been crying.

'I know,' she said to them all. 'I know we're all feeling this. We can mourn and we can grieve Lawrence.' She held tears back and she felt the pressure of them bulging behind her eyes. It wouldn't do for her team to see her emotional. 'But I think Lawrence would want us to solve this case. Don't you?'

Silence.

'I'm sorry that I'm not coming to you all with better news, but…'

'Christ, what now?' Arlow asked.

'I got the word that Leah Putney has died,' de Silva said. 'Murdered. We lost another officer, too.'

'Who?' Braxton asked.

'DC O'Meara,' de Silva said. 'She was FLO to Leah Putney. Arlow, she was murdered in the same way as your previous victims. You and your team will want to get on that after the briefing.'

Arlow nodded. 'Yes, boss.' He was already typing at his computer.

She had to press on. 'We know that Mitch Whitley was the man who removed Bea Tredwell from Allerton House. We don't know why.' De Silva knew that they might never know why. 'News this morning from Murphy is that DCI Collins from GMP has been charged. His bank account shows regular payments from T & K Holdings. A holdings company which has direct ties all across this case. Not least because they funded pro-bono work at the law firm which represents Tom O'Brien, and which represented Mitch Whitley himself.'

'Fuck,' Braxton said.

'You can say that again,' Harris said.

'Last night, Law… I arrested Peter Tredwell, Lee's brother,' de Silva said, taking in each of her team in turn. 'He admitted to having had a sexual relationship with Beatrice Tredwell.'

'That poor girl,' Yates said.

'He also admitted to knowing about her pregnancy, that she'd told him,' de Silva said. 'We need to await genetic testing, but I think it's safe to say that he is the father. He also told us about how he connected with other… people like him. How he'd shared Bea with other men. How it had turned nasty, and they'd become insistent that they see her again. I think it's more than likely how Mitch Whitley became involved.'

'Did he connect with these monsters through The Woulds app?' Braxton asked.

'He says not, but we will seize his phone and any personal devices from his property,' he said. 'Given Mitch Whitley's involvement, though…'

There were rumbles of disgust across the incident room.

De Silva's voice cut through it all. 'All right, listen! We don't have the luxury of time here. He also claims that Lee was there the night he met with these men. Peter also states that these men attempted to blackmail him. If he didn't bring Bea back to them, they'd release videos and images of that night.'

'So,' Braxton said, leaning forward on his chair. 'Do we think Lee and Peter Tredwell orchestrated Bea's disappearance with Mitch Whitley?'

'We can't rule it out,' de Silva said. 'But given the time and organisation it would have taken, I'd say no. We already have Lee in custody, and Braxton, I'd like you to speak with him this morning. Charge him. Harris, did you take a look at the CCTV footage from outside the ICU the day Beatrice died?'

'I did,' he said. He stood up, took a sheaf of papers from his desk and handed them around. 'This doctor you see entering the ICU five minutes before Bea's death was a locum from an agency called Care+ Solutions, which is owned and financed by a holdings company called Compass Care.'

'And who owns Compass Care?'

'One guess,' Harris said. 'T & K Holdings.'

'Get me an address of that doctor.'

'I tried,' Harris said. 'Compass Care offices are shut down, the company dissolved. Southport hospital records have him listed as a Dr Kieran Blackman. And I can't find a single bit of information on him. The General Medical Council have no record of anyone by that name.'

'So, T & K Holdings put him in that hospital to do what?' Arlow asked.

'Bea was a witness,' Lavery said out of nowhere. 'Any witness is a threat.'

'You're saying a holdings company had a teenage girl killed?' Patel asked, her brow furrowed.

'Whoever is behind the holdings company clearly has a vested interest in cases like this one. It's why they fund pro-bono work for men connected with The Woulds and Rainford Lane case,' Lavery said. 'I'd have thought that was obvious given what we now know.'

'Well, we can't rule it out,' de Silva said, knowing in her heart that Lavery was right. 'Lavery, do we have anything from PVPU on Sarah or Scarlet?'

'I'm sorry, no,' Lavery said. 'There's nothing to update you on.'

'Jesus,' Harris said.

'We're doing our best, Harris!' Lavery said, defensively.

'Yeah, well maybe you should be doing more.'

'And what exactly are you doing?' Lavery bit back. 'Looks to me like you're sat around twiddling your thumbs in this bat cave waiting for evidence to drop in your lap.'

'Stop it!' de Silva roared. 'That's enough. We've got work to do. We haven't got time for pissing contests and dick waving.' The room fell silent. 'Arlow, any updates from you?'

Arlow turned to face the room. 'As a matter of fact, boss, yeah we do,' he said. 'We know that the Simmonses have a direct link there to Rainford Lane School for Boys. And we know that Christine Jones was a deputy head there, too. The report didn't mention the lad's name, and naturally there are no school records to speak of.'

De Silva thought on that for a moment. 'And you've spoken to the constabularies where the other murders took place, I assume? Established identities?'

'We have,' he said.

'And?' de Silva asked, trying not to let her impatience show. 'Were they in some way related to Rainford Lane School for Boys?'

'One of them was,' Patel said.

'Not directly, though,' Yates chimed in.

'The victim in Devon, Maureen Robbins,' Arlow said. 'Her son, Raymond, attended a summer camp down there. Guess who owned the camp?'

'Jeremiah Sure by any chance?' De Silva shook her head, not needing an answer. She knew the truth. These men, they swooped in and destroyed the lives of so many children. Some of them they may never know about. 'Any evidence of The Woulds app there?'

'No,' Arlow said. 'This was the early 2000s, before apps really took off. I found no mention in the case notes of the other two victims about any app on their personal devices.'

'So, we've got one case related to The Woulds app,' Braxton said. 'And the other two are what? Copycats?'

'Not quite, no,' Arlow said. 'Patel, do you want to share what you found?'

'Each of the other two victims who were murdered with the same MO as Charlene Khan, Christine Jones and the Simmonses, and… now Leah Putney, too. They all had a kid. Each one had a child who spoke of abuse, whether at their schools, somewhere in the family, or even in therapy. There was no commonality as to where it took place,' she said. 'Nothing like The Woulds or Rainford Lane. They didn't know each other or have any other connection than the way they were murdered.'

'So, we're missing something,' de Silva said. 'Each one of them had an abused child.' She paced, chewing her bottom lip, hands on her hips. 'There are only similarities going back to the Simmons case in the nineties, am I right, Arlow? There we no similar cases before that?'

'That's right, yeah,' he said.

'Let's say the killer is this lad from Rainford Lane, the one they sent back after he'd escaped to their farm,' she said. 'Why do you think he'd kill them?'

'If it was him, and he wanted to get away so badly and they turned him back to the people who were harming him, you'd be pretty pissed off wouldn't you?' Braxton said, tapping his pen on his desk.

'So, it's a revenge killing then?' Lavery asked.

'No, I think it's more than that.' De Silva stopped still as the thought hit her, like a punch to the jaw. 'It's punishment,' she said. 'He punished the Simmonses for what they did. For letting him continue to be abused.'

'So, what does that have to do with the other victims?' Patel asked, her face crumpled and confused.

'Each of them had an abused child,' de Silva said. 'Was he punishing them for letting this happen to them, too?'

Harris was nodding along, de Silva's reasoning clearly making sense to him. 'And Christine Jones, according to Meeks's manuscript, was a perpetrator of abuse at Rainford Lane. He punished her too.'

'But why the stabbing?' Arlow asked. 'Why the pre-mortem burn marks and the fire?'

De Silva had been giving that some thought while the rest of the incident room caught up with her rationale. 'It's unique, isn't it? An MO I've not seen before. A repeated pattern, and the thing about repeated patterns is that they have to start somewhere.' She locked eyes on Arlow. 'I think we're on the verge of something here, Arlow. Could each of you three grab a section of Jacob Meeks's manuscript? There should be a digital version somewhere.'

'What for?' Arlow asked.

‘A pattern starts somewhere, as I said,’ she said, ‘and I wonder whether that somewhere is Rainford Lane. We have a first-hand account of a victim of that place. See if there’s any mention in there of one of the boys running away. Or scalding, fire, stabbing.’ Her phone rang out. Joel Matthews calling.

‘Right then, everyone,’ she said. ‘Let’s get on with it.’ She stepped outside into the corridor and answered the phone. ‘Hello?’

‘Sefton Park,’ Matthews said. ‘Two p.m. If you’re late, she’ll leave. If you’re with anyone other than me, she’ll leave.’ He took a breath, and de Silva was sure she could hear his smile down the line. ‘She wants me to be there, too.’

–

De Silva was sitting alone in a side room off the basement corridor. Alone time was becoming more of a necessity than a nice-to-have in recent days. When the lights turned themselves off due to lack of movement, she didn’t flinch. Didn’t raise her arms or stand to turn them back on. She felt happy in the cold black. Comforted by its familiarity.

Eventually, she heard the incident room door open and close further up the corridor, and footsteps made soft by the corridor carpet. Braxton walked by and the lights in the room came on, stinging at de Silva’s eyes. Braxton screamed like de Silva had never heard a grown man scream before. She couldn’t help but laugh as his face turned from sheet-white to pink then crimson.

‘What the bloody hell are you doing sat in the dark like some bleeding gargoyle?’ he hissed at her, checking no one had come out of the incident room to check on the commotion. ‘You casting a spell or holding a séance?’

‘I think you need more than one person for a séance,’ she said.

‘Just witchcraft then,’ he said, regaining his composure and leaning against the doorframe. ‘They were right about you after all.’ He looked at her, his face a picture of concern. She looked down at her fingers, picked at the skin around her thumbnail. 'What's going on?'

'I'm not sure I can tell you,' she said.

'You can tell me anything.' Braxton entered the room and closed the door behind him. 'Come on.'

'That was Joel Matthews,' she said.

'That dirty little scrotum,' he said with disdain. 'What does he want?'

'He set up a meeting.' De Silva looked at him then. The tired, balding middle-aged man in front of her. In the absence of Barclay, she had no one else she could trust completely. 'With me and Breaker. You remember her, the hacker from last year?'

If he was surprised, his face didn't show it. 'What for?'

She shrugged. 'She has information,' she said. 'Apparently.'

'Want me to come with you?'

'No,' de Silva said. 'Then the hospital in Hull called.'

'About O'Brien?'

She nodded. 'He's regained consciousness,' she said.

'And you're sat here conjuring up demons in the dark to try to reverse that?'

She laughed again. 'I'm just not sure how I feel about it all,' she said.

'Do you want to talk about it?'

'No,' she said. 'We've got enough going on without adding him into the mix.'

Braxton lowered himself into a chair opposite her, groaning and letting his weight collapse into it. 'I think he's already in the mix, boss. He's been in the mix since the nineties. Earlier than that probably.'

'I've been so angry at him,' she said. 'I wished that he'd feel pain. I said that to his face and now look.'

'Well, I was joking about the witch stuff, but…'

'Oh, shut up, Braxton,' she said, slapping his forearm playfully. She settled back in her chair, exhaled through her nose. 'He was in my life for as long as I can remember.'

'He and your dad were as thick as thieves for as long as I've been about.' Braxton looked up at the ceiling, a smile on his face, as though remembering. 'People used to call them Hinge and Bracket.' He laughed, the kind that rakes at the lungs of smokers and drinkers. 'They were like an old married couple.'

'Yeah,' de Silva said; her eyes drifted down to her hands. 'And that's what I'm worried about.' She let those words hang in the air between them, something unsaid that probably didn't need to be vocalised.

'Because of what Arlow found?' Braxton asked. 'The report with your dad's name on saying all was well at Rainford Lane?'

She nodded, too scared to speak in case a sob clawed its way out of her throat.

'I get you,' he said. 'Your dad was an honest man, boss. If you think about it... he did what any of us would have done. He went and checked it out. They told him everything was fine. God, the report says even the lad himself said he was fine.'

'But he didn't take the lad's name.' De Silva looked at him then. 'Or if he did, he didn't report it. He and O'Brien were always together; you said that yourself.'

'That's right.'

'Except that day Dad went to the school.' De Silva swallowed hard. 'According to the report he went alone.'

'You don't know that for sure, boss.' Braxton tapped her knee, softly. 'Maybe O'Brien didn't sign the report. Maybe your dad wrote it to save time and submitted it under his name. Reporting back then wasn't what it is now.'

'No, I know.' She groaned, covered her face, then rubbed her eyes. She was exhausted. Her back ached from sitting in that chair, and if she didn't get some sleep soon, she was sure her body would shut down.

'So...' Braxton started.

'So what?'

'Are you going to visit him?' he asked. 'O'Brien I mean. In hospital.'

'No,' she said without hesitation. 'I don't know, actually. He's a… well, you know what he did, Braxton. How can I visit him like some concerned friend after all of that?'

'Look, we all had a different relationship with him,' he said. 'Every single one of us in that incident room knew him before all of this. Liked him. Respected him.'

'So, you're saying I should forget what he's done?'

'Good God no, he's a disgusting nonce who deserves to swing for it.' He took a breath, closing his eyes, then started again. 'You can't forget the awful stuff he's done just as much as you can't forget how he was there for you after your dad passed.'

'And that's just it, isn't it?' De Silva felt the memory of her dad's passing swell in her chest and throat, threatening to burst from her in the shape of a thousand tears. 'The respect I had for him. The love I had for him even. It's confusing me. I'm disgusted by him. Being around him makes my skin crawl. When I think that he might be one of the men who…' She couldn't finish.

'Hurt Ritchie?'

'Yeah,' she said, barely a whisper. 'But all of this case is still dragging on, and that monster that was once someone I admired and looked up to might have answers.'

'Well, now he might take them to his grave,' Braxton said. 'Just because he's going to live doesn't mean he's going to be able to communicate. He might not even know who you are even if you do visit.'

'I know that.' She knew that more than most. Her own mum was wasting away, mind and body, in a care home. That pained de Silva every single day.

'You might never get answers, boss,' Braxton said. 'Not about whether O'Brien hurt your husband. Not about why he did what he did and covered up what he covered up. Or why your dad went to that school and didn't record the lad's name on an official report. It's all done and it's all out of your hands. History is history, and that's all there is to it. Sooner or later, everything we ever did is covered over by sand or dirt, and if we're lucky enough, people will come and cry at our gravestone.'

'Bloody hell,' de Silva said. 'I felt better sat in the dark on my own than hearing this soppy bollocks.'

The pair of them laughed.

'But thank you though,' de Silva said, standing. 'I appreciate it.'

Footsteps out in the corridor.

'You're welcome, boss,' Braxton said. 'Any time.' The wink he gave her made her feel only slightly uncomfortable, but she accepted it with a smile.

Arlow at the door. 'We've finished with Meeks's manuscript,' he said.

'And?' de Silva asked, hopeful. 'Anything?'

'Nothing. I'm sorry, boss.' Arlow turned away down the corridor.

'Well, that's it then, isn't it?' De Silva looked to Braxton. 'There are no school records remaining, there's nothing in the manuscript, and the only man who might have a memory of that time has had a stroke and can't communicate.'

'You're forgetting two people,' Braxton said. 'Billy Thompson and Mike Crosby.'

In truth, she hadn't forgotten them. She knew that they were rotting in prison, just like O'Brien, and she had no desire to see them ever again.

'I can put a request in to question them,' Braxton offered. 'If you don't want to.'

'No,' she said. 'I'll do it myself.'

Forty-One

When Barclay's phone rang and he checked the caller ID, he excused himself and went upstairs. 'Where have you been?'

'I'm sorry.' It had only been a few days since he'd last heard Rob Ayris's voice, and Barclay was surprised by how it made him feel. Comforted somehow. Safer. 'I've been on assignment. I've not had phone access. What's going on?

Barclay didn't know where to start with what was going on. 'It's Sarah.'

'What about Sarah?' Ayris asked. 'Is she okay?'

'No…' Barclay's eyes stung with the heat of his tears. 'No, she's missing. And we think…' He took the phone away from his ear, could hear Ayris's voice saying something, and wiped at his face. He took a deep breath and controlled the trembling of his lips. 'We think this is connected to The Woulds app.'

'I'm on my way.'

Barclay could hear Ayris moving around down the line, the slamming of drawers, the sound of a zipper. 'Really?'

'Yes,' he said. 'I'll drive. Get a hotel in town. I'll be there as soon as I can.'

Barclay didn't know how he'd explain Ayris's sudden return to Nick, but right then he didn't care, and that realisation stung deep. 'I'll see you soon.'

'Ben…' Ayris said. 'I'm sorry.'

Barclay held his breath, unsure of what would come out of his mouth next. 'I'll see you soon,' he said, and hung up the phone.

When Barclay entered the living room, Nick was pacing, pale and ghostly, as the sun reached ever closer to the roofs across the street. In just a few hours it would be black outside, and another day would have passed without them hearing anything about Sarah.

Barclay sat down and watched him. He wasn't sure why he needed to be at Nick's. Company, he supposed, until Ayris arrived, despite everything he'd said to Nick the day before. All of that still held true, but even Nick seemed to appreciate having someone other than Char around the house.

He'd expected de Silva to call, to berate him about his actions the previous night, but she hadn't. To Barclay, that spoke volumes. She was angry with him, and that was something he felt deeply ashamed of.

Nick jumped out of his skin when the doorbell rang, raced past Barclay and into the hall to answer it, but found Char already opening the door.

'Am I all right to come in?' Lavery was standing on the doorstep in her camel-coloured coat, seemingly unaffected by the freezing February air, as though she was made from ice herself.

Nick's shoulders slumped and he went back into the living room and Barclay moved forward, said, 'Come in.'

'I'll put the kettle on,' Char said, leaving them to it.

'What's happened?' Barclay asked. 'Is it Sarah? Have you found her?'

'No,' Lavery said. 'But we do have some updates. Can we go through to the kitchen?'

Nick followed them through and slumped into a chair. Barclay wished he'd take himself off for a bath or a shower and try to get some sleep. Still, he'd only managed half an hour himself before waking up. He'd wished the whole thing was some awful bloody nightmare, but it wasn't. When he woke up in his own bed and looked out of the window, the snow was falling. Sarah was still missing. And all around these missing girls, people were dying.

The nightmare was real, he decided, but he was awake and living through it.

'Go on then…' Nick said, impatient.

Char placed a tray of steaming mugs in the middle of the table, then leaned against the fridge, listening. Barclay clocked Nick eying her with utter contempt, as though any of this was her fault. He'd have to have a word with him later.

'The public response has been phenomenal,' Lavery said. 'We've had sightings as far as Somerset. Though, as you know, not all of them can be true sightings.'

'None of them could be true sightings,' Nick said.

'Nick…' Barclay put a hand on Nick's, but he pulled his away.

'It's the truth, isn't it?' Nick glared at Lavery. 'It could be that none of those sightings are her.'

'The main thing that matters is that the public are invested,' Lavery said. 'They're looking out for her, and that's important. We're following up each and every report and we've sent pictures out to all local constabularies to follow them up, and they're reporting in directly to me. It's going to take some time.'

'That's all we've heard,' Nick said. 'It's going to take time.'

Barclay almost told Nick to calm down, but why should he? He should be angry. Someone had taken their daughter and there was clearly no intention of bringing her back; that realisation had already dawned.

Nick picked up a mug and launched it at the wall, narrowly missing Char, who shot back with a scream. Hot tea sprayed everywhere, stained the wall and dripped down it. The mug shattered and splintered and fell to the ground. 'My little girl is out there for another night, and we're all sat around drinking tea and catching up like a fucking knitting circle? WHERE. IS. SHE?'

'We're doing our—'

'If you tell me you're doing your best, Lavery, I swear to God, I'll throw all of those mugs at your bastard head.' Nick was on his feet, pacing, tears gushing down his red face.

Barclay stood and turned to Nick, wanted to pull him in close, but thought better of it.

'Ben,' Lavery said. 'Nick, please take a seat. There's something I need to discuss with you.'

Nick sighed heavily and sat back down. Char picked up the remnants of the broken mug from the floor and put them in the bin.

'Leave it,' Nick barked.

'I'll just—'

'I said leave it!'

Char dropped the pieces she held, raised her hands in surrender to Nick and backed away.

Barclay turned to Lavery. 'What's wrong?'

'Leah Putney was found murdered early hours this morning,' Lavery said, as though delivering the day's weather. 'A similar MO to the Christine Jones case you know about, Ben, and the Simmonses from the nineties.'

'And Charlene Khan,' Barclay said.

'Who are these people?' Nick asked.

'They were victims of brutal murders,' Lavery said. 'We found a connection between all of them.'

'What's that then?' Nick asked.

'Each one of them, in some way, had a child…' Lavery looked up to Char then back at Barclay. 'Who had reported sexual abuse.'

'So, someone is targeting the parents of abused kids?' Barclay asked, his head throbbing. 'What does that have to do with us?'

'Leah Putney and at least one other victim had a child who had used The Woulds app,' Lavery said. 'We don't know that there is a definite connection there, but we're not taking any chances.'

'What are you trying to say, Lavery?' Nick asked.

'No fucking way,' Nick exploded. 'You think I'm going to hide out somewhere while Sarah is out there? You've got another thing coming. I'm not doing that again. Not without her.'

'Nick, I wouldn't ask you to do this if it wasn't for your own safety,' Lavery said. 'It's here in Liverpool, so you're close enough if anything changes. Look, you've seen the news. Leah Putney, Charlene Khan. They're parents of missing kids. They're both dead now.'

'What if it's just a coincidence?' Nick asked.

Lavery shook her head. 'There are historical instances of similar cases across the years,' she said. 'This *is* a pattern; we just don't know what it's telling us yet. But de Silva is working on the theory that…' She trailed off, shaking her head.

'That what?' Nick asked.

'That these parents should be—'

'Punished,' Barclay finished her sentence for her. It was all there and had finally become clear to him. 'He's targeting the parents of missing kids as punishment for not protecting them, isn't he?'

Lavery nodded. 'De Silva seems to think so, yes.'

'We didn't do this to Sarah,' Nick said. 'Why would he come for us?'

'In his mind, his *warped* mind, you should have kept her safe,' Lavery said. 'You should have protected her. That's what he believes in all of these instances. According to de Silva, anyway.'

'We got rid of that app as soon as we found it,' Nick exploded. 'We got new devices. We kept checking. We checked! Ben, tell her.'

'So then, how does he know?' Barclay asked.

'I'm sorry?' Lavery asked.

'If he's targeting or punishing parents of children who were abused, and some who had The Woulds app on their phones or tablets or whatever,' Barclay started. 'How does he know they were abused or that they even had the app?'

Lavery's face was blank.

'Please tell me you've considered that?' Barclay asked.

'I've considered it,' she said. 'I just don't have an answer for you. I'm sorry.' She took out her phone. 'I need an answer from you both right now. You can pack a few things, but we need to leave now. So,' she said. 'Are you coming with me or not?'

'I'm not going anywhere,' Nick said. 'She might ring or turn up, and if we aren't here, well she'll think we've left her.'

'Nick,' she said. 'Ben, I can't impress on you the importance of what I'm asking of you. Just like I can't imagine how big a decision this must be for you both. But this is important. If something happens to you both, then when we find Sarah, she won't have a home to come back to.'

Forty-Two

De Silva was ushered into the room by two prison guards, both taller than her and twice as wide, packed with muscle. The room was smaller than the one she had spoken to O'Brien in, where his face had contorted, where he'd fallen to the ground.

She'd wanted to head back to the station to get moving on everything and take control of the incident room. She'd left Braxton in charge and trusted him to do a good job.

As she entered the small room, where the air stank of sweat, she did her best to control her breathing. Slow and steady. In through the nose and out through the mouth. Eventually, the heavy, urgent drumming of her heart caught on and slowed its pace.

Mike Crosby was handcuffed to the table in grey tracksuit bottoms and top, and white pumps. The kind you'd find in cheap shoe shops. He stared at her, taking all of her in; to her, his eyes felt like hands moving all over her body. Once upon a time, his hands had touched all of her. But those days were gone. Any love she'd had for him had eventually died.

'I was surprised you wanted to see me.' His voice was lower than she remembered, deeper. It didn't sound like him, and if it weren't for those eyes of his, she'd have asked to see the real Mike Crosby. 'Are you going to sit down?'

The last time she'd seen him, he looked pale and frail, almost as old as O'Brien had done. But now, he looked different. There was colour in his cheeks, muscle on his frame. She was sure that he was taller than she'd remembered.

She sat down opposite him, panicked that Crosby might hear the thud of her heart as it started up that rhythm again. 'There's someone out there killing innocent people,' de Silva said. 'And I need your help.'

He laughed. 'You can fuck right off if you think I'm helping you.'

'I can't say that you'll ever get parole, Mike, but helping a police investigation would look good to a parole board.'

'Is that the best you can do?' Crosby asked. 'I'm sat here day in and day out, looking over my shoulder in case *they* come to tie off this particular loose end. And you want me to help you with a fucking case?'

'I don't need you to do anything,' she said. 'Just remember something.'

'Did you know that Tommo is in intensive care? That he was attacked?'

'No, I didn't know that.' In truth, she didn't care about Billy Thompson. She had no empathy for the man who had tried to kill her, who had taken her finger like he'd taken it from so many of his victims. She rubbed at it now, slightly discoloured and cold compared to the others. 'What happened?'

'He got done in the shower,' Crosby said. 'An inmate that had transferred into the high-sec wing. There were supposed to be guards.' He looked up to the prison guards who'd escorted de Silva in. 'But they all seemed to vanish, didn't they, boys?'

'Watch your mouth, Crosby,' one of them said.

'Well, maybe something'll come out in the investigation, 'ey?' He looked at de Silva again. 'What do you think?'

'You, Lewis Lamond, Billy Thompson, Ritchie and the others,' she said. 'You made a pact to keep quiet about that night Bob Brendan…' *Died?* she asked herself. *The night Bob Brendan was murdered?*

'The night your loving husband killed that rapist nonce?' He sneered. 'We did the world a favour, but yeah. We had to. It'd be us up in court, despite what he'd done to us. Maybe even the judge who would sentence us had fucked us once or twice. You never know. They'd come from all over the place.'

'Were there any others?'

'Any other what?'

'In that school, were there any other pacts? Allegiances? Cliques? Gangs?'

'Oh no,' he said. 'If you want me to help, then you'll tell me everything. It's nearly teatime, and I can just as easily head off and have my evening meal by candlelight.'

De Silva didn't want to tell him anything. She'd made her mind up on that as she drove out here. She knew it was useless. If she needed his help, she would have to tell him some of it.

'There's someone out there killing parents of abused kids. Some who have connections to The Woulds app,' she said.

Mike shrugged.

She tried again. 'We think this all leads back to a particular murder which has connections to Rainford Lane.'

'Singing Tommo's tune, are they?' he asked with a laugh. 'Not very original, is it?'

'Barclay's daughter is missing.' She couldn't say Sarah's name, not in that place, not to that man.

He sat up right then, and she saw a shift on his face, something close to concern. 'How old is she?'

'She's young,' de Silva said. 'Younger than the others who are missing.'

'Tell me about the people you think are connected to the school.'

'Christine Jones,' she said quickly, keen to have this conversation over with and be on her way. 'She was the—'

'Oh, I know exactly who *she* is.' Crosby scowled, nodding his head. 'One mean bitch. When the men were… when they'd finished with us, it was her job to take us back to our dorms. We'd stop by the shower block first. She'd turn off the hot water.'

'Mike, I don't have time for a trip down memory lane,' she said. 'Barclay's daughter is missing and I need to find her.'

He pressed on, as though he hadn't heard her. 'Sometimes, she'd get the hose pipe, and we'd hear boys screaming. There was this one kid, God love him, he was her favourite to torment. She'd—'

'The other related victims are a couple. The Simmonses. They were murdered in the nineties,' she said, talking over him. 'In 1999. They lived on a farm right near the school.'

'Oh,' he said, laughter causing him to cough. 'Oh hoh! I know about the Simmonses.'

'Tell me.'

'And I know who you're looking for,' he said. 'They were stabbed if I remember correctly. Their house set on fire.'

Her heart thundered. Sweat trickled down her back, itching her skin. 'That's right.'

'I heard all about it,' he said. 'A little escape artist tried to get away, but they clawed him back. They always do.'

'Who?'

'I suppose we're all still trying to claw our way out of that place. One way or another.'

'Mike, what's the guy's name?'

'Well, to be honest with you, I'd heard he'd died,' he said. 'Killed himself, like—'

Like Ritchie, she thought. 'Mike. Do you know his name or don't you?'

'Well obviously I'd heard wrong if he's still knocking around,' he said. 'You asked me before about cliques and gangs and allegiances,' he said. 'This was fucking wild. The kid I said about earlier, Mrs Jones's favourite. That was him. She took pleasure in trying to break him, I think. She never did though, not until the very end. After he ran away, the things she did to him.'

'Did she burn him?'

'And worse. That kid had cuts all over him. Deep ones. Needed stitches.'

She didn't want to tell him about the recent cases. How they'd been scalded. The violence of the attacks. She stared at him instead, willing him to continue.

'It doesn't matter I suppose,' he said. 'You've got your work cut out for you, Win. I would hate to come up against him.' He laughed again. 'You've probably already figured out the reason he's doing this, haven't you?'

'He's punishing those he thinks should have protected the children in their care, isn't he?'

'Reenacting what was done to him,' Crosby said, nodding.

'Mike, I need his name.'

'No.'

'What?' She should have known better than to trust him. Now he was armed with an update on their case and de Silva had nothing in return. 'Mike, Barclay's daughter is out there somewhere. Frightened. She'll want to come home.'

'What are you going to do for me?'

'I...' She had nothing to offer him. His life going forward had already been decided, and soon he would receive his sentencing.

He lunged at her. The chains clanked against the table. The guards ran forward, but it was too late. His hands were on her chin, cupping her face. He stared her in the eyes, and she could smell tea on his breath. 'This will have to do then.' He kissed her, his wet tongue in and around her mouth, gliding across her closed teeth. She pushed herself back as the guards gripped his elbows.

'It's fine!' de Silva shouted. 'It's fine, just leave him.' The guards lifted their hands in surrender to her and backed away. 'Get off on that, did you?'

'One for the wank bank for sure.' He laughed, eyeing the guards.

She shook her head. 'What happened to you, Mike? You should be on this side of the table helping me put an end to all of this. To The Woulds app. Those bastards from Rainford Lane.'

'There's no ending any of that, you stupid bitch,' he said. 'It's always happened and it always will.'

'I refuse to believe that, Mike.'

'Then more fool you.'

'Do you have a name for me or what?' She looked at her clock. 'Time's ticking on, and I need to get back to Liverpool.'

'Terry,' he said. 'Terry Thompson.'

De Silva's eyes flicked to the blank ceiling as she thought. 'Thompson? Like—'

'Like Billy Thompson, yeah,' he said, a smile on his curled-back lips, exposing his teeth which looked yellow in this light. 'They were brothers.'

Forty-Three

Snow had fallen and settled over Sefton Park, leaving the banks of open fields white, like fresh sheets on laundry day. Any footprints had been covered over in the most recent snowfall, but the paths that wound their way around the pavilion and lake were slush. Mist hovered over the top of the water, where not even the swans and ducks swam. De Silva imagined them cosied up somewhere, staying close and sharing warmth.

She'd arrived early, with well enough time to head slowly through the park to the coffee shop at the centre, where Joel Matthews had said he would meet her. She hadn't yet called ahead to the incident room to brief the team on the things Crosby had told her. She wanted to do that in person.

The trees were bare naked branches that twisted and turned like old, gnarled fingers, reaching upward. Outward. As de Silva reached the café, where people were sitting outside enjoying hot drinks, she heard the flap of wings somewhere up ahead. A tiny white feather see-sawed down in front of her, the calamus of which pointed her on in the direction she was already heading.

Ahead of her, she saw him waiting, shifting from one foot to the other, bundled up in a thick padded coat, scarf, gloves and a hat. An outfit that put her in mind of Kevin McCallister from *Home Alone.* He spotted her and headed straight toward her.

'Afternoon, Detective,' he said, grinning.

She didn't know the reasons why Breaker had wanted Joel Matthews to accompany them in their meeting, but whatever that reason was, de Silva resented it. She had a physical hatred for this man that she felt in every fibre of her being, right down to her bones.

'All right,' she said with a slight nod, by way of greeting. 'Where are we meeting?'

'A bench up there,' he said, nodding on ahead in the direction of the Palm House.

De Silva had just come from that general direction, and she was furious he hadn't just told her to meet him there. It would have saved her the walk down to the middle of the park in the freezing cold. Joel Matthews had this way of getting under her skin just by existing; she recognised that and had made her peace with it a long time ago.

'What's in this for you?' de Silva asked. 'You write a story on all of this, and the *Liverpool Journal* welcomes you back with open arms?'

'The *Journal*?' He snorted a laugh. 'I wouldn't go back there if you paid me a million.'

De Silva sensed that he was baiting her, wanting her to ask for more information. She left it there. He'd tell her if he wanted to.

'I've got plans,' he said. 'And I've got backing.'

'What're you talking about now? Speaking with you in person feels just as much a riddle as one of those salacious pieces you write.'

'Salacious? I've only ever told the truth.'

'Told in a way to get people salivating over dead girls and serial murderers,' she said, dodging ice on the path. 'And who's backing you? For what?'

'I think all of this is crying out for a documentary, don't you?'

De Silva stopped in her tracks. 'I'm sorry? A documentary?'

'True crime stuff is huge now, all over Netflix and stuff.' He stopped with her, looking at her with the most earnest of faces. 'I pitched the idea around. There's this new streaming service coming out in summer. TrueCrime+ it's called. Like Netflix for true crime documentaries and podcasts.'

De Silva tutted and carried on walking ahead. 'You want to tell the story of how Rainford Lane School for Boys became The Woulds, don't you?'

'No, I want to tell the victims' stories,' he said. 'All those boys at that school, all of the children since. The story of how Lewis Lamond became a serial killer of teenage girls due to trauma brought on by the suffering he endured at that school. His childhood.'

'I think the past is better left in the past,' she said. 'Once this investigation is over, that's where I'm leaving it. I'm moving on. We should all do the same, you included.'

'The past isn't a place, de Silva,' he said. 'It's a moment. You can't just dump history somewhere and expect it to break apart and dissolve. For some of these people, that moment is still happening. Imagine what seeing a documentary about this could do for all of those victims that haven't yet stepped forward.'

'Don't pretend you're doing this for the victims, for God's sake, you'll make me sick,' she said. 'You're doing this for your own gain. How much are they paying you?'

'That's none of your business, Detective.'

'Too much then.'

A quiet balanced on a knife edge between them and above that, the chattering of people, the whistle of the biting wind through bare branches and the sing-song tweets of small birds somewhere in the shrubs.

'It's happening, de Silva, whether you like it or not. You're doing a good job of bringing the truth out; I just want to bring it to a wider audience.'

'You do what you like,' she said. 'You always do, and to hell with the consequences to anyone else. But like you said, the past for some people isn't a moment, it's now. It's every day. You think about that when you're bringing it all back up for people who aren't ready to deal with it.'

'Are you talking about the victims or yourself?'

'What's that supposed to mean?'

'Your old mentor is heavily involved in all of this,' he said. 'It doesn't take a genius…'

'Doesn't take a genius to what?'

'Oh,' he said, laughing. 'Maybe it does. Do I really need to spell it out for you, de Silva? Your dad and O'Brien were best mates. You're telling me your dad knew nothing about what happened at Rainford Lane? The extent of O'Brien's involvement? Don't make me laugh.'

De Silva's jaw tightened. The wind cut across her face, sharp and cold, carrying the faintest scent of smoke from somewhere distant. She had convinced herself that she could put everything that had happened these last two years behind her when the case was resolved. When they'd shut down the people behind The Woulds for good, when Lee and Peter Tredwell were behind bars. When they'd found Sarah and Scarlet safe and sound.

Her dad had made mistakes, she was convinced of that, but that he himself had lurked in the shadows of Rainford Lane School for Boys, she knew wasn't true. Right there in the freezing cold of the mid-afternoon in Sefton Park, it all appeared laid out in front of her; Joel Matthews at her side hovering like a vulture waiting to rake the bones of the dead, of her own past, she realised the truth.

For some people, the past is both a place and a moment, somewhere and some-when you choose to forget. Somewhere you can leave the awful things that have shaped you behind. But for others, the past isn't something you can leave. It's something that lives and breathes alongside you, feeding on your memory of it, a parasite; it grows even stronger each day you let it linger.

For some people, their past cannot be outrun or evaded, and for others that's their only way to cope: to attempt to get ahead of it. Get away from it.

For others, there's no place left to run.

A woman was sitting on a bench up ahead, a cold metal thing with black flaking paint. Her breath misted in front of her face and the low winter sun turned the steam orange until finally, it dispersed, as though melted by the light.

She stood as she saw de Silva and Matthews approaching. 'Thank you for coming,' she said. De Silva recognised her voice from their phone call the year before instantly. That was a day she was not likely to forget, given what that conversation had led to.

'Breaker?' de Silva asked, feeling bloody stupid for using that name, despite having no other reference.

The woman nodded. She was nothing like what de Silva had expected. Her hair had been tied back perfectly, not a hair out of place. She wore business clothes, heels even in this weather and a long green peacoat which suited her dark hair and eyes.

'I'm DCI Win de Silva.'

'I know,' she said. 'You're shorter than I imagined though.'

'Do you have a name?'

Breaker shook her head. 'That's unimportant,' she said. 'Sit down, Detective, Mr Matthews. I don't have long. And you never know who is watching.'

She's paranoid, de Silva thought. Her thoughts must have been written all over her face, because Breaker added, 'There doesn't need to be anyone around to watch.' She pointed up at the sky. 'Drones are everywhere these days, aren't they, Detective?'

So she knew about the particulars of Mitch Whitley having found Beatrice Tredwell's baby. She was flexing, clearly. Showing that she had knowledge. Had answers.

'Why have you asked us to come here?' Matthews asked, not sitting down either. 'You said you have answers for us.'

'I do have them,' she said. 'Some of them. But here's the deal. I tell you both some of what I know. The parts that won't have me immediately killed. They already attempted to have your colleague killed.'

'Barclay,' de Silva said. 'The car at the hospital?'

Breaker nodded. 'DCI de Silva here will use them to wrap up this case. And you will use them in your documentary once the arrests are made, are we clear?'

'I can't make that deal with you,' de Silva said. 'I'm a detective with Merseyside Police. I have to understand what you're going to tell me before I let you dish it all to this man here.'

'Let me?' Breaker smirked. 'I could walk away from this bench right now and you'd know nothing, Detective. But I know that's not what Jacob would have wanted.'

'You mean Jacob Meeks?' Matthews asked. 'The man who was murdered last year?'

De Silva eyed him; his face seemed lit up. He was enjoying this. Meeks was another victim of Rainford Lane. From their conversation last year, de Silva knew that Breaker and Meeks worked together via some internet sleuth online message board which had since been deleted. She had always wondered whether there was something more between them both, and as a tear swelled in Breaker's right eye but didn't fall, de Silva knew she had been right.

Breaker nodded. 'He was hellbent on getting his word out there. Did you know that publishers are asking for his manuscript?'

No, de Silva did not know that. 'It's evidence in an investigation. It's not going anywhere.'

'Not yet,' Breaker said.

Joel sat down next to her. 'Whatever you tell us stays with me until after the investigation is concluded. Until the arrests are made.'

Breaker nodded. She looked up at de Silva. 'Well?'

De Silva moved closer to the bench but didn't sit down. If Murphy were there, she'd be screaming at de Silva to act in a professional manner, befitting of a Merseyside Police detective. Finally, de Silva nodded.

'After Jacob's death, I received a letter from his solicitor inviting me to a one-on-one meeting at their offices. A tiny little place off Victoria Street you wouldn't even know was there unless you were looking for it.'

'What did they want?' Matthews asked, hands in his pockets.

'To give me a letter from Jacob,' she said.

'What did the letter say?' De Silva felt her brow aching, knew she must have been frowning, keen to work out how this was connected, why this was important.

'Some personal things which I'll keep to myself,' she said. 'Nothing of any importance other than to me. But he told me of some work he'd been doing. He'd rented some office space out in the Cains Brewery district. Just a small office. One desk. Hard drives. Three screens.'

De Silva held her breath, waiting for Breaker to continue. 'Is that it?' she asked finally. Her mind flashed back to Whitley's house on Gloucester Road. 'What was on the hard drives?'

'A web,' she answered simply. 'I had no idea he was working on all of this. His book, yes. The unsolved deaths of some of those people from Rainford Lane, yes, we all knew.'

'I don't have time for this,' de Silva said, her patience wearing thin. 'There's a little girl out there whose parents are worried sick. A teenager whose mother is lying dead in a mortuary. I need to find them both alive.'

Breaker nodded. 'It's all connected,' she said. 'Does the name T & K Holdings mean anything to you?' She looked up at de Silva and shaded her eyes from the low winter sun.

De Silva eyed Joel Matthews, who was looking at her now too, expectantly. 'Yes,' she said.

'It meant something to Jacob, too,' she said. 'It was founded in the year 2000 and—'

'Founded by whom? The Companies House website has the director listed as Stephen Aubrey. Does that name mean anything to you?'

'I'm getting to it,' Breaker said.

Get to it quicker, de Silva thought.

'Anonymous donations got it on its feet,' Breaker went on. 'It grew over its first five years, became national.'

'Grew through further donations?' de Silva asked.

'Partly,' Breaker said. 'But mostly due to their product. The one thing their entire client base was interested in. The reason everything they invested in was so important to them. Another five years later and it was a global operation, with investments in businesses running cybersecurity, prison services and other contracts for governments around the world. It invested in rail freighter services, imports and exports off the continent.'

'So?' Matthews asked.

'Girls,' de Silva said, the realisation dawning on her. 'And boys. Kids. They exported kids out of the country...'

'And imported others,' she said. 'Jacob's research showed they were never in the same place for too long.'

'You say research,' de Silva said. 'How did he get this information?'

'He did what we always did,' she said. 'He hacked.'

'He hacked his way into an organisation that had contracts in cybersecurity?' De Silva sounded incredulous and meant it.

Breaker shook her head. 'The cybersecurity aspect of the business was a money-making scheme,' she said. 'They sold the government nothing that they couldn't have gotten themselves easily enough from anyone else. It was a smoke screen.'

'For what?' Matthews asked.

'For The Woulds,' Breaker said. 'Jacob found his way in through a weak spot in the organisation's cybersecurity defences. A fault in a VPN used by these people made an IP address pop up somewhere in Southport, and just like that, Jacob was in.'

Southport, de Silva thought. *Whitley's house was in Southport.* 'Is that where these girls are now?' she asked. 'Sarah and Scarlet? Are they on their way out of the country?'

'If they haven't already gone, they'll be going soon,' she said.

'What's the name of the import-export company?'

'I've emailed it to you,' she said. 'There are others, but I've sent you a list of the most likely.'

De Silva took out her phone and forwarded the whole email to Braxton with instructions to get onto Interpol, to contact every border patrol in the country to stop any shipments to or from this registered company.

'I'll need the full list,' de Silva said. 'And I need answers. About you. Where do you fit into all of this? How do you have these answers?'

Breaker looked at de Silva for a length of time that made her feel uncomfortable. 'Let's just say that Jacob getting access to these systems was no accident.'

'You helped him?' Matthews asked.

'No,' de Silva said. 'She let him in.' Silence. 'You work for these people, don't you? How could you, knowing what they do to these kids?'

'I have my reasons,' she said, standing. 'I'm afraid I have to go now.'

'Wait!' Matthews gripped Breaker's arm, and she glared at his hand until he removed it. 'You said you knew who set this T & K Holdings up back in 2000.'

'That's right,' Breaker said. 'The founders were two men. Thomas O'Brien, former DSI at Merseyside Police.' Breaker looked to de Silva then. 'And the late Carl Brophy.'

Forty-Four

'I have the preliminary post-mortem report on Beatrice Tredwell back from Dr Carey,' Harris said, a printout in his hand. In that moment, the entire incident room fell silent.

'Right then.' She handed Harris a board marker and followed him to the evidence board, where he began scribbling.

'There was widespread internal bleeding,' he said, reading from the report. 'Multiple small haemorrhages from… words I can't even begin to pronounce.'

'Could that have been caused by her injuries from the fall or from childbirth?' Patel asked.

'Hmm…' Harris scanned the report quickly. 'Carey says it could be, but these haemorrhages are more "prominent than expected". She also notes here a massive intra… sorry, I'm due an eye test. Intracerebral bleed, which she proposes is the cause of death.'

'Has she sent tissue and blood samples to toxicology?' de Silva asked.

'Yeah,' Harris said. 'Be a few weeks, I suppose. They always seem backed up.'

'So, we have this doctor no one has ever heard of from a company that is now defunct, Bea's death due to the bleed on her brain. I dunno… something about her death isn't sitting right…' de Silva said out loud, hoping the words would form something solid in her mind.

'You think that she didn't die because of her injuries?' Braxton asked.

'I'll be honest, I'm not sure what to think,' de Silva said. 'On the one hand, we have this alleged "clean-up" operation O'Brien told us about, and on the other, the whole thing's a fucking shitshow.'

Yates was looking down at her phone. 'Widespread internal bleeding and intracerebral bleeding are both common causes of death in a patient who is over-anticoagulated.' She looked up, and when all eyes were on her, she shrugged. 'Google.'

'But she already had a bleed on her brain,' Braxton said.

'So what're you thinking, boss, that this doctor could have drugged Bea? Brought on her death?' Arlow said.

'A bleed on the brain...' de Silva said low, her mind in flux. 'Like a stroke.'

Braxton caught her eye, and he glared back at her, mouth ajar. 'Like O'Brien.'

'Bloody hell,' Harris said.

'Well, we won't know anything until we get the toxicology results back for Bea. Like you say, Braxton, she had a bleed on her brain due to her injuries already.' She nodded to Braxton. 'I'll call the hospital and ask if there were any anomalies in O'Brien's bloodwork.'

'I can do it,' Braxton said.

'No,' she said. 'He has me down as his in-case-of-emergency person for some reason. They'll speak to me.'

'What're you hoping to find?' Arlow asked.

'Something in his bloodwork would mean something bigger is going on,' she said. 'And then maybe he was right; there really is a clean-up operation. Arlow, could you call HMP Hull, tell them we have reason to believe that Crosby's life could be in danger. Billy Thompson's too.'

Braxton and Harris eyed her, and she felt the heat of their judgement on her.

'If they die then they won't ever face justice,' de Silva said. 'Besides, it could be nothing.'

'You're the boss,' Harris said. 'But there is something I do need to update you on.'

'We're all ears.'

'I went through the security records sent over from Allerton House,' he said. 'Their security manager, Marcus Blakeman, was on duty that night. That seemed unusual for him, looking at the staff rotas. He usually worked in the day, handing over to a guard for the evening and overnight shift.'

'And?' de Silva asked, impatient.

'And, none of the security team require access to any of the patient rooms unless there is some sort of risk. Either to themselves or to another patient. Blakeman gave himself access to Bea's room two weeks before she disappeared. He maintained that access until the day after she disappeared.'

'Right,' de Silva said. 'Look into him. Financial background specifically,' she said. 'These people know who to target and when, and so far, it always seems to be about money.'

'Already done it, boss,' Harris said. 'Blakeman seemed to have a gambling problem. Loans coming out of his ears. A kid. A wife. He was barely keeping his head above water. Two days after Bea disappeared, he receives three lump sum payments of ten thousand pounds across three days.'

'From T & K Holdings, by any chance?' Even saying the name out loud made her feel sick, knowing what she now knew. A massive global conglomerate she knew nothing about, and she'd been wrestling to find money to keep her mum in care and comfortable. If her dad had been involved, where was the money?

'Well, sort of,' he said. 'Through the private firm that pays him, MediSec, they specialise in security provision for medical and clinical settings. They've worked with Allerton House for a decade.'

'Are they owned or funded by T & K Holdings?' Braxton asked.

'Yeah,' Harris said. 'They're one of two holdings companies that have shares and financial interests in the security company.'

'You've got enough to make an arrest, Harris,' de Silva said. 'Get him in an interview room.'

'I'll get on it when we're done here.'

'No, go now,' de Silva said. 'Is he Manchester based?'

'Yeah.'

'Call Veronica Fairhurst from GMP; you'll need the backup. I'm going to call ahead and have an armed response team with you.'

'That seems a bit—'

'Necessary given everything that's happened?' de Silva asked. 'I agree. Head off, and I'll call you to update you when I've spoken with DSI Little.'

Harris grabbed his big coat and headed for the door.

'Arlow,' de Silva said. 'Anything on this Terry Thompson?'

'Well,' Arlow said. 'Terry is briefly mentioned in Meeks's manuscript. Quiet. Sullen. Prone to violent outbursts.'

'Sounds just like our man, doesn't it?'

'Well, that's what I thought…' Arlow said.

'Terry Thompson's dead,' Patel said.

'He hung himself when he was just twenty-one,' Yates said, grimly. 'He was found, slung over the banister, by his little brother.'

A quick flash of Ritchie over the banister in the house they'd shared together. The house she'd had to move away from. She breathed in slowly, until the image dissipated. 'Did he attend the school, too?' de Silva asked.

'No,' Arlow said. 'He attended a mainstream school.'

'Right,' she said.

'So Mike Crosby lied to us,' Braxton said.

'No,' she said. 'Mike did say that he'd heard Terry was dead. Maybe it's not Terry we're looking for. Arlow, find out as much as you can about this younger brother of his, won't you?'

De Silva's phone rang out from her pocket, and she hurried to collect it. She'd still not had the cracked-screen work phone replaced, though it sometimes cut at her fingers. She knew she should at least get a screen protector for it, if only to save her own fingers. Holden calling.

'Holden,' she said. 'Yes, I'm still here. Mmhmm, yeah, I'll be right up.' She slipped her phone into her pocket. 'Look, I know it's a lot to ask and I know it's getting late, but I feel like we're onto something here.'

'I'm fine staying for a while,' Braxton said.

'Same,' Arlow said.

Patel and Yates nodded.

'Right,' she said. 'I'll be back down as soon as I've spoken with Holden. I've been expecting his analysis of Sarah Barclay's tablets.' As she left the incident room, she took out her phone again. 'Lavery,' she said. 'Holden's ready with his analysis. Where are you?'

'I'm home,' she said. 'I'll head in.'

'Don't, I'll dial you in.'

–

The open-plan office floor of the Digital Forensics suite was empty. Holden's team must have already left for the day. Holden had squeezed himself into a chair in his little office off the main floor. It was all glass windows, and without a door, de Silva wondered what the point in it was.

'De Silva!' Holden said, a joy in his voice despite the gloom of the moment, and the snow falling down outside. 'Sorry to keep you here on a night like this. I suppose we all want to be home, tucked up in our onesies watching films, don't we?'

'A onesie, Holden?'

He didn't even blush. 'They're warm!' he said, defensively. 'I used to have a tiger one with a tail, but my sister's dog Troy attacked me. I had to throw it away.'

'That's a sad story, Holden,' she said. 'I've got Lavery on the phone.' She waved it at him then pressed the speaker button. 'You hear us, Lavery?'

'Loud and clear,' she said. 'Though thinking of either of you in a onesie is making me wish I couldn't.'

You and me both, de Silva thought.

'Okay,' Holden said. 'First things first. Sarah's tablets. Both of them had previously downloaded the In2Web VPN. On the one we received from Nick's home, it had been deleted. But it had been downloaded and deleted multiple times in the three weeks leading up to her disappearance. Same on the tablet from Barclay's.'

'So Nick or Ben were downloading the VPN?' Lavery asked.

'Not necessarily. The tablets had both been connected to both IP addresses at both properties, so they'd been used interchangeably at each address. They look the same, so I'm assuming they were easily mixed up.'

'Right?' de Silva asked.

'We're looking into linking the IP addresses with the downloads themselves, but we're not quite there yet.'

'Was there any evidence of The Woulds app?' de Silva asked.

'No,' he said. 'Nothing.'

'So, so far, you have nothing?' Lavery asked.

Holden looked to de Silva, winced and mouthed, 'What's her problem?'

De Silva shrugged. 'Well it's not nothing. We know that the VPN has been on both tablets at one point or another.'

'Hmmm.' Lavery sounded unconvinced.

'Well,' Holden said. 'I actually called you here for something else.'

'Go on,' de Silva said.

'We've managed to break into the hard drives from Mitch Whitley's,' he said. 'Endless coding, seamless firewalls. But we got there.'

'What did you find?' Lavery asked.

'Well, we're still digging through it all, but I can show you,' he said. 'It's not pretty. But I will.'

'Okay,' de Silva said, nodding.

'This is… not easy viewing.' He pressed play.

The image was of the loft space they'd found in Whitley's property. A girl, post-pubescent, de Silva could see, was chained to the wall, sitting up on a filthy mattress. The window displayed several angles. Some zoomed in on her face and her body, covered in bruises.

'Look at the camera,' a man's voice said. 'Look at the camera now.' He hit her so hard the girl fell back into the mattress. He grabbed her by her chin and moved her back into frame again. 'Look down that lens and tell them what you are.' His voice was low, menacing, thick with what sounded like hatred. Disgust.

'I…' the girl said, crying.

He hit her again and this time her nose burst with blood. 'Tell them you're a whore.'

De Silva reached over and paused the footage. 'For God's sake.' There were tears in her eyes, already slipping down her face. 'I can't watch any more.'

'I'm sorry,' Holden said. 'I know.'

'We're going to have to watch it,' Lavery said. 'To identify that girl. The others I'm assuming who are just like her on those hard drives.'

'Have you found Scarlet on there?' de Silva asked Holden. 'Sarah?'

'No,' Holden said. 'But we're not even a quarter of the way through all of the… er… content. There were some videos in there with Mitch Whitley on them, we know that much.'

'I'm coming in,' Lavery said. 'I need to go through this with you, Holden.'

He mouthed to de Silva, 'Fucking why?', but said out loud, 'That's fine. I'll see you soon.'

'Right, Lavery, come see me when you're done, won't you?' de Silva said.

'I will.'

'See you soon.' De Silva hung up. 'I don't know how you're going to get through all of this, Holden.'

'Me too,' he said. 'Some of the team have already requested alternative assignments. I don't blame them.'

'They were keeping a record,' de Silva said. 'A catalogue of their abuses. This is torture. Rape. I can't even begin to comprehend what happened in that room.'

'You won't have to,' Holden said. 'It's all in those hard drives. But, de Silva, that's not everything…'

'Jesus Christ, Holden, if there's any more, I'm not sure I want to hear about it.'

'These videos weren't just recorded and kept,' Holden said. 'They were live-streamed.'

Forty-Five

The Airbnb had two spacious bedrooms, a large living space and a separate kitchen on the first floor of an old, converted house that overlooked the park next to Crosby Marina. These houses reminded Barclay of *Mary Poppins* and *Peter Pan*, of Victorian-era London in films and on TV. There was magic about them, a sense of wonderment that had captured his imagination since he was a kid, on those rare occasions they came to the beach as a family.

Nick chose the room closest to the door, while Barclay's overlooked Marine Crescent and a park which backed up onto the marina itself. This time of year, it was quiet here, but in summer, families bustled, kids screamed and played. Just last summer, Barclay had taken Sarah there for a walk on the beach. She'd met dogs on leads with fluffy ears, and she'd squealed with delight and surprise as they licked her face and hands.

They'd bought ice creams from the vendor near the Waterloo Sunset café and said hello to even more dogs. He wondered whether that was the time they'd spotted her. These people from this app. Whether they had scouts out there looking for vulnerable kids, ones they knew rich old men would like to pay for.

He sat down on the bed and looked out of the window. Took out his phone to send Ayris a text to tell him they'd moved to an Airbnb in Waterloo and to call him when he was in Liverpool. He slid his phone into his pocket and peered out of his bedroom window onto the snow-banked paths and the icy roads, slick like wet glass; he wondered whether he would ever bring Sarah here again. Whether, in fact, he'd ever get to take her anywhere again.

He and Nick had had plans for her, the silly, fragile plans that all parents have for their kids. Good marks in exams, university to study some impossible subject that neither Nick nor Barclay understood, a really good job in finance or maybe a vet. She did like animals. They knew that, one day, these plans would slip them by as Sarah made her own decisions. Navigating her own way through life.

Barclay had hoped secretly that she would not make the same mistakes that he had made. That she wouldn't follow him down a path of one broken career to the next. The navy had turned into a nightmare and all he had wanted to do was serve his country, to follow rules and keep his head down. Get the job done. But that's not what God had in mind for him.

Later, he came to the police. Another way to serve, another set of rules to abide by, and even here God showed his true hand. Nothing in Barclay's life was to be easy. He sometimes felt, when the gloaming mood came on him, that he was created to suffer. Like that was his purpose. That was God's plan for him all along.

'You all right?' Char at the door.

Barclay turned to see her, felt something hot and wet slip down his cheek and he wiped it away. 'I'm fine,' he said. 'I'm sorry, I didn't expect to see you here.'

'You're not getting rid of me that easily,' she said with a laugh. 'I'll be around in the daytime. We've hired the apartment across the corridor there. Me and two uniform officers. I'll get them to introduce themselves in the morning. You and Nick should get some sleep. It's late.'

Barclay knew that there was no sleep to be had that night as the black crawled its way across everything, outside and in, and extinguished the sun. A strange apartment, a strange bed, his husband asleep in a bed next door. Maybe even lying there, staring up at the ceiling like Barclay knew he would.

'Okay,' Barclay said. He checked his watch. It was after ten p.m. 'See you in the morning.'

'DI Lavery will be around in the morning, too,' she said. 'Nothing to worry over, she just wants to make sure that you're settled in.'

'Okay.' Barclay nodded. He was convinced that under any other circumstance, he would like Char, but right then he wished he never had to see her ever again. Not because of anything she had done, he knew that, but because of what she had become to represent to him. If Sarah was still around, Char wouldn't be dogging their every move. She was Barclay's albatross.

But doesn't the albatross come before the bad stuff? he asked himself. *Like a warning? Oh, who cares!*

Char disappeared, he heard her saying goodnight to Nick and then the front door closed behind her. He walked out into the corridor and Nick was there, leaning against the wall.

'Do we need to talk?' Nick asked.

Barclay supposed that they did have to talk but wondered whether right then was the best time. Still, they walked into Barclay's bedroom and sat down on the hard mattress. They talked about Sarah, about what would happen when she came back, how things would be now that they had made the decision to end whatever was going on between them.

Somewhere in the early hours, the talking stopped. Nick fell asleep on top of the covers, and Barclay's eyes grew heavier until finally they closed too. In his sleep, he dreamed of Sarah. He could see her across the marina lake, her back to him as she was standing on top of a sand dune, looking out at the Irish Sea. There was screaming and shouting and banging and as Barclay ran toward her, the banging grew louder.

As the sound built to an awful crescendo, Barclay woke up. Nick was still fast asleep next to him, facing away to the bedroom door. Barclay crept out of bed and closed the door behind him. He sat on the couch for an hour, looking out at the street; the soft amber of the streetlight bathed the living room. Snow came down in drifts now, thick and heavy. Finally, when he knew sleep would evade him, he pulled on his coat, grabbed the key and headed outside into the snow. Some fresh air would do him good.

Barclay walked the length of Marine Crescent and back again, looped around onto South Road, passing the closed and shuttered restaurants and bars until he reached Crosby Road North. He turned right and walked until the junction with Cambridge Road, and headed back toward the Airbnb. There was a smell of smoke in the air, and somewhere, someone screamed.

His phone rang. Ayris calling. He answered, but Ayris's voice was muffled, tinny, made gappy by the lack of phone signal.

'Ayris?' Barclay said. 'I'll call you back when I get inside.'

His legs had started to hurt, and his eyes felt tired. He walked almost clumsily, and knew then that his body was finally, at last, ready for sleep. Smoke plumed over the tops of houses, all with lights on in the windows. He heard the roar of it before he saw it: somewhere there was a fire burning. Raging. And in that second, he knew...

He rounded the tall hedges which blocked the lower floor of the property and front garden from the view of passersby. Neighbours were out in the street, someone said they'd called for the fire brigade, and fire tore through the Airbnb building.

The old gate, painted white, squealed on rusted hinges as he pushed it. There, on the path, a young man in a pyjama T-shirt and shorts set lay, covered in blood. His green eyes wide. Stab marks all over his arms and chest and neck.

Barclay checked his phone again. He'd left his harness upstairs, with the PAVA spray and cuffs, and now all of it would burn.

A scream came from somewhere behind him. He turned and it came again through the evergreen trees of the park fenced in behind black railings.

There was no time for anything else. As it came again, he realised—

Nick.

Forty-Six

The rest of the team had left a little before midnight, exhausted and desperate for their families and their beds. De Silva understood that but knew that if she went home to her big empty house, she'd lie awake trying to piece all of this together.

She woke up slumped over her keyboard, the screen locked, and the cursor in the password box of her log-in screen typing away some key she'd leaned on. She wiped at her mouth with her fingers, which came away wet. She deleted the extraneous letters in the password box and logged in, the clacking of the keyboard loud in the quiet of the incident room. She had to move her arms above her head so the lights would come back on. When they did, they stung at her tired eyes.

She reached for her mug, sipped at the freezing cold coffee and spat it back out. She stood, stretched and turned toward the door. In the doorway, the silhouette of someone watching her from the dark of the corridor. She dropped her mug to the floor, heard the handle snap and the liquid splash into the carpet.

The figure stepped into the light. Lavery.

'Jesus Christ, what're you doing lurking around like Hannibal fucking Lecter?' De Silva bent down to pick up her broken mug, the one with rabbits on that Bonnie had gifted her last Easter.

'I'm sorry,' Lavery said, her voice gruff but soft. If de Silva wasn't mistaken, Lavery was almost smiling. Maybe she had wind. 'You were sleeping,' she said. 'I didn't want to startle you.'

'Well, you've done a piss-poor job of that,' de Silva said, throwing her mug into the bin with a clatter. 'What're you doing here so late?' She looked at her watch. 'So early,' she corrected herself.

'I just finished with Holden,' Lavery said.

'It's been hours; I thought you'd gone home already,' de Silva said. 'And you owe me a new mug.' She looked down at her computer. 'I was just…'

'Napping?'

'Doing research.'

'Into what?'

De Silva huffed and sagged into her chair. 'God, where do I even start?'

Lavery pulled up a chair next to her. 'At the beginning.'

'Well, it all started in 1986 when Rainford Lane School for Boys was opened by—'

'Very funny.' Lavery's straight face told de Silva she found her anything but funny. 'Those videos, de Silva.' She shook her head, pulled her full lips between her teeth then let them go. 'I've seen things tonight I didn't think I'd ever see. And he's still not even a quarter of the way through. This could take weeks. Boys. Girls. Some of them so young, de Silva. Some didn't even speak English.'

De Silva didn't even want to imagine what was in those videos but knew that one day she would have to. Maybe when all of this as over. When Sarah and Scarlet were found safe and sound.

'So, your research,' Lavery said, sitting down on a spare chair. 'Is it something that could help me find Sarah and Scarlet?'

De Silva nodded. 'I think so,' she said. 'Maybe.' She turned back to her computer and pulled up the notes she'd been making for a progress report to DSI Murphy. 'You know about T & K Holdings, so I can skip that part. They have investments in import and export companies, haulage, rail freight. All of that comes under one company, Litchfield's Haulage, Imports and Exports.'

'Catchy name.'

'Careful, Lavery,' de Silva said. 'You smile and your face might crack.'

Lavery's nostrils flared, almost imperceptibly, but de Silva caught it.

'A source of mine believes that this is how they're getting victims in and out of the country,' de Silva said.

'What source?'

'Breaker.'

'The person who leaked The Woulds client list to you last year?' Lavery couldn't keep the incredulity from her face. 'Can you trust her?'

'I'm not entirely sure, but it's more information than we had before tonight, er yesterday. You know what I mean,' de Silva said. 'We'd have got there, but slower without her help. Anyway, listen, T & K Holdings also have investments in a company called Granite Warehousing, who specialise in corporate storage facilities. They have warehouses in London, Swansea, Plymouth, all over the UK. Including right here in Liverpool.'

Lavery frowned, and she glanced away for just a second. 'They're all port cities.'

De Silva nodded. 'Now you're catching on. I called the Port Control Centre earlier,' she said. 'They confirm that Litchfield's Haulage have cargo ships docking there weekly.'

'That's interesting.'

'There's more.' De Silva's mind had begun to turn again, the cogs spinning quickly and smoothly now. 'The port is operated by The Gateway Group.'

'Right?'

'And guess who is a key stakeholder of that group?'

'T & K Holdings.'

'Correct.' De Silva turned to her computer and brought up Google Maps. 'Now, Granite Warehousing owns a building out on Brocklebank Dock.'

'So what are you thinking?'

'I… and tell me if you think I've lost it… but what if the warehouse at Brocklebank Dock is a storage facility. A holding place until the shipments can be delivered to Litchfield's Haulage at the port.'

'Shipments of…?'

De Silva paused, turned to look at Lavery and said, 'The boys and girls you saw in those videos.'

The buzz and whirr of de Silva's computer filled the silence that followed. A quiet in which she was sure she could hear Lavery thinking. 'De Silva,' Lavery said finally. 'I think you've lost it. But, if I'm honest, I think that happened a long time ago.' She studied de Silva's face, and she wondered what the DI was looking for there. 'But I think you might be onto something. And if you're right, we'll need to arrange a team now. We can't go down there on our own; this isn't an episode of *Cagney & Lacey*. We do things properly, or we don't do it at all.'

De Silva got to her feet. 'We can scramble a team on the way.'

Lavery stood too. 'No,' she said. 'I'm not getting myself caught up in a shoot-out or some other danger the way you and Barclay seem to find yourselves.'

'Then stay here and organise everything.' De Silva pulled her harness from the back of her chair and slipped into it. 'I'm going and I'll update Murphy on the way. You can stay here if you want to.'

'If you go out there without proper backup, without following protocol, I'll include it in my report to DSI Murphy, and I *will* make recommendations based on the recklessness of your actions.'

'You do what you need to do, Lavery.' De Silva locked her computer, grabbed her mobile phone and coat and headed for the door.

–

Lavery was sitting in the passenger seat, barking orders down the phone to someone on her team. When she was done, she looked out of the window as the dock road slipped by in a blur of run-down buildings and grey metal fences. 'I can't believe I'm doing this,' she said.

De Silva turned on the wipers, flicking away the snow that fell now in thick, heavy clumps, covering the roads and paths quickly. She'd called DSI Murphy to beg for a warrant to search the property of Granite Warehousing, based on the evidence they'd amassed. Murphy hadn't called back yet. De Silva sighed, pushed it out of her mind, and said, 'There is something else I need to discuss with you.'

'Of course there is,' Lavery said. 'I knew your reputation wasn't just hearsay and slander.'

Slander, de Silva thought. *What exactly do people say about me?*

'We thought we had a name for the killers Arlow's team have been looking into,' de Silva said.

'Right?'

One of the tyres skidded in the snow, but de Silva managed to correct it and slow down. 'Fuck,' she said. 'Look, you let me know a method to tell you two things at once, and I'll employ it. The name's Terry Thompson.'

'Thompson...' Lavery pondered. 'I know that name. Any relation to Billy Thompson?'

'His brother,' de Silva said.

'Did he go to Rainford Lane School for Boys, too?'

De Silva nodded. 'And Mike Crosby indicated that Terry was more than just abused. He was tortured. By Christine Jones.'

'So he killed her,' Lavery said, nodding. 'Do we have an address?'

De Silva shrugged. 'The fella's dead, Lavery. They had a younger brother, though. Arlow's looking into it.'

Forty-Seven

Barclay could barely make them out in the dark and the heavy snow. Two shadows chasing each other down the marina path toward the sand dunes he'd seen just an hour or so ago in his dreams. Though he wished he'd find Sarah there, that his dream would be some sort of prophecy, he knew that was a folly.

'Nick!' he shouted out, but only his own voice replied to him in thinning echoes until finally it stopped. His phone still had no service. He was sure that the scream he heard had belonged to Nick. He could run back to the Airbnb, find the dead PC's radio and call for help, or he could run after shadows. As the ashes from the burning Airbnb fell with the snow, he knew there was no reason for him to go back.

If one of those people is Nick, he told himself, *he might need me. He might need help.*

It was against procedure and protocol. It went against every fibre of his rule-abiding nature. But it could be his ex out there. His husband. The father of his daughter. Barclay was on his toes and heading down the path as the figures disappeared over the sand dunes.

The path ran between the dunes on either side, opening up onto another larger path, the beach beyond. He could see one of them standing out there, staring out at the ocean or looking right at him. He couldn't tell which.

There was another of them.

Another.

They were all over the beach, all standing straight and staring.

The realisation overcame his fear as finally he knew that he was seeing the Antony Gormley sculptures. He'd always found them a bit creepy. Some half-buried in the sand like they were clawing their way out of the earth or burying themselves like crabs when the tide has gone out.

'Nick!' he screamed at the Irish Sea, but all that came back was the shush and collapse of waves he couldn't see somewhere out in the dark.

'Ben!' It was him. His voice seemed to come from everywhere and nowhere all at once. 'Ben!' His scream filled the air, shrill with terror.

Barclay ran down the concrete steps and onto the beach, the wet sand kicking up onto his shoes and jeans as he darted toward the tide. He didn't know where else to go.

He sprinted past one of the iron men, could smell the blood-like stink of it in the air. Then it moved. It reached out, grabbed him and pulled him down into the sand. He felt wet instantly, grains finding their way into his jumper, his jeans, even into his shoes.

The flash of a knife. He groaned, tried to shove the man off him, but it bit solidly into his shoulder. Somewhere nearby, he could hear coughing, spluttering, the glug-glug of a blocked drain.

The man on top of him raised the knife again, glinting in the moonlight. Barclay gripped his wrist and tried to push the weapon backward. Footfall somewhere else on the sand.

The knife came down again, the handle cracking into the side of his skull. White light burst bright behind his eyes and the beach spun around him. The snow seemed to fall from the ground upward. The sky somehow upside down, and above him, two men among the Gormley sculptures. Two men with the same wild snarl. Two men leaning close to Barclay's face, hissing something, two men whose breath Barclay could smell, coppery.

Two knives in identical fists raised above him as the footfall came again, closer this time. 'Hold him still,' a low, ragged voice came from somewhere.

'I've got him.' Another voice, higher this time, almost frightened. 'Do it, Terry,' he said. 'Do it!'

Barclay blinked hard, trying to rectify his vision, to stop the pounding in his temples. Wind raked down the beach and the iron men watched on, faces blank. A shadow moved out there somewhere beyond them and as the man on top of Barclay swung the knife down toward Barclay's chest, the man grunted. The weight on top of Barclay shifted sideways. He heard something skitter and crunch in the snow or the sand.

A hand reached down to take hold of Barclay's, and he took it. He got to his feet to find Ayris there, sweating, drenched, shoulders and hair covered in snow. 'Are you okay?' he asked, his Scottish accent stronger than Barclay had ever heard it before. 'Jesus Christ, you're bleeding.'

They turned to look down at the man who had been on top of Barclay, flat out cold. 'Who the fuck is that?' Ayris asked.

'I've no idea,' Barclay said. The ache in his head throbbed, brought him out of the dull haze. 'Nick,' he said, moving forward. 'Where's Nick?' He took his phone out of his pocket, still no signal, and turned on the torch. But, in truth, he didn't have to look. He could hear. Above the crashing of the waves, the screaming of gulls even at this hour, was that glugging sound.

A few yards up the beach, a black silhouette against the white of the snow, something lay in front of one of the iron men. Barclay raced toward it, almost slipping in the snow. The phone light found the object, found Nick, and all around him the white snow had stained red. The image of Lawrence outside the flat in Manchester flashed quickly in his mind before he managed to take in the sight in front of him.

If it weren't for the fact that he had Nick's clothes on, Barclay would have thought this person lying there was some stranger.

Someone he could never possibly recognise. Blood bubbled and foamed at Nick's mouth and a hand reached up for Barclay as he sank to his knees.

He took off his coat, not knowing where to apply pressure first. His body was covered. Blood. Deep, dark, rich. Nick's eyes flicked to Barclay, wide and desperate. For the first time, Barclay felt as though the tide in his mind had completely receded, as though readying itself for a tsunami. An onslaught of destruction.

Screaming behind him now.

Ayris's voice boomed in the open expanse, 'Stay down!' Then, 'Ben! Watch out!'

Barclay felt it strike him in the shoulder blade, like a hammer blow. He rolled sideways so that his weight didn't crush Nick, and as he did so, something snapped. He felt it more than he heard it.

The man was standing over him, just the one of him, clear as a bell now that the haziness had lifted. 'Don't let him get away,' the man said, in a voice so low and rasping that it sounded like a metal grinder.

'I won't.' A completely different voice from the same mouth. The man got to one knee and thumped Barclay about the head with closed fists.

Then, his weight shifted again. The man was pulled off Barclay, who got to his feet quickly to see Ayris dragging the man to the ground. He looked down to Nick, still and quiet beside him, his eyes staring hauntingly at Barclay.

Barclay ran forward, grabbed the man by his shoulders and pinioned him to the ground. Ayris reached for the cuffs from his pocket, spun him over and fastened them to his wrists. 'Who the fuck is this?' Ayris asked.

Barclay shook his head. Words wouldn't come to him. He knew why this man had come. He knew why he'd attacked Nick, why he'd wanted to kill Barclay, but didn't know his name.

'Get up to the main road,' Ayris said. 'See if you get a bloody signal.'

'But—'

'I've got him,' Ayris shouted. 'Just go!'

The restrained man struggled against the cuffs and the weight of Ayris, his chest heaving. 'Say nothing,' he said, in that hellish voice. 'Say nothing and we'll be sound.'

'What's your name?' Ayris asked.

The man just laughed.

'Ben!' Ayris shouted. 'We need help!'

The throbbing in Barclay's head had turned into a ringing, and the wounds to his shoulder and back burned. He swallowed down the metallic taste in his throat and mouth, painfully aware of something jagged and sharp stuck in his shoulder blade. He looked back to Nick, lying there in the sand, his chest rising and falling in uneven, jagged motion.

He'll be cold, Barclay thought. *He'll get sick.*

'BEN!' Ayris's voice boomed, annoyance fortifying it. 'FUCKING GO.'

Barclay staggered away toward the concrete steps and the footpath, his phone in his hand. As he walked away, the sound of the sea became quieter, and across the snow and sand, he heard the man speak in that voice that gave Barclay chills. 'He's scared of the dark you know.'

'No, I'm not!' The other voice then. 'I'm not, Terry!'

Barclay turned back as he reached the top of the steps. The snow still fell, covering the sand and the sea and the shape of Nick's body. The iron men stared out at the tide, rusted and freckled with snow. The icy wind worried at Barclay's torn jumper. He looked back across the marina, to the twirling blue lights of emergency services. Smoke billowed up into the black sky, and the fury of the fire still raged.

He ran toward the chaos.

Forty-Eight

'I haven't got time for you to call and check,' de Silva said to a fat security guard in a hi-viz jacket and a woollen hat with a reflective stripe around it. 'I need you to give me access to the grounds immediately.' She snatched back her warrant card from him and shoved it into her pocket.

The security guard's jaw worked as though he was chewing on a decision, then he reached for a loop of keys fastened to his belt. 'All right, girl,' the man said. 'Calm the fuck down.' He unfastened the heavy padlock on the gate and slid them open. 'Granite is just down there,' he said, pointing. 'Middle right. But I'm ringing through now to make sure you're genuine.'

'Do what you've got to do, mate.' De Silva climbed back into the car and drove down toward the warehouse.

The snow still came, turning the grey dock white. The carpark outside Granite Warehousing was a square of concrete fringed with high metal fences and topped with barbed wire. Security lights on the exterior blazed white light down on them, reflecting in the snow, and Lavery covered her eyes from the dazzling of the light.

Lavery was out of the car before de Silva, pulling the collar of her coat up high, her breath steaming in front of her. A sign on the fence read *GRANITE WAREHOUSING*, the paint faded and peeling. The warehouse itself was nondescript, a grey block that matched every other warehouse around it, though it was smaller than de Silva had imagined.

The security guard joined them finally and unlocked a small gate into the warehouse's empty carpark. 'They're here every night,' he said, 'so don't be shocked if they show up and ask what the fuck you're doing. Show me that warrant card again; I want to know exactly who I'm asking about when I ring.'

De Silva showed him it again and he snapped a photo of it on his phone. 'We'll be inside when you've checked me out,' she said.

Lavery pushed open the gate with a groan of old hinges, the sound reverberating through the metal fences. A wooden door seemed to be the only way into the warehouse. Not even a roller-shutter for easy access. That struck de Silva as unusual. Surely it would be needed for deliveries.

'I suppose that's locked as well,' de Silva said, nodding toward the door, which seemed as though a good shove would have it open anyway.

'Can't help you with that one,' he said. 'We leave anything like that to the businesses to manage.'

De Silva walked over to the door and tried the handle. Locked. 'Help me,' she said to Lavery.

'No,' she said. 'We don't have a warrant to access this space.'

'Murphy is working on it,' de Silva said.

'And until we get a response from DSI Murphy, I'm staying right here.'

De Silva shoved at the door, and something splintered and cracked.

'Should she be doing that?' the security guard asked.

'No, she shouldn't,' Lavery said. 'Maybe best if you leave us to it. You weren't here; you saw nothing.'

The guard nodded and wandered off, chunnering to himself about police feeling like they can do whatever they want to do.

De Silva gave the door her shoulder one more time, and the whole thing fell apart. Inside, darkness lay on top of darkness. They both turned on the torches from their harnesses, cutting through the black. Plastic sheeting had been hung from the ceiling and shifted lazily on the breeze coming through the door. De Silva could see the roller-shutter at the back of the warehouse then, only half closed. There was a stink of rust and shit, and through the roof, snow fell in patches onto the concrete floor.

The space was small and empty, save for the sheeting, scattered pallets against the wall, some spools of abandoned cable. Nothing moved.

'There's nothing here, de Silva,' Lavery said.

'Then you won't mind if we have a quick look around.' De Silva stepped inside the warehouse and Lavery followed her. Their torchlight swept over the space and found nothing.

A crack came from outside, like a car door shutting. The grumble of an engine. Headlights shone through the windows at the side of the warehouse and before she even considered her actions, de Silva had spun on her heels, raced around to the side of the warehouse as a lorry barrelled toward her.

'Stop!' she screamed.

It didn't brake. The engine revved and the headlights grew brighter. De Silva dodged it just in time. Her boots slipped; she sprawled in the snow, her hip cracking against the concrete beneath it. She felt the heat of the van's engine as it sailed past. It collided with the open door of her battered old Ford Kuga and spun it to the ground in a shower of sparks and clanging.

'Fuck,' she said. 'Fuck!' De Silva jumped to her feet, launched her torch somewhere and ran to her car, starting the engine and putting her foot down on the gas. The car spun in the snow and ice but eventually gained traction and moved off. The security guard was shouting something at her from his little hut, but she didn't have time to stop.

Her palms were raw on the steering wheel, her heartbeat hammering beneath her ribs. She followed the lorry out onto the main road, almost colliding with the fence. Ahead of her, the lorry fishtailed, its back doors rattling. It straightened and accelerated down Regent Road.

The tarmac, turned white by snow now, stretched ahead like a strip of frozen steel, lamp posts turning everything yellow and orange. The van roared ahead of her, its diesel engine working hard. De Silva pressed her foot flat. If she lost the van now and it got to the port, then whatever was inside, *whoever* was inside, could be lost forever.

The tyres screamed as her car bucked across the ice and snow. Her fingers clenched the wheel, knuckles white and bloodless as bone. With each revolution of the tyres, she felt the car slip.

The lorry slewed left, skidding onto Seymour Street, almost colliding with the Dockside Lodge building on the corner.

She followed.

The back end of her car slid out, skittering across the road. She tried to brake, but they must have locked. She slid. She lurched. The snow and ice won. The vehicle spun once. Twice. The world around her was a blur of buildings and parked lorries, of streaks of orange light.

Metal shrieked. The car tipped, rolled onto its side, and de Silva was sure that she was upside down for just a second. It crashed into a parked lorry on the junction and the windshield cracked, a spiderweb in glass.

The world seemed to slow.

Something hot and warm coursed down from her hairline. The steering wheel lodged in her ribs. Her legs felt cold. The airbag had inflated, smashed into her face. Ahead of her, the lorry's red taillights disappeared as it turned left off Seymour Street.

Her head felt heavy and sagged forward.

She heard the blaring of the horn. An endless scream that filled the dark night.

De Silva couldn't say how long she had been out. She heard a voice. Not Lavery's icy tone, but a man's voice. A foreign accent. 'Come on,' he was saying. 'Come on, you can do it.'

She felt his hands on her, hot and steady and strong. He was lifting her, pulling her, reaching around her. There was a smell of smoke that hung in the air, acrid. She coughed and her eyes opened, to see the man finally. He was dark skinned, hair shaved short, with a heavy moustache that reminded her of one her dad had grown in the eighties.

She couldn't move, couldn't make it easier for the man. He hauled her out of the car window, arms hooked under her shoulders. She groaned as pain sliced through her abdomen and her head. He dropped her down to the snow and dragged her backward. She saw tiny reflections out of the corners of her eyes.

Snow, she thought. *No, not snow. Glass.*

She saw it then. Smoke rising from the front of her car. Yellow flames crackling from under the bonnet. She had collided with a lorry container. The fire grew, a muffled roar, and she could feel the heat from across the street.

The man carried her into the shadow of a lorry, where the cabin door was open. He put her down against the tyre and staggered back to the front of the lorry, his phone to his ear, talking to someone.

De Silva fumbled for her radio, the plastic slick with blood. 'Control...' she said, her throat aching and dry. 'This is DCI de Silva. Officer down. We need backup at Brocklebank Dock. Granite...' Talking hurt her head. 'Granite Warehousing.'

She got to her feet, her knees almost buckling under her own weight. She had to get back to the warehouse. To Lavery. 'Lavery,' she called down the radio. 'DI Lavery, come in.'

A distorted voice replied. 'De Silva! Jesus Christ, where are you?'

'I'm—'

A whoosh. A boom. A ringing in de Silva's ears. Instinctively, she ducked down, the lorry beside her swaying, the windows of the cabin blown out. The foreign man on the phone, hands flailing in front of the cab. His cab.

There was no time to waste, she knew that. She pushed herself up to her feet, legs quivering, and staggered back down the snow-covered road toward the warehouse.

She wanted to vomit. Felt it burn at the back of her throat as her eyes struggled to focus on anything in front of her. The security guard from Brocklebank ran to her, arms outstretched, ready to grab her. 'You need to sit down,' he said. He cast a glance over her shoulder. 'Jesus, love, what the fuck have you done?'

'They're gone,' she said, her voice hoarse. 'Wait here,' she managed. 'Backup is coming.'

She walked on to the warehouse alone, and inside Lavery's torchlight seemed brighter that it had done before. 'De Silva!' She raced toward her, the light bouncing in her hand. 'Bloody hell!'

'I'm fine,' she said. 'I just need to sit down. Did you find anything?' De Silva was sitting on a rough-wood stack of old pallets and behind her something squeaked and shuffled off into the shadows. She radioed control. Asked to divert the backup to converge on the docks instead. 'We need to stop that lorry.'

'You need more than to sit down, de Silva,' Lavery said, eyeing her. 'Look at the state of you.'

'Did you find anything?'

Lavery's breath caught in her throat. Hesitating. 'Yes,' she said. 'There's a door leading to the basement.'

'Okay.' De Silva got to her feet. 'Show me.'

De Silva leaned on Lavery as she limped across the space to the back, where there was a small office that de Silva doubted anyone had ever sat in, and an open metal door with concrete steps leading down into even more dark. There was a smell of shit, of stale air, of damp and festering. Sour. Rotting.

They descended slowly, Lavery supporting de Silva every step of the way, the torch beam jerking across the mould-ridden walls as they descended. Then, they heard it.

A whimper.

They both stopped, stared at each other. It came again.

Small.

Human.

'Hello?' de Silva called into the dark.

Below them, shuffling. Whispering.

They edged forward and stepped off the bottom stair, swept their beam across the basement room. Steel crates. Large. New. Bolted to the floor and ceiling. Padlocked.

Behind the bars, faces blinked in the sudden light. Filthy faces. Gaunt and bruised. They were the faces of children. Boys and girls. Ten, twelve, some no more than five years old, if de Silva had to guess there and then. They were dressed in old clothes that didn't quite seem to fit them, hair lank with grease and filth.

'Oh my fuck...' Lavery managed.

'Get back upstairs and radio again for ambulances,' de Silva barked.

'De Silva—'

'Now!'

Lavery turned and ran up the stairs.

De Silva moved to the first crate, pulled at the padlock. It shone bright and brilliant in her torchlight, and she knew that it too was new. It wouldn't budge. 'It's okay,' she said softly, trying to smile. 'I'm going to get you out. You're safe.'

Whispers among the kids. De Silva looked around. There were four more crates just like this one, each packed with kids. There had to be over a hundred, she guessed, maybe two hundred.

'We're going to get you out,' she said again. She moved forward, her legs throbbing and cold. She scanned the faces quickly. 'Sarah?' she called out, her voice rasping. 'Sarah Barclay, are you here?'

The kids started to cry. The sound swelled in the basement, but none answered the name. De Silva knew Sarah could still be there, could be too frightened to answer to someone standing in the shadows of this hell.

Lavery's shoes thudded on the concrete floor behind de Silva. 'They're coming,' she said, breathless. 'A few minutes away.'

'We'll get you out,' de Silva called again. 'Just hold on.'

Their sobs hurt her head and broke her heart and then suddenly, Lavery shouted, 'Oh my God, de Silva. Over here!'

De Silva turned to look at her, pressed up against the bars of the crate opposite the first one. Her little face was dirty, and tears had left tracks in the filth, but it was her. Unmistakably her. Her hands held out and de Silva took hold of them.

Her face was hollow, eyes wide in the half-light, but she was alive. She gripped de Silva's hands with white knuckles, and she cried.

Behind her, the children cried and wailed, their voices rising like smoke, like a tide, and they echoed off the damp concrete walls.

De Silva's knees almost gave out, but she steadied herself against the bars. 'Scarlet,' she said. 'We've been looking for you.'

Forty-Nine

Nine Days Later

De Silva had more black clothes than the average person, she assumed. The snow had lifted three days ago, but still the air was icy, and she knew that a dress wouldn't be a sensible choice. It would be black trousers, a thick but smart black coat; she'd like to wear a heel, but her leg was still giving her gyp, so it would have to be flats, and that made her thankful she could wear socks. Not that the day was about style, nor was it about DCI Winifred de Silva.

The call came as she climbed into her car and turned off the radio, some incessant chatter about the latest celebrity scandal. Brennan said, 'Hi, Win.' His voice was neutral, not his jolly self. Though, she supposed, joviality was not the order of the day. 'I'm sorry to call you today, but I knew you'd want to know.'

'It's all right,' de Silva said. There was an old saying that an officer was never off duty. That there was no such thing. De Silva had come to realise that was a truth bobbies didn't seem to speak about. 'What is it?'

'I've got Holden on the line,' he said.

'Morning,' Holden said, awkwardly stumbling over the single word.

'You asked us to look into something for you,' Brennan continued.

She remembered. Specifically, she wanted to know whether there was any evidence that Sarah Barclay had ever been there in that room where they'd seen those awful things happen via videos on hard drives. From Holden, she wanted to know whether Sarah appeared in any videos on those hard drives, beneath the layers of encryption.

'And?'

'We found hair samples that matched samples we took from a brush taken from Nick Barclay's property. She was in that room,' he said.

She had thought as much. Feared as much. Soon, she would have to inform Lavery of this development, and in turn, Lavery would have to update Barclay. 'I see.'

'And for us...' Holden said. There was a quiet then, where Holden bumbled, tried to think of a way to say what he needed to say, but all that came out were sounds. 'She is on one of the tapes,' Holden said, finally.

De Silva closed her eyes. Willing this conversation to be some awful nightmare. As she opened them and saw mascara running down her cheek in the rearview mirror, she knew that this was very real. 'Is she...?' De Silva could barely finish.

'Is she alive?' Holden asked. 'In this video she is. But, de Silva, what they did—'

'I can't hear this today,' she said. 'I'll talk to you about it tomorrow. With Lavery.' Her heart was heavy; her stomach grumbled. The only thing that kept her from breaking apart was knowing that, on that video at least, Sarah was alive. 'I'm going to be late,' she said. 'I'll speak with you tomorrow.'

She disconnected the call without saying goodbye. She wiped away the black scars on her cheek, quickly reapplied some make-up to her cheeks and turned on the engine.

She had told Braxton that she would pick him up as he didn't live too far from her, and the others said they would meet them there. He walked out of his front door, head bowed low, shoulders hunched. When he climbed in, he gave de Silva a tight smile, and neither of them spoke as they made their way to the crematorium.

In the quiet, she thought of her father. His apparent connections to T & K Holdings. His omitting Terry's name from his report when he visited Rainford Lane. Was it all connected? Had he known about O'Brien's own involvement, his sick, perverse tastes? She'd have to find out. She'd have to clear his name or, if it came to it, damn it.

De Silva turned off the main road, rolled into the carpark and reversed into a narrow space. Braxton turned to her. 'Have you heard from him?'

'No,' she said, simply. In truth there was more she wanted to talk about. How Barclay had buttoned every call she'd made, had ignored each text message since that night. She wondered, with a sinking sense of contrition, whether Barclay blamed her in some way.

They'd rescued Scarlet that night in that grim warehouse on Brocklebank Dock, but Sarah was nowhere to be found. By time the diverted team reached the port, the cargo ship owned by Litchfield's Haulage had gone. The port control office had no listed destination, and despite de Silva putting out a notice to Interpol, the ship had never pinged at any port or dock.

These people had operated out of the Port of Liverpool with impunity for only God knew how long, and de Silva doubted that they didn't have the power to hide themselves at any port in the world if they needed to, especially in a world where billionaires owned private islands.

Mourners streamed from the carpark up toward the crematorium, eager to get in out of the cold. As de Silva and Braxton followed them, she spotted Harris, Arlow, Yates and Patel up ahead with Lavery. De Silva was glad to see that O'Connor was there, too. Yates gave a little wave and smile, then remembered where she was.

'It's a good turnout,' Harris said by way of a hello.

'Shall we head up?' de Silva asked. 'Sit at the back, all right? Let the family and friends fill up the front first.'

'We are friends,' Braxton said, walking off ahead of the others.

That jarred with de Silva in a way she couldn't quite recognise and made her question her own words. Her own thoughts.

She had worked with Lawrence for the last two years and had gotten to know her; but de Silva wondered whether Lawrence was only ever a colleague to her. If so, was that not okay? Was that not enough?

She had kept everyone at a distance since she had returned to work after Ritchie's death. Even more so since they'd found out about O'Brien. The things he'd done to innocent boys. How he'd betrayed her. DCI Collins had betrayed them all, too, and disgraced himself and Greater Manchester Police, and every other police officer in the country. He'd withheld evidence, and despite intense questioning, he'd said nothing. His reasons remained unknown. The reasons for the T & K Holdings bank transfers would probably remain unresolved. She tried not to imagine what work he had done for them, but sometimes, in the nighttime and the comfort of her bed, it was all she could think about.

And then there was her own father.

Carl Brophy.

He'd been her hero. The man she had looked up to, doted on, admired, wanted to be like. Her devotion to him had led her on her career path, had dragged her up the ranks to DCI. And now his name was linked to T & K Holdings and to this whole sorry mess. That was a fact she would have to keep to herself for the time being. She knew that there were questions to ask, but whether she was willing, or prepared, to answer them was something she would have to save for another day.

'De Silva.' Murphy approached from behind, arm in arm with DSI Graeme Little from GMP. 'Do you have a second?'

De Silva turned back to the others. 'I'll be along in a minute.'

Murphy excused Little, and he passed de Silva with a curt nod. They sat down on a wooden bench off the main path, mourners passing them like crows. 'How are you holding up?' Murphy asked.

'Tired,' de Silva answered. 'Worried about Barclay. He won't speak to me.'

'He's processing everything.'

'Have you spoken to him?'

Murphy nodded. 'I'm afraid to say that he tendered his resignation this morning,' she said, her voice grave. 'In light of everything with Sarah, I don't blame him.'

'And Nick?'

'Well, he's going to need a lot of time to recover,' she said, 'but…'

'But what?'

'What Robert Thompson did to him… he could heal, but he'll never be the same again.'

'Jesus.' De Silva looked down at her lap, felt tears pulsing behind her eyes and not for the first time that day.

'How is it going with Thompson?' Murphy asked.

'We had to hand him off to a mental health facility,' de Silva said. 'Speaking to and for your dead brother… I doubt he'll ever stand trial for what he's done.'

'The world is cruel.'

'Those men and women at Rainford Lane were cruel,' de Silva said. 'When he… when he *was* himself, Rob told us about what happened to Terry. The abuse he suffered like the other boys. But the extra attention Christine Jones paid to him during his stay there. She'd burn him with boiled kettles. Stab him with a compass. A screwdriver. When the school finally closed, their parents couldn't deal with their sons' behaviour. Sent them to a therapist. Turns out he was abusing them too. I meant to update you on this one, but we found the therapy tapes on the hard drives we found at Whitley's house.'

'He recorded their therapy sessions? Did the parents know?'

'I doubt they knew about it, based on what we saw on the recordings,' de Silva said. 'We're still unpicking everything Whitley had stored at his house, ma'am. But I think it'll be more of the same. We found kids showering, changing, people giving them instructions on how to move or dance, to put their tongue out to…' De Silva trailed off. 'Some of it recorded from their own smart devices.'

Murphy shook her head. 'I'll never understand it,' she said.

'Have you heard anything about Scarlet Putney?'

'She's safe,' Murphy said. 'And she'll live, despite the abuse she has endured. I think that's the best we can hope for. She'll go into the foster system.'

'Not the best place for kids like her.' De Silva had to believe that there was more to hope for. That, one day in the future, Scarlet could put behind her everything that had happened and find a way to move on. Not to forgive. Not to forget. To live with the memory of what had happened to her. The abuse. The death of her mother.

'So much death,' de Silva said. 'So much hurt. How do you heal from something like that?'

'You move forward,' Murphy said. 'What about the toxicology results from Beatrice's post-mortem?'

'They came back,' de Silva said. 'She'd been over-anticoagulated with a common drug called warfarin. The effects would look like a stroke. Blood tests when Tom O'Brien was admitted to hospital showed a similar amount of the drug in his system.'

'Something else to look into,' Murphy said. 'Tomorrow.'

The service was a beautiful one. Lawrence's dad spoke about how much of a good girl she'd been as a kid. Always followed the rules. How she was a netball champion who played for Merseyside in her teenage years. How she had befriended everyone at school, resulting in her popularity; how she always wanted to help those in need. Those who couldn't help themselves.

Her brother, a tall man with a buzzcut, read a poem he said was called 'When Tomorrow Starts Without Me' by David M. Romano. De Silva had never heard it before, but the words were beautiful, the sentiment authentic, even as the brother's voice wobbled under the weight of his own emotions. De Silva couldn't help but notice the bulk at the bottom of his suit trousers. She knew that underneath there was an ankle monitor, something else she didn't know about Lawrence.

Later, when the coffin was pulled toward open curtains, de Silva allowed herself a moment of weakness in front of her team. She cried, not loudly, not sobs wringing out of her body like water from a sponge.

If anyone noticed, they didn't say a word.

Fifty

The bedroom was to be kept dark. They were the instructions. Not from the doctor or the surgeon, but from Nick. 'I don't want to see outside,' he'd said. Barclay had wondered whether Nick didn't want to see the world outside, or whether he was more worried the world outside would see him.

The nurse had come to change the bandages earlier and had shown Barclay how to do it, how to keep the wounds clean. He cried each time he left the room, sobbed every time Nick lost his temper and threw something at the wall, glass shattering everywhere.

He couldn't imagine what his husband was feeling or going through. They'd lost their daughter, she wasn't among the children de Silva and Lavery found in the basement of that warehouse, and now Nick had lost himself. The face he looked on in the mirror wasn't his own.

'It's hideous,' he'd said. 'It's disgusting.' He'd shattered the mirror with his fist and had needed eight more stitches. Another scar for his collection.

Barclay was barely healed himself; though the knife that had broken off in his shoulder blade was removed, it had left some lasting nerve damage. A numbness to his shoulder and arm that he may never recover from.

At night, when he slept in the guest bedroom, watching videos of cow hoof injury repairs on Instagram, he heard the sucking sound of Nick choking on his own blood. Felt the icy wind thunder down the beach. The snow land like tiny fingertips on his hair and face, the hard concrete pavement under his feet. He'd see faces on the iron men at the beach. Sometimes he saw Rob Thompson's face. Other times it was Nick's face he saw. Or what was left of Nick's face.

Nick was asleep in the gloom of the bedroom they'd once shared, and next door, Sarah's room hadn't changed. Barclay needed to get out of the house, to feel the winter air on his face. He'd promised Nick he'd run an errand for him when he next went into town, and right then was as good a time as any. He took out his phone and called Ayris.

They met in town an hour later, when Barclay's legs ached from walking all that way in the biting cold. Ayris had ordered Barclay an oat milk latte and it steamed on the table as he sat down. There was a small overnight bag on the floor at Ayris's feet and Barclay eyed it with a jealousy he felt unjustified feeling. Ayris was leaving again. Escaping while Barclay stayed. While he cared for a man he no longer wanted to be with.

'How is everything at home?' Ayris asked.

Barclay nodded. 'The same.' He sipped his coffee, and it was so hot it burned his top lip. He didn't care. 'I can't help but think how different things could have been.'

'If what?'

'If you'd have not gone back to London,' he said. 'If you'd have stayed.'

'I came as soon as I could,' Ayris said. 'I'm sorry.' Ayris looked down at the table, his face pale.

'You don't need to apologise,' he said. 'You came, and that's the important bit. If you didn't show up that night…' *Nick would be dead*, Barclay thought. 'So, what's now for you? Back to London?'

He sighed. 'De Silva, you and the team, you've split the case wide open. But there's more to do now. I feel like this is just the beginning. I'm not going anywhere.' He reached out and put a warm hand on Barclay's.

Barclay looked away, out of the steamed window as shoppers rushed by with their bags, mothers with their prams, small children bundled in coats and scarfs, and he thought of Sarah. His chest caved under the weight of his guilt, and he covered his face. Ayris moved around the table and held him close. 'Oh God, Rob,' Barclay said. 'I should have done more. I could have done more.'

'You couldn't,' Ayris said. 'But listen. We'll find her. I promise you.'

'Don't make promises you can't keep,' Barclay said. 'I should go anyway.' He took one last sip of his latte and headed for the door, where Ayris followed him carrying his overnight bag. 'I don't know when I can see you again,' he said. 'Nick needs me right now and—'

'I'll be around when you're ready,' Ayris said.

Barclay took a step backward. 'Thank you.'

Ayris nodded.

As Barclay walked away from the Nero on Bold Street, he felt the pull of something between him and Ayris; it tightened and finally it snapped. His empty backpack sagged on his back and with every step, a slicing pain in his shoulder reminded him of that night on the beach when Ayris saved his life. Saved Nick's life, too.

-

The Grey Room gallery was a small one, a clean, light grey space that smelled of nothing. It reminded Barclay of his first visit to an autopsy room over two years ago. There was no smell then, either.

'You didn't have to come,' Stefan said. 'I'd have dropped it off.'

'He's been asking for it.'

'Right,' Stefan said, nodding. 'It's just through here.' Stefan led Barclay through to a small office. It smelled like Nick used to smell. Bright and floral and like fruit. He wondered whether he would ever smell that scent on Nick again.

On the table was a plant in a white ceramic pot, with thick leaves the shape of coins. Next to it, in a matching white frame, was a fingerpainting. The beach in summer. Sarah playing with a ball. Mingo, her stuffed penguin, watching on. The smiling faces of her two dads. The words *My Wish* handwritten at the top. Barclay felt tears slip down his face and he wiped them from the glass of the frame.

'He used to always look at this,' Stefan said.

'It was a school project,' Barclay said, almost to himself. 'She had to paint something she wished for the most.' *And she wished for all of us*, he thought. *Together and in the sun*.

'As I say, he used to always have it in his hand and—'

'He's not dead, Stefan.'

'I'm sorry, I meant—'

'I need to go.' Barclay slipped the framed painting into his backpack and secured it with both straps to his back.

'I'm sorry about all of this,' Stefan said. 'His job will always be here if he wants to come back.'

'I don't think he'll be back,' Barclay said. 'You'd know why if you bothered to visit him.'

'Ben, I can't—'

Barclay put a hand up. 'I get it. You're not interested now he doesn't look like himself.'

'That's not it at all,' he said, almost earnestly. 'I care a great deal for Nick.'

Barclay headed for the corridor that led to the gallery. 'Yeah,' he said. 'I'll let him know you care a great deal.'

'Ben!'

Barclay ignored him and bounded down the corridor, passing open doors on his right and left until something caught his eye. He took a step backward and peered through an open door into what looked like a storage area. Filled with paintings and sculptures in various stages of readiness for transport elsewhere, or maybe they were new in.

'Excuse me,' Stefan said. 'This is a private area.' He stepped in front of the doorway and Barclay shoved him to the side.

Bubble wrap hung out of open wooden crates, and there in faded blue ink printed onto the wooden slats were five words.

Litchfield's Haulage, Imports and Exports.

Acknowledgements

I can't believe I'm sitting here putting the finishing touches to my third book. This has been a particularly challenging novel to write for a few reasons, really. Not just because of the (as always) challenging subject matter, but because this book had to do two things: it needed to be the final part of a trilogy of sorts, but also the third book of a series, springboarding into a possibly fourth novel, and so on. It had to offer enough answers, but it also had to leave so many questions unanswered. For that, I am both sorry and particularly proud of myself. HAH!

Before I kickstart any thanks, many of you know that I used a lot of family names in writing my books, with de Silva being the maiden name of my grandad, James Watkin. The nurse who features in several scenes in this book is named after his sister, Doreen Day, who celebrated her ninetieth birthday while I was drafting this novel.

There are so many people to thank, so let's get started:

To my wonderful agent, Francesca Riccardi, for taking a chance on me, and for always telling me the honest truth. And, of course, for always having my back and being excited about where I want to go with de Silva and my career.

To the superb folk at Canelo: Louise Cullen, Alicia Pountney, my editors who always champion me and my work. Kate Shepherd, publicist extraordinaire, for always being switched on! Aidan Kavanagh, though we didn't work together much, I appreciate your super speedy responses, and all of your help with this book and more.

To each editor who has worked on this novel, huge thanks, particularly Sian Heap, who was the first at Canelo to see something in my work and in de Silva and Barclay.

My brilliant and supportive friends and family, you're a constant source of humour, reflection and honesty. Sounding boards, inspiration and support, all of you!

As I'm writing this in late 2025, this year I've met some lovely people who have gone above and beyond in terms of their support of me. The Theakston Old Peculier Crime Writing Festival, Bloody Scotland, Newcastle Noir, Stockport Noir, Cheshire Crime Writing Festival, Write Blend on South Road, Pritchards in Crosby, Messrs Fletcher and Frost, and the lovely team at Isla Gladstone. Love you all.

A particular shout out to some of the loveliest book blog folk I've ever met. You know who you are, and you know there are far too many of you to mention. But specific thanks to two lads who I've loved working with, who have been nothing but supportive and encouraging: Kev (@thefirstelevenminutes) and Nick (@nick_picksbooks). I appreciate everything you've done for me.

Keepingcowsmoovin on Instagram has been a lifeline for me, something to watch that really calmed my mind. Thank you for allowing me to feature you in this book; I appreciate it.

Finally, a massive thanks to everyone who has read de Silva's adventures so far. I know that I have more stories to tell with de Silva and Barclay, and I can't wait to share them with you all.

As I look ahead at what's next, I can promise you this… the end was just the beginning.